SPECIAL MESSAGE TO R[E...

24/60

...[TION
[...]4873)
[...]nds for
[...] diseases.
[...]by the

[...]Eye

[...]Great
[...]en
[...]treatment
[...]University

[...], Institute

[...]Ophthalmic

[...]val

[...]ndation
[...]y. Every
[...]vould like
to help support the Foundation or require further
information, please contact:

THE ULVERSCROFT FOUNDATION
The Green, Bradgate Road, Anstey
Leicester LE7 7FU, England
Tel: (0116) 236 4325

website: www.ulverscroft-foundation.org.uk

WARTIME WITH THE TRAM GIRLS

July 1914. Britain is in turmoil as WW1 begins to change the world. While the young men disappear off to foreign battlefields, the women left at home throw themselves into jobs meant for the boys.

Hiding her privileged background and her suffragette past, Constance Copeland signs up to be a Clippie — collecting money and giving out tickets — on the trams in Staffordshire, despite her parents' disapproval.

Constance, known as Connie, soon makes fast friends with lively fellow Clippies, Betty and Jean, as well as growing closer to the charming, gentle Inspector Robert Caldwell.

But Connie is haunted by another secret; and if it comes out, it could destroy her new life.

After war ends and the men take back their roles, will Connie find that she can return to her previous existence?

LYNN JOHNSON

WARTIME WITH THE TRAM GIRLS

Complete and Unabridged

MAGNA
Leicester

First published in Great Britain in 2021

First Ulverscroft Edition
published 2023

*A catalogue record for this book is available
from the British Library.*

ISBN 978–0–7505–5005–5

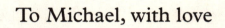

To Michael, with love

1

June 1913

Constance Copeland wiped the sleep from her eyes as Alice drew open the curtains to let in the brightness of the day.

'Are you looking forward to yer birthday treat, Miss Constance? Looks like a fine day for yer travelling.'

She appeared a mere shadow framed against sunlight. 'Oh, I hope so, Alice.' Constance yawned, stretching all her limbs, and sat upright. 'Have you seen Mother and Father yet?'

'Yes, miss. They're already taking breakfast.'

'What a pity you aren't coming to Epsom with us, Alice. We could have a simply wonderful time comparing the latest fashions and spying on all the young gentlemen.'

Alice blushed. 'It's not for the likes of me, miss. Being among all them posh people.'

'Oh, Alice, Derby Day isn't just for posh people, as you call them. It's like a carnival. They let anybody in.' Constance's hand flew to her mouth. 'Sorry, I didn't mean that in the way it came out.'

'No, miss, be sure and have a good day anyroad. I'd best get down to give Mrs Williams an 'and — I have ter scrub the kitchen so as she can get some baking done, before yer come back.'

Alice disappeared through the door as Constance drew her legs out of bed watching her thoughtfully.

1

It would have been nice to have Alice accompany her — even if she was only a servant.

And that wasn't meant the way it sounded, either.

She really must learn to control her thoughts about people, particularly if she was going to repeat the words out loud. It was rare for her to have a young companion to accompany her anywhere since she had returned home from boarding school. It was all so boring.

Their horse and carriage would take them to Stoke station where they would board a train, first class of course, to London and stay overnight in the West-End. The following morning, they would catch a train to Epsom. Oh, what excitement the journey held!

The weather had been sultry, just the sort of weather for thunderstorms. How awful if rain were to interrupt such a fine day, the biggest day out on the racing calendar.

Constance had no illusions about the purpose of the visit. Her father was determined to introduce her to people of influence with a notion of seeing her married off at the earliest opportunity. After all, she was in her nineteenth year now, and plans had to be made, or so her father said. After selling his business in Manchester, he had moved his family to The Potteries in 1909 and bought a fine house, Holmorton Lodge, in need of some renovation but at a very reasonable price. He had ideas of living the life of a gentleman but much to his dismay he missed the cut and thrust of business and sought employment which, given his advanced age of fifty-eight years, failed to materialise.

Constance had been his next project — finding her a suitable husband among the well-connected. It mattered little to her for she had no plans on settling down yet, although she would confess to having dreams of meeting the man who would sweep her off her feet sometime in the future. She certainly didn't expect to meet him at a racecourse accompanied by her parents.

She made her way down the wide staircase towards the dining room, frowning as she heard the heated voices of her mother and father. Tilda, the housemaid, wore a grin on her face as she passed Constance on her way to the kitchen.

'I am not a child, Agatha. I should be pleased if you would remember that.'

'Then you shouldn't act as a child, Edwin. Why do you have to be seen to be the grand gentleman for the crowds? A gentleman does not need to put on an act.'

'How dare you, woman.'

An angry chair scraped across the wooden floor. Constance sighed and closed her eyes. They argued a lot these days, mainly about money. It was his strong opinion that money, in all forms, was strictly a man's domain. Here again, mother and father didn't see eye-to-eye. Her mother felt that as a modern woman, she had every right to be included in financial matters affecting the household.

Constance was determined to enjoy herself; they owed her that courtesy, after all it was her birthday treat. A day with a difference, and she would make the most of it.

She painted a smile on her face and walked into the dining room.

'Good morning, Mother.' She dropped a light kiss on to her mother's forehead and glanced towards her father. 'Good morning, Father.'

'I'm just telling your father, Constance, my dear,

3

that we will need to stay together. There will no doubt be pickpockets and other undesirables about. And we don't want to get drawn into . . . I hate to mention it . . . betting with those awful men who are so intent on taking money from people.'

Before coming to The Potteries, her father had developed a passion for horses, going out regularly with the hunt to enjoy the fresh Cheshire air. Now he was older and did not ride himself he enjoyed visiting local racecourses. What Father really looked forward to was going to see top class horse racing at famous courses, like the Epsom Derby where he could mix with high society and enjoy having a bet.

'Can't a man enjoy himself once a year, for heaven's sake, woman?'

Agatha raised her eyebrows. 'Throwing money away is not akin to enjoying oneself, Edwin.'

Constance pouted at them. 'Have you forgotten that this is my treat? How can I enjoy myself on my birthday if you two are determined to argue all day?'

'Constance! This conversation is between me and your mother. You will kindly be quiet.'

Constance helped herself to some toast. 'I do have some say, Father, as it is my treat.' She flounced around the table and slid into a chair next to her mother.

'She's right, Edwin.'

Mother gave Constance a warning look to keep quiet. Father sniffed and turned his head towards the newspaper laying on the table beside him.

Agatha smiled at Constance. 'Are you all packed, darling?'

'Yes, Mother.'

'Very well. We shall leave within the hour. I asked Bainbridge to bring the carriage from livery to take us

4

to the station. Do be sure not to delay us.'

Bainbridge, the gardener, also stepped in as groomsman when required, which wasn't often. Father refused to pay someone to sit around all day.

★ ★ ★

They arrived at the racecourse, crowded with people looking to enjoy themselves in the carnival-like atmosphere. It was the first time Constance had been to such an event. Her excitement mounted as they paraded around the ground. Father refused to allow her to move beyond the area reserved for people of importance, and thus potential husbands which, after all, was what her father cared about. She wished she had siblings, and then his determination to make an advantageous marriage for her could be diluted among them.

She missed company. At school there had been plenty of young ladies she could count as friends and with whom she could talk and share confidences. As it was, her family had made its home in The Potteries — dirty, noisy, with small, cramped terraced houses and the air full of smoke from the mass of bottle ovens. She still missed the cleanliness of Cheshire, with its green rolling fields, hedgerows of wildflowers and houses that were more than a row of front doors with no gardens.

She couldn't tell her parents how she felt and she didn't know anyone else she could talk to in confidence. One night, when she was home for the holidays and had discovered she was entering that most disgusting thing that all women have to go through in order to have babies, her mother had sat her down and explained what would happen now that she was growing up. Constance had asked whether it was the awful experience of childbirth that had put her off having any more children. Her mother's face twisted, as if to stop her from crying. There was almost a younger brother or sister, her mother said, but she had been very ill during the pregnancy, nearly died, and the baby was lost.

After her mother returned to full health, the doctor said there would be no more babies. Constance felt her eyes glisten as she remembered putting her hand on her mother's knee. Her mother had ignored it. There was such a wistful look on her face. She was in a place that Constance could not go.

Constance had finished school six months ago and, of late, the only young people of her acquaintance had been the servants at Holmorton Lodge, Tilda, the housemaid, Sal the scullery maid and Alice Tucker, taken out of the workhouse, where Constance's mother had been a Workhouse Friend. Alice had been employed as a trainee cook during the time Constance was away. She was younger than Constance, and easy to talk to. But not someone her father would countenance accompanying them to the Epsom Derby.

Now, walking demurely alongside her parents, Constance longed to experience the hustle and bustle and revelries going on in the centre of the course. That was where she found sympathy in her mother. Having seen signs of boredom creeping into her daughter's face, her mother had winked, strolled over to her husband, and engaged him in a conversation which required him to turn his back on his daughter. With a huge grin, Constance took only seconds to

6

disappear from the enclosure. She could always rely on Mother to indulge her.

Free of constraints, she strolled through the crowds, enjoying her own company and was able to stop and start as she pleased. Fewer women were about here. The Betting Ring was the place for men where book-makers used a secret language of their own, and none of it made any sense, but she watched nevertheless.

Some distance away, she noticed her father pushing his way towards the betting booths. She chose to ignore him, not ready to give up her freedom quite yet, and headed towards the white railings at Tattenham Corner where, she had been told, she would get an excellent view of the horses as they rounded the bend.

Tension in the crowds mounted. The Derby was the big race of the day, and the king's horse, Anmer, was running. The rush of excitement became physical as the crowds at the railings grew larger and the noise louder.

She edged her way forward, person by person and until she was close enough to peep between the bodies pushing against the railings. There was hardly room to breathe, and the shouting was deafening.

'They're off . . . they're off.'

The steady thumping of hooves grew louder. The ground shook as the horses thundered towards them. Quick as a flash, the leading horses passed where she was standing, and shouts of excitement went up, causing her to worry about the effect of the noise on the poor horses.

There were three or may be four horses in the second group. It all happened so fast. Someone, a woman, dressed in a long, dark coat and hat, ducked under

7

the rails about twenty yards to Constance's right. The woman ran out on to the course, startling the horses galloping towards her at full pelt. The men on each side of Constance closed in, and her view was lost. Shouts went up, first in anger, then dismay. No one near her knew what was going on. People ran onto the track and separated into two groups, one surrounding the jockey, and a few steps further on, another group around the body lying still on the muddied ground. The horse struggled free.

Somebody screamed.

'A woman ran onto the track, and she's been killed, I'll bet. Kicked in the chest like that.'

'Somebody's brought down the king's horse. Did you see the animal roll over?'

'Is the jockey dead?'

'I bet on Anmer to win. Which stupid beggar brought him down?'

'It was some crazed suffragette woman!'

Shouts of concern about getting a doctor onto the course grew louder. Many of the witnesses to what had happened were more annoyed about the interference to the race. Constance prayed hard that whoever the woman was, she was not badly hurt.

★ ★ ★

It wasn't until the next day that Constance found out more. Newspapers reported that Emily Wilding Davison, a member of the Women's Social and Political Union, had deliberately run onto the course with the wish to bring down the king's horse and thereby kill herself. Constance didn't know Miss Davison to speak to, but knew her to be a friend of Mrs Pankhurst, an old neighbour of theirs before they left Manchester.

Constance and her mother had attended some of the meetings run by Mrs Pankhurst until they became too militant, for her mother's sensibilities. Constance had read their journal to keep apace with news but that was all. Witnessing the shocking events at Epsom had made her realise this was not a game to be picked up on a whim. The dedication of women such as Emily had set fire to something inside her. Women didn't need men to look after them; they could look after themselves if only they had the chance. Women had a voice and they needed to express it for themselves. They needed a vote. Miss Davison had been carrying a suffragette flag and many people believed it to be a display of sensationalism, or a suicide mission, or both. The suffragettes had become much more militant in claiming their rights to vote in recent months.

How much dedication did it take to believe in something so intensely that you were prepared to die for that belief? Constance barely slept that night. She felt the thud of hooves, heard the shouting crowd, and she screamed into the darkness. Her face was wet, and her breath was coming too quickly for her liking, but she was asking herself a question. Could she rise to the challenge?

Could she ever give her life for a cause?

★ ★ ★

Miss Davison died without regaining consciousness and Constance cried for the woman, for the death of the spirit that had both created Emily and was ultimately to be her downfall.

Constance joined the WSPU the very next day.

9

2

July 1913

The Suffragette journal carried numerous reports of Miss Davison's bravery and held the ultimate epitaph: *she died for women*. Pictures of silent women marching behind a flower-laden coffin appeared etched on Constance's brain every time she closed her eyes. She could almost hear the continual pounding of marching feet and covered her ears until it went away.

Constance decided that she would lend her support to one of the demonstrations. *The Suffragette* journal listed campaigns and almost every week something was happening. She soon found what she was looking for; Sylvia Pankhurst, recently released from prison, would be speaking at a meeting in Trafalgar Square on 27th July. Word had it that she was going to speak to the working women and men of the country on the theme of 'deeds not words' and would present a letter to the prime minister, Mr Asquith.

'You look miles away, Miss Constance.'

Alice's voice made her jump, so taken was she with the pictures inside her head. She tried to slide the journal into the drawer of her dressing table, but Alice's sharp eyes caught sight of it before it disappeared.

'You're not reading one of them suffragette papers are you? I thought you'd given up all of that bunkum.'

'Shush, Alice. And for goodness' sake keep your voice down. Close the door.'

Alice did as she was bid and came back to the dressing table. 'It is their journal. Oh, Miss Constance — do yer know what yer doing?'

'Alice, it is not your place to question me. And it is certainly not 'bunkum', as you put it.'

'Sorry, miss. Beg your pardon.' Alice's face turned to stone.

'I didn't mean it. I'm so excited, that's all. There's a meeting taking place in London, and I want to go.'

'Not on your own all that way, surely? The Mistress would never agree.'

'Who says I'm going on my own?'

'You know someone what'll go with you?'

'I'm looking at her right now.'

'Yer mean me?' She pointed at her chest.

'Why not? We could travel together quite easily. I've been doing some planning. I could pretend to go to see a couple of school friends who live in the city and take you with me as my companion?'

'Oh, I dunno, miss.'

'We'll be fine. Think of all those women, cheering Miss Pankhurst. They're doing it for all of us, Alice. Women everywhere who want to have a say in what happens to them.'

The thought of hearing one of the Pankhursts speaking again was almost too much, and any doubts she might have had were subsumed by an overwhelming excitement.

'We'll have such fun. But you are to speak to no one about it, Alice. And I mean, no one.'

A ghost of a smile crossed Alice's face.

'Cross me heart, miss.'

* * *

It was easier to plan than Constance had thought. Talking to her mother a few days later, she pretended to be more than a little melancholy over Miss Davison's death and suggested a trip to London might help cheer her.

'I've been thinking of visiting two schoolfriends, Eunice and Lavinia, who live in London and I was thinking that Alice might come along and keep me company.'

'It sounds an excellent idea, Constance. What do you think, Edwin?'

'Capital — if they can show her how to snare a man as well you have my consent,' said Father.

Constance rolled her eyes at her mother, who gave a wink in return.

★ ★ ★

'There — that was easy,' Constance boasted to Alice later. 'I had to lie. I knew Father would agree to anything that involves me meeting 'young ladies'. Mother would be more concerned about me getting into trouble if she knew about the rally. She doesn't agree with the suffragettes becoming militant. She's a suffragist. They believe that only political means should be used.'

'Oh, I see,' said a doubtful sounding Alice. 'Are them girls real what you was talking about then?'

'They were at my boarding school. I don't suppose I'll ever see them again. I mean . . . what need would they have to come to The Potteries from London?'

'D'yer miss 'em?'

Constance sighed. 'I miss them so much you wouldn't believe.' She had taken them for granted at

12

school. Her friends were just . . . there. Now, she was only friends with people chosen by her father.

Alice began to put away some clothes that Constance had worn earlier. Constance watched. Alice was slim and her dark hair was gathered at the nape of her neck and tied with a plain cream ribbon. At five foot three she was shorter than Constance. She tried to imagine Alice dressed in finer clothes and her hair in a becoming style. She could pass for a lady and it would give her a little confidence.

'How old are you, Alice?'

Alice appeared startled and Constance wondered if anyone had ever asked her before.

'I'm fifteen, Miss Constance,' she said finally.

'And how long were you in the workhouse?'

'Couple of years. It was good of Mrs Copeland to give me a job. Dunno what would've happened ter me if she hadn't. Probably be in the Big House with the rest of the inmates.'

Constance raised her eyebrows. How matter-of-factly Alice spoke of that dreadful workhouse where children were parted from their parents and married men and women forced to live separate lives. Constance had visited the workhouse children's hostel one Christmas, a couple of years ago, to help her mother, a Workhouse Friend. She had marvelled at the children who lived there, all dressed the same, boys with shorn heads and girls in frocks that were either too small or too big.

There was one girl Constance remembered, small, dark-haired, with big sad eyes, who appeared to help in the kitchen. She couldn't have been more than ten or eleven, but her face had remained in Constance's mind ever since. Now, she could imagine Alice in her place, and she felt her eyes water a little. She blinked and jumped up to brush her hair vigorously, glad that Alice would accompany her.

* * *

They travelled the day before the march and stayed in a small but comfortable hotel. Even so, Alice was clearly out of her depth and almost hid behind Constance every time someone spoke to them.

Constance smiled. She would have to educate the girl — although she couldn't see her father agreeing to them coming to town too often.

After an early breakfast, they walked to the nearest tube station and took the train to Euston Square. They came up behind a small group of women walking towards the outer doors. It was the way they walked that had caught her notice, moving swiftly without the appearance of urgency, eyes darting everywhere, missing nothing. The woman who appeared to be the leader turned and spoke to a woman behind and her coat blew open. She pulled it closed quickly but not before Constance had seen a suffragette badge pinned below the woman's collar.

Constance hurried after them. She caught up with their leader and whispered urgently. 'You're suffragettes, aren't you?'

The woman gave her a sharp look. Constance opened her lapel fleetingly to reveal her badge. The woman nodded.

'Are you going to Trafalgar Square?'

Another brief nod.

Constance linked arms with Alice and relaxed her steps to match with the group. They continued in

14

silence, glad to be part of something. It gave her a feeling of solidarity.

'Have you been to one of these meetings before?' Constance asked. 'This is my first time.'

Again, the woman nodded. 'The WSPU needs more supporters. You will be surprised how many women feel the same way we do and will show it in any way possible. What led you to become a member?'

Constance hadn't really thought it through until now. 'I want women to have the same rights as men. Not just women like us, but all women. It seems simple when I think about it, but I am beginning to realise that there is nothing simple in this world.'

'Stay alert, and be very careful. You will need your wits about you is the best advice I can give you.'

On arriving at a packed Trafalgar Square, the woman turned to the rest of her small group.

'Right, you know what to do. And may we all return safely.' She nodded at Constance and Alice and moved on.

Sylvia Pankhurst appeared through the crowds and was helped up onto one of the lion plinths flanked by women acting as bodyguards. The plinth faced the National Gallery, with Whitehall at their backs.

A cheer went up. Being some distance away, Constance could barely make out her words.

Miss Pankhurst held a sheaf of papers high above her head and raised her voice. 'We are all here today with a common purpose. The papers I hold in my hand are from men and women all wanting the same thing. Deeds Not Words —'

A shout went up.

She waited until it died away. 'And we want votes for women this year —'

The roars grew even louder.

'When do we want the vote?' she shouted.

'This year!' The reply was deafening.

'We are taking our requests to the prime minister.'

Miss Pankhurst marched off towards Whitehall, the crowd with her. Mounted police were stationed across Whitehall blocking their way to Downing Street and Parliament, their horses prancing skittishly on the spot as riders fought to stay in control. Both sides of Whitehall were lined with police constables.

'Come on, Alice.'

Constance shouted over her shoulder as the crush of people from behind, mainly women, surged forward. She staggered as the crowd pushed against her. Fighting broke out behind her. She moved swiftly forward and lost sight of Alice.

'Alice! Alice! Where are you?'

She was on her own. It was both frightening and exhilarating as she drew closer to the spot where Sylvia Pankhurst had been standing. She had to hold on to her hat more than once to stop it taking flight.

'Alice!'

Constance had to find her. The girl would be lost on her own in such a place as this. She had never been out of the borough before, as far as Constance was aware.

Suddenly Miss Pankhurst disappeared from her sight. Police constables moved in from the side of the road to break up the march. Two women were thrown to the ground and beaten by policemen. Panic turned to hysteria as the police tried to disperse the march and detain the ringleaders.

Two police constables held a woman down as she kicked and screamed at them, blood running over her cheek from a cut above her left eye. Her eyes were wide open and filled with terror.

Revulsion encompassed Constance. How could English policemen act in such a manner to a fellow Englishwoman?

A woman with a pram full of stones passed close to Constance. Without thinking of the consequences, Constance picked one out and hurled it through a nearby window to distract the policemen who had the bleeding woman pinned to the ground.

Constance stood rooted to the spot, shocked at what had come to her so naturally. A policeman grabbed her arm and forced it up her back. She screamed, but still they held her. She struggled, panicking now. Whatever had possessed her to throw the stone? She couldn't just stand by and let the constables assault the woman. The woman mouthed a silent thank you and closed her eyes. Constance was glad she had at least helped the poor woman, even if it had meant getting herself in trouble.

Her eyes darted everywhere. Where was Alice?

* * *

Constance was pulled through the crowds and bundled into the back of a waiting police wagon along with others, all women, packed like sardines. The doors closed. They moved off, rocking back and forth as the wagon lurched through crowds that seemed to be growing wilder by the minute. Her heart pounded with shock, horror and not a little excitement as she stared at the faces of the other women, her comrades, some hugging each other, some in tears. Their progress was slow and the heat unbearable. Rank smells

17

of body-odour mixed with the sickly smell of cologne. Constance recognised none of the faces around her. Where was Alice, alone and petrified? All she could do was wait and hope to meet up with her at the police station which, no doubt, was where they were headed. And if she wasn't there, what would she do? How could she have been so thoughtless, getting poor Alice involved in such a mess?

The wagon jerked to a halt and the back door opened.

'Right you lot. Out you come. Single file. Give your name and address at the desk. No talking!'

They filed through the doors of the Cannon Row police station and lined up, one behind the other, as they were taken through the booking-in process. Constance couldn't hear what they were saying, but judging by their accents, she wasn't the only one to have travelled a distance that day.

She was pushed into a small room in the middle of which was a table with a chair at either side. A man and a uniformed constable entered and slammed the door shut behind them. The man pointed Constance to one chair, and he took the other, leaving the constable on guard at the door.

Once again, she recited her name, address, and her reason for being in London.

'I came with my maid, Alice Tucker. Have you seen her? Has she been brought here?'

'I'm the one asking the questions. And you'll be good enough to answer them.'

'But she is only young. She'll be worried. I need to find her.'

'Nothing to do with me. If you were so worried about her welfare, you shouldn't have put her in harm's way. Why did you throw the stone?'

The sharp tone startled her.

'A woman was being attacked by two police constables. She was in so much pain. She was screaming. I thought she was going to get badly hurt. I just wanted to gain the constables' attention so they would leave her alone.'

'You certainly did that . . . miss,' he said with a grin, staring down at her hands and taking in the lack of a ring. 'But I'll have to ask you again, miss. You threw a stone through a window of government property. Why?'

'I told you. I just picked it up and threw it. I didn't plan it. It could have been any window.'

'You didn't aim for that particular building?'

'No! I . . . didn't . . . think. As I said, I just wanted it all to stop.'

He nodded encouragingly. She thought she was getting somewhere, but the smile hardened and the kindly face turned to granite.

'And you thought the best way was to commit a crime and cause deliberate damage to government property? You have put a stone through the window of the War Office. You could have killed anyone working in that room. Good job it's Sunday. Do you realise the seriousness of the crime you have committed?'

Constance hung her head. She had not the strength to say anything more. Their minds were closed.

'Miss Constance Copeland, I arrest you for causing a breach of the peace and wilful damage to government property. You . . .'

The rest of the caution was lost. The seriousness of her predicament hit her as heavily as the stone must have hit the window of the government building. How would her father take the news? What will Mother say? How was she going to get home — and if Alice wasn't at the police station, where on earth was she?

* * *

It all happened so fast. Constance was held in a police cell overnight and there was still no sign of Alice.

The following day Constance was taken to Bow Street Magistrates' Court. The clerk asked her to confirm her name, age and address and whether she was guilty or not. She had been told by the woman leading the group from Euston to plead guilty. As it was her first offence, she would most probably get off lightly.

After hearing testimony from the arresting officers the magistrate asked if Constance had anything to say.

'Just that I am truly sorry and promise not to do it again.'

'I thank you for your apology, but if you think you are going to be treated leniently then you are much mistaken. You committed a premeditated act of wilful damage. You may not have carried the stone to the site, but one of your kind did and you took advantage of it. Your constant attacks on property cannot and will not be tolerated. I therefore sentence you to four weeks imprisonment for wilful damage and one week for breaching the peace. The sentences are to run concurrently. Take her down. Next case!'

Constance couldn't swallow. Her legs shook as one of the guards grabbed her arm and forced her towards the door. Her eyes smarted with unshed tears as she determined not to let them flow. She held her head

high. She regretted the outcome, but she knew without a doubt she would do the same again if she had
to.

★ ★ ★

She was transported to Holloway prison along with
other women, mostly from the march. On arrival at
Holloway she was taken to a cell and pushed inside.
The door slammed with inevitable hopelessness. The
key turned and she was alone in the tiny cell that was
to be her home for the next four weeks.

She eyed the room with its cold, painted walls helplessly. Her questions on the whereabouts of Alice had
been ignored. The more she thought of the poor girl
alone in the city with no money, as far as Constance
was aware, the more panicked she became. How could
she sleep until she knew the girl was safe?

She banged on the door until a small square panel
slid across, and the eye of a wardress appeared.

'Where's Alice Tucker? What have you done with
her?'

'We've booked in forty today. Give you all their
names, shall I, madam?'

Constance was about to nod until she saw the woman's lip curl.

She tried again. 'I only want to know if she's in
here. We came to London together. She has no one
else. She's only fifteen.'

'Then you should've took care of her a bit better,
shouldn't yer,' the woman sneered. Her face disappeared, and the panel banged shut.

Eyes smarting, Constance turned back to the room.
The floor was cold stone, and wooden planks pro-

vided a harsh bed. On closer inspection of the wall below the bed, she saw that someone had scratched words into the bricks.

'*Deeds Not Words.*'

The very same words Sylvia Pankhurst had shouted at the meeting that had led her here. It was comforting to know someone else with her beliefs had stayed in this very room. A warm feeling spread through her chest. If only she hadn't brought Alice with her, she could have accepted her punishment with grace and dignity.

She had no idea of time; the whole establishment appeared to be governed by food, exercise and emptying the slops. The day started at six o'clock with breakfast, exercise at ten, lunch time, teatime between four and five, and lights out at eight o'clock. Apart from these times, Constance saw no one. If only she'd had a book or something to do with her hands, anything that would help pass the time. Had her parents been informed? How would they know she was safe? It was not knowing the answers to the questions that hurt the most.

The first couple of days passed without news of Alice and Constance barely ate a thing. The wardresses tutted and warned her they would be obliged to force-feed her if she went on hunger strike. She told them she wasn't on hunger strike, nor was she hungry.

On the third morning, someone spoke to her in the exercise yard, where around forty or fifty women paraded under the watchful eyes of the wardresses. Most walked with their arms folded, holding themselves taunt. Some shuffled, others trudged, their bodies following the mindless tramp of their feet — women from all walks of life.

Constance, too, stared at her feet as she followed the woman in front. There was a sudden scuffle behind.

'Don't turn round.' A woman's voice whispered close to her ear, and Constance felt a slight tap on her shoulder.

With her heart in her mouth, Constance did as she was bid.

'Are you Constance Copeland?'

Hardly able to breathe, she nodded. 'I hear you. What do you want?' she hissed back.

'Alice says she's all —'

'Alice di —'

'Be quiet. Don't say anything.'

They carried on, plodding their way. After a moment or two, the voice came again.

'She's at the safe house down the road. She was taken in when she told them you was in 'ere. She'll stay there till you get out. She wanted you to know that she's safe. We look after our own in 'ere.'

'May the Lord be praised,' Constance muttered, tears of relief coming to her eyes.

An ear-piercing whistle blew and they were led back to their cells. As she headed down the corridor, a woman behind her bumped into her, knocking her against the wall. Constance turned to give her a piece of her mind. The woman smiled and laid a finger on her lips and nodded.

Constance understood. It was the woman who had given her the message about Alice. And now she knew what the woman looked like.

At last, there was a smile on Constance's face. Her world had just grown a little brighter again.

* * *

23

Now she knew Alice was safe, Constance's only thought was to get out of prison and take the girl home. She owed it to her. She'd heard whispers about women being force-fed. They would last four days of abstinence and then the sound of the trolley could be heard wheeling its way insidiously along the corridor. The sounds that followed were terrible and frightening: women's voices getting louder, a man's voice cursing because a wardress wasn't holding a prisoner tight enough to avoid her flailing arms. She heard screams and the sounds of choking until she had to cover her ears to blot out their anguish from the pain of having a tube forced through their captive mouths or noses. It didn't always go in the first time and was forced repeatedly until the woman had no strength left. The women told her, out in the yard — and every time she heard the sound, she gagged until she was sick.

She could not go on hunger strike. Mrs Pankhurst wouldn't allow girls under twenty-one to do so. Constance asked herself if she could have supported her sisters if it came to it. She didn't have an answer. All she knew was she had to keep herself well so she could take Alice home.

3

August 1913

Constance was one of six making their way to the exit of Holloway prison the day their sentences ended. The sun was bright, and a small group of women were waiting on the far side of the road, all dressed in WSPU sashes of purple and green and each holding a small posy of flowers. A woman smiled at Constance and moved towards her, fastening a small badge onto her lapel. It depicted the portcullis of the House of Commons with small chains either side. The badge of a suffragette who had been imprisoned for the cause.

'For your first stay in Holloway. We thank you for your support. May you have a safe journey back to your family.'

She handed over the posy, and Constance lifted it automatically to her nose to smell the fresh fragrance of the flowers after the musty, sickly odours of the prison.

Tears came to Constance's eyes as Alice hurtled towards her.

'I'm sorry, Alice. I'm so sorry.' It was all Constance could find to say as a tearful Alice led her to the safe house where Constance knew her father was waiting to take her home.

Alice would have none of it. 'I was scared. I'd be fibbing if I said I wasn't. But it weren't your fault, Miss Constance. One of the women at the safe house told me you was trying to help a poor woman what was in trouble, and I thought you did right.'

'Thank you, dearest Alice.' Constance put her arm around Alice's shoulders, and they entered the safe house together.

★　★　★

Father was standing in front of the fire with his arms behind his back, rocking on his heels.

'I'm so glad to see you, Father.' She threw her arms around him, but he stood to attention, almost rigid. She backed away, suddenly conscious of her appearance, her crumpled dress and coat, dirty and with a tear at the shoulder from the rough handling of the constables.

Her father was looking at the opposite wall when he spoke to her.

'We will depart for home as soon as you can make yourself ready, Constance. We will leave questions until we get there. You, Alice Tucker . . .' he pointed a finger towards her '. . . will pack your bags and leave my house within the next twenty-four hours.'

Alice's face turned white. She darted a pleading look at Constance.

'But Father, please don't do this. I asked her to come with me.'

'The girl is not to be trusted. She should have come to me as soon as she heard your ridiculous plans.'

Alice bowed her head, wringing her hands. 'But how am I to manage, sir? How'll I get another job if you kick me out?'

He glared back. 'That, young lady, is no concern of mine.'

26

His voice sounded distant. Constance searched his face, but he refused to look at her.

* * *

The journey home was a silent one. She did not see Alice. Father bought her a third-class ticket and sent her off to sit by herself well away from their own first-class carriage, so she might think about how much she had let the family down. Constance was mortified that her father could allow a young girl to travel on her own, with the prospect of losing both her job, and her home, hanging over her.

Constance climbed into their carriage and sent Alice a quick apology over her shoulder. How could she have been so thoughtless about the effect her jaunt might have on her companion? Had she been so caught up in her own political principles that she had had no thought on what it might cost Alice?

She desperately wanted to defy her father but knew that she would need to be circumspect if she was to get him to change his mind about poor Alice's future.

* * *

Bainbridge was waiting at the station with the carriage. The three sat in silence. Once home, Father left them and shut himself in the library.

Constance hugged Alice. The poor girl had been in tears since they had arrived home and nothing Constance could say seemed to help. 'Don't worry, Alice. I will explain it was nothing to do with you. That I required you to accompany me and you had no choice.'

27

Alice shrugged and sat alone in the kitchen.

Constance knocked on the door of the library and slid inside and waited for her father to look up. 'Father, please do something to help Alice. She doesn't deserve to lose her job over something that was entirely my fault.'

'Perhaps it will teach you to think before you act in future.'

He wouldn't listen. She asked her mother to intervene too but even she could not persuade him to change his mind.

No matter how many times Constance told him, he wouldn't listen.

★ ★ ★

When Constance rose the next morning, the first thing she registered was the quietness around her. She was in her own comfortable, clean bed and could please herself when she rose and went about her business. She revelled at a long soak in a bath full of hot water and looked forward to going for a walk in the town rather than the walled-up exercise yard of Holloway.

Constance felt more and more shaken and disturbed, doubting her ability to talk her father round. Supposing he refused to allow Alice to retain her job? Being sacked would surely prevent her getting another post. Father was too angry with her to listen to anything she had to say. She could well have destroyed the poor girl's life and all because she, Constance, had wanted a little excitement.

'For God's sake, Constance. How am I ever to find you a good match of a husband after this disgusting behaviour? Do you ever think of anyone except yourself? You deliberately set out to disregard my intentions for you. How do you think all of this non-sense will affect your future prospects?'

She supposed she deserved everything her father said. A certain annoyance rose inside her. Had he never done anything for a good reason that had back-fired on him?

'Have you ever thought, Edwin, that there would be no reason for this behaviour if women had been allowed to vote for themselves on matters that affect their lives?'

'Agatha, you would challenge me?'

'Most certainly, if I believe you are wrong. But, dearest, think about it. I don't believe that our daughter would have planned to commit a criminal offence or be imprisoned. I think she regrets the heartache she has put us through. I'm right aren't I, Constance?' She glanced at Constance seeking confirmation. 'But it's over now. Can you find it in your heart to forgive her — and poor Alice too, who was only doing her duty by our daughter?'

'And be made a laughing stock of by everyone because I can't control my own child?'

'I'm not a child, Father.' Constance was trying her hardest to button her tongue, but this was too much. Her mother flashed a warning glare at her and, some-how, her own temper fizzled out.

'No one else needs to know, Edwin. Nothing has been reported in *The Sentinel*. I'm sure Constance will be only too keen to ensure that word doesn't get out. Isn't that right, Constance?'

Once more Constance caught the look from her mother; the look that was meant to be obeyed.

And then it was over. Constance would keep the

whole affair to herself. After all, it had happened in London and thus the family would be spared the ignominy of a report in the local press. She would continue her work as a suffragette, handing out the magazine and attending local meetings, but would refrain from attending any demonstrations in the future. In return for this promise, Alice would be allowed to retain her employment with the family until Constance had her own home to manage. At that point, Alice would go with her. Edwin seemed content to lay the blame for the whole event at Alice's door. She didn't deserve to be treated like this.

'Thank you, Miss Constance,' said Alice, later. 'Dunno what I would've done if Mr Copeland had thrown me out. The workhouse or summat, till I gorra job, I was feared.'

'But it wasn't your fault.'

Constance felt worse than ever. Here was Alice, in trouble for something that was not her fault, and thanking Constance for trying to ensure she didn't lose her job.

When Constance didn't speak, Alice continued.

'If you don't mind me saying so, many families are happier to put wrongdoing on servants rather than their own kin. Sorry for saying that, Miss Constance, but it's true.'

'Alice . . . I swear you will never go back to that workhouse while there's a breath in my body. After what we've been through, do you honestly think I would send you there? You will stay with me. And you will call me Constance when we're on our own. That's what friends do.'

Alice threw her arms around Constance. In a flood of tears, brought on by relief, uncertainty, or happiness, or very possibly all three, they hugged each other.

It was the least Constance could do.

4

July 1914

Constance felt she had grown up quite a lot since completing her prison sentence. Now, twelve months on, Constance continued her work with the WSPU, handing out pamphlets and generally doing what she could to help her suffragette colleague, Sarah, who delivered her speech to anyone who stopped to listen.

They were at their regular spot at the bandstand opposite the meat market in the centre of Burslem. Today, her mind wasn't really on the job — not that there was anything difficult about it; nothing was required from her apart from polite responses to those in the audience who wanted to see women given the power to vote on their own destinies.

From the moment Constance first saw him, she couldn't take her eyes off him. She put on her very best voice as she moved through the crowds. The day was bright and cheerful and she wished she had thought more about the clothes she wore. Sarah, one of the better speakers in the local branch of the WSPU, was standing on a box trying to explain the case of women's suffrage to passersby.

Constance edged her way through the crowd towards the tall, dark-haired man, conversing politely and handing out her pamphlets as she went.

'Could I offer you one, sir?'

32

'You're a suffragette?'

'I am, sir. I'm here for the Cause most weeks. My name is Miss Constance Copeland. I am pleased to make your acquaintance.'

'Matthew Roundswell. At your service.'

His voice was deep, luxuriant; a voice she could listen to for ages.

He gave a sweeping bow, and Constance was quite overcome. He glanced at the pamphlet briefly. 'It sounds fascinating, Constance. I like a woman with a brain.'

She was about to reply when an attractive young woman stepped forward and caught his arm. She was laughing at something someone had said and was hardly aware of Constance. Dismayed, Constance had to admit they made the perfect couple.

'What's this, Matthew? Do you wish to support these ladies? I wonder you even noticed.'

There was laughter in the woman's voice. Constance grimaced behind her hand.

'Surprisingly, my dear Louisa, I do have more to think about than your good self.'

Although Matthew was talking to Louisa, he was looking in Constance's direction and she beamed at him.

He inclined his head.

Excitement mounted in Constance's chest although she would have liked to know more about Louisa's role in his life before allowing herself to swoon completely.

Disappointed, but not entirely without hope, Constance watched them continue on their way. She felt sure they would meet again. Somehow, she would arrange it.

★ ★ ★

The following week, after a particularly busy morning, someone tapped her shoulder.

'Excuse me, miss.'

Constance gulped and turned to face Matthew again, hoping that the tightness of her skin didn't mean she was too red of face. Within seconds she discerned that he was both smiling and alone.

'Can I help you?' she squeaked, annoyed at her breathlessness.

'You gave me a pamphlet recently, Constance, if I recall correctly?'

'You do indeed, Matthew.'

'Those green eyes of yours are ... most striking. I have never seen the like. I would like to discuss the matters raised in your pamphlet, Constance.'

'And I would be very happy to discuss them with you. I shall be free in ten minutes if you would care to wait?' She held her breath.

'Of course.'

For the sake of propriety, she asked Sarah to accompany her walk with him as they paraded slowly around the town. They talked mainly of women's right to vote and she liked what she heard. Most of the men her father had introduced her to were dull and more interested in what they were looking at rather than what a woman talked about.

He was perfect in every way. Except for Louisa. Who was she? 'And how is Louisa?' she asked, as casually as she was able.

'Louisa Pendleton? She accompanied me the last time we met. I believe she is quite well ... She was visiting us from London. I was her chaperone.'

34

Later, as she took her leave of him, she suspected her father would be quite pleased with him. He looked just the sort of man her father would have in mind to take his wayward daughter in hand.

*　*　*

Sarah's voice was like a continuous drip in the back of Constance's mind, until she was hardly aware of the words. After all, she had heard it all before. She was thinking of her meeting with Matthew on Sunday. Looking forward to getting to know more about each other.

Strolling through the dozen or so people surrounding Sarah's box, she found herself looking at a young girl staring at Sarah, taking in every word. Although working class, she looked familiar.

Constance stepped towards the girl and handed her a pamphlet. She looked startled.

'I know you,' Constance puzzled. 'But I can't remember your name.'

'Ginnie . . . Gin-Ginnie Jones from —'

The poor girl could scarcely say the words and looked about to run.

'I know where you're from.' Constance didn't want her to have to say the words *Haddon Workhouse Children's Hostel* out loud.

'You come to the . . . with yer mother,' Ginnie faltered.

'Stay, please. I would love to talk to you. A lot must have happened to you since we met that Christmas. I'm nearly finished.'

Constance continued to hand out pamphlets, sending the odd glance Ginnie's way. The girl stood, reading the sheet that had been placed into her hand.

'That's it for today, come on, let's walk to the park. I'm Constance, my mother is Mrs Copeland, you remember her?'

Ginnie's mouth fell open. Constance smothered a laugh, not wanting to put Ginnie off.

They began to chat. She was so easy to talk to. Constance thought her life had been lonely, but it was as nothing compared to Ginnie's experience of life, where good things were always followed by bad.

The very next topic of conversation was something that was on every young woman's mind — a young man to walk out with. Ginnie had confessed to having feelings for a boy from the workhouse named Sam White.

'Me and my friend Clara and Sam were best friends. They looked after me when I first went in. Me and Clara shared a bed until . . . until.' Ginnie stopped talking and her eyes filled. 'I conner talk about it.'

'Was it something very bad?' asked Constance.

Ginnie nodded, sniffing. She rubbed her nose on her sleeve.

They entered the park and headed towards the grass bank overlooking the empty bandstand. Constance sat quietly, allowing Ginnie to regain control. After a moment she continued. 'And what about Sam?'

'He's in the Big House now. The workhouse. He's got nobody 'cept me. His dad went away when his mum died. Back to sea. He would love to sit in the park like this. He loves flowers. He used to work the veg patch back at Haddon. He's the best person in the whole world.'

'And what about you?'

36

'Me sister, Mabel come for me a couple of months back, and now I live with her and her 'usband.'

Ginnie finished with a huge sigh. It was obvious to Constance that she was missing Sam. Her face softened as she said his name and it was evident that she was smitten by him. From what Ginnie said, he sounded decent and good-natured.

'You are so lucky to have Sam waiting for you, Ginnie.' Constance spread out her skirts to allow her legs to breathe in the warm July air and leaned back on her arms, her eyes closed.

'Do you have a special friend, a boy?' Ginnie asked.

Easy as it was to talk to Ginnie, Constance still found her face feeling faintly flushed at the direct question.

'I do have a gentleman friend. His name is Matthew, but we've only recently become acquainted. It's early days yet, but I am hopeful that he likes me as much as I like him.'

They chatted on. Constance even told Ginnie that she had been on a suffragette march and had been to prison for a month. She said she hadn't told Matthew because she didn't want to put him off.

Why had she been so quick to tell Ginnie? It was a lot to take in when you've only recently met.

'As I said, Ginnie, it's early days yet.'

After arranging to meet the following week, the girls parted. It had been a lucky first meeting that had the potential to grow into a friendship between two most unlikely girls. It had surprised Constance and she was intrigued to know more about the girl who was so different to anyone she had met before. She was even more surprised to find herself slightly envious of Ginnie having someone in her life like Sam.

* * *

The following Saturday was another bright day and once again Constance suggested a walk in the park to end their suffragette session for the day.

'I'm sure our Mabel wonders what I'm up to,' said Ginnie.

'Have you told her about me?'

'Just a bit. I doubt as she believes me. Why should a toff want ter walk about with me anyroad? I dunner think as I believe it meself.' Ginnie laughed.

'Whyever not?'

'Me? A girl from the workhouse? I was told to say now't to nobody if I want to make me way in the world.'

'Poppycock! Ginnie, the world is changing.'

Ginnie's eyebrows lifted. 'Dunno as it's changing that quick,' she retorted. 'Sorry,' she said with her hand over her mouth.

Constance laughed. 'Oh, Ginnie, you're like a breath of fresh air to me.'

* * *

Later that evening, when Constance and her mother were alone, she broached the subject of Sam.

'Mother, I have made the acquaintance of a girl we both met on one of our Workhouse Friend visits three years ago. She was listening to one of Sarah's speeches and we got chatting. She lives with her sister now.'

'Really? What is her name?'

'Ginnie Jones. You may not remember her. She helped Mary Higgins in the kitchen mainly. She's left Haddon now, but her friend Sam has been sent from

38

the children's hostel to the workhouse and she's missing him terribly.'

'It often happens. Friends get split up and leave. It's a great shame for those left behind.'

'She's living with her sister, Mabel, now and she has a job. She seems to be doing quite well.'

'That is good news, to know we have helped someone to make a new life for themselves. I wish we could help more.'

* * *

The last week of July brought the tensions in Europe to a head. Country after country were reported to be mobilising their armies — for attack, or in self-defence. So far, England remained neutral but war was beginning to seem inevitable.

5

August 1914

Germany demanded that her troops be allowed passage through Belgium to attack France. England's threat to mobilise against them didn't stop them. The newspapers reported that the British Armed Forces were preparing for war. Poor Mr Bainbridge, the gardener, who was in the Territorials, received a telegram to join his unit, the South Staffordshires, that same evening.

Constance had a sinking feeling in her stomach. Talk of war in the newspaper was as nothing compared with the shock of a servant going off to fight. It made it all real. Still, no doubt they would get a replacement soon, otherwise they would have no one to tend the horse.

On 5th August, Constance awoke to a Britain at war with Germany. It was all there, in black and white. All over Europe, troops had been mobilised. So many men, ordered to fight for their countries. It happened so quickly. Regular soldiers were already on their way to Belgium and each day Constance opened the newspaper with trepidation, scanning the headlines for good news but fearing bad. Mrs Pankhurst had ended all acts of militancy as soon as war was declared and suffragettes were instructed to help with the fight in any way they could.

Matthew Roundswell was a never-ending source

40

of information and was always ready to talk about it. He sounded so knowledgeable and manly. Then, out of the blue, he made an announcement. She should have expected it, she reflected afterwards.

When they met that evening, there was an added excitement in his eyes. She hadn't seen him so charged up before. It suited him but she didn't dare ask what had brought him to such a pitch.

They had barely greeted one another when the words he truly wanted to say burst through his lips.

'Constance, my dear. I have important news for you, and I hope that you will appreciate why it must be done.'

Her heart buzzed. She could scarcely breathe.

'You are aware of my family's need to show its total commitment to this country and to be true in all things?' He paused, watching her face carefully.

Then she knew. She wanted to interrupt, to stop him saying the words that would make her world fall apart.

'Dearest Constance, I went to the recruiting office yesterday and enlisted in the army. I will serve my country, possibly in France, or Belgium after basic training.'

He stopped momentarily, searching her face for her reaction to his news. News that would put him in great peril no matter how long the war lasted.

'Oh, Matthew! When will you go?' Constance felt a tremendous pride that the man she was walking out with was going to serve king and country, but the reality of what he had committed himself to shook her.

'Basic training starts in September and lasts four months. We'll soon sort out the Kaiser and his boys. People in the know say it will all be over by Christmas anyway, so I won't have finished training by then.'

'But if it's not, then you could be going into battle in January or February? We've only just found each other, and now you have to leave. I will miss you so much.'

'I'm glad to hear it. I would be devastated if you didn't. I want you to think of me while I'm fighting for our country. Darling Constance. May I call you darling?'

'Oh, Matthew! Of course you may, and I will think about you all the time.'

His arms came around her — strong, firm, caring arms. He was beginning to steal her heart. At school, she would have chortled at such language but now, it suited the occasion perfectly.

There was no time to think of words. She waited impatiently for his lips to meet hers but it couldn't happen quickly enough. She reached up and pulled his head towards her. His lips crushed hers, sending tingling sensations through her arms to her heart. By the time his lips pulled away, she was breathless and hungered for more.

'Oh, Matthew, I wish you didn't have to go. When will you come home again?'

She sounded petulant and selfish, and that would never do. Her heart screamed 'but what about me?' She put a hand to her chest to try to stem her racing heart but all she could think of was that kiss and knowing that it could be weeks before she felt his lips on hers again. He would go because it was expected of him. He was an honourable man. She doubted it would enter his head not to. But thinking of him fighting, killing others, or being killed seemed like a horrific nightmare.

If, as he said, the whole ghastly thing would be over by Christmas, then he wouldn't be called upon to fight, thank goodness.

She could only pray it came true.

* * *

In late August, Father had word that poor Mr Bainbridge had been killed at a place called Mons in Belgium where the British had been forced into retreat. A month at war and already she knew someone who had lost his life. What would she do if the same happened to Matthew?

6

October 1914

'I want to get him out.'

Constance's mother stared at her.

'Get who out, dear?'

'Sam, Ginnie's friend. I spoke of him, if you remember. I want to get him out of the workhouse. We must be able to help, Mother. Neither of them will be happy until they can be together again. Sam has nothing to look forward to.'

'Does he have somewhere to go?'

'I doubt it. His father is a seaman so it's unlikely anyone will know where he is, and his mother is dead.' Constance took a deep breath. 'Ginnie is a lovely girl but I sense she's lonely. I would like to help them. If we could help to find Sam a job, and get him a place to board, he could leave the workhouse, couldn't he?'

'Well, yes he could. But I really don't —'

'There must be something we can do. I believe he's too young to fight, but I thought that maybe some manufacturers might be short of men. Or he could try one of the pits? They may be looking to recruit replacement workers.'

'Mmm. And where would he live?'

'We . . . could ask around. Somewhere temporary, until he finds his feet.'

'Constance! You're not thinking of here, are you?'

'No Mother. I think he would probably feel quite

uncomfortable and out of his depth. If you can get him out, I will find somewhere for him.'

Her mother smiled. 'I will do as you ask, but please don't say anything to your father that you have a friendship with a former workhouse girl!'

★ ★ ★

Mother had spoken to Mr Hardcastle. The workhouse superintendent had confirmed that she could assist Sam White to leave at the earliest opportunity as he was a friend of a friend. They would help him look for work and see him settled somewhere. Mr Hardcastle said the fewer inmates the better in these times, what with men leaving to join the Colours. Sam could be allowed out of the workhouse to look for work, but would be warned that he must return the same day, or be charged with theft of his workhouse uniform.

★ ★ ★

Constance called at the workhouse the very next day, to make Sam aware of the arrangements. As she walked through the great iron gates, she stared at the huge, austere building as if through the eyes of a child, the way Ginnie would have seen it the first day she entered. Imposing, rows of windows, no signs of the inmates outside. It reminded her of Holloway. An icy coldness settled around her heart. How brave Ginnie must have been.

She entered the porter's lodge and was shown to a small empty room. Through the window she could see men walking round what appeared to be an exercise yard. Most were looking at the floor. She thought

45

of the sixteen-year-old Sam, and her heart went out to him.

The door opened and a tall, angular boy was pushed into the room. His head was shaved, with a glimmer of dark hairs. Clear, blue eyes frowned at her as she motioned him to sit.

'My name is Constance Copeland. You must wonder why I have asked to see you, Sam,' Constance began.

His eyes opened wide. ''Ow do yer know me name?'

'I'm a friend of Ginnie's.'

It was a positive joy to see his eyes light up when she said the name, but they clouded over suspiciously. 'You know Ginnie? 'Ow could she 'ave a friend like you?'

What he really meant was, how could a former workhouse girl have a toff for a friend, Constance translated. 'I assure you she is a friend and I have promised to help you to get out of here.'

He started up at that. 'I've gorra have a job. Somewhere to live. 'Ow's that going to 'appen? What did yer say yer name was, miss?'

'Constance Copeland,' she smiled.

'Copeland?' Sam frowned, staring at the wall behind Constance's head. Then his eyes widened. 'Were you the wench what came to give us presents one year, one Christmas?'

'That's right,' Constance nodded. 'And call me Constance as we are to be friends, Sam. I believe there are some jobs going at Etruria pit. You have permission to leave the workhouse and to make yourself known to them. Once you have work, we can sort out board and lodgings for you. You don't have any objections to the pit, do you, Sam?'

'No, miss. I'll do anything to get out and be with Ginnie again.'

'She's a special girl, I know.'

'The best. 'Course, I couldn't tell 'er that. Not in Haddon. We was just kids then.'

Constance smiled again and Sam grinned back. Immediately she saw what Ginnie had seen in this boy. Yes, Ginnie wasn't the only special person Constance had met.

They deserved each other.

★ ★ ★

Constance hadn't said a word to Ginnie, but today she would be taking Sam to see her. It was all arranged. She couldn't wait to see the look on Ginnie's face when she saw Sam.

Just as they arrived at Ginnie's door, Sam stopped. 'I want ter thank yer for all you've done for me and ma wench, Mis . . . Constance. Her's done alright to get a friend like yerself.'

'You are welcome, Sam. I'm glad I could be of help.'

Sam stared at the door, Number 25. He moved back a step. 'Er's living with 'er sister. Is 'er alright? She was a bit worried about why her Mabel had asked her to stay an' all, given as she never came to see Ginnie.'

'It's early days, Sam, but I believe they are getting to know one another again and that must be a good thing. Ready?'

Sam's lips thinned. He nodded.

Constance knocked on the door and indicated that Sam should move to one side so he couldn't be seen. It was Mabel who answered.

'Miss Constance!'

'Hello Mabel,' she said brightly and chuckled at the lifted eyebrows on the woman's face as Sam followed her inside.

And there was Ginnie. Staring open-mouthed at the boy who needed no introduction.

'Sam! Sam! I can't believe it.' Her grin spread from ear to ear.

'Hello lass. It's grand to see yer.'

His arms went around Ginnie. Constance watched, delighted with her surprise.

Ginnie reached up and held Sam's cheeks, staring into his eyes as if unable to take it in. Constance felt her eyes water and blinked to stop tears from forming at such a special moment.

A red-faced Ginnie turned to Mabel, eyes shining. 'This is Sam. He's a friend.'

'I should hope he's a friend after that greeting,' said Mabel.

Ginnie's face turned a bright red.

After the pleasantries were over, it was arranged that Ginnie would see Sam at Holmorton Lodge where they could get to know each other again. Constance couldn't have been happier.

7

1915

Last year, going to war was looked upon as a big adventure that would be over with by Christmas. Thousands of young men had answered Lord Kitchener's call to arms, ready to do their bit.

But now things were very different. The war on the Western Front had reached a stalemate. Both sides had dug in for the winter and the newspapers had said the front lines stretched from the English Channel to the Swiss border. Constance shivered. All those men, living out in the open through the harshness of winter.

Father had sold Star, the horse. The carriage had also been sold. Horses were in demand by the army and Constance did not want to think of that poor animal thrust into battle. He would be all alone with no one to give him his carrot each day.

★ ★ ★

It was late February when Constance received a letter from Matthew. It was sitting on the silver tray on the hall table where all the post was placed after each delivery.

'I'm going to my room, Tilda, could you bring me a pot of tea, please?'

'Yes, miss.'

49

When she got to her room, her heart was pounding. She hoped this first letter would say how much he was missing her and how he longed to come home. She sat in her favourite chair by the window and started to read.

My dear Constance,
*   I hope this letter finds you well. As you will appreciate, I cannot tell you where I am, suffice to say we are working hard to end this war.*
*   I miss you so very much and cannot wait until I return to The Potteries. I hope things will change for the better when the spring arrives. It's dashed good that we are doing so well in other theatres of war. I don't know when I will next have leave and I can see you again.*
*   Dearest, I hope you are missing me. Write to me as soon as you can.*
*   Your loving Matthew*

Constance started to weep. He was alone, facing danger every day. She was a little disappointed the letter wasn't longer, but then, she supposed, he wouldn't have a lot of time. There was a knock at the door and Alice entered with a tray of tea and some of Mrs Williams's fruit cake.

'Oh! You haven't had bad news, have yer?'

Constance dried her eyes and composed herself. 'It's a letter from a friend. Put the tray down on the table, I'll pour for myself.'

'Is there anything else I can do for you, Constance?'

'No, that will be all, thank you, Alice. I need a bit of time to myself.'

A terrible thought suddenly occurred to Constance

— the papers were full of the new expedition to Gallipoli and the heavy fighting there.

Could Matthew be in Gallipoli?

★ ★ ★

It was April. She had hoped to receive a letter every week where Matthew would pour his heart out, telling her how much he missed her and that he was longing to see her. But she was disappointed again. The length of time between letters made her wonder if he even thought of her. Maybe she was just someone to pass the time of day with and now he was settled into the serious business of war, he was no longer interested.

A job had not been high on her list of priorities before the war started but women, in all walks of life, were taking on jobs and mucking in to support the war effort. She needed something to keep her mind firmly fixed on the here and now, rather than thinking about what might be.

She broached the matter with her mother. 'What would you think of me getting a job?'

'Why would you want to get a job?'

'I can't bear the thought of my life continuing in this manner. Every day is the same. I need something to take my mind of this horrible war. I want to help. I want to meet people of my own age. I think I am just treading water between school and marriage.'

'I respect and commend your wish for independence. What do you have in mind?'

Constance shrugged. 'I'll know it when I see it.'

Mother smiled. 'No doubt you will, my dear. You have already taken over some of my role as a Workhouse Friend after we helped your friend Sam and you

51

have increased your work for the WSPU. You learned to type and help with office duties at the branch.'

Constance thought for a moment. 'It is quiet in the office now and I want something more.'

★ ★ ★

Tilda and Sal were the next to leave. They had both applied for jobs in a munitions factory in Birmingham and been accepted.

'We're sorry to leave yer, Mrs Copeland but yer canna look a gift horse in the mouth. The pay's much better and we'll 'ave time for ourselves an' all. Be fools not to.'

Constance sat with her mother to hear the news. She couldn't blame either of them. Only Mrs Williams and Alice would be left to look after the house, garden and all the meals.

'How on earth will we manage, Mother?'

'It's wartime, Constance. We will manage because we have to. Your father has already decided not to replace Bainbridge in the garden. And in any case, it would be difficult to get an able-bodied man who isn't in the army.'

They discussed staffing matters at dinner that evening. Her father was quite adamant. 'I am not going to employ a gardener. We can get a man to come in for half a day to keep the garden tidy.'

'You can help him, Father!' Constance giggled.

'Certainly not. And I'm not going to take on any more servants. Mrs Williams will do the cooking and Alice can do the rest.'

'But that's too much, Father.'

'So, you can help her, Constance.'

Constance declined to comment.

It only occurred to her later that families like hers would be helping the war effort if they kept their own houses clean and tidy and left young girls like Tilda and Sal free to work in the munitions factories. She would do her bit.

★ ★ ★

By June, it was becoming clear that more men were needed if the war was to be won. Constance now worked regularly in the local WSPU branch office undertaking clerical duties and taking notes at all their meetings. She enjoyed supporting her activist colleagues without potentially getting involved with the police, just what she had promised Father.

During a meeting in early June, discussions took place on what the branch might do to help and support the war effort. The Army Recruiting Committee had welcomed the latest suffragette strategy of shaming and humiliating men not in uniform. By pinning a white feather on to a man's collar or lapel they instantly branded him a coward. How could he then look his lady in the eye? It wasn't fair, it was argued, that able-bodied men could let others fight while they stayed at home in safety and comfort.

Helen, a rather outspoken individual, was keen to play an active role in using the white feathers.

'It's been very effective elsewhere. We should try it out as a branch. We must.'

Constance tried to imagine a young man's horror at being confronted by a strange woman in the street and presented with a white feather for all to see.

'I don't know if I could do that,' someone said with

a frown. 'Isn't there something else we could do?'

'It might make them think twice about leaving the fighting to others,' said Helen, mutinously. She had even procured a box of feathers from somewhere. She banged it down on the table in front of them. 'I suggest we test it out at the earliest opportunity, ladies.'

There were nine of them sitting around the table. Constance felt their mixed views and uncomfortable shuffling. Four were all for it, three against and two dithered, unable to make a decision.

'I am concerned it might backfire on the WSPU. The public might lose sympathy for our cause. It is already a source of controversy across many branches,' said Mrs Bracegirdle, one of the founder members of the branch.

'How do we choose our targets? Some boys of my acquaintance could quite easily be mistaken as young men of greater age. How can it be right to approach an unknown man and pin a feather on him?' ventured Constance.

'It's not for you to speak in this committee.' Helen glared at Constance. 'You're here to take the notes. So shut up!'

'No, no, Helen. Constance is a member of this branch and has the right to be heard,' said Mrs Bracegirdle. She turned to Constance. 'Go on, my dear.'

'Thank you, Mrs Bracegirdle. What I was going on to say is any man wandering the streets with a woman on his arm may have a multitude of reasons for being here and not in France or Belgium, or indeed any part of the Empire. I agree, the men who stay behind are not being fair to those who have already come forward but does anyone have the right to so much power over another human being?'

'If he's fit and healthy-looking and not in uniform, I should want to know why, wouldn't you?' said Helen, scornfully.

Constance wasn't sure how she felt about Helen's extreme views. A couple of the group members tittered, although that could have been from nerves.

'The man might have been ill or be an invalid. How do we know?' said Mary, one of the doubters.

'Whatever would the constables say?' another member asked.

Questions came in quickly and Constance had difficulty in keeping up with them.

'Look, ladies, the Army's Recruiting Committee is keen for the WSPU to help,' said Helen firmly. 'And I think it's the very least we can do. We all know of young men fighting at the Front, don't we?' Her eyes scoured the table. Most heads were nodding furiously. 'We have a duty to help them by sending more men over.'

Constance was nervous of doing something which could send her back to prison. And, even if the WSPU committee condoned such behaviour, what would Matthew think? Her father would certainly be against it and so would Mother. After all, she left the WSPU because of their rising militancy.

At the end of the discussion, the branch agreed to try it out before formally adopting it as policy. Helen asked for volunteers to work in groups of two and Constance reluctantly agreed.

★ ★ ★

On this sunny, summer Sunday there was determination in the air. Half a dozen branch members gathered together, ostensibly listening to the band playing in the park. Many people had gathered dressed in their Sunday best. Some of the members hung back, not wanting to be the first to give out a white feather, but the leader insisted they must follow it through; she had to make a report to Head Office.

After a quick nod, the women split into pairs and spread out to target specific areas of the park, conscious of the need to make quick their escape, should the situation turn unpleasant. To her dismay, Constance was paired up with Helen. All she really knew about the woman was that she worked in Burton & Dunn's in Hanley, she had a loud mouth and she seemed to find it impossible to do anything quietly.

'Come on, Constance. The country needs as many soldiers as it can get. It's our duty to search out cowards.' Helen grabbed Constance's arm and linked it with her own as if they were the best of friends.

The two walked side by side along the footpath, admiring the array of colour in the flowers lining their way. Helen whispered in her ear. She was ready to do the deed as a well-dressed man in his mid-twenties and a woman strolled towards them, arm in arm. He was laughing, and the woman was looking up at him, oblivious to everyone.

'I'll take this one.' Helen had a look of immense satisfaction on her face as she strode swiftly towards the man.

How could he be a coward when a woman loved him so much? Constance wished she could back away but Helen reached out and pinned the feather on to his lapel. He raised his arm to push her away, but Helen was too strong.

'Hope you have second thoughts and join the

Colours, lest your lady friend here thinks you a coward.'

The woman screamed and burst into tears as the man's face turned an ashen colour. That was all Constance saw as she and Helen covered their faces and scurried off before his surprise turned to violence. The woman screamed again, causing everyone around them to witness the event.

As they rounded a bend in the path, Helen panted, 'Your turn, Constance.'

Thinking back to the poor woman whose life they had probably destroyed, Constance hesitated. She wasn't frightened, but she was horrified at the reaction of the woman. Such a devastating event in the middle of such happiness. Surely it hadn't been fair to upset her. It was her husband or friend's fault for not enlisting.

When they were out of sight of their target, they slowed down to a steady walk. Constance's breaths were coming in sharp, painful spasms which she tried desperately to control.

Their new target was a man on his own, and therefore the only one to be upset would be the guilty party himself. He looked about thirty and his hair — what little she could see not covered by his hat — was a pale blond. As they drew closer, she could see his eyes had a glazed and vacant look. He was an easy prey, a perfect prey if she genuinely believed in their mission. She doubted he even saw them. But there was something about his stance and manner that made her hesitate.

Helen pushed her forward.

Constance closed her eyes, took a deep breath and asked for forgiveness before dashing towards him.

Momentarily, he looked startled. Then, as he realised what she was about to do, he caught her hand firmly.

'Ouch . . .' she cried out.

He let go of her without speaking. She thrust the feather into his top pocket. As she did so, his eyes caught hers, blue, turning to grey. How light they were. Haunted, full of pain.

But she'd done it, and it was too late to stop now.

She glanced over her shoulder as she and Helen ran towards the park gates. He hadn't moved. He stood in silence, staring at the feather he had taken out of his pocket.

When she went to bed that night, those blue-grey eyes were the last thing that came into her mind as she tried to sleep. She tossed and turned, but every time she closed her eyes, the man's haunted eyes looked at her with such sadness, she almost cried. She told herself she had done it for the cause, and for Matthew, but she couldn't help but feel ashamed.

There was so much talk of war over the next few weeks. It was in everyone's mind, never far away. The suffragettes kept up their coercion tactics, to make those who stayed behind feel like the cowards they were, they said, and the local Recruiting Committee continued to welcome their actions.

Constance couldn't help thinking of the pain she had seen in the man's eyes as he stared at the white feather.

8

July 1916

Seeing Ginnie and Sam so happy together caused Constance happiness, but sadness too. Matthew, who seemed so keen to woo her, had barely written during the time he had been away. She had male acquaintances, mainly those on leave from one of the armed services, and many were officers, but none made her heart race as Matthew had. She had even considered approaching his mother for news. She couldn't, of course, because they hadn't been introduced, and she didn't know how Matthew would feel about such an intrusion.

The Sentinel was sitting on the table in the morning room. It was full of news about the new offensive on the River Somme in France. Constance read all she could about the battle and hoped Matthew was safe. The British were doing well and making ground. Perhaps the war might end soon.

★ ★ ★

She was visiting the Queen's Hall to buy tickets for herself and Ginnie to attend a performance of the Burslem Amateur Dramatic Society. Their annual show was a highlight Constance looked forward to, and this year she wanted to share it with Ginnie who had never been to the theatre. Unfortunately for her, the tickets had not gone on sale. Disappointed and concentrating on putting her purse away, she bumped into someone on the pavement outside.

'S-sorry. I didn't mean —'

Constance found herself looking directly into Matthew's eyes, which appeared to light up when he saw her. She couldn't look away. And neither, it seemed, could he.

She threw her arms around him. 'Oh Matthew, thank God you're alive. I prayed you weren't injured or worse in the terrible battles on the River Somme. The newspapers are full of it.'

'Thank you for your concern, Constance, but as you can see I am quite well.'

Embarrassed at her show of affection, she pushed him away and fiddled with her purse, putting it securely in her handbag. He looked debonair in his officer's uniform. Her heart skipped a beat.

'Are you continuing with your shopping or would you allow me to escort you home?'

She took a deep breath. 'You may escort me, Matthew.'

She delved into her bag, pretending to look for something, determined not to give away the effect he was having on her. 'Am I right in assuming you're on leave at present? You definitely aren't injured in any way?'

He held out his arm and she took it. Although it felt good to feel his presence beside her, she was a little annoyed that he hadn't written to her recently. Had he tried to see her or, if she hadn't bumped into him, would he have returned to his regiment without contacting her? She had been thinking of him often and couldn't bear that he didn't seem to feel the same.

'You are quite right, my dear. I return within the

week. I've missed you so much, Constance. I was planning to pay you a surprise visit this evening. You have been in my thoughts day and night and I couldn't bear the thought of going back without seeing you. Dearest Constance, I didn't think it fair to ask you to wait for me.' He curled his other hand over hers tenderly. 'Christ, Constance, I only have to look at you and I find I want to believe you will, very much.'

'Of course.' Her annoyance melted away. 'I've missed you, Matthew. I didn't know if I'd ever see you again. How is Mrs Roundswell keeping?' Good manners demanded she had to ask.

'Mother keeps herself to herself these days. She isn't one for socialising.'

He gripped her arm tightly. Her heart fluttered. Just the touch of him excited her. He was still the man of her dreams.

'Matthew, I was beginning to think you had another lady . . . or worse . . .' She couldn't bring herself to say the words on the tip of her tongue.

'I'm sorry for my neglect, Constance. Please forgive me. You don't know what it's like over there, continually on the alert, the men's lives depending on me.'

She felt guilty for raising the matter, but she extracted a promise that he would write faithfully in the future and, with that, she had to be content.

He talked about his bravery overseas and his family business in The Potteries, and she told him about her work with the WSPU and various outings with her parents.

All too soon, they arrived at Holmorton Lodge, and he escorted her to the door. Constance felt this wasn't the time to invite him in, so early in their re-acquaintance. She wasn't even sure when their next meeting would be.

'You were buying theatre tickets? I would be honoured to have the pleasure of your company, and we could go together?'

Her excitement grew.

'What is your ticket number?'

'My ticket number?'

'I believe that when one accompanies a young lady to the theatre, it is acceptable for them to sit next to each other.' There it was again, his dry wit. But this time, it made her smile.

'I didn't get one,' she confessed. In answer to his perplexed frown, she carried on. 'I mean, they haven't gone on sale yet; it is for a performance in September. It appears I am too eager.' She gave a self-conscious laugh.

'Then perhaps you would allow me to get tickets for tomorrow's performance? I don't know what it will be, but I think that hardly matters.'

His gaze burned into her, leaving her to dwell on where his thoughts might be heading.

Her breaths came quickly. 'That would be . . . most acceptable, Matthew. And now I must leave you, as my mother is expecting my return. I bid you good day.'

She walked away, her back straight, pleased at the restraint she was exercising.

★　★　★

He kissed her on the lips after the theatre the following night. She felt alive, her whole body tingled with promise. She wanted it to go on and on, not wanting it to end and have him leave her bereft and alone on the doorstep.

Over the next two days they saw each other often, walking and talking incessantly. It all looked very promising. The more she heard, the more she liked and when he asked to see her parents before he left, she couldn't have been more thrilled. She had been on the point of asking him every time they met, conscious of their limited time together, but didn't want to appear too forward. It was unlike her, but nothing had seemed as important as this in her life before.

He was meant for her.

Was she being overly sentimental? The war had changed everything for so many people. It would be easy to be swept away by the romance of being parted sweethearts.

No, she wasn't that shallow. There was much more to it than that. She couldn't deny that her feelings for him were deepening. She thought about him all the time and, as the days progressed, she didn't know how she was going to cope without him. They arranged that he would meet her parents shortly before he was due to return, and she found herself increasingly nervous, hoping it would go well.

9

August 1916

'Edwin, you'll be pleased to know that we are four for dinner this evening. Constance has asked if she could bring a gentleman friend and I have agreed.'

'I'm sure you will like him, Father. Matthew Roundswell is a much-respected member of the community. A refined gentleman of means.'

'I know of Mr Roundswell, he's a member of the Chamber of Commerce. He could make a good husband.' He frowned. 'Don't you go telling him about your suffragette escapades if you want to stand a chance of snaring him. I understand his mother is quite protective.'

'He already knows I am a suffragette — that's how we met,' Constance said, triumphantly. 'My past appears to mean more to you than it does to him.'

'What? You've spoken of . . . ?'

'I met him when I was with Sarah, handing out my pamphlets. He even said he liked a woman with a brain,' she finished smugly.

'But does he want a criminal for a wife? Have you asked him that?'

Constance's face was on fire. 'Of course not. We've only just become acquainted, Father. How can we be talking of marriage or any such thing?' She mustered her anger to deflect his thoughts. 'And I wasn't a criminal; I was a political prisoner.'

'Take heed, Constance. If I'm ever going to get you off my hands and into your husband's, you need to promise me that you will, under no circumstances, inform Mr Roundswell, or any other potential husband you may feel justified in bringing to our door, of your stay in that place we don't speak of.'

* * *

Matthew rang the doorbell of Holmorton Lodge at precisely seven o'clock. Constance had chosen to wear a pale blue silk dress, fitted at the waist, with a fine lace shawl which would do nicely if they should happen to take a stroll around the gardens later.

Alice showed him into the drawing room, threw a glance at Constance, and quietly withdrew. He ignored Constance and her mother and strode over to shake hands with her father, which rather pleased him, Constance could tell. She concluded that Matthew had read her father's personality very well, knowing he would enjoy the flattery.

'Mother, can I introduce you to our guest, Mr Matthew Roundswell?'

He took her mother's raised hand. 'Charmed to meet you, Mrs Copeland. I hope you are well? And call me Matthew, both of you.'

'Certainly, Matthew,' her mother said with a smile. 'Do come and sit by me and tell me more about yourself. My husband tells me you belong to the Chamber of Commerce?'

Constance smiled to herself. Mother always rose to the occasion. That Father was put out about Matthew spending so much time listening to her mother, was easy to see. He sat in his leather chair beside the fireplace drumming his fingers on the arm.

There was a knock on the drawing room door. Alice entered and announced that dinner was being served. The party moved into the dining room.

At the end of the meal, her father rose. 'Matthew? Let us withdraw to the library and leave the women to talk among themselves. I want to hear about your business plans for the future. It could be a good time to invest, I'm told.'

Matthew nodded politely and joined him at the door.

Her father put his arm across Matthew's shoulder and their heads came together. 'I've been meaning to ask . . .'

The door closed behind them.

Constance had a smug smile on her face as she turned to her mother. 'Well, that went better than I expected. Father obviously feels they have much in common.'

'Yes, I believe so. I feel that young man has more in common with your father than you realise.'

'Whatever do you mean?'

'They are men of business used to getting their own way. Emotions and business do not sit well in your father's life and I fear that Matthew might be the same.'

'Oh no, Mother, Matthew is very attentive. He's wonderful. He's kind and considerate. I thought you, of all people, would be happy for me to meet some-one like him.'

'So was your father at first. Sometimes I feel he needed a wife to complete his portfolio of achievements to make him successful and I was most suitable in that regard. For all his faults, I do love him.' She stopped for a moment, staring ahead.

Constance was shocked into silence. Such an admission from her mother did not come lightly.

Her mother continued. 'There is something about Matthew . . . he seems to be concerned greatly about his family's standing within the community, but do you not think he is somewhat . . . cold in his manner?'

'Cold?'

'When he smiles, it doesn't quite meet his eyes.'

Was that truly how Mother saw him? No, he would never be so inattentive. Not to her.

'How can you say that after so brief an acquaintance, Mother?'

'Take it from someone older and more experienced than you, Constance. Be very aware of what you are looking for and satisfy yourself that you can achieve it with Matthew.'

Her mother's words gave Constance food for thought as they moved into the drawing room to await their men.

The door to the library opened and the men joined them, each smoking a cigar, her father talking about the war. Matthew gave an almost imperceptible nod and Constance knew that all had gone well.

'. . . it seems we are giving the Huns a terrible beating on the Western Front. How long do you think it will be before the war is over?'

'No one knows. The Germans are very resourceful and brave and are putting up a strong and spirited defence,' said Matthew.

'Judging by the casualty lists reported in *The Sentinel* if we are winning then it would seem to be at a terrible cost,' interjected Constance.

'It is the way of this war, I'm afraid. If we are to win

then this sacrifice will be worth it,' said Matthew.

'Just been showing this young man my whisky collection, Agatha. He appears quite knowledgeable himself.' His raised eyebrows gave away his impressed demeanour.

Later, Constance and Matthew wandered around the garden, densely packed with budding flowers, making polite conversation. Constance didn't say a good deal. She was quite content to hear him speak. He certainly had plenty to say.

'Your parents are very approachable, Constance, particularly your father.'

Constance choked back her surprise. Her father was at his most charming when he wanted to get his own way and having Matthew as a son-in-law would undoubtedly give him that. She should be pleased but her mother's comments were in her thoughts.

'What did Father want to talk to you about?' Constance hoped it would be all about her. After all, it was his opportunity to tell Matthew what a wonderful wife she would make.

'About the war, mainly. Your father clearly wanted to impress me with his business skills.'

He laughed to himself, except Constance didn't think it funny.

Nevertheless, they continued their walk. At the end of the garden, in the cover of the hebe bushes, she pulled him close to her. She didn't care if he thought her forward. They were out of sight from the downstairs windows, and it could be her only chance to be alone with him and she wanted him to remember it. She also wanted to prove to herself that Matthew was far from cold towards her.

Tomorrow, they would visit his mother and then on

Saturday morning, he would make his way back to his regiment, and heaven knew when she would see him again.

* * *

After he'd gone, she returned to the drawing room to hear the verdict, particularly from her father.

'He seems like a very personable young man to me. If you want to keep him, I suggest you say nothing of your imprisonment. He holds his mother's feelings in high regard, which is praise indeed for any man. But I don't think his mother would take kindly to a criminal for a daughter-in-law, no matter how well-bred she may be.'

'He's open-minded and is not concerned about my being a suffragette. And I wasn't a criminal. Father, we were all political prisoners placed there for what we believed in.'

'Whatever, the Pankhursts or the rest of your kind think, it was wilful damage in the eyes of the law. You were not imprisoned for protesting, but for throwing a stone through a window. Do you really want to tell him about Holloway? Are you prepared to take the risk?'

'Father! For goodness' sake!'

* * *

Constance dressed in her best conservative outfit to meet Matthew's mother, as he had instructed. When they first discussed her attire for the evening, he'd said she should wear something smart but nothing that would make her stand out, as his mother was quite conservative in her dress. That his mother could dictate such a matter was somewhat disconcerting, but she could see his reasoning about treading softly on a first visit. There was absolutely no point in antagonising the person who was so important in his life. If anything, it showed how important the meeting was to him, and she wanted to create a good impression, didn't she? She chose a dark blue day dress, not her favourite, but it would do. It did show off her auburn curls and green eyes very well.

Matthew was half an hour early picking her up and had the motor waiting outside. It was naughty of her, she knew, but as she entered the drawing room, she could almost feel him assessing her with his mother's eyes. Had he deliberately arrived early so that he could ask her to change if the need should arise? Such behaviour would normally cause her to do the opposite of what was demanded, but today she told herself she was pleased to adhere because it showed he wanted his mother to like her.

Matthew helped Constance from the motor — a Lanchester 40hp he said it was — and escorted her to the house, which looked more substantial than her own, standing in its well-kept grounds. At least that would please Father if he should ever receive an invitation.

The door was opened into a large square hallway by a woman Constance imagined was the housekeeper, dressed smartly in black with a white collar and cuffs. Her face was plain and her hair scraped back into a tight bun in the nape of her neck. It was difficult to assess her age.

Matthew nodded to the woman and swept Constance in front of him. He took her hat and coat and handed both to the housekeeper. He made no effort to introduce her, so Constance concluded that she would, hereinafter, be known simply as The House-keeper.

Matthew looked Constance up and down one final time and, seemingly satisfied, led her to a partly open door. Matthew's rather diligent attention to his mother's sensibilities was beginning to make Constance feel ever so slightly nervous, and the prospect of meeting her almost had her tongue-tied. A niggle of annoyance began to build inside her. She would not act in this almost subservient way for anybody.

Constance strode forwards without waiting for Matthew's intervention and stopped in front of the older woman, sour of face and dressed in black, sitting in a chair beside the fire with her tiny feet perched on a footstool. She gave no sign of getting up to greet her guest and there was no vestige of a smile.

Constance felt her breath constrict. This meeting was so important. She had to try to make a good impression, as Matthew had done for her. 'How do you do, Mrs Roundswell? I am so pleased to make your acquaintance.' Constance held out her hand and left it there.

Matthew rushed to his mother's side. 'Mother dear, this is Constance Copeland, the young lady I have been speaking of this week.'

Mrs Roundswell inclined her head graciously at Constance and when their hands met, her touch was cold and so light it hardly made an impression.

'Please take a seat, Constance,' said Matthew, steering her towards the ladder-back chair placed away from the fire, directly opposite his mother.

Constance felt she was being interviewed on a

71

matter of some importance. Maybe that was how Mrs Roundswell saw it. She sat demurely and waited for someone to open the conversation. The fighter in Constance wanted to take control, but the thinker had to curb her emotions, and she reminded herself that power resided in those who could retain control when needed.

'Good evening, Constance,' said Mrs Roundswell at last. 'Welcome to our home.'

Constance was quick to notice the emphasis on our and chastised herself for being over sensitive.

'I have been hearing a lot about you from my son. You seem to have made quite an impression on him.'

'Thank you.'

'How are your legs today, Mother?' he said.

'As well as could be expected after spending the day alone with no conversation.'

Constance was surprised to see Matthew's face redden at the implied criticism.

After some small talk they moved into the dining room. It was during the meal that the conversation took an unexpected turn.

'Constance is a member of the Women's Social and Political Union, Mother. She helps them in the branch office. We became acquainted when she was handing out pamphlets. Most informative, they were. Did you produce them yourself, Constance?'

It wasn't a subject she had expected him to talk about in front of his mother.

'I er I . . . no. I wrote an article and do some typing and various office duties.'

'I never told you. Mother also believes women should have the vote. But she is a suffragist.'

72

'I couldn't possibly lend my name to such goings-on as the suffragettes get up to. Breaking the law. They are troublemakers and I'm surprised that you give them the time of day, Constance.' Mrs Roundswell shook her head. 'No, dear, we suffragists feel the only way to tackle the matter is through the political system, not rampaging through the streets committing needless acts of violence. It's hardly lady-like is it?'

'My mother is a suffragist, but she keeps an open mind and allows me to have my own views.' Constance could feel her hackles rise as Matthew shot her a warning glance. Her head was swimming. She managed to ease her napkin off the table so she had to bend to retrieve it. The conversation was too close to her secret for comfort. Why hadn't Matthew told her? She could have been more prepared.

When she sat upright again, she at least had a reason for her red face.

'You should have much in common, ladies,' said Matthew.

Constance wondered if he was oblivious to the friction swirling between them, but his mother chose this moment to change the topic of conversation.

'How is dear Robert, Matthew? He's a delightful boy,' she said by way of explanation to Constance. 'He and Matthew have been friends for more years than I can remember. He worked in London for a while and had opportunities to meet the most important people. I believe he lives locally now. I haven't seen him for a good while. Have you spoken to him, Matthew?'

'No, Mother,' said Matthew and changed the subject.

'Then you should invite him to take tea with us the

next time he is in the town.'

As Matthew tried again to change the subject, Constance frowned detecting an underlying current to their discussion. One she was not party to, deliberately so and effectively cutting her out of the conversation. She thought it rather rude.

The rest of the meal was a quiet affair. Constance decided she had a headache and asked Matthew to take her home. She was sure his face held a trace of thankfulness as he led her into the hallway and The Housekeeper brought her coat. Constance smiled at her. She looked startled, as if no one had smiled at her before.

Constance's first meeting with Mrs Roundswell was over. She hoped Matthew would be more of a help to her if there were to be another.

They walked down the pathway to the car. She stopped walking and turned to face him.

'Why did you not warn me that your mother was a suffragist? That was highly embarrassing, Matthew.'

'I thought it would provide some common ground between you.'

'And who is Robert?'

'I went to school with him. He's just a friend.'

'Is there something going on, something you've not talked about?'

Matthew shrugged. 'He's just a friend.'

'She wanted to make me feel out of it. Talking about someone I've never met. She was making a point, Matthew.'

He sighed. 'She doesn't want to lose me. She'll get used to it.'

'I understand her concern. Many mothers are reluctant to lose control over their only son as he gets older. Only you can challenge her, Matthew.' Constance started to walk away.

Matthew grimaced.

Clearly, he wasn't used to being spoken to in this way, but his expression mellowed.

'Mother may not like the idea, but I will get married. And it will be my choice and not hers.'

In the midst of that minor argument one word had stood out — married. Was he thinking of marrying her, or was he talking in general terms? After all, she barely knew him. At home, with his mother, he appeared different. She couldn't quite put a finger on it and she could think of nothing else.

★ ★ ★

In view of his impending departure, they agreed to spend the day together. Matthew picked her up in the Lanchester and drove to the Peak District. It was a glorious day. They stopped at Rudyard Lake and again at The Roaches to overlook the vast Cheshire plain with the smoke of Manchester and Liverpool in the far distance. As they sat there, taking in the views, Matthew said something that astounded her.

'Dearest, our visit went well after all. Mother and I had a long talk last night, and she thinks you are most suitable. She likes your independent manner. I think we should get married in September. What do you say?'

'Marriage! In September? How . . . I mean . . . it's too soon.' Constance was shaking.

He was due to depart in the morning, and the word marriage had only once entered their conversations, and even then, she hadn't known whether he was talking about her. She flushed with such heat she was in danger of exploding. Marry Matthew Roundswell?

He took up her hands and brought them to his lips. 'We can do it . . . if you want to, Constance.'

'But there's no time.'

'There's a war on, if you've noticed. Everybody's getting married before they go. The war has speeded up people's commitment to each other, that's all.'

'I've known you for such a short time, Matthew. Might people think we have to?' It was but a whisper. She had never talked to a man about such an intimate subject before.

'Darling Constance. No one will dare to think such a thing. We're from highly respectable families. I would need to get leave granted, of course.'

'I . . . I don't know what to say —'

'Then say yes and be done with it.'

'What about your mother?'

'She might make a fuss but she will want to please me. She always does.'

The comment jarred momentarily but was forgotten as his lips descended on hers.

He made her feel so alive. With sparkling eyes, she nodded, and the nods became more vigorous. 'Yes,' she said breathlessly. 'Oh, yes, let's get married. I love you, Matthew.'

'And I'm crazy about you, Constance. I don't want anyone else, only you, waiting for me each time I come home.'

He pulled her towards him and kissed her firmly on the lips even though they were standing on the doorstep for all to see. She couldn't believe she would soon be married to a soldier.

'Shall I come in now and we can tell your parents together?'

'No!' She laid both hands flat on his chest. 'No, I'll tell them. I can prepare them rather than it coming out of the blue.'

'You think they need preparing? I would have thought they would be expecting it.' His surprise was obvious.

'Father doesn't like surprises. Let me talk to them. You can come back tomorrow morning, and we can all talk together before you leave.'

He frowned but nodded. Then, he took a bow and departed.

Constance stood alone, the smile on her face gradually fading. They would, no doubt be very happy about the marriage; it was what her father had wanted for her, after all. Except he would have been assuming a grand wedding would take place between two successful families. This way there would be no time for splendour, just a simple wedding. They could make up for the rest when the war was over.

And there was still the dreaded problem of what to say about Holloway. How on earth could she break it to Matthew now?

★ ★ ★

She told them the moment she walked in, very much doubting she could keep it to herself. She wanted to tell the world about it. As she had expected, her father looked particularly pleased.

'That's wonderful news, Constance. He will make an excellent husband!'

Mother crossed to Constance and embraced her. 'I hope you will be very happy, my dear.'

'Might I remind you to say nothing about Holloway

to him, Constance. Are you listening to me?'

'But Father, it's his last night before he goes back. I have to —'

'You don't have to say anything. Your ridiculous infatuation with those women is putting your possibility of marriage and your whole future at serious risk. Do you want that?'

'No. But —'

'No buts, Constance. You will obey me in this matter.'

'Edwin, we must speak of —'

'Agatha! That is an end to the conversation. I will have no more of it. A daughter will obey her father at all times until she has a husband to lean on. You will do as I command, Constance.'

Constance paled. Matthew was calling tomorrow to officially ask for her hand on his way back to the barracks. Throughout her life, she had obeyed her father's command; as a good daughter should. But this was too big.

'I hope you're right, Father. I really do.'

She left her parents arguing, but she could tell by her mother's resigned acceptance that her father had already won.

★ ★ ★

Matthew arrived early on Saturday morning. Alice answered the door.

'Good morning Mr. Roundswell.

'I have an appointment with Mr. Copeland, be good enough to tell him I'm here.'

Constance and her mother were waiting in the hall. Matthew nodded his head at them and followed

Alice to the library, knocked, and entered. There was no noise or conversation to be heard as she stood, wringing her hands, wishing she was in there. She was surprised he hadn't come to her first. What if she had changed her mind? She doubted such a thought would have entered Matthew's head.

Within a short space of time the door opened and the two men stood in the doorway and shook hands vigorously; both seemed satisfied with the outcome of their talks. Constance heaved a huge sigh. And that meant . . .

'Constance, my dear, I am delighted to —'

'No sir,' her father interrupted. 'It is I who am delighted. Constance, you have a husband-to-be, and I have a son-in-law to care for my beautiful daughter.'

Constance beamed at them both. Her hands flew to her cheeks. It was actually happening. 'I can't believe it!'

'You must,' said Matthew. 'We have much to organise if we are to arrange our nuptials for September.'

'Oh my word! September. It sounds so close now. What about your mother?' She had to pose the question again, to be sure.

'Mother wants me to be happy, and if I have found the woman I wish to marry, she will not stand in my way. When I took over my father's business Mother was a considerable help to me and will instruct you in business and social matters to ensure you succeed in your new position in society.'

Matthew glanced at her parents as if to press home the point. 'Mother has worked hard to achieve what we have and will enjoy helping us continue to grow and expand our business and when we are blessed with children, she will help Constance to raise them correctly.'

Constance frowned at the suggestion that she would need to be educated into the ways Mrs Roundswell felt acceptable. But, once they were married, she would show Mrs Roundswell she knew very well how to fulfil her role and there would be nothing Mrs Roundswell could do about it.

★ ★ ★

She went to see Ginnie at the first opportunity. She was thrilled, and they spent a happy time making wedding plans, although this conversation stopped when Ginnie announced that Sam had enlisted in the army even though he was fairly sure he wasn't old enough. He didn't know when he was born, and there was no one to tell him.

He'd told Ginnie he felt uncomfortable walking the streets as an able-bodied man who wasn't in uniform. He said he knew where his duty lay. Constance flushed at his mention of duty and felt uncomfortable. Was he talking about men being given a white feather?

Constance couldn't believe he had enlisted without knowing if he was required to. His attitude was the opposite to that of the men the suffragettes were campaigning against.

And what about poor Ginnie? You only had to see the two of them together to know that he adored her. So many times they had come together only to be split up again. Constance was even beginning to believe Ginnie's adage — that good things were always followed by bad. It took a very special young man to put himself into so much danger when he was not obliged to. After all, his job in the pit was dangerous enough for anyone and it was a reserved occupation, so he didn't need to enlist at all.

Immediately, Constance thought of the white feather she had given to the man with the blue-grey eyes. Even now, she could see the pain written on his face as he stared at the feather. She hadn't given one out since. She could see how it could so easily have happened to Sam. Sam, who was only around sixteen but who felt guilty because he had not taken the Colours.

She hadn't told Ginnie she had been a part of the campaign. She had felt uncomfortable at the time but had done it for the right reason. How could she have been so insensitive? How many other lives had been destroyed by someone who thought they were doing the right thing!

A pang of guilt took away some of the pleasure of the day. How long was this hateful war going to last?

10

September 1916

Constance smiled at the girl in the full-length mirror and her green eyes smiled back, broadening until she was laughing with delight. How could she be so happy when the war had brought devastation and heart-break to so many homes across the country, across the world even, and still showed no signs of ending?

She rolled an auburn curl around her finger, and it sprang back like a coiled spring. The rest had been swept back and held in place by a silver clasp to show off the clear, unlined skin of her forehead. Her slim figure was shown to its best advantage in the fitted, silk dress with a décolletage finished in lace, the colour matched her eyes perfectly. She nodded to the mirror, satisfied that Matthew couldn't help but be stunned at his good fortune in his choice of a wife. She would wear it as her going-away outfit, after the formality of the wedding ceremony.

Since the war started, everything had become urgent. Plans that would typically take months or years were now completed much quicker or done away with altogether. Women rushed to pledge un-dying love before their beloveds left for foreign fields. Fortunately for her, but not for someone else, a cancellation at the church had created an opportunity, and she had snatched it without troubling to think how it had come about. It was better not to ask.

In all the excitement, she felt nauseous.

She began the long process of undoing the many buttons of the dress to change into the one she would wear tonight, twisting and struggling without Alice there to help now she had other duties to perform. Constance would have to get used to being without Alice. How could she take Alice with her and leave her parents bereft of help? Mrs Roundswell had assured her she would have a lady's maid of her own after the wedding. No doubt she would also assist in the choosing too.

Tonight would be the last time she would see Matthew before they walked down the aisle together to exchange vows that would bind them together for a lifetime. She was determined he would find no fault in her appearance and manner.

She wished she had ignored her father and told Matthew about her stay in Holloway. What Matthew would do if he ever discovered her secret didn't bear thinking about. Even so, she couldn't bring herself to regret what she had done when she thought about that poor woman.

There was still much to do. Her wedding dress was quite plain with a flourish of lace at the end of the sleeves and around the hem, not as fanciful as she would have liked, given the short timescale. Mother said that its very plainness added to her beauty rather than detracted from it, for which she received an unexpected hug. Flowers were mainly from the garden, and Alice had agreed to help decorate the church and the Albert Hotel on the corner of Moorland Road, where the celebrations were to take place. No expense had been spared on the menu although shortages would determine its content on the day.

She hummed to herself.

There was a quiet tap on her bedroom door. 'Is that you, Alice?'

Alice hurried into her bedroom. 'Mrs Copeland says you are to go down to the drawing room immediately, Constance. Mr Matthew's arrived.'

'He's a little early. Very well. Can you help me to button this dress back up? I didn't want him to see it until after the wedding, but if I'm required so urgently, it'll have to do.'

'Mrs Copeland said you were to come directly, and that I was to accompany you downstairs.'

Alice's fingers stumbled with the tiny buttons as she tried to help Constance.

'Mr Matthew looks a little . . . angry, if I might say so.'

Constance frowned. Her steady heartbeats had become a little erratic. 'Has anything been said? Anything at all?' Surely nothing could go wrong at this late stage.

Alice shook her head. 'You don't think he knows, do you?'

'I . . . I hope not. Otherwise, there will be serious trouble. Pray for me. I have a feeling I might need it.'

As she made her way downstairs, she could hear low voices coming from the drawing room. She took a deep breath and opened the door.

'Good evening,' she said, in as cheerful a voice as she could manage.

Mother and Father were standing beside Matthew, who had his back to Constance.

Matthew turned. His hair was standing on end over his temples and his face tinged with a redness that had not emanated from the flames of the coal fire.

His mouth fell open as he took in her special dress and her hair pinned up, decorated with its silver clasp. She was pleased she had taken so much care over her appearance and stood tall as she looked into his eyes.

'I understand you wanted to see me quickly. I'm sorry, Matthew, but you were not supposed to see me in this . . .' she swept her arm across the dress as if to show her disappointment, ' . . . until after the wedding.'

Her breathing was difficult to control. Her hand flew to her chest as if to calm her heart.

'You took your time,' said her father.

He shook his head, clearly annoyed with whatever had passed between them. Constance got the impression he would have said more but for her mother's restraining hand on his arm.

'I think we should leave them to talk over . . . matters, Edwin.' Mother's pointed expression harboured no discussion.

Despite herself, Constance smiled. No one could argue with her mother when she was in one of her forthright moods. Constance believed she had inherited this trait too. Her father blustered a little but allowed himself to be led away. Alice threw a backward glance at Constance and followed them out of the room, closing the door quietly behind her.

Constance's eyes locked on to Matthew. The redness had left his face. His Adam's apple nudged against his collar as he swallowed and his eyes bore into hers then slid away. He was feeling uncomfortable, that much was obvious.

'Will you take a seat, Matthew?'

'I prefer to stand.'

No apologies. No suggestion of what was troubling

him. No suggestion too that she could help matters.

She pulled herself as upright as she could but still didn't reach his shoulder. 'What is troubling you, Matthew, my dear?'

'You dare to ask me as if you have no idea of the anxiety and heartache you have caused me this night? And still, you call me your 'dear'?'

His voice contained a wave of anger she had not heard in him before, and it was getting louder. His mouth set firmly in his square jaw. She could almost hear his teeth grinding and backed away. His eyes were almost black.

'It appears there is a matter of some importance which you have neglected to discuss with me.'

Constance's face tightened. The moment she had dreaded had arrived. What else could it be?

It wasn't that she'd had no intention of telling him. Once she was no longer under her father's roof, she could please herself with what she did. Matthew might even find it laughable, a prank. After all, she wasn't the only woman of her class to have thrown herself into a fight for her beliefs.

'Even now, you can't bring yourself to tell your future husband something so important, can you?'

She swallowed. There was a slim chance he didn't know and was referring to something entirely different. She said nothing, although her eyes lowered, unable to stay connected to his.

He sprang forward, startling her, and grabbed her wrist. She cried out as he twisted her arm and pulled her towards him. For the first time in her life, she felt what it was like to be at the mercy of someone stronger.

'You *will* tell me, Constance.'

'It was only the once, I swear to you,' she whispered. 'A misunderstanding.'

His grip tightened. 'Tell me, damn you, woman.'

Her shock turned to rage. She tried to shake his hand away, but it only fastened tighter.

'All right, all right, I'll tell you. Now take your hands off me and never do that again.'

He stretched his hand, clenching and unclenching it to get the blood flowing again. Then, as if nothing had happened, he sat in the wing-backed chair and crossed his legs as if he had all the time in the world.

'I apologise, Constance. That was uncalled for. But you do see how disappointed I am. What are you are keeping from me?'

She rubbed the red marks left by his fingers and studied his face. This wasn't the Matthew she knew.

'I never meant for it to happen.'

Disdain crossed his face. Even before he'd heard what she had to say, he was refusing to keep an open mind. How dare he treat her like this? She wanted to challenge him and to say that actually, she had meant it; she would do it again if she felt the need. It had happened before they had met, and he loved her, didn't he? That was all that mattered.

She stood tall and talked him through the events of that day as she had done to the police at the time. It felt cathartic to let it go. Nothing else could come between them after this. It was right to be honest now so they could spend the rest of their lives together.

'Why did you do it, Constance? Whatever possessed you?' He shook his head, unable to comprehend her motives.

'I believed in what we were doing, Matthew. You knew I was a suffragette; I'd given you a pamphlet.

We even talked about it. You have said on more than one occasion that you love me because we can talk so widely about important matters of all sorts. You believe women should have the vote,' she rounded on him. 'You told me.'

'Handing out pamphlets doesn't usually lead to a prison sentence.' His voice was calmer but full of sarcasm.

'How did you find out?'

'Does it matter?'

She shook her head. 'I suppose not.'

He continued anyway. 'You remember Robert, a friend Mother mentioned when you visited?'

She nodded.

'Your stone smashed his window at the War Office. He wasn't in there at the time, but he remembered your name and put two and two together when he received the invitation to the wedding.'

'Your friend's office?' Constance stared at him in disbelief. 'I swear I never meant to hit anyone. I just wanted the violence to stop.'

'How? By creating more? How long before everyone in the borough knows I have a convict for a wife? How will I hold my head up? Did you not stop to think about anyone but yourself, woman?'

His anger was building again. He jumped up and paced the room, agitated.

'What concerns me most is that you kept it from me. Deliberately withheld it from me.' He shook his head. 'I'm having great difficulty in accepting your deceit in the matter. I suppose you thought you'd be safe after the wedding — that it wouldn't matter because I would have made you acceptable again.'

He shook his head and thought for a moment and

then snapped. 'Which prison?'

'Holloway.'

He groaned and ran agitated fingers through his hair. Why had she not noticed he did that when under pressure?

'Mother is mortified by the whole thing. She says she'll have to take to her room permanently after this.'

'Your mother? What has she to do with it?'

'You ask me that? My wife, the criminal?' A laugh which was not a laugh escaped from his lips. 'How will she ever hold her head up in polite society?'

'But you love me, and I love you. Surely that is all that matters?'

'I'm sorry, Constance. I need to talk to your father.'

'Is there anyone else you would like to invite to discuss the matter? I'll drag someone off the street. You can tell them too!' She stamped her foot in frustration, her arms folded as if she needed a barrier between them.

'Sarcasm doesn't become you, Constance. I will talk with your father, and that's the end of the matter.'

He stormed out of the room and banged the door shut behind him. Father must have been close by, for she heard voices in the hallway. And then silence.

Frustrated, she paced up and down, growing angrier with each step. She should storm into Father's library right now and demand an apology from Matthew but knew that, even in these circumstances, her father would not forgive her for forcing her way in. She would wait for them both to come out. By that time, she may have calmed down sufficiently to have a meaningful conversation.

When neither man returned, she sank into a chair. For better or worse, the whole mess was now in the open whether her father liked it or not. She could only hope that something could be salvaged from the wreckage left in its wake.

The door opened. Her mother walked into the drawing room and sat in the chair opposite. She stared without speaking.

'Oh, Mother, I did what Father asked. I should be getting married. What if it all goes wrong? What about our guests . . .'

'Hush, child. Your father should never have ordered you to keep silent on the matter. You should have done what you felt was best, and we would have had to live with the consequences, good or bad.' Mother shook her head. 'Believe it or not, he did it for your own good. He felt you would cut off all chances of marriage with a man of good standing if Matthew discovered you had been to prison, even if it was only for a month.'

'But that's who I am, Mother. Why should I change because it makes him uncomfortable? It was my misfortune that the stone I threw smashed the window of an office where a friend of his worked — can you believe that? His friend remembered my name when he received the wedding invitation and felt obliged to tell him. No doubt he embellished it with gory details. It's such a mess!'

Her mother sighed. 'This friend of his must have thought he was doing the right thing, Constance. Wouldn't you have done the same for your friend, to save her?' She stopped and thought for a moment. 'Sometimes I feel that I have wronged you, Constance. I certainly didn't bring you into this world to wait on a man and pander to his needs. I want you to have what I never had — the right to choose for yourself.'

'But you chose Father because you loved him, didn't you?'

Somewhere, a door closed with a thud. The door to the drawing room opened. It was her father, and he was alone.

He sat down heavily in the high-backed chair beside the fireplace. 'I think I've talked him round, my dear. I advised him that there are no more skeletons in the cupboard and that your 'misdemeanour' was a mere 'telling off' by the authorities. I said you had been led astray by ladies who should have known better.'

He took out a handkerchief from his breast pocket, shook it open and dabbed away the beads of sweat that had accumulated on his forehead.

Her initial sadness for putting him into this position was outstripped by her annoyance at his words. How dare he say she had been led astray? Her twenty-one years made her more than capable of making her apologies if they were warranted, which they weren't. She took a deep breath.

'Where is he now?'

'I let him out through the French windows. I thought it best. He had calmed down, and I didn't want to aggravate the situation further by him running into you again tonight.'

'How could you? We're getting married on Saturday, Father. These things need to be resolved if that is to happen.'

'No Constance. I am your father, and I am telling you I have resolved the matter. You will be getting married as planned; you have my word. Now I think that you ladies should go and attend to whatever you have to do at this time of impending matrimony and leave me to a little peace.'

'But I need —'

'Constance, I said I have sorted the matter. Please do me the courtesy of believing me.'

Constance rose; she could stay in the room no longer. 'I hope you're right, Father.' She raised her head. 'I fear the wedding is going to be a day we shall regret for some time to come.'

How dare her father discuss her future, and whether or not she had one, with Matthew as if she were a mere child who didn't know her own mind? Now that the matter was in the open, she should be the one to talk to Matthew to see if they had any future together. She was a grown woman able to fight her own battles.

She called Matthew's home on the telephone several times, but each time The Housekeeper said that he was out. She left her number, but he did not reply.

She spent most of the time until the wedding sitting in her room unable to believe what was happening. Should she threaten to cancel everything until she had spoken to him? She didn't see how she could do that. It was all arranged, and he would be going back to France within days. If she could set the matter straight, maybe, their marriage could go ahead.

There was still the disturbing memory of Matthew's violent reaction after discovering her secret. It was a side of him she had never seen and hoped not to see again, and she would tell him so.

11

September 1916

Standing outside a church, staring at the clock on the
*   tower.*
Twelve o'clock. Noon.
Wind screams through the trees.
My hands try to blot out the sound.
I'm dressed in white and a ghostly veil swirls like clouds
*   around my face.*
I see nothing more until the church door swings open.
Where is Father?
Can I do it alone?
Walking among people seated, staring upwards with
*   stony faces.*
The echo of shoes against stone.
And then the swishing of wings.
Black wings. Ravens wings, circling in the rafters.
Where's my Father?
Can I do this alone?
Ravens swooping towards me. Dark eyes grown bright.
*   Huge raven wings.*
Claws held out. Bill open.
Ready to strike. Coming for me . . .

Constance fought her way out of the bed coverings,
panting hard, desperate to breathe again. She ran to
the window and forced the curtains apart. Her window
opened on to a lovely sunny day, surprisingly warm

93

for the middle of September. Her breath came in short bursts and caught the smell of smoky air belching from the chimneys of the potbanks in Burslem. She closed her eyes, thankful to be in her bedroom. Her sleep had caught the worries of the previous day. Nothing about it had been real.

Today was her wedding day, and the sun was shining. Surely that was a good omen? She must put everything else out of her mind.

She closed the window again and crossed the room to sit at the dressing table. The sparkle that should have been there on this most momentous of days was lost. She rested her chin on her arms and closed her eyes.

Alice brought her a letter. She said it must have been pushed through the letterbox late last night for it wasn't there when she locked up. With trembling fingers, Constance tore open the envelope and with a deep breath began to read.

My dear Constance,

It is with a heavy heart that I write to you this evening. I can only apologise for my recent behaviour. It was inexcusable, I know. I felt I had good cause to speak out after receiving such shocking news days before my wedding.

It was inappropriate, but understandable in the circumstances. However, I am willing to put it behind me as I understand it was a slight aberration on your part and, with Mother's guidance, we can ensure that it will not happen again. Having spoken to your father, I believe him when he says you are contrite and looking forward to becoming part of my family.

I will see you at the church tomorrow. You can rest
assured that Mother will come around and accept
you as her daughter-in-law in due course.
Your loving husband-to-be
Matthew

The letter became a blur of words. He may indeed put the whole of the blame squarely on her shoulders, but to think she would become a better person under the tutelage of his mother! An uncontrollable wave of anger rose in her chest.

There was a knock on the door. She expected to see Alice, but it was her mother.

'How are you, my dear?'

The anger subsided. 'I don't quite know how I should feel at this moment, Mother, honestly I don't. I am to be married today, if I believe what his letter says. It would appear that it is all in the hands of my father and my future husband and I have no say in the matter.' Constance folded her arms, hugging herself. 'This wedding shouldn't be a gentleman's agreement as Father put it; it should be a marriage between two people who love each other. I saw the bad side of Matthew on Thursday evening and it was not pleasant.'

'We can call it off if you are unsure, Constance.'

There was a hint of anxiety in her mother's voice which surprised Constance. Her mother could always be relied on to offer a sensible approach to any problem.

'Yes, no . . . oh, I don't know. I want to marry him but he has to understand that I've got values and opinions of my own. I know I can change him when we get married. I believe it was shock he displayed on Thursday, nothing more.'

'Women sometimes have to give up their opinions when they get married.'

'You didn't, Mother.'

'I gave up a lot to marry your father.' She lowered her voice. 'My parents believed I had married beneath myself and could have done better. I suppose I was stubborn, and I loved him. My father disliked him. In the end, Father said that he would not see me again while I was married to Edwin. And that was it.'

'Oh, Mother. I never realised. You must have loved Father very much to go against Grandfather's wishes.'

Mother looked thoughtful. 'I did love your father. I still do. Matthew reminds me of him. They both have grand ideas, and expectations that the world owes them something. I can see why you care for him, believe me. And Edwin's mother doted on him in the same way. Perhaps that's what a domineering mother does to a man.'

Before Constance could butt in, her mother continued. 'My father made me choose between my husband and my family and I couldn't forgive him for that. I only wish I could have seen more of my brother. Your Uncle James and I were inseparable once.' She sighed.

'I knew something was wrong because I never saw my grandparents.'

'I'll tell you some day. Not now, dear. Today is your day, yours and Matthew's.'

'All Matthew is concerned about is whether I will upset his precious mother.'

'Constance, there is no call to speak discourteously of your elders. Although I rather wish that I, as your mother, was as high up on your list of priorities at times.' Her mother gave a wry smile.

'Oh, Mother, of course you are.' Constance ran to

her and hugged her until her mother begged her to stop.

Another knock came on the door.

'Come in.'

It was Father.

'I suggest we get ready for the church, Agatha. I expect you ladies will have some last-minute titivating to do.' He made a move to go.

'Father?'

He turned.

'All is resolved, isn't it? The wedding is going ahead?'

'We have a gentleman's agreement. Matthew is a gentleman, and I have no reason to suppose that he will renege on his promise.'

'Shouldn't his promise have been to me, Father?'

'You will have a wedding to remember, Constance, even if it was arranged at short notice. I wish I could have invited more guests but there was no time. *The Sentinel* will no doubt want to cover it. So, don't be late!'

He left the room without a glimmer of a smile.

'I do wish I could have spoken to Matthew,' she said wistfully. 'Today would have been much easier if I could have talked to him.'

Mother rose and patted Constance on the shoulder. 'Well, we shall know soon enough, my dear.'

★ ★ ★

Before they left home, she gave her mother a big hug.

'Oh, my dear Constance. I do hope you will be happy. You're a young woman with a mind of your own, but I worry about you all the same. Are you sure you're doing the right thing?'

'Mother, I —'

'Agatha, you need to go. At once. We shall be late, and that would never do.' Father's voice was sharp.

Constance held her mother a fraction too long, taking in the fragrant smell of her cologne, the firmness of her voice, the strength of her arms. Her mother placed a kiss on her forehead. 'You'll always be in my thoughts, Constance.' She turned on her heel and departed, leaving Constance alone with her father.

His eyes held a glazed stare. 'You'll be fine, Constance.' He cleared his throat but didn't once look in her direction.

'I wish I could believe that Father. Matthew wants to please his mother rather than me. How can that be a good start to a marriage? And he has a temper which is not at all pleasant. I told myself I could change him after we are married. But I don't know if I can.'

'Of course you can, my dear. You of all people should know that. He was suffering from shock, nothing more.'

She wished she could believe him. It was not like her to have doubts. She was surprised and reassured by her father's confidence in her abilities. Perhaps he was right.

She linked his arm and they stepped outside the house and entered the waiting carriage. She was having last-minute nerves, like most brides.

As Constance stepped down from the hired carriage outside St John's church, the sun, which had shone brightly all morning, all but disappeared behind a cloud. Matthew was nowhere to be seen and she felt a momentary panic. Then she realised that of course, he would be inside the church. Her nightmare and nerves were muddling her thoughts.

She turned at the sound of footsteps approaching. Matthew had followed them from the lych-gate. Her first impulse was to smile at him in relief. He was here, just as he had said he would be. Everything was going to be fine. But then, why was he outside when he should be in the church, waiting?

'I will escort Constance from here, Mr Copeland.'

She opened her eyes quickly. No! That was not supposed to happen. Her father's last role in her unmarried life should be to walk her down the aisle and Matthew should be inside the church waiting to receive her. Her stomach churned. Anxiety or fear? She didn't know. But the outcome felt the same.

Father began to speak but his words made little impact on Matthew. Her father let go of her arm and stood hesitantly by her side. He wasn't usually a hesitant man, but beside Matthew, he looked positively insecure.

'Mr Copeland, you may leave us to sort out this mess by ourselves. It is, no doubt, something Constance is used to doing.'

Constance was struck dumb. She tried to make some sense of what was going on, but it eluded her. She didn't want her father to leave her, but he had been left with no choice. She shivered, recalling the nightmare loneliness of her dream. If Matthew noticed, he didn't comment. Her father, red-faced, walked up the uneven pathway alone, his back stiff and entered the church without so much as a glance behind.

A small crowd had started to gather around the church. Old ladies whispered to each other.

'Matthew . . . ?'

She put a hand on his arm. He ignored it. Her hand

99

slid away. As if he had come to a decision, he took hold of her arm and strode past the open church door and stopped where well-wishers couldn't hear.

He paced to and fro rubbing his hands as if he was cold, but the sun had come out, and it was too bright for that.

'I told Mother about your escapades. She was furious.'

'Are you obliged to tell her everything that happens in your life?' Anger made her voice sound cold.

'Contrary to your family, my dear Constance, I am obliged to discuss matters of damaging importance with my mother. When it becomes known to her friends and acquaintances, this whole thing will hurt her dreadfully. I don't suppose that occurred to you?'

Her skin felt tight and her neck ached. She didn't like the direction the conversation was heading. His eyes were cold and hard. He had never looked at her in such a manner before. There was only one question she could ask.

'Are you thinking of not —'

'We have no time for thinking, Constance. If you had wanted time for thoughts, you should have come to me earlier. I will remind you: everything that happens today is down to your selfishness.'

He reached for her hand and linked her arm through his. She tried to pull away, but his hold was firm.

'We had better not keep our guests waiting any longer.'

She blinked a couple of times. Under no circumstances would she let fall the tears that were beginning to well up. She ground her teeth in an attempt to stay in control.

With her head held high, they walked back towards

the open door of the church. Her hand gripped the posy of carnations and freesias she carried. She almost felt sorry for them. Already two had lost the last of their petals. They looked as sad as she felt.

As they reached the inner door of the church, she couldn't hold back a gasp that took her breath. She didn't want to pass through that door into the sanctity of the church. No matter how hard she tried to convince herself that everything would somehow right itself, it felt wrong to celebrate, with God, the beginning of a life together feeling as she did right now.

A flurry on their right announced the arrival of Ginnie and Sam. Ginnie was dressed in light blue, which complemented her large brown eyes, and Sam looked smart in dark trousers and jacket. As she drew level with them, he removed his cap. She nodded at him.

'How do, duck?' he grinned.

Constance could have broken down there and then. Sam's down-to-earth voice sounded so normal.

'You're . . . beautiful,' said Ginnie in an awed voice.

Constance wanted to thank her for coming but was sure she might burst into tears. She inclined her head and held her lips tight in a thin line. Ginnie's face changed in that instant to concern.

'What's —'

'Don't ask, Ginnie. Everything's fine.' She took hold of her friend's hands and pulled her close. She whispered. 'If you say anything, I shall cry.'

She pulled away and raised her voice. 'Go in, you two, unless you aim to walk in behind the bride and groom.' She tried to make light of it, but it didn't work.

With a last look back, Ginnie pulled Sam's arm and walked into the church.

The organ started to play. Constance gave Matthew one last glance. His face was closed to her. Was she about to make the greatest mistake of her life? She almost stopped walking as all her thoughts screamed that she was. But how could that be? They loved each other.

Matthew's arm pulled her forward.

As she walked down the aisle, the congregation turned to look at her, eyes wide with curiosity as they saw she was not accompanied by her father. Whispers buzzed, echoing on the stone of the pillars as they passed. She was thankful that her veil prevented anyone witnessing her distress. Her future would be set by what happened next.

The priest smiled at each of them in turn.

'Dearly beloved, we are gathered together here in the sight of God, and in the face of this congregation, to join together this man and this woman in holy matrimony.'

Constance fastened her eyes on the statue of Mary beyond the altar. She wished she knew what was in Matthew's mind. But she knew what was in her own. She did not want to spend the rest of her life with a man dominated by his mother. He was a bully with a temper, and she knew where that might lead. She would never change him.

'If there is anybody here present who knows of any just impediment why these two people should not be joined in marriage speak now, or forever hold your peace.'

She took a deep breath, lifted her chin, her back straight as a ramrod, and turned towards Matthew. Before she could say anything, Matthew spoke.

'I do.'

She closed her eyes and stumbled forwards but managed to remain upright without Matthew's assistance.

He stepped away from her, shaking his head. 'I can't do it.'

'But you said . . .'

'I know what I said . . . but I can't.'

He ran his hands through his hair, looking distraught, and suddenly, the priest was ushering her towards the vestry. Constance stepped inside, and she had a vague notion that Matthew had followed. She sank into the chair where, in a little while, she would have been signing the marriage register. It lay open at today's date, but she knew without a doubt that her hand would not be writing in it. Not today. Not ever with this man.

And she was relieved.

Any anger she felt was with herself — that she had not been more decisive sooner.

'Be seated everyone, please. I must talk to the congregation and apologise for the delay.'

The priest hurried out and closed the door.

Gossip must have been rife as their guests attempted to make sense of events. The priest returned to a silent vestry with her parents. Surprisingly — or perhaps not — Matthew's mother was not with them. Constance didn't recall seeing her in the congregation. And there was no best man. Then again, she hadn't really noticed anyone during that walk, just a sea of unrecognisable faces.

If Mrs Roundswell and Matthew's best man were not sitting in the church then it could only mean one thing. Matthew had never had any intention of going through with the wedding today. A surge of white-hot anger rose deep inside her. But she didn't move.

Her mother came and sat beside her in the chair that Matthew should have occupied.

Father stood in front of Matthew, back straight, arms pinned to his sides, his fists clenched. 'How dare you treat my daughter in this disgraceful manner? We had an agreement, man. Do you realise you could have destroyed her? You, sir, are no gentleman.'

'I believe it is your daughter who has wronged me, sir.' Matthew's speech was derisory in its tone.

Her father's face turned red.

Matthew continued. 'Do you want me to outline to you the unfortunate events that have led us to this position?' he asked the priest, rhetorically. 'This poor man who is trying to wed us is unaware of your daughter's past crimes. I'm sure that, in the circumstances, he would advise me not to proceed and . . . shackle myself, for the rest of my life, to this . . . this woman. My mother has found this whole thing most distressing.'

Constance looked down, anger growing in her breast. Anger at Matthew for putting her parents through this painful day. Anger at herself for following her father's wishes. Anger for not deciding her own course of action. Anger for embarrassing the congregation beyond the door. Someone would have to go out there and explain to them that there would be no wedding.

'Why wait until we are in church about to make our vows? Why couldn't you have sent word this morning and we could have put an end to this . . . this farce?' she asked in a steady voice.

'And have the world pitying you and believing

that you were the wronged person in all of this?' he snapped. 'No Constance, I'm sorry, but you don't have the right to be pitied.'

She felt light-headed, as if the stone floor was moving beneath her feet. 'How could you hate me so much? I thought we were in love.'

'Nothing you could bring to this marriage is worth what you might have put my mother and me through.'

'But it was reported in London, Matthew, not here in The Potteries. Nobody had a right to know. It was none of their business.'

'But it was my business.' He prodded at her several times, each one more pronounced than the last. 'You should have told me. Just because the story might not reach as far as The Potteries, doesn't make it right to pretend it didn't happen. As you well know, I have been away serving my country. It was only brought to my attention a few days ago. I came to see you as soon as I knew.'

Constance got to her feet, clutching the table and holding herself as upright as she could.

'And you left it until now before deciding to end it? Two nights ago, you said you would marry me. You could have ended it then. Why didn't you? Why send that letter?' She stared at him, her eyes blazing. 'You had no intention of going through with it. You wanted to make me suffer, didn't you?'

She slapped his face so hard her hand tingled. The shape of her hand gradually appearing in the redness of his face gave her so much satisfaction, she was sorely tempted to plant a second.

With her back rigid, and her head high, she spoke calmly and firmly. 'Matthew, I apologise for the unfortunate circumstances which have led us to this moment. I admit I was ill-advised. I should have followed my own sense of justice and told you sooner. But I will not apologise for doing something I steadfastly believed in.'

She did not look at her father during her speech. This was on her head and nobody else's.

Slowly and deliberately, Matthew took a handkerchief from his pocket and wiped a drop of blood from his lip. 'You don't think I would allow you to become the injured party by failing to attend my own wedding, or call it off at short notice, do you? I had to be sure my side was heard and that I would be the injured party and not tainted by your indiscretions.'

'My father is right. Matthew. You are no gentleman. I can see why you, and your 'poor' mother might have been upset by my actions. And I agree that all the money in the world could not recompense you for the upset of finding yourself married to a criminal. You may rest assured that I will not make any fuss. I assume you will tell our guests there will be no wedding today.'

It was not a question.

Maybe Matthew expected tears or anger, but she had left him in no doubt about her feelings, or lack of them, and she was glad. He thought he could break her. But there was admiration in his eyes.

'Constance . . . I . . .'

'Please leave us now, Matthew.'

'But —'

'You heard what my daughter said, Mr Roundswell.'

Her mother was at her haughtiest, and Matthew seemed to shrink before her eyes.

Constance felt exhilarated, alive with a fire she had not experienced since her time in the suffragettes.

Matthew shrugged. 'Very well. I'll get rid of the guests.'

He looked at each of them as if expecting someone to stop him. No one did. He stepped out of the vestry and closed the door, leaving silence behind him.

Left on their own, her mother held her hand, patting it from time to time in consolation. Constance could only imagine the thoughts in the heads of their friends and families who, by now, were most likely leaving the church.

The priest had left Constance and her parents to themselves, but now he was back.

'I'm afraid I'm going to have to ask you to leave, my child. I have another wedding in less than half an hour, and I need to prepare the church. I am sorry for the terrible upset of the day. If I can be of any assistance, you must not hesitate to call on me.'

'Come, my dear, let us go home,' said Mother, resting her arm around Constance's shoulders.

12

September 1916

Constance felt tearful as she left the vestry and walked into the church. Her heart had slowed and her breathing was easier. Behind her, Father mumbled about unladylike behaviour and how he would have no alternative but to wash his hands of her . . . or some such . . . for she was barely listening. Her eyes filled with tears at the sight of Ginnie and Sam standing in the empty church, Ginnie tearful, Sam puzzled.

Overcome, she rushed to the only person she wanted to see at this moment in time. Constance sobbed into Ginnie's shoulder. Words weren't needed. Ginnie's arms were strong. Steady as a rock. It seemed to Constance that she was the sixteen-year-old girl, and Ginnie, the older friend.

Ginnie guided her to a pew at the back of the church and eased her down. She gave her a white handkerchief from her coat pocket.

Constance composed herself and the next time she looked up she was alone with Ginnie. 'You were right. I should have told him about prison. It seems Matthew can just about cope with me being one of the mad women who are fighting for the right to vote, but he can't have his family besmirched by someone who has been to prison for her beliefs. The march took place in London, so it was never reported in *The Sentinel*. A friend of his broke the news about my sentence to him a couple of days ago.'

'Oh, no.'

Constance lifted her head and her whole body was shaking. 'Matthew said he could have tried to understand if I had told him. Instead, he felt I was being underhand. I swear I was only carrying out Father's wishes by keeping quiet, and I told him so. Matthew said I should think more about my future husband. He's not the man I thought he was, Ginnie.'

'Good job you found out now then.'

'Last night, he said he was willing to go through with the wedding.' Constance sniffed and burst into tears again. Perhaps the shock was catching up with her.

'Look, if he could leave you at the altar like that, he's definitely not the man for you. And he has to be more than *willing*. You want someone who will love you for who you are; friendly, funny, beautiful and helpful. Look what you have done for me and Sam.'

Constance smiled. 'Thank goodness I have you both.'

They clasped each other and Constance realised how much Ginnie and her friendship meant to her.

★ ★ ★

It was Uncle James who helped Constance into the coach where her mother sat waiting patiently. Her father was nowhere in sight. Constance turned and waved to Ginnie and Sam as the coach set off for Holmorton Lodge.

'How are you, Constance?' Her mother's voice held a note of anxiety that very nearly set Constance crying again but she managed to hold it back. She would not spend any more tears on the man who had hurt her so much. 'Your father has gone to inform the hotel of the change in plans.'

'Why did he wait until you were at the church to tell you he wasn't going through with it?' asked Uncle James.

Mother must have given him much of the background to the day's events. Constance's eyes glittered. 'He wanted to embarrass me in front of my friends and family. He came to see me a couple of nights ago. He told Father he would go through with the wedding. He even sent me a note apologising for his behaviour assuring me that he wanted to marry me. That was Friday evening! I could've understood if he'd called it off as soon as he found out, but to walk me down the aisle and stand in front of all those people . . . just because his mother wanted him to shame me in public? Spiteful old —'

'Constance!'

Mother's eyebrows lifted. Even after such a day as this, she had standards to uphold.

Uncle James shook his head. 'Didn't you sit down and talk about it?'

'I wanted to, but Father more or less ordered me not to.'

'But what could be more important than talking through a problem before you get wed?'

Mother spoke up. 'He's not good enough for you, Constance. He may think he has a lot to offer but he's weak. If he could leave you at the altar like that, he isn't the man you thought he was.'

Constance snatched off the veil that had been held in place by carnations above each earlobe. Petals scattered on the floor of the carriage like snow.

'He was in love with me, Uncle James. I couldn't have dreamt that.'

'Why don't you come and see me soon, Constance. I could think of no one else I would rather see.'

She threw herself into his arms. 'I'll be sure to. Thank you, Uncle James.'

★ ★ ★

The next morning, Constance entered the dining room half an hour later than usual. Her parents were already eating breakfast. Her father got to his feet, his face flushed. She crossed to her mother to place a kiss on her uplifted cheek.

'How are you this morning, my dear?' Her mother's face was full of sympathy.

'You should say, what is left of the morning, Agatha.'

Constance flashed her father a sharp look. Doing his bidding had been the cause of all her troubles.

'It's too late to dwell on what has passed, Edwin,' said Mother. 'Would it not be more sensible to discuss what is to happen from this point onwards?' She glanced at Constance. 'Perhaps you could answer my first question, my child. How are you?'

'As well as can be expected, Mother. Yesterday I was looking forward to marrying the man I loved in the presence of my family and friends and spending the rest of our lives together. Today, I am a spinster with no thoughts of a future, married or otherwise.' She dropped onto the high-backed chair, which required her to sit up straight. On reflection, it made her feel a little better.

'This mess is all down to you, young lady. If you

hadn't got yourself involved with those . . . those . . . suffragettes,' Father spat out the word as if it was distasteful even to say it out loud, 'we should never have had to cross this bridge. No, I take back what I just said. You, Agatha started it all. You set Constance along this path by joining the suffragettes. You created chaos in a world where none would have existed if I'd had my way.'

'Father, Matthew had one problem only. I didn't tell him about my time in Holloway. He cared less about my being in Holloway and more about my not telling him.'

Father cringed as she referred to the prison by name. 'And you believe that, do you?'

'I do. If Matthew had known, he could better have prepared his mother for discovering the truth.'

'Then I have raised you to be a vandal and a gullible fool.'

'Would you rather have me become a fraud, trapping a man into marriage for his money? That was your only concern. I might have been happy to do that, provided that I could look up to my husband and be proud that he is mine. I am not ashamed of what I've done. It was less about causing trouble and more about helping a woman who had been set upon by the very people who should be protecting her. I'm only disappointed that I didn't have the courage to bring the matter to Matthew's attention sooner. And, if I have to become a spinster for having the courage of my convictions, then at least I will have the knowledge that I have not sold my soul to the devil!'

'How dare you speak to me like that? My own flesh and blood.'

Father rose from his chair, his face red. Embarrassment or anger? Constance wasn't sure which. She hurried from the room before she said something she might later regret.

Could she say with all honesty that she had known Matthew well enough to contemplate marriage? Her heart already knew. She had realised in the church, staring at the statue; she couldn't marry him. He was a bully with a temper. Ginnie had been right about her lucky escape. Constance only wished she had been the one to break the news.

★ ★ ★

Ginnie called a week later.

Constance was in the library trying to decide which book to read. She reached for *Frankenstein* with its mix of horror, shock and deep sadness. Just what she needed.

She heard Alice whispering to Ginnie as they came along the hall although she couldn't make out the words as Ginnie whispered back. They stopped talking. Ginnie's anxious face popped around the door.

'How are you, Constance?'

'Come in.' How could she explain what she felt? She had barely slept. Her eyes felt like two orbs on fire and her shoulders too heavy to prevent sagging.

'Has Matthew been round ter see yer?'

'I don't expect him to. He said all he wanted to say on that dreadful day. He was due to return to his regiment last Wednesday.'

'Did he say how he found out? You said there was nowt in the paper at the time.'

'A friend of his works in London and you'll never

113

guess, the stone I threw smashed the window in the office where he was working! When he was invited to the wedding and saw my name he realised who I was. He felt obliged to enlighten Matthew.'

'Well I never!'

Constance laughed. 'Let's go for a walk around the garden. I need to feel the wind on my face.'

A sharp breeze met them. Constance was glad she had picked up a jacket before leaving, a sure sign that summer was over. She took in a breath of air. She hadn't realised how tense she was.

'How are you, Ginnie?'

'I'm fine . . . well, not really.'

'What do you mean?'

'Our Mabel's husband, Frank, has had his call-up papers. He's got to leave soon. Mabel's scared witless about being on her own with little Florrie.'

'Oh, poor Mabel.' Constance and Mabel were the same age, although Mabel seemed much older. 'She must be frantic. How old is Florrie now?'

'Two, very nearly. Mabel's worried she won't get to know her dad.'

'And I think I've got problems.'

'I don't know what to say to her, Constance.'

'Just be there for her, Ginnie. Let her see she's got you. You'll cope. You both will.'

★ ★ ★

Constance had no doubt she would be the topic of conversation at every dinner table for the next few weeks. *Did you hear about poor Matthew Roundswell? people would whisper; the poor man had no alternative, did he? Some dreadful story that could not be ignored had*

114

come to his attention. Too upsetting to disclose to the congregation, they would sympathise.

She no longer cared what Matthew thought. She hadn't joined the WSPU to break the law but to fight for women's right to vote. It was important to bear witness to what was happening rather than to read an interpretation in the newspapers. Constance had remained true to her principles that women should have the vote now and not wait for the politics of society to decide.

She thought of Mabel, about to be left alone for who knew how long, with little in the way of money, to bring up her daughter. It was for the likes of her that the fight had to go on, with no apologies to society.

Yes, Constance had had a narrow escape from a potentially loveless marriage but life would carry on and the business of the wedding would become a distant memory — for everyone.

13

Autumn/Winter 1916

Constance accompanied her mother to the milliner's on Queen Street to choose their new winter hats. Mother was afraid that if Constance went alone, she would choose something fanciful and unsuitable for winter weather. Miss Waterhouse stocked the most exquisite hats and the latest fashion items. The atmosphere in her shop was always so very pleasant, with plenty of time to choose styles and materials.

'Ah, Mrs Copeland and Miss Copeland, good morning. I hope you are both in good health?'

'Very well, thank you.' Mother explained to Miss Waterhouse what was required and received her full attention. Styles were chosen, and materials selected. As usual, Miss Waterhouse wrote down the costs in her order book, and Mother signed it.

'How will you be paying for the goods?'

Miss Waterhouse's face tinged pink. Constance thought she looked embarrassed for some reason.

Mother was taken aback. She frowned. It had been many years since she had been asked such a question. 'By account, as usual.'

'Beg your pardon, Mrs Copeland, but I don't think that will be possible.'

'Why might that be?'

Constance was surprised that her mother wasn't offended by her words. It was almost as if she suspected what the answer would be.

'Your account is outstanding for the hats I made in both the summer and autumn, and I'm afraid I will not be able to extend any more credit until the balance is cleared. I'm terribly sorry, Mrs Copeland.'

Constance felt her mother's deep embarrassment. Her eyes roamed the shop, but she felt unable to say anything.

Her mother drew herself to her full height. 'How much is the total outstanding, Miss Waterhouse?'

'Twenty-seven guineas including today's order,' Miss Waterhouse said in a quiet voice.

'Very well. I will ensure my husband pays your account in full, by return. I can only apologise for this oversight on my husband's part. You can be assured that it will not happen again.'

They left the shop and walked towards the tram stop in the centre of Burslem.

'That was embarrassing.' Constance glanced in her mother's direction, but she was looking directly ahead. 'I don't know if I shall dare to go in again.'

'I'm sure it a mere oversight on your father's part. I will make sure it is corrected immediately.'

★ ★ ★

Preparations for Christmas were well underway at Holmorton Lodge. Mrs Williams had been working day and night in the kitchen. Alice had taken over much of the housework and day-to-day management under Mrs Williams's tutelage and was doing a good job.

Constance and her mother were sitting in the morning room taking their tea. There was a knock on

117

the door and Mrs Williams, along with a tearful Alice, entered.

'Sorry to trouble you Mrs Copeland, but Alice here's had a problem at the butcher's.'

'Whatever's the matter, Alice?' asked Constance.

'They have put up the meat we ordered but won't give it to me unless I pay for it. Oh Miss Constance, they say we're behind with the bill. I dunno what to do.'

'She's right, ma'am, I have checked the book. Nothing's been paid since October,' said Mrs Williams.

Constance turned to look at her mother. 'Surely that can't be right?'

'Mrs Williams, would you and Alice mind leaving us, and I'll get it sorted?' Mother asked.

When they were alone, her mother continued. 'I will speak to your father immediately.'

'Before you go, Mother, I would like to understand a little more about our finances. We have a very nice lifestyle, but I have no idea how it's funded.'

'Your father deals with all of that, but I can tell you a little. The proceeds from the sale of the business and our house in Manchester enabled us to buy this house,' her mother waved her arms about her, 'and renovate it.'

'I remember, it looked very sad when we moved in. I imagined it to be haunted or fancied some other terrible event had taken place!'

'It's a substantial property and your father could see its merits. The remainder of the money was invested equally in Government Bonds and shares in solid British companies.'

'What are Government Bonds?'

'I believe it's money lent to the government by

people like ourselves. In return, we get guaranteed interest periodically. The shares pay dividends which are not guaranteed but the income we get is higher, so it makes sense to have a mix of both. We live on the interest and dividends.'

'I think I understand.'

'Things have not gone too well for us recently. The war has had a considerable effect on our income. Many companies are paying very low dividends or none at all.'

'Is that why he hasn't replaced any of the servants?'

'In part. We would have had considerable difficulty finding anyone when factories are paying such high wages for women, and conscription has taken most able-bodied men.'

Constance's cheeks felt tight. How could they be in such a predicament without her knowing? She might have helped in some way. 'Why didn't you tell me?'

'We didn't want to bother you. You had enough on your plate. Your father thought we could manage without selling investments which are perfectly sound and will pay out again once the war is over and things get back to normal. We didn't think that the war would last so long and it is affecting all incomes. Add this to the increase in living costs and we are feeling the strain of it all.'

'My wedding fiasco hasn't helped, has it?'

'In all honesty, no. But we shall manage.' Her mother got to her feet. 'I must talk to your father.'

Constance didn't understand much of what her mother said, after all financial matters were the domain of the man of the house and her education had done nothing to change that. All this information about shares and bonds and equities was beyond her current understanding, but that could be resolved in time and Constance decided that would be her first priority.

She could understand now why her father had been so eager to see her married, but she was not and never would be another commodity to be bought and sold. She would get a job as soon as she possibly could, where she could start immediately, and get paid. She might not earn very much initially, but at least she would make a contribution.

A job that was different, where the pay was the same for men and women. A job that gave her some freedom.

14

January 1917

'There must be lots of jobs you could do, Constance. You'd be welcome anywhere. You could work in an office, or a fancy shop or you could teach kids, or nurse. I'm sure there's lots more. Places must be crying out for workers with all the men what's gone overseas.'

'I've thought of all manner of jobs, including those you mention, but nothing appeals to me, Ginnie. I've looked through *The Sentinel*, but I can't see anything that takes my eye.'

'Well, you don't have to like what you do. Most of us have to work because we've got no choice.'

A flush rose up Constance's cheeks as she was reminded of the differences between them. 'That's not what I mean,' she said in a small voice.

'So, what have you thought about?' Ginnie folded her arms and sat back in the high-backed leather chair in the drawing room.

'I don't know. I want something interesting. Something that will give me some freedom. I want to do something that . . . oh, I don't know. Something that someone like me wouldn't necessarily do. If I had a choice, I would do something outrageous. Something that would upset Father.'

'You're still angry with him then?'

'Sometimes I want to scream at him. It's not the

121

olden days, Ginnie. Daughters are not products to be bought and sold between families, even if the family needs the money.'

'I don't think as yer dad had thoughts like that, Constance. He was most likely thinking of yer future. Yer only twenty-one for goodness' sake. You're not exactly on the shelf just yet.'

'You do make me feel good, Ginnie. I'm so glad we became friends. How would I ever manage without you?'

★ ★ ★

After her talk with Ginnie, Constance took a solitary walk around Burslem Park to clear her head. The flowers were dead, and the flowerbeds empty of colour. Gardeners, mainly older men and young boys, were working hard at their winter chores, weeding and generally tidying up, getting ready for spring. There had been some talk of replacing flowers with vegetables to help with food supplies, but Constance didn't know whether they would or not. It might make people feel worse. Show that the war wasn't likely to be ending shortly.

What did she want to do? Nursing? She didn't know if she could stand seeing people in pain or bleeding. Teaching could be a possibility, but she would probably need qualifications. Working in a pottery? Too dirty and Ginnie said the workers were looked down on. Shopwork? Possibly, she could look into that, after all she had spent enough time in them! She was able to type quite proficiently in her work with the WSPU so working in an office could be a possibility. But, any job that could be termed a career would need qualifications she did not have. She sighed, feeling no further forward.

Four soldiers in full uniform, with kitbags slung over their shoulders, crossed the path in front of her. They were laughing over something when one of them looked her way — but she'd had her fill of soldiers. She turned sharply down a pathway leading towards the Town Hall. The old Constance, before her wedding day, would have laughed back, maybe even have walked provocatively towards them, wished them good luck on their travels. This new Constance had promised herself she would stay away from men in general and soldiers in particular.

Once out of the park, she crossed the road and headed towards the town. A tram glided by with the occasional jerky movement, as it made its way down towards the cobbles at the crossroads.

Burslem was always busy on Saturday afternoons. Constance wandered in and out of shops — not because she wanted to buy anything, for money should not be spent lightly and anyway many of the shops had empty spaces that used to be lined with goods now in short supply. Before the war, she had taken a liking to coffee. Now there was none to be had anywhere.

She caught a tram home and sat towards the front, staring out of the window as it began the steady climb up Moorland Road past the park, Moorland Pottery and the hospital. The clippie appeared at her side.

'Fares, please.'

'Sneyd Road would do nicely.' Constance smiled back.

'That'll be fourpence, if you please.'

Constance held out the coppers and the clippie

dropped them into a thick leather bag draped across her body. She took out a fourpenny ticket, slid it into her ticket machine, and pressed a lever. The machine clipped a hole in the ticket, and she handed it over.

'Do you mind me asking if you like your work?' Constance blurted out.

'Sorry, miss?'

'I asked if you enjoy your work,' said Constance. 'Do you find it lonely standing by yourself on the platform all day? Don't think I am being nosey. I am interested in how you feel about it.'

'Beg your pardon, miss.' The woman's face turned pink. 'Nobody's ever asked me that before.' She grinned broadly. 'Truth be told, I like it fine. Better than being in service, I'd say. That was the loneliest job in the world. I was the only one — servant, I mean. Had nobody to talk to. Now, I meet lots of people, and I get better pay an' all — the same rate as the men. I've got freedom, you see. When I've finished me shift, me times me own. Worth a lot that is . . . well, it is to me, anyroad.'

'How long have you been working as a clippie?'

'Started Christmas 1915, I was one of the first what was took on. The company had lost so many blokes to the war they had no choice if they wanted to keep the trams running. Conscription made it worse. They're always on the lookout for clippies. Anyroad, I'd best get on, miss.'

The clippie moved down the tram, turning one way and then another, asking brief questions and, more often than not, receiving one-word answers before returning to the platform. When her stop arrived, Constance walked down the tram, nodded to the clippie and descended to the road below.

The journey had given her much to think about. What the clippie had said about working as a servant caused her to think of Alice. Was she lonely? The thought had never occurred to her. After all, she had Mrs Williams for company. Then again, there was a vast age difference between them.

The more thinking Constance put into her future, the more she realised she wanted something different from those jobs she had been considering.

And what could be more different than doing a man's job and getting a man's pay?

★ ★ ★

A few days later, she watched another tram creeping up the slight incline of Waterloo Road towards the crossroads, before heading north towards Goldenhill. She watched its steady progress, a little world where people boarded and embarked, leaving behind only the coins with which they had purchased their tickets. As it passed, she could make out a lady conductor working her way through the tram, but not well enough to determine if it was the same young lady she had spoken to on her previous journey.

Something came to mind and wouldn't go away. Supposing, just supposing?

No, she couldn't possibly, could she?

Supposing for a moment that she found out a little more about becoming a lady conductor? A clippie! Where would be the harm in that?

A thrill of excitement invaded her body. She felt more alive than she had for the last two months, perhaps even longer than that. Becoming a clippie must be better than sitting at home trying to make herself useful. She would have a uniform and would be just another woman working to help the war effort. She tried to recall what the clippie had said about working, and then remembered the woman saying she had not felt as lonely working on the trams than she had when she was in service. Even the words 'in service' suggested a lack of freedom. Becoming a suffragette had taught her to take unexpected paths, hadn't it? Showing the world that women could do the same jobs as men perfectly well!

Patience was not a virtue of hers. She had come to a decision and she acted on it without further ado. She penned a letter to the manager of the Potteries Tramway Company, known as the PTC, based in Stoke, requesting an appointment with him regarding work as a lady conductor and posted it the very next day at Burslem post office to ensure its delivery as soon as possible.

What if they turned her down? She had already been subjected to rejection when Matthew deserted her at the altar. She didn't know what she would do if she were to be rejected as a clippie too. After all, there couldn't be that much to the job, could there? Taking fares off passengers and handing out tickets.

When she told Ginnie later, she laughed at the concerns Constance expressed.

'Now you know how us ordinary girls feel most of the time. We try, but we never expect much, so we're not disappointed when it all goes wrong. I can't think of anyone who would dare to turn you down, apart from . . .' She rolled her eyes.

'If they turn me down, I'll just look for something else.' She shrugged her shoulders to show she didn't care and pulled her lips into a thin line. A steely deter-

126

mination rose in her chest. No one was ever going to say no to her again. She'd make sure of it.

* * *

When Alice appeared with supper that evening, Constance determined to quiz her regarding the pros and cons of being a paid worker in someone else's house. Constance had fulfilled lots of roles in the past, helping her mother with charity work, voluntary work at the WSPU and accompanying her father to functions. But she had never actually had paid work anywhere. She had been taught to look attractive and be on display when in company. Schooling had ensured she had become accomplished and well-read. She could sing and was able to play the piano well enough for the pleasure of her future husband, rather than for material gain. None of these had ever introduced the real Constance.

Alice looked surprised, and not a little concerned when Constance indicated she should sit after she had laid the tea tray on the table. She sat on the edge of her seat fidgeting and looking vaguely uncomfortable.

Constance had asked for two cups and a pot of tea so, not surprisingly, Alice glanced around the room looking for signs of a visitor.

'No, Alice, there's no one else. Just the two of us.'

'Have I . . . have I done summat wrong?'

'No, of course not. I didn't ask you here to chastise you.'

'You didn't? That's a relief. Couldn't think what I'd done wrong. I only come in this room to bring you things and to tidy up and lay the fire, and I've done all that, haven't I?' She gave a short laugh tinged with embarrassment.

Constance laughed too and was pleased to see Alice's shoulders relax. 'I asked you to stay because I want to talk to you.'

Alice went quiet. The flames from the open fire cast reflections across her face.

Constance felt strangely uncomfortable. Was it so bad being a servant in this house that the poor girl couldn't meet her employers in anything other than a working capacity? She tried to remember how she had got Ginnie to talk to her in those early days.

She poured out two cups of tea, took one and bid Alice take the other. Then she relaxed into her chair.

'Alice, you've been here quite a while now.'

Alice nodded warily.

'Are you happy?'

'Course I am. It's a good job. I'm not complaining.'

'I know that, Alice. Please don't feel worried. That's not my intention at all.'

Alice picked up her cup of tea and sank into her chair.

'That's better. So, tell me,' said Constance, 'what sort of things do you do when you're not working?'

'Well . . . I don't get much time. I like to walk in the park. I wander round the town looking in the shop windows, although there's not much in them these days. What else? Oh yes, I sometimes meet up with a couple of girls what I knew from Haddon Workhouse, but it's not often we all get time off together. Mostly that's on a Sunday, at church.'

'I had a conversation recently, with a lady conductor on the trams.'

Alice's eyes widened. 'You spoke to a clippie?'

'Yes. I asked if she liked the job.'

'What did she say?'

'That it was much better than being in service. She'd been the only maid and had no one to talk to most of the time.'

'I have Mrs Williams to talk to but she likes an early night after her's finished the cooking and baking.' Alice thought for a moment. 'I suppose it can be lonely, sometimes. I don't think about it too much. A job's a job, after all.'

'Have you ever thought about doing something else? Something completely different — munitions work, for example?'

'I did think about it. A friend managed to get a munitions job, but it scared me a bit. I'd be worried the factory might blow up and I don't think it'd be worth it.'

Constance smothered a giggle then straightened her face. It wasn't funny. Alice was making decisions that might impact on her whole future life.

'Do you have any family?'

'From what I was told, me mam left me at the workhouse when I was eight. Said she was going to look for work — and she did, a couple of times. She didn't have any family herself, and I was in the way. She said she'd never get a job with me trailing around after her. She went out one day and never came back. They tried to find her. I should've expected it, but you don't think about things like that when you're eight. They never found her, as far as I know.'

Constance blinked quickly. Alice talked so matter-of-factly. She remembered Ginnie saying that her Sam had had a similar time after his mother died and his father went back to sea. He had just upped and gone a couple of days after the funeral. How often

129

must that happen? Parents put in the position of trying to help their family by getting work and then leaving them behind because they can't have both?

'I was at the children's hostel until your mam came as a Workhouse Friend and got me out, as you know.'

'What would you say if I told you that I am thinking of becoming a clippie?'

'You — a clippie? Never had you down as one of them. You're too much of a lady, if you don't mind me saying so. You talk proper an' all. People would see you as a rich woman playing at work. I conner imagine a clippie going by the name of Constance, can you?' Alice coughed as she tried, without success, to cover up a chortle.

'What's in a name? It says nothing about the person or their ability to do a job.' But Constance knew what she meant. She didn't want to stand out as someone different. Dressed in the uniform, the girls would all be the same, but the name would still be there as evidence of her class.

Soon after that, Alice collected the dishes and left Constance to her musings.

'I might just prove you wrong on that, Alice Tucker,' she said as Alice smiled and closed the door.

15

February 1917

Constance received a letter from the Potteries Tramway Company inviting her to attend the Stoke depot on 5th February. She had never been to Stoke and she had never had an interview for a job so the day would be both challenging and exciting.

She descended from the tram and walked under the railway bridge towards the town. She had to ask for directions from a police constable who was standing outside the Glebe public house, next to an imposing building he said was the Town Hall. He pointed across the road to the church, surrounded by stark, bare trees.

'Right, miss, follow the road round the church, cross over and mind the trams, of course. You'll not be far away from the depot there. It's opposite the Red Lion public house.' He smiled. 'Di'st tha'come on tram, duck? For yer could've stayed on it an' saved yer legs.'

'I'm much obliged to you,' she said having difficulty in deciphering the broad Potteries dialect, so different to that used in the north of the borough. She set off across the cobbled street and, after a little back-tracking, arrived at the entrance to the depot. By the side of the red-brick building, there was a large open yard housing a couple of tramcars where she could see three or four men working. She decided against walking boldly into the yard. Instead, she headed for the arched double doors in the centre of the building. She took a moment to look around, feeling suddenly nervous.

Opposite, just as the constable said, was the Red Lion. Glazed windows with a frosted design covered most of the front of the ground floor, with long windows above, and finished off with a castellated roof. Connie wondered if the male conductors regularly spent much of their hard-earned wages inside the public house. She couldn't imagine the owners made much money out of the lady clippies, for it would hardly be seemly for them to frequent it without male company.

She turned back to the depot and opened the door into the entrance hall. There was a large model of a tram in a glass case and on the wall above it, a portrait of a very stern and portly man, probably the founder. She tapped on the enquiry office window. The window slid open revealing a woman of indeterminate age and an expression similar to the founder.

'May I help you?'

'My name is Connie Copeland and I have an appointment with Mr Adams.'

'Ah yes, I see your name in the diary. Could you please take a seat and Mr Adams will see you shortly.'

A whole ten minutes passed when a man with a walking stick approached her.

'In yer come, miss.'

The man opened a door marked private and ushered Connie into a room. He walked round to the other side of the desk, pushed a pile of folders and papers to one side and motioned her to the chair facing him. He looked to be in his mid-thirties although his receding hairline may have given him a more aged appearance, especially as there were touches of grey scattered among the dark hairs.

'So, you're wanting a job?'

Connie nodded. 'Yes, I would be pleased to work here.' She glanced down at the papers littering his desk and caught sight of the letter she had posted only last week. She could even read it upside down too. Miss C Copeland, Holmorton Lodge, Sneyd Road, Stoke-on-Trent. She had taken note of Alice's words and had decided that Connie sounded more approachable than Constance. She had even practised in front of the mirror. After all, she was donning a new identity.

'And what did yer have in mind, Miss, er, Copeland? Office work maybe? Something light? Not too strenuous?'

She hesitated and tried to disregard his condescending manner. She thought for a second, what would Connie say?

He was of medium height. His cheekbones were pronounced, giving his eyes the dark, sunken look of someone lacking in sleep.

She brought her mind back to his question. 'Well, Mr—?'

He coloured, and blustered momentarily, then stood to attention. 'I'm sorry ma'am. Mr Adams, depot manager at Goldenhill, is who I am.'

'Thank you, Mr Adams. I would like to work with you. As a clippie.'

He spluttered and struggled to turn it into a cough. 'You . . . a clippie?' He stared, open-mouthed. 'I'm sorry, ma'am, but you don't want to be a clippie. Not hereabouts. We get all sorts travelling with us. We can talk about other jobs, of course. But I don't think you've thought it through.'

She lifted her chin. Her eyes bored into his. 'I assure you, Mr Adams, I have thought about it very carefully. I want to do something constructive to help. I am strong and healthy and can hold my own in conversations requiring,' she paused for effect, 'a little determination.'

He looked at her curiously, seeming to weigh up the pros and cons of accepting her request.

'If you take me on, Mr Adams, you can be sure that you will not regret it. I am punctual, hardworking and reliable.'

'We employ lady conductors in a temporary capacity. You'll have to finish come the end of the war when our blokes come home.'

'I believe that to be the case, Mr Adams. I also read in *The Sentinel* that lady conductors receive the same rate of pay as the men?'

'Indeed, miss. Tis fair that way. They work the same hours under the same conditions. That includes shift work. The trams run from five o'clock in the morning to midnight, seven days a week and you work for forty-eight hours per week split over a number of shifts. You happy with that? It's all agreed with the London and Provincial Union of Licensed Vehicle Workers,' he said smartly.

Connie's smile stiffened. She hadn't thought of early starts and late finishes, but she was sure she would get used to it. After all Alice worked these hours and so could she. She nodded.

'I shall be obliged to take up references, Miss Copeland. We have to satisfy ourselves as to your character.'

'Of course, Mr Adams.'

She almost stumbled at that. What if her prison sentence became known? He might not be so obliging then.

He glanced at her and looked at the letter carefully. 'No, I don't think it will be necessary, but I will need to have sight of your birth certificate as evidence that you are who you say you are, regarding your name and nationality which, of course, must be British.'

'Naturally.'

'And we'll need a photograph.'

Connie relaxed. 'Anything else, Mr Adams?'

'No, Miss er Copeland. You'll be working in my depot at Goldenhill. I'll give you a trial run. See how you get on. How's that sound?'

'Perfect, Mr Adams. You will be pleased you did, I can assure you.'

They stood up, and she held out her hand. 'I'll bid you good day, Mr Adams.'

His eyes bulged. He looked at his hand, spit on it, and clasped hers, warmly. She stared at their two hands, willing herself not to alter the expression on her face, and then smiled as best she could.

He picked up the walking stick propped against the side of the desk and limped towards the door.

'We've got two more clippies starting on Monday. You can start training together. You can let me see your birth certificate then.' He pondered for a moment. 'I'll send you a letter Miss . . . er?'

'My name is Connie, Mr Adams.'

'. . . a letter in the post, telling you what's what. We'll get you kitted up in no time.'

Connie beamed and headed off.

The town of Stoke was smaller than she had expected, given it was the chosen town of the borough.

It had a complicated mass of streets criss-crossing in all directions, plus a row of small shops and a market. She took great delight in glancing in the shop windows and wandered across to the market which, unlike Burslem's, covered all produce, including meat.

It was late afternoon when she arrived back at Holmorton Lodge. She let herself into the house quietly, not wanting to encounter her parents just yet. Alice peeped her head around the door of the kitchen.

'Constance? Oh, there you are.'

'Ssh,' Connie said in a loud whisper and placed a finger over her lips. She beckoned Alice forward, and the two of them ran up the stairs and into her bedroom and quietly closed the door.

'You all right? Your mother was looking for you earlier.'

'Did she say why?'

Alice shook her head. 'Your father's after going to the club this evening, I do believe.'

Connie sank onto the chair by her dressing table and stared into the large oval mirror. She found it surprising that she looked no different than she had earlier, except that maybe there was a sparkle in her green eyes that had been missing for a while.

'You'll never guess where I've been, Alice.'

'No, I conner.'

Connie shook her head. 'No. I mean, you'll never guess where . . . I mean, I want you to guess.'

Alice shrugged her shoulders. 'You could've gone anywhere. Miss Ginnie's? Or somewhere else in Burslem?'

Connie shook her head emphatically. 'No, and no.'

'Hanley?'

'Somewhere much more exciting.'

'You haven't been in no trouble, have yer? Your father wouldn't —'

'No, I haven't been in trouble. Although when I tell him my news, he might think it'll bring a whole lot of trouble with it. But I don't care!'

'Oh, no. You've gone and done something stupid, even if it's not my place to say so?'

'You're getting closer.'

Alice's eyes widened. 'You haven't, have you? Not done what I think you've done?'

Connie took a deep satisfying breath. 'You will call me Connie from now on.' She nodded as if to rubber-stamp her words.

Alice's eyes very nearly stood on stalks. 'You have, haven't yer?' She repeated. Her hands shot to her bright red cheeks. 'Whatever will Mr Copeland say?'

'I shall break the news to Mother and Father this evening before he leaves. In the meantime, you are to say nothing, Alice. I wish to start as I mean to go on. So, from now on, you will call me Connie.'

Alice gave her the broadest of smiles. 'Best not show me face then, for if Mrs Copeland were to ask me what's going on or why I'm wearing this stupid grin, I can't tell no lies.'

Connie beamed. 'I think there's a chance I might have the same trouble too.'

★ ★ ★

Connie took a leaf out of Alice's book and kept herself to herself. She wasn't worried — well, she was a little, but she had set her heart on this new pathway. It had a sense of purpose and she was old enough to make up her mind.

She dressed for dinner carefully, wanting to create an aura of confidence, whether she felt it or not. Alice appeared half an hour before dinner, looking anxious, her face pale, and even her hands were trembling.

'Oh, Constance. Do think about what you're doing. Remember how your father took against you over the suffragette business. He's bound to say as this has all come about cos of your involvement with the likes of them.'

'And that's precisely why I'm doing it. I do have a mind of my own, and neither he nor the likes of Matthew Roundswell will persuade me to do things I don't wish to. Not any more. And don't forget, Alice, from now on, I am Connie.'

'Yer on, Connie,' said Alice. 'I didn't really forget. But it feels ever so strange.'

Connie's words sounded determined, but later, as she made her way down to the dining room, her heart found its way into her stomach rather than its usual place in her chest. Mother and Father were already seated.

Father rose as she entered the room.

'Good evening, Constance. Are you well? You appear to have been in your room for most of the day.'

'Quite well, Father. I have been catching up on my correspondence mainly and reading for some light relief. I also had a lovely walk too. It was rather a successful day.'

'You are looking improved, my dear,' said Mother with a smile. 'You have a touch of colour about your cheeks. Your walk must have done you some good.'

'I'm glad you think so, Mother. I have some good news for you both.'

'Then we are all ears and shall hear it directly we

have finished dining.'

Connie inclined her head, glad to have a few minutes to decide what to say as they ate their meal of pea soup, baked fish with potatoes and leeks, followed by fruit cake. A glass of wine, drunk more quickly than she would normally drink, brought a look of surprise to her father's face and a flush to her own.

She waited until Alice had cleared away all the detritus of the meal, and they were relaxing in the drawing room. Father was smoking a cigar, his eyes closed as he savoured the smoke. His contentment wouldn't last once she'd had her say. She swallowed hard. Alice gave a cautious wink as she closed the door.

'As I said, I have some news to share,' she said with an overly bright smile that made her mouth ache as she tried to hold on to it. 'I have got myself a job, and I hope you'll be as pleased as I am.' Father wouldn't be, but she needed them to know, right at the outset, that she wanted this job.

Her father opened an eye and raised an eyebrow, no doubt surprised she had taken the matter into her own hands. He smiled at her mother, although Connie spotted that there was an element of concern too.

'Well done, Constance. I believe we are recovering from our, shall we say . . . unfortunate events of last year. But why didn't you say you were looking for employment? I could have found you a nice little office job somewhere. To keep you occupied.'

'I know you could, Father, and if you don't mind me saying so, that is precisely why I didn't tell you. I wanted to get my own job and anyway, I didn't know what I wanted to do until recently.'

She paused and studied their faces. Their expressions hadn't changed in any way, except perhaps for a

139

faint deepening of curiosity.

She carried on. 'I want to do something for the war effort. Something that will benefit the community while our gallant young men are fighting for our freedom. There are, of course, lots of jobs I could do but I wanted to meet people from all walks of life. I think I must get that from you, Mother dear.'

It was a blatant ruse to get her mother on her side. If anything, it brought anxious looks to both her parents' faces.

'So, what are you planning to do?' Her father's eyebrows knitted together. The hesitation in his voice told her he was preparing for the worst, and now the moment had arrived, she was not sure how to tell him that she truly wanted this job and was not doing it to annoy him. Should she come right out with it in a devil-may-care way, or take it a step at a time and try to encourage him to her point of view?

She made her decision and took a deep breath. 'Having looked at several possibilities, I have decided . . . to become a clippie.'

The room went silent. They stared at her as if they hadn't heard. She might even have been talking in some foreign language.

'A what . . .? Clippie?' said her father, in the voice he used when he was stalling for time. 'What do you mean?'

'I have applied for a job as a lady conductor . . . on the trams. And they have accepted me.' She looked from one to the other. 'Your daughter will shortly be working for the Potteries Tramway Company, Father.'

'Lady conductor on the trams? Have you lost your wits?' He jumped to his feet, his glare moving between the two women in his life. 'Heaven and all the saints preserve us. What on earth has she got herself into now? Agatha, is this your doing?'

'Of course not, Edwin. This is the first I've heard about it. Darling, please tell us you don't mean it? That it's all part of some huge joke?'

'I can't say that Mother because it wouldn't be true. I mean every word. I am going to become a clippie.'

'No daughter of mine is going to become a clippie, even in a joke.' Her father's mouth contorted into a contemptuous sneer. 'Out on your own on the dark winter nights with no one to protect you? Are you determined to ruin your life once and for all, Constance?' He pointed his finger. 'What self-respecting man would want a . . . a woman who works on the trams for a wife?'

'I do not intend to ruin my life at all, Father. That has already happened. And by the way, my name — Constance — doesn't fit with my new role. From now on, I shall be known as Connie, and I am very keen to get to know her. It will keep me out of trouble, as you call it, Father. You should be pleased.'

'Now you're being —' he spluttered.

'But Constance is a beautiful name —' her mother interrupted at the same time.

They were both on their feet, trying to out-talk each other. Connie sat calmly watching their animated conversation, which was rapidly turning into a blazing row, her father insisting her mother talk some sense into her daughter while her mother took pains to remind him that Constance was his daughter too.

'I have to present evidence that I am who I say I am. There is always a possibility the company might not accept me.'

'Of course, they'll take you. A young woman daft

141

enough to throw away a chance of a decent marriage and work with all sorts of common people?'

Connie sat down muttering to herself, 'Father, thanks to you I don't have a chance at marriage . . . decent or otherwise.'

When she decided they'd had long enough to discuss the terrible ordeal she was about to put them through, she rose.

'I am pleased with the thought of my new life. I had hoped you would both be pleased that I have finally decided to get out of this rut. I will leave you to talk among yourselves. Perhaps we can talk again tomorrow when you are both calmer and able to discuss this matter. But I do intend to do this.' She walked towards the door.

'Constance, come back here —' her father began.

Connie turned sharply. 'Connie, Father. My name is Connie. This job will not be a career. I know it will end when the war ends. But, for the first time in months, I feel excited. Interested. And I shall be paid the same rate as a man. I will be valued as a man would be valued, not for doing some little office job to keep me occupied, as you so helpfully put it.'

Until that moment, Connie hadn't realised just how much this job was beginning to mean to her. She was embarking on a new period in her life, and her decision would impact on everything she did from now on.

16

February 1917

Two days later she received a letter confirming she would commence her duties as a lady conductor on Monday 12th February at eight o'clock prompt at the Goldenhill depot. She dressed with care. Not knowing what to expect on her first morning she decided on a conservative approach, hoping the plain dark blue skirt and long jacket would help her to blend in more easily. Her auburn hair was held in place by a rather neat hat newly bought only last week from Miss Waterhouse, her usual milliner.

Mother called from her bedroom and Connie opened the door.

'I'm off to work, Mother,' Connie whispered.

'Are you doing the right thing, Constance? I do worry about you.'

'I'll be fine. Has Father said anything?'

'No. He's having difficulty taking it in. Young ladies didn't act like you in his day. They did as they were told.'

'But Mother, I really want this job and not just to annoy him.'

'Well, if it's what you want . . . but do take care. I don't like to think of you alone, late at night.'

'I shall be fine.'

She stooped and placed a light kiss on her mother's cheek before running down the stairs.

She caught a cream and red tram to Burslem and then another to the small mining community of Goldenhill, the most northerly tram stop in the borough. She couldn't believe that she would soon be in charge of her tram full of people.

Only two other women were left on the tram as it stopped outside the depot. They both looked younger than Connie and sat side by side at the front watching the world go by, excitedly pointing at things through windows as if seeing it all for the first time.

The two women descended in front of Connie. Their drab coats had seen better days. Immediately, Connie regretted her own choice of dress, expensive by comparison. The outfit gave her confidence, but in doing so, it took away any chance of anonymity. Instead, it only added to the differences between the three of them.

The other two stood together, whispering. Connie was convinced they were to become her new work-mates.

She put on her brightest smile. 'Good morning to you.'

The smaller of the two women returned her smile. 'Morning, duck.' Her eyes looked Connie up and down.

'Er . . . good morning, miss,' said the taller one.

Connie was right in her assumptions. 'Are you here to be a conductor?'

The small woman nodded, her eyes like saucers.

'I am too. Pleased to meet you.' She held out her hand.

The taller woman stared at the proffered hand, unsure what to do. Self-consciously, she wiped her hand on her coat and took hold of Connie's, in a firm grip.

Connie took an instant liking to her. 'I'm Connie Copeland.'

'And I'm Jean Wright,' the tall woman said.

Her light brown hair was tied in a bun at the base of her neck. Her clear hazel eyes held warmth although she had bitten nails. She looked reserved but seemed to want to make a good impression, Connie thought.

'I'm Betty Dean. You really going to be a clippie?' said the other woman. She grabbed hold of Connie's hand with both of her own and shook it vigorously. 'You look a bit posh for it.'

Connie grinned back. She wanted to be accepted by the two of them and was surprised how nervous she felt. 'It's all so new, isn't it? I'm a bit nervous.'

'Me too.'

Jean relaxed her shoulders as if she was glad to get the introductions over.

'It was Betty what persuaded me to come. She said it'd be a good laugh.'

'Better than being beholden to some toff and never having no time for yourself, Jean duck —' Betty stopped and slapped a hand over her mouth, her face a bright pink as she stared at Connie.

★ ★ ★

'Right, ladies.' Mr Adams, in a uniform and with his walking stick in his left hand, appeared beside them. The talking stopped immediately. 'You've made your acquaintances, I see.'

'We have,' said Betty, with a broad smile.

Connie smiled at him but didn't speak. She would have to tread carefully in the presence of Jean and Betty if she wanted to be accepted as one of them.

145

She would do well to hold her tongue for a while.

'Follow me.'

He led them across the yard to some low buildings that appeared to be a mix of offices and storerooms. Another door led back out into the yard to where the maintenance men worked. Betty immediately brightened and turned on another huge smile. Jean looked more interested in the machinery.

'This way,' said Mr Adams.

He entered through a door and walked up the stairs and took the first door, leading into a small room with a table and four chairs. He motioned for them all to be seated and cleared his throat. His face flushed as if suddenly aware of the three pairs of eyes staring back at him.

He cleared his throat. 'Now then, you three have been successful in getting jobs with the Potteries Tramway Company which, I am proud to say, has been going for twenty years now. We are part of the British Electric Traction Company. The first tram ran from Stoke to Longton in May 1899, and we've gone from strength to strength ever since. We now have thirty-two miles of track.'

He paused for effect as if he'd had a hand in building it all.

The girls took the hint and nodded to each other, attempting to look as impressed as he was. They had obviously done the right thing because Mr Adams nodded, and there was a vestige of a wry grin on his face.

Connie hid a smile. It was plain that he was uncomfortable talking to staff who were not men. This could be very interesting, she thought.

'Following the loss of a good number of our men to

joining the Colours, we took our first lady conductors on in November 1915, and we've had no problems with our passengers so far. Our drivers, all men, of course, will be responsible for the tram at all times, and you will take instructions from them. But while the tram is in motion, you will, of course, be on your own in the saloon.'

'I'm sure we are all looking forward to working on the trams, aren't we, girls?' said Betty, eyebrows raised, waiting for a word of agreement or nod of the head.

'Oh yes,' said Connie.

'And me,' said Jean, quickly following suit.

Connie had watched them throughout the conversation and quickly reviewed her thoughts of the two women. Jean looked to Betty before commenting as if she didn't have thoughts of her own. Jean may look a force to be reckoned with, but it was Betty who was the leader. She would do well to remember that.

'If you need any drivers, I wouldn't mind giving it a go an' all,' Betty beamed.

Jean's mouth fell open.

Mr Adams narrowed his eyes and thought for a moment. 'Like I said, Miss er . . .'

'Betty Dean.' She held the smile fast as if her lips were permanently stuck.

'As I said, all our drivers are men. The company believes driving trams is not a job for ladies. Turning the tram and changing the trolley pole in the trolley head is far too heavy work for ladies to consider.'

He stopped talking as he took in their blank looks. 'The trolley pole links the tram to the wires by fitting into something called a trolley head. We'll look at it when we go out, but as I say, you won't need to know about that.'

147

He waited for some signs that they had the remotest idea of what he was talking about; only Jean seemed capable of taking it in.

'What I was going on to say before I was interrupted,' he looked sternly at Betty, 'was that when the tram is moving you clippies will be in charge of the passengers.'

Connie smothered a giggle. Mr Adams actually believed what he was saying about heavy work. Maybe if the three of them worked on him, he might be persuaded to change his mind.

'First of all, your hours and wages. I'm sure those are uppermost in your minds, ladies.' Mr Adams smirked. 'You will work eight hours a day and six days a week. You'll work four hours, have two hours' rest and then work another four hours, same as the men. Some days, you might have four hours off during the day and a late shift until ten in the evening. If you don't live in Goldenhill, you most likely won't get home and back between some of the shifts so you could be in work for ten hours a day. We've got a temporary room upstairs for you and the other clippies to use when you're not on shift. It has washing facilities and . . . other necessities.' He coloured slightly but chose not to mention the privies in front of ladies. 'You might find a bicycle handy for earlies and lates.

'We tell yer on Friday your shift times for the next week. You won't work the same shifts each week, and you'll sometimes cover sickness at short notice. You'll get paid for the extra hours at your daily rate. The rate for the job is four shillings and sixpence per day, making twenty-seven shillings a week and on top of that you'll get the war bonus of two-bob a week, same as the men, making a total of twenty-nine shillings.'

Jean kept a straight face, but Betty clapped her hands, nodding approval. Connie felt a tingle of excitement run down her arms. She would be delighted to receive a pay packet for the first time in her life. She kept her mouth shut. It wasn't the right time to mention such details.

Having got the key points out of the way, Mr Adams told them he had arranged for each of them to take a short test. He gave them sheets of paper, on which were columns of numbers, to add up. Then they were given a variety of coins and asked to give out change for a range of fares.

'How would you handle a drunken passenger?' said Mr Adams.

'I might ask him to sit still and attempt to calm his manner,' said Connie.

Jean said, 'I think I might gather support from other passengers.'

'What if you were alone? It could be a late-night tram,' shrugged Mr Adams.

'I would summon the driver, Mr Adams. You said the driver would always be a man?' Betty said quickly. 'And that he would be in charge?'

'And you would be quite right, Miss Dean.'

Privately, Connie felt a mixture of all three answers might be the best approach. Sometimes, bringing a man into an argument might make matters worse. Young Betty had her head screwed on right though, as she clearly knew the answer that would impress Mr Adams, who had made it plain that he felt it was a man's role in life to uphold the peace. Betty positively glowed for the rest of the day.

Next, they were shown around a tram, including the driver's compartment — although they would never have cause to enter it on a shift, he reminded them again. He also said that clippies shouldn't find the work too onerous as the company had only single-deck tramcars which meant clippies wouldn't have to run up and down the stairs, for a start, a task that was both tiring and dangerous if their skirts got in the way. Shorter skirts had reduced the possibility of accidents. The women looked at each other knowingly, and Betty grinned, appearing to have no qualms about showing her ankles.

Later, they went into a small office where a lady clerk met them, with paper, pen, and a measure to determine sizes for their uniforms.

'Good afternoon, ladies. I'm Emily Norton. Take off your jackets, and I'll run a measure over you all.' Miss Norton began with Connie, twirling her to measure from neck to mid-calf. 'Don't expect high fashion and made to measure. I just need to know whether you are small, medium or large and tall or short or normal.'

The girls looked at each other and burst out laughing. 'What's normal?' chortled Betty.

'The uniforms'll come from the Stoke office sometime later this week, if they remember. They are well made, so look after them. They're only for use at work,' she said, staring at Betty. 'You'll have a set for wearing and one for the wash. And you can wear these overcoats until your uniforms arrive. They have the PTC badge on the lapel, so when you're on the tram the passengers will know you're an employee.'

Connie tried not to notice that Betty's own coat had holes at the cuffs.

All in all, it was a good day. Connie found herself taken with Jean and Betty and was glad that she wouldn't be the only one learning the ropes. Despite not working on the tram yet, being on her feet all day was more tiring than she had anticipated. Working in the big airy depot building was exceedingly draughty and chilly.

At the end of the first day, Connie liked to think that the three of them had become friends. Jean was nervous and rather quiet, whereas Betty was quite sociable. She was rather taken with the work and glad she had followed her wishes rather than look for a 'suitable job for a woman'.

Jean had been a flower-maker on one of the pot-banks near to Hanley while Betty had been in service. Now they were close neighbours and Hanley had everything they could want. They were bound to enjoy the travelling and the freedom, thought Connie, surprised at how pleased that made her feel.

★ ★ ★

They all arrived on a later tram the following day. Jean and Betty had been chatting away at the front when Connie got on in Burslem. She nodded at the conductor. Now they were in their PTC overcoats they didn't have to pay a fare. Today, each of them would be going out on a tram with either a conductor or a clippie, to show them the ropes.

'Connie, I'm a bit nervous,' said Jean. 'I'm bound to get a conductor and I won't know what to say to him. He'll think I'm a stuck-up cow.'

Betty's eyes lit up at the prospect then faded. Most of the male conductors would be middle-aged and not exactly eligible bachelors. Connie grinned.

When they arrived in the yard, they went straight

through the door to the office and were greeted by Mr Adams before going upstairs to the restroom.

After a bit of a chat they were introduced to the tools of their trade, beginning with the ticket machine. Mr Adams swung the machine into the air.

'Ticket machines weigh about two pounds each. Not overly heavy, you might think, but heavy enough at the end of a long shift. You'll keep your new tickets in your money bag. Ask your passenger where he or she wants to go to. There are several stops in a stage, and you'll do well to memorise them. Take a ticket for the correct fare out of your moneybag and insert it into this little groove at the top, press the lever and it'll punch a hole in the stage number.'

He stopped and checked that each of them was giving him their full attention. 'This number,' he pointed to a number on the front, 'clicks round with every ticket punched so we know how many have been issued. At the end of each day, check the number issued with the number on the dial and they should tally. Put the day's takings in one of these here bags and the clerk in the office, or whoever is managing the depot when your shift ends, will put it in the safe. On Friday morning take the machine to the office and someone'll reset it for you with a special key. You will be told of any problems with your cash and tickets if they don't balance. The cashier will go through this on Friday.'

'What if they don't agree?' Jean said, biting her nails.

'You'd best make sure they do; it'll be docked out of yer wages.' Judging by the look on her face, the answer was of little consolation.

They were given a spare machine and a money bag

each and shown how to wear it. Both had straps which would slide through the epaulettes on their jackets and greatcoats. This would stop the straps rubbing against their shoulders. Connie's view was that this was for the benefit of the coat rather than the prevention of bruises. Trying to see the small numbers, turn the cogs and stamp the ticket made their arms ache, but nobody complained.

17

February 1917

When the three of them arrived at the depot the next day, there was none of the usual banter going on. It seemed quiet. Fred Parsons, a driver, was in the corner opposite the office, and he beckoned them over.

'One of the bosses from Stoke's here. Dunno what he wants. You lot had best look busy while he's here.'

'Perhaps he's just visiting?' said Betty.

'Doubt it,' said Fred. 'Inspector Caldwell don't do just visiting. He only comes when summat's up.'

'Well, it's useless to try to speculate. No doubt we'll find out in good time. We need to clock on.' Connie smiled and headed over towards the office door.

She was about to open the door when it swung open and banged into her hand and then bounced back into the man who had thrust it open.

'Ouch!' She couldn't help but cry out.

'I'm sorry. Did I hurt you?'

She looked down at her hand and rubbed it furiously. 'Nobody's fault. It'll be fine.'

She glanced up and tried to smile. There was something about the man, something familiar. Blond hair peeked from underneath his cap. He was tall, but it was his eyes, blue-grey, framed with long blond lashes she noticed most. He was very handsome.

Mr Adams came up behind him. He nodded to Connie and then continued to talk to the man standing next to him as if Connie wasn't there. She was about to walk away when the man spoke again.

'Look, Miss . . . er . . .' He tried to get the words out, but they somehow got entangled, and he had to take another breath.

Before he could repeat his question, Connie spoke out. 'It's Connie, Mr . . . ?'

Mr Adams butted in this time. 'He's not Mr anything. He's Inspector Caldwell. And you, Connie, need to get back to work. Connie's one of our new clippies,' he explained to Inspector Caldwell.

Inspector Caldwell ignored him. 'Are you sure your hand isn't hurt? You're still rubbing it. I'd hate to think I'd hurt you.' He frowned and took her hand in his. She noticed at once the scarring on the back of his hands. It was a tender act, and it caused goose pimples to shoot up her arm. Again, she looked into the lightness of his eyes, and then, suddenly, most awfully, she remembered.

It was the pain she remembered. Pain swimming in blue-grey eyes. She snatched her hand away. She knew exactly who he was.

'S-Sorry . . . it's kind of you, Inspector Caldwell, but my hand feels quite well now. I am not incapacitated —'

'Connie, I'm sure Inspector Caldwell will be satisfied that you are well when you return to your post.'

That was undoubtedly a cue to get back to work if ever there was one, and for Connie, it brought a certain relief. She clocked on and returned to the yard. The bosses weren't in sight, so she beckoned Fred over.

'I've just spoken to Inspector Caldwell. What do you know about him?'

155

'The inspector calls occasionally. He's a quiet bugger, never says much, at least not to us. Seems to only talk to Mr Adams. What's-her-name in the office, Miss Norton, says they know each other outside of work. He has to check we're all doing us jobs proper. You ladies will be doing yer tests soon so as yer can be proper clippies and it's most likely him what'll test yer.'

Connie groaned at the ceiling. Could things get much worse?

Fred grinned at her shocked face. 'Why? Yer've not gone and upset him already, have yer?'

'I'd better get upstairs. Jean and Betty will be there already.'

She hurried towards the restroom to stow away her belongings and digest the information she had received. The man who might determine whether or not she would have a job as a clippie was none other than the man to whom she had given a white feather. Oh, the coincidence of it all. She might as well end her employment right now. She felt hot and cold and could scarcely breathe.

She took several deep breaths. It would never do for someone to see her like this, and she could hardly run away.

She reassessed the event that had just happened. If she looked at it sensibly, she could see reason. The feather-pinning might have been only an event in her eyes. Inspector Caldwell might have forgotten all about it. She had seen no signs of recognition on his face.

Was it possible that the white feather, with all its connotations, had not consumed his being as it had hers? Was she worrying unnecessarily?

On Wednesday, they were greeted by a beaming Mr Adams.

'Ladies, your uniforms have arrived. Collect them from the office in half an hour.' He handed each of them a piece of paper. 'And this is your rota until next Tuesday. There are going to be some immediate changes; you'll be working typical shift patterns and will be the conductor in charge on the tram. The best way to learn is by doing it yerself.'

They gasped in unison, some more than others. At last, they were going to be in charge of a tram.

'You'll have an experienced conductor with you to help in emergencies. See them as your guardian angels,' he grinned.

'At some point in the next few days you'll be joined by an inspector. He'll introduce himself and will watch how you get on. I'll be checking your work back at the depot.'

When the time came to collect their uniforms, they could hardly contain their excitement. Miss Norton told each of them to check their pile and to tick the items off on a list, which would be held on each of their files so as the company could be sure to get them back when the clippie left her employment.

Their uniforms were laid out in piles on a table under shelves of heavy-looking account books similar to those Connie's father used to keep the household accounts.

Connie, Jean and Betty each collected an armful of clothes and a pair of boots and made their way to a small storeroom in which they were to change. Each item had a heaviness about it, and Connie had no doubt they would be much warmer standing on their platforms now. The skirt was rather daring, ending at the mid-calf of the leg — or ten inches off the ground — leaving her lower leg quite exposed but knee-length boots and gaiters ensured ankles were not on show and thus protected her modesty. A double-breasted jacket with five buttons fitted snugly at the waist. Epaulettes on each shoulder held the straps to the money bag and ticket machine in place as instructed. They were also given an overcoat lined with flannel and a military-style cap.

Connie felt proud to be in her dark blue uniform, although the skirt was slack at the waist and needed the button moving.

They grinned at each other, each as excited as the next. Connie wished she could see herself, but there were no mirrors. Jean looked very smart and marched up and down the corridor as if preparing for some military campaign. Surprisingly, the uniform appeared to have bolstered her confidence. Connie's mind shot back to something Ginnie had said; that if you looked capable of doing the job, it would be easier to convince others you could do it. In Connie's view, Jean was the one who needed to convince herself that she was capable, but only time would tell. They were all clippies doing their bit — the same job for the same pay. And they all looked the same. With the jobs and the uniform, the differences between them had all but disappeared.

They made their way out into the yard. Bert and Fred and a few others were there to welcome the somewhat embarrassed clippies. Betty drank it all in. Jean's height, added to her uniform, did give her an air of quiet superiority which had been missing. Connie couldn't wait to get home and take a look at herself in the long mirror in her bedroom. All that was left was to pass the test.

They were each given their money bags and ticket machines and were reminded that the money bag sat on the right hip with the ticket machine sitting on the left. They spent the next hour sorting out all the paperwork with Miss Norton and signing for their ticket allocation and cash float.

'I really do feel like a clippie now,' giggled Betty.

Fred leaned over and whispered in her ear. Her face burned in answer, but a sharp glance from Mr Adams brought her attention back.

'Right ladies, work out when your tram will arrive and be sure to be there. It will usually be at Snape Street terminus rather than from this depot. The driver and conductor will be expecting you.'

* * *

Connie called to see Ginnie at the weekend and she was agog for news. She was looking after Florrie for Mabel, who had gone into Burslem to do some shopping.

'What d'yer think, then? Is it anything like you thought it'd be?'

Connie laughed at Ginnie's excitement and sank into a chair. Her feet ached, and she had rubbed cream on her shoulders where they were reddened by the straps of the ticket machine and money bag. Her skin felt tender, and she thought about putting a piece of linen or other material between her skin and clothes lest the next week's work made it worse.

She stretched her neck and shoulders. 'Jean and

159

Betty are rather nice. They live in Hanley, so they have further to travel than I do. I think Betty needs the money, judging by the state of her coat but . . .' she held her hand up as Ginnie was about to speak, 'don't worry, I haven't said anything to her. The old me might have been tempted to offer her one of mine. But,' she smiled, 'I have you to thank for not embarrassing her. And now we have our uniforms, and we are all the same.'

Ginnie's face tinged with pink. 'How old are they?'

'Jean's twenty, quiet and reserved, but strong as an ox, I should imagine. Betty is eighteen and a hoot. She would've made a good suffragette. If the men in the depot say anything inappropriate to her when Mr Adams isn't around, she gives as good as she gets. She could help to bring Jean out of her shell. They were friends before they started on the trams.'

'How long before you're allowed out on your own?'

'We've been working on our own since Thursday, but we have an experienced conductor with us just in case we need them. Sometimes it's a man and other times a woman. When it is a woman, we get lots of useful advice. They come out with such daring comments, Ginnie. One clippie, Doris, advised me to put a newspaper down the back of my drawers! To stop the men doing what they shouldn't when they have had a bit too much to drink on pay-day.'

They both blushed and then laughed.

'This training will carry on until Tuesday afternoon. That's when we'll be told if we are suitable to be clippies. Honestly, Ginnie, Mr Adams is so concerned that we poor women — his words not mine — will be taken advantage of that he might be tempted to employ a man to look after us, but if he

160

could find a man then he wouldn't need clippies!' Connie fell into a spasm of laughter.

'How's your job going, Ginnie?'

Ginnie scowled. 'Same as always. I'd love ter have a go on the machines, but you know how it is.'

'Perhaps you should look for something else?'

'Dunno as I'd be good for anything else.'

'Have you heard from Sam since he went back?'

'No. I hope as he's alright, Connie.'

Connie hesitated, as if she was going to say something, but changed her mind. 'I'm sure he will be in touch as soon as he's able.'

Back home, Connie went through to the library to choose a book to read later that evening. She felt like immersing herself in *Wuthering Heights*. What would it be like to be loved so much by one man? Was it love, or was it possession? Matthew couldn't have loved her the way she had loved him.

A week ago she had seen his mother in Burslem about to enter the draper's shop. Even though their eyes met, Mrs Roundswell ignored her. The thought that she would never again be received by the woman pleased her.

What would Matthew have thought of her new employment? She could never have taken on the job if he'd had anything to do with it. She had surprised herself by how much she had enjoyed her first week and was looking forward to the next one.

18

February 1917

Connie couldn't begin to say why she enjoyed being a clippie so much. It was more satisfying to be doing the job than merely watching what the other conductor was doing. Also, she enjoyed the company of others.

The second week started in the same way. Connie met Jean and Betty as she stepped aboard the tram to Goldenhill. Today, they smiled happily and wished her good morning as she took the seat behind them and relaxed. It felt good.

Connie leaned forward to speak to them. 'My legs were aching every day last week. I do hope it gets easier this week.'

'Expect yer not used to standing around, like what we are, I suppose,' said Jean.

'Oh, come off it, Jean. You mean you never had a twinge in yer legs when yer got in, and yer had to put yer feet up?' said Betty.

Connie caught a faint flush rise up Jean's neck, the bit she could see. She didn't want to cause any unpleasantness, so she pretended to laugh. 'I have to confess that I rested my feet in a bowl of warm water.'

Betty giggled and looked Connie in the eye. There was a warmth in her eyes, and Connie couldn't help but smile. She glanced at Jean and was pleased to see a slight upturn in her mouth. Connie smiled and relaxed back into her seat, determined to enjoy the rest of her journey.

The tram pulled up outside the depot and, as the three of them entered the yard, a couple of maintenance men passed them. Once again, Betty's smile was visible. Connie swore she pouted at one of them as they walked by. Whatever she did, it received a reply from the shorter of the two men who threw a glance that took in every part of her. Betty turned a smug face forward and appeared pleased with the outcome.

It was the week of the test and Monday passed off with only one sighting of an inspector. Betty was out with Fred in the afternoon when an inspector got into her tram's cab. She thought this was it, she said when she told the others, but the inspector, who she'd never seen before, got off after ten minutes or so. When she asked Fred, he said it was usual for drivers to be checked too.

Tuesday was the last day of training so the clippies knew they would meet an inspector who would report back on their suitability, all three were nervous. Connie was surprised to see Bert waiting for her. He was to be her experienced conductor for today. She remembered him saying he had been a conductor before he became a driver, but she had forgotten.

'We're going on the long 'un today,' said Bert. 'From Goldenhill to Tunstall, Hanley, Longton, Longton Depot and Fenton and then to Meir. Nice run out for you, plenty of chances for the inspector to get on.' Bert gave her his stage sheet so she would have it to hand. She would need it.

Towns in this area ran into one another, and it was difficult to ascertain where one ended and another began. She had never visited Longton, although she had been through it several times on the tram now.

It was a place littered with well-known potbanks with names like Royal Albert, Aynsley China, and Beswick's. She was looking forward to it.

Bert had a quick word with the driver and then beckoned her onto the platform at the back of the tram. He checked Connie's ticket machine and bag were correct and off they went to Snape Street and the start of their journey.

'Fares, please. Fares please.'

One by one, fares were collected, tickets dispensed, and change given, in that order. There wasn't much time for talking in a busy carriage. As the tram moved towards Hanley, the main town in the borough, it grew more crowded. Connie had to push her way through the people standing in the aisle. More than one man winked at her. She flushed but thought it best to ignore them until she had learned the correct response.

On the return journey, things were quieter. They stopped in Hanley and there he was. Inspector Caldwell. He was standing at the back of a queue of passengers. This was it. She'd been expecting it, of course, but had rather hoped that Robert Caldwell would not be the inspector she had to impress.

The passengers boarded the tram. An old lady dressed in black was first, and Connie stepped forward to give her a hand up onto the platform. Inspector Caldwell got on last. She smiled at him, but he was straight-faced and merely nodded to her. He spoke briefly to Bert, who was sitting on one of the back seats in the saloon. She swallowed. If Inspector Caldwell was determined to keep his distance, so be it.

Connie rang the bell to inform the driver that their passengers were all seated, and the tram rolled forward. Relieved to move away from him, and wearing her friendliest smile, Connie greeted her first fare. It was the woman she'd helped on. Dressed in a black coat, with a sombre black hat, she removed black gloves to delve into her purse for money.

Connie's smile faltered a little. It was possible that the poor woman was in mourning and her beaming smile was not likely to help.

'Tunstall, please,' the woman said quietly.

'Certainly, madam.' The woman had given Connie the correct fare, and so she took a ticket for the relevant fare out of her money bag, clipped it and gave it to her, hoping her face now wore a more sympathetic smile.

'You women should be more loyal to your employers.'

The statement, coming out of the blue, shocked Connie. 'I beg your pardon, madam?'

'Leaving us in the lurch when we most need you.'

Behind her, she could feel Inspector Caldwell's eyes boring into her back, waiting for her reply. They were statements rather than questions, so they didn't call for a response. But not to reply seemed discourteous.

'Servants! Domestic help, I suppose you'd call it. You abandon us when you think you can get more money . . . you lot, and those working on the munitions. Do you not think that you owe us any loyalty?'

'I can assure you, madam, that I have abandoned no one. Furthermore, the servants who are working on the trams and in the munitions factories are doing important work for the war effort,' said Connie in her best voice. 'We're all required to do our bit. Now, I must see to my other passengers, madam. Please excuse me.'

165

She nodded and moved on before the woman could say more. A glance over her shoulder revealed Inspector Caldwell busily writing at the same time as trying to retain his balance.

Should she have been more sympathetic? Just her luck to have that woman as the first passenger of her test, but she couldn't allow her to get away with such remarks just because she had lost a maid-of-all-work. If that was what the woman thought of her staff, it was no wonder the poor thing left. Her mother would never treat Alice in such a manner. She felt embarrassed for her class.

The next fare said nothing. Just barked out her destination, with not a please or a thank you. Perhaps she shouldn't expect any more. An older man kept calling her duck and said she was an improvement on the last one. But then the final woman who got on the tram at the first stop, was very talkative and friendly. The passenger kept Connie talking until the next stop.

The rest of the fares were picked up with no problem at all, much to Connie's relief. Inspector Caldwell remained silent for the whole journey. She was careful to avoid eye contact with the woman in black.

When they got to the Flying Horse stop in Tunstall High Street, the woman in black rose slowly to her feet and made her way to the platform without so much as a glance at Connie. And to think, she had felt sorry for her! That was a lesson for the future if indeed she had one on the trams. The inspector gave Connie a quick nod, before he also left the tram.

Connie felt drained. Even Betty would've had difficulty in raising any sign of emotion from this enigmatic man.

Bert joined her on the platform, grinning.

'Bert, that was awful. Is he always so quiet?'

'Suppose 'e is. I don't see him that often now I'm a driver. Passes the time of day and then gets on with his job. You have to respect the inspectors, Connie, not like them. I supposed he has to do the same. I 'ave to admit, he didn't 'ave much ter say. You 'aven't been upsetting 'im, 'ave yer, duck?'

Connie shrugged.

When they arrived back at Goldenhill depot, the relief must have shown on her face. Mr Adams, who had arrived to meet her, looked a trifle disconcerted.

'Everything went well, I trust?'

Connie gave the briefest of shrugs and a slight shake of her head.

'Inspector Caldwell was very quiet and stern-looking the whole time.'

The thought that her job relied on that man was too annoying to contemplate. She tried to quell her indignation.

'Well, take yerself up to Miss Norton in the office. She'll go through the cash sheets and tickets and reset your ticket machine.'

Miss Norton confirmed that all was correct and Connie strolled into the restroom. Jean was there, deep in thought. Connie hoped Jean had been able to cope with Inspector Caldwell's cold stony demeanour. The whole experience had been quite off-putting. She forced a smile on to her face in case Jean should look at her as she passed, but she needn't have worried. Jean kept her eyes to the front, looking at no one.

Connie knocked on the door of Mr Adams's office.

'Come in.'

Her disappointment must have been evident as she paced up and down.

167

'Wasn't that bad, was it?'

Once Connie got going, she couldn't stop. She told him everything, about the woman who had lost her maid, the passengers who never spoke a word, the lovely woman she passed the time of day with right at the front of the tram, and how uncommunicative Inspector Caldwell had been during the whole journey.

'It wasn't fair,' she wailed. 'I didn't know what he expected of me. Should I have spoken up for myself to the woman in black and should I have stayed talking to the woman who was nice to me? Do you think I'm taking things to heart too much, Mr Adams?' She stopped pacing and turned to face him. 'I mean . . . is he always like that or has he taken against me?'

'He does an important job, Connie. He has to satisfy himself that you can cope when you're alone on the tram and he has to justify the decisions he makes. Seems to me that you didn't do so badly from what you say. Dunner be too hard on yourself. It's over and done with. In the future, you won't have anyone breathing down your neck. You'll just be your natural self. You'll find it so much easier.'

'You think there'll be a next time then, Mr Adams?'

'Get yerself up to the office at five o'clock, and you'll find out.'

He smiled and walked off, whistling, leaving a frustrated but heartened Connie behind.

She arrived at the office to find Jean and Betty waiting. 'What do you think?' Connie said anxiously. Surprisingly, it was Jean who looked the most confident.

'I can't see them turning us away. They need us too much. We would have to be pretty useless for them to fail us. And Inspector Caldwell was ever so nice, wasn't he?'

Connie could hardly believe her ears. Had he remembered something? Was he deliberately ignoring her? Or had he guessed that she was a woman who didn't need the money?

'I was so nervous, I could hardly speak,' Jean continued. 'But Mr Adams told me I didn't need to worry. He told me to take deep breaths and to stay calm. Apparently, he told the inspector that I was competent once I stopped worrying. Anyroad, when he got on the tram, he chatted a little, asked if I was all right and told me to carry on and pretend he wasn't there.'

Connie's eyes widened. So, why had he been so horrible to her? Unless he had realised who she was? She certainly couldn't think of anything else she had said or done to cause his standoffishness. She was glad the test appeared to have gone satisfactorily for her friend. Once they were true clippies, there might be no reason for her to speak to the wretched man again.

'I had a horrible woman on my tram,' said Connie. 'She was annoyed that I was working on the trams when I should be in service. She said I should show more loyalty to my employer. I nearly said, can you blame them if they're earning more money that way. I didn't know what to say. I certainly didn't want to get into an argument with her. Goodness knows what the inspector thought of it all. He never spoke to me about it.'

'There was a lady on mine who was disgusted about our short skirts,' Betty added. 'She said we were a disgrace.'

Something in Connie's brain clicked. 'Was your lady dressed all in black . . . with a quiet voice that led

169

you to think she was in mourning?'

'How did you . . .'

'A lady in black told me I should be in service and not taking up men's jobs,' said Jean.

Connie could see the light dawning on their faces. It was the same woman. She had been part of their test.

Connie couldn't believe it. She had spent half the afternoon worrying about whether she'd done the right thing and what she would do if the woman were a frequent passenger. And it was all a game? Inspector Caldwell was responsible for how she was feeling right now. 'I'll give him a piece of my mind, I will. What a mean, underhand —'

'So, you've been talking —'

The three would-be clippies rounded on the man who interrupted their chat.

'Mr Adams!' said Betty. 'Did you know Inspector Caldwell was going to trick us? It was mean —'

He put a hand up to stop Betty in mid-flow. 'He did no such thing, and I did know. That lady only said some stuff that our regular clippies have to face, not every day, but regular enough, and you need to deal with it.'

He looked at each of them in turn, and then his face broke out into a broad grin. 'I'm happy to tell you that you are all now clippies of the Potteries Tramway Company and I have pleasure in giving you this brass cap badge of the British Electric Traction Company. It's a horseshoe-shaped magnet and a wheel with electricity shooting out of it. Clip it to your cap and wear it with pride. Your employee number will sit below. That is, of course, if you still want to be clippies after today?'

'Yes!' they shouted in unison.

Their smiles were broad and, although each tried to look demure, they all joined in the little jig that followed. Jean was staring at Mr Adams with a rapt face.

Connie smiled to herself. Jean couldn't take her eyes off him.

19

March 1917

A couple of weeks later, the clippies were gathered in the office to be given their jobs for the following week when Inspector Caldwell called into the depot. Even Betty jumped to attention. He looked surprised to see a room full of women and his face became tinged with pink.

'Er . . . Good morning, everyone,' he said.

Startled at his sudden appearance, Connie inclined her head towards him and joined everyone in a chorus of good mornings.

He opened his mouth to speak again but appeared to have second thoughts. Connie lowered her head to avoid his gaze. The fact that Inspector Caldwell and Mr Adams were friends before he was engaged in his current job concerned her a little. She must be careful what she said in their presence.

'And how have you settled in?' Inspector Caldwell's eyes found Connie.

'Very well. Mr Adams is a good man to work for; he is most considerate as far as we clippies are concerned.'

The inspector's eyebrow raised, and he gave a wry smile. 'You think a lot of Mr Adams?'

Connie realised that in her rush to acknowledge Mr Adams's good points, she might have led Inspector Caldwell to believe she had developed an affection for Mr Adams.

She blushed, feeling even more embarrassed. 'I mean he is helpful and friendly, unlike some people.'

'Do you have anyone in mind?'

'No, just men in general.'

The rest of the clippies murmured their agreement, at which Connie felt satisfied.

Inspector Caldwell gave her a lingering look, nodded and walked out to the yard.

Connie let go the breath she wasn't aware she was still holding, then grew annoyed. Robert Caldwell wasn't the type of person to engage in idle chit-chat without reason. Why had she drawn attention to herself? She knew why; she had wanted to get the upper hand. When would she learn that it was often better to keep her mouth shut?

★ ★ ★

The early spring flowers were in bloom with the promise of sunshine and warmer weather to come. At work, there were good days and not so good days, as would no doubt be the case in any job. Connie discovered a liking for being outside in the fresh air and especially on the platform of the tram. Much to the amusement of Alice, she was learning how to ride a bicycle without falling off. She had bought a second-hand bicycle to ride to and from work as suggested by Mr Adams, but it would come in useful for getting about more generally. Unfortunately, she could pedal and she could steer but not yet at the same time.

★ ★ ★

The woman in black, Connie's very first passenger and the cause of a certain amount of stress, boarded the tram again. She gave Connie a quick smile and sat down near the back of the tram, close to the platform on which Connie would be standing for most of the journey. Even though the old woman had been part of a test, Connie wondered if she had recognised her. She decided to treat her as she would any passenger. She would collect her fare with a smile and move on.

Before Connie could make a move, the woman beckoned to her. Connie responded, thankful the decision had been made for her. She took a deep breath and took a couple of decisive steps towards her, casting a quick look at Fred, her driver today. If her passenger continued to rant, Connie would be ready. Not argumentative, but firm.

'Can I help you, madam?' She stood with a straight back, trying her best to look efficient.

The woman was smiling.

'I am so sorry, my dear. I hope I didn't put you off during our little charade the other day?'

'No, of course not, madam, but it did come as a shock to find out you were part of the test.'

'And you did admirably, my dear. I told my son so too.'

'Your son?'

'Stephen.'

She must have seen doubt written on Connie's face. 'My son, Stephen. Stephen Adams.'

'Mr Adams is your son?'

'You didn't know?'

Silently, Connie shook her head, her mind in a whirl.

'I do these things for the tram company occasionally. Both he and Robert Caldwell believe it's necessary, and I have to agree with him. You young women have a lot to put up with in your job, and they have to be sure you can cope. There have been court cases . . . still, less of that. I'm sure Stephen will tell you in due course.'

Connie gave her a brilliant smile. She seemed quite nice. 'I felt sorry for you . . . you were dressed in black. I thought you must have lost . . .'

The look of intense pain that shot across the woman's face stopped Connie in her tracks. Oh, no, that part was true, she thought. Quickly, she laid a hand on the woman's shoulder. 'I'm so sorry.'

The woman patted her hand with cool fingers and waited a moment, blinking away the tears that had set her eyes awash. 'My youngest. Stephen's younger brother, Walter. 1915. He was nineteen . . . just a lad. It seems like only yesterday.'

There was nothing Connie could say. New passengers had come aboard, and there were fares to be taken.

'I'm very sorry for your loss, Mrs Adams. I am so pleased to have met you again but I'm afraid I must collect the fares. Will you be all right?'

Mrs Adams reached inside her pocket and took out a lace handkerchief. She nodded briskly. 'Of course, dear. You carry on. I'm fine. Just a bit maudlin, that's all.'

The old lady alighted from the tram in Hanley. As she stepped down, she gave Connie another smile. 'If it's any consolation, I told my son you would do well and that the passengers would be lucky to have you.'

Connie's face felt tight and hot. Whatever would

she find to say to him when next she saw him, knowing what she knew? She almost wished she hadn't met his mother today. On the other hand, she rather liked her compliments; who wouldn't want to know they had made such an impression?

She was still deep in thought when the tram pulled into the depot.

'You all right, Connie duck?' said Fred as he sauntered around the tram towards her with his hands in his pockets. 'Not too busy today.'

She jumped off the platform and accompanied him into the building, taking her hat off so that her head could breathe.

'There's summat on yer mind. Yer look dazed. Shocked, I'd say. Come on, out with it?'

Connie looked at him through the corner of her eye. Like Bert, Fred knew everyone. She hadn't been there long enough to decide who she could trust and didn't want to be known as a tittle-tattler. 'I don't know if I should say anything. I don't think it's up to me to tell.'

Fred thought for a moment. 'Have you been speaking to Mrs Adams?'

'How did you know?'

'Saw her waiting for the tram. Put two and two together.'

'I'm hopeless. I shouldn't have said anything.'

'Who says it's a secret? Are you talking about Stephen's brother or —'

'Or what?' Connie's head jerked up.

A red flush crept up the part of Fred's neck that was visible. 'Well . . . I . . . er —' he blustered.

'Come on, Fred. I'll tell you what's on my mind if you do too?'

Fred gave a deep sigh. 'Betty says as you're pretty smart. I'm beginning to think she's right an 'all. Come on. We'll go into the mess room before anyone else gets back.'

They opened the door. It was empty. Connie flopped down into a chair, relieved. Fred nodded at her to get on with it. She took a deep breath. 'You're right. It is about Mr Adams. Mrs Adams . . .' She stopped. '. . . Stephen's mother . . .'

Fred nodded at her to continue.

'She got on the tram this morning, as you rightly said. But she was the lady in black who boarded when I was doing my test with Mr Caldwell. She . . . she . . . wasn't very nice.'

Fred put his head back and laughed heartily. 'She was testing yer, was she?'

'You mean you know?'

Fred nodded. 'I should think everybody does, Connie. She does it to all the new clippies. Wants to make sure Stephen can trust you all to do a good job.' He relaxed into his chair. 'Started about three years ago. It gave her summat to do when her husband died. She stopped when Walter got killed in March 1915, just two months after he was sent over there, at a village called Neuve Chapelle.' He looked across at her and carried on. 'Only nineteen, he was.'

Connie's heart went out to poor Mrs Adams, and Stephen Adams. How soul-destroying to lose a father and a brother. He must have been devastated.

Fred carried on talking.

'The two of them enlisted at the same time. Went to the recruiting centre in Hanley and signed up together. Joined the North Staffords in the October after the war started. They did their basic training

177

and went off to God-knows-where. From what I can remember, they went over to Belgium at the beginning of January 1915 — around Wipers. And, believe it or not, Stephen got badly injured two months later also near to Wipers. It was so bad he was invalided out of the army.'

'Poor Mr Adams. He must feel so guilty that he came back and his brother didn't.'

'Just the luck of the draw, duck. If it's got yer name on it, you're a goner. He used to be a right good laugh before he went over there. Drank with the lads, he did. Now, look at him. Hardly hear a word out of 'im during the day. Works all hours so's not to spend too much time thinking, if you ask me.'

Connie shook her head sadly. Ginnie's friend, Sam, had been in the army for nearly a year now. Nobody had known whether he was old enough to fight, but he had enlisted anyway. She could understand a little of what her friend was going through right now. He had his basic training and had been in England. Now he could be anywhere. She thought of Ginnie getting up every day and wondering whether he was still alive or not. Connie hadn't been affected by the war so far if she didn't count Matthew. She'd had no news from him and didn't expect to.

'Thank you for telling me. I understand. I promise I will keep it to myself. I assume everyone would know by now if he had wanted to share it?'

'Only us what was here when he come back knows. He and his mam don't talk about it outside the family.'

'I won't breathe a word, Fred.'

He set his mouth grimly, nodded and got to his feet, about to walk away.

'Fred . . . do you think Inspector Caldwell is aware of Mr Adams's background?' Connie didn't know why she asked the question. She was hardly going to be talking to Inspector Caldwell about Mr Adams, or vice versa. But the words had flown from her mouth before she could stop herself.

'I should think so. They knew each other before the inspector started to work on the tramcars. I think he's been to their house a couple of times. But you've seen him. Another one as keeps himself to himself even more than Stephen. Doesn't say much at all unless he has to. The war does that to some men.'

Connie nodded in return.

The door opened and in walked Jean, accompanied by Inspector Caldwell and Bert. The inspector frowned.

'Still here?' Jean said. 'Thought you'd have gone long since.'

'I was just leaving.' Connie picked up her coat and fumbled her arms into the sleeves.

'I'll come an' all,' said Fred.

She could feel the inspector's eyes boring into her back as she followed Fred to the door. He opened it and stood back with a grand, sweeping gesture.

'Bye, you two,' Jean called.

Connie gave a slight wave and departed, heaving a sigh of relief as she closed the door behind her. They met Mr Adams on their way out, and she couldn't help but wonder if Jean had hung back deliberately to talk to him. He was a nice man, and his mother seemed very nice too if she wasn't testing you for a clippie's job. But his age disturbed her as well as his recent history. If they were getting close, she certainly didn't want to see Jean get hurt.

179

20

Spring 1917

A very pleased Connie joined her parents relaxing in the drawing room.

'Have you seen the news, Father? The Allies have forced the Germans into retreat. Perhaps the end of the war is coming.'

'I read that too. But they've retreated to the Hindenburg Line. It's playing right into German hands.'

'How could that be if we are winning?'

'They've already built defences there and the Front is shorter — more concentrated. They can take pot shots at our troops and there will be nowhere for them to go.'

'But the newspapers say . . .'

'The papers can say what they like. It's not good news, I'm telling you. Damn war.'

Connie raised her eyebrows. Her father rarely swore in the house, but he looked so glum.

'Is it good news and bad? Like electoral reform? Women being told they will get the vote, but only if they have property and are over thirty?'

Her father shook his head. 'No point in votes for women if we lose the war, Constance.'

'Is it really bad?' she asked.

'It'll carry on forever at this rate and our dividends will never go back to where I need them to be. All this uncertainty is playing havoc with the financial markets.'

'Do we have financial problems, Edwin?'

Her mother's face looked pale and strained. It wasn't like her to look on the black side.

'Yes . . . and no . . . our income has gone down but it's nothing for you and Constance to worry about, Agatha. Even I have my bad days when it all gets a bit too much.'

Shortly afterwards, Father made an excuse to leave, taking his glass of whisky with him.

'Have we really got money problems, Mother?' She whispered even though the two were alone.

'Your guess is as good as mine,' said her mother, thoughtfully. 'We must get him to tell us what he's so worried about.'

★ ★ ★

At the beginning of April, the Americans declared war on Germany and Father's depression on the news from the Western Front, like the weather, seemed to have lifted.

'The Huns have done it this time. They've tried to starve us out by attacking any ship coming to Britain, no matter what country it sails under. That's angered the Americans and they've joined the war on our side. They will send their army to the Western Front and that will make up for the Russians who seem to have stopped fighting in the east. The Russians are more concerned about their internal politics than the war.'

'It seems strange to celebrate more men getting thrown on to the battlefield.'

'This war is putting pressure on us all and the sooner it finishes, the better.'

181

Jean was definitely developing feelings for Mr Adams. Connie had been watching her during the last couple of weeks. Infatuation, or something deeper? It was too soon to tell. Jean was always on hand to help or work an extra shift should the need arise. In Connie's view, Jean was trying too hard. Fred had said that Mr Adams had changed since he had returned from the war. He must still be grieving for his lost father and his brother, possibly feeling guilty for being the one to come home.

She was afraid for Jean. Was she mature enough to take on such a damaged man?

It was a few days later when she got the opportunity to talk to Jean alone. Connie was in the restroom, and Jean walked in, smiling.

'Hiya Connie! How are you?'

Connie grinned back. 'Not bad. More importantly, how are you? Did I hear you singing in the restroom the other day?'

Jean flushed a brilliant red. Her long, straight brown hair was twisted into a becoming roll, giving prominence to her hazel eyes. She looked more attractive and grown-up than Connie remembered from their first few days in the depot. She had made an effort with her appearance. Was today something special or had it been going on for a while and she hadn't noticed?

'I . . . it's my birthday.'

Connie grinned broadly. This was the time to speak out. 'Happy birthday! And how old might that be?'

'Twenty-one.'

'A true woman. A proper lady!'

Jean blushed delicately. 'I feel marvellous. As if the next stage of my life has begun.'

'And what do you think it might involve? Male company, perhaps?'

Jean blushed violently.

Connie grinned and continued. 'I think you have a young man in mind.'

'Don't say anything. He doesn't even know. We've only talked, I swear.'

'I'm not judging you. Would you like to talk about it?'

Jean shook her head. 'Oh, I couldn't say anything. You know him. It wouldn't be right.'

'Ah, someone I know. It couldn't be Mr Adams, could it?'

'How . . . did you know?' Her face was now truly in flames.

'I didn't. You just told me.'

'You tricked me! But don't tell anybody. Please!'

She let Jean recover before saying more. 'I won't tell, I promise. Does he feel the same?'

'We have only had a couple of conversations so far. Dunno what he thinks of me, if anything at all. You probably think he's too old?'

'Are you sure it's not a response to him being nice to you . . . to us all?'

'He is a lovely man, and I know you're right, Connie. Why should there be anything more in his mind other than a caring employer looking after his workers?'

'Because employers don't usually care about their workers. Do you know anything about him?'

Jean twisted her face and shrugged. 'As much as any of us do, I suppose.'

They both turned as they heard voices approaching. 'Let's meet somewhere more private the next time we are off together,' Connie hissed.

'We'll talk then.'

The door of the office opened, and they both turned to their money bags as if checking the contents. Fred walked in. If he was suspicious of their silence and deep concentration, he didn't say.

21

May 1917

Connie had seen Ginnie at the weekend. The girl had arrived at the house in a complete panic and had difficulty speaking. A worried Connie took Ginnie through to the library.

Ginnie blurted out that she had received two letters from Sam, and that he couldn't read or write, so someone must have written them for him. She stopped, clearly expecting Connie to be quite disgusted but there was worse to come. Ginnie's face became bright red and the poor girl was unable to look her in the eye.

'You mean you . . . you can't —'

'I can't . . . I can't read, neither.'

'Oh, you poor love. I should have realised what you meant instead of forcing you to speak of it.'

Never had Connie felt so helpless, knowing she had made Ginnie articulate words too awful to speak in that heart-rending moment. Ginnie had spoken of it to no one, not even Mabel, ashamed that she was so stupid.

'What about my pamphlet? Oh, I remember — you took it to read later.'

'When I got home, I asked our Mabel what she thought of it. So I'll understand if you throw me out.'

'. . . because you can't read?'

Ginnie said nothing.

'Listen to me.' Connie grabbed Ginnie's shoulders. 'I would never throw you out. Do you hear me? Darling Ginnie, don't you realise how important you are to me?'

'You really mean that?'

Ginnie passed the letters over to Connie. 'Would you . . . ?'

'Of course.'

Connie read the letters and Ginnie's face broke into a smile. She desperately wanted to help but had to tread carefully. 'I want to help, if you'll let me? I would be more than happy to teach you to read. If you like. I'm happy to get together whenever I'm not working.'

'I'm such a dunce. My friend, Clara, tried and didn't get anywhere.'

'Oh, I don't give up very easily.'

'When you see how stupid —'

'You're not. It's because I'm your friend that I want to help, Ginnie. I promise it won't make any difference to us.'

Ginnie shook her head and admitted she was a dunce.

They made arrangements to meet the following Saturday and Connie helped Ginnie to write back to Sam.

Connie thought about it as she rode into work the next day. How awful for Ginnie to carry that burden with her all this time, to hide it from everyone. Connie had wept when she had gone. When she'd welcomed Ginnie into her life she hadn't reckoned on this.

★ ★ ★

Connie was wearing her overcoat as the winds were still on the cool side when she was standing on the platform, especially on late evenings. She thought about books that Ginnie might enjoy as she adjusted the money bag's leather strap on her shoulder. It was heavy with coins and its weight was wearing her down. She closed her eyes and rubbed her forehead. It was her last trip of the day, and she was ready to finish. Friday afternoons and evenings were always busy. There would be a lot of money to count up before she could head off home.

A small group of young men, not much more than boys, had gathered in the centre of the saloon, with lots of singing and joking and merriment going on. Their wages must have burned holes in their pockets for they were already inebriated. Drunken behaviour wouldn't normally have bothered her. A group of young men, full to the gunnels with drink, and lacking any modicum of self-control in the confines of the tram, disturbed her greatly.

She gave the group time to settle before approaching them for their fares.

'What's a good-looking wench like you doing conducting?' said the boy closest to her sprawled across a double seat, his arms wide open.

Close up, they were even more disturbing, with strong, sneery faces. Connie was determined to do her job.

'Fares please,' she said in her pleasantest but firmest voice, attempting a fine line between not playing along with their games, and not sounding overly officious.

'Yer didn't answer me question,' said one lad.

'Yer didn't answer his question,' another mimicked.

Connie tried again. 'Where are you going?' She had the ticket machine ready to punch a ticket.

'Hey, you lot. D'yer think the wench wants to come wi' us?' repeated the first lad. He was the ringleader. She glanced around quickly. Apart from the trouble-makers, there were few other passengers still on board.

'Tell me where you're going, and I'll give you your tickets.'

'Sounds like we got a posh 'un here, or her's pre-tending 'cause she wants us ter think so. What d'yer reckon, lads?'

The ringleader stood up beside her. He was much taller than Connie and well-built. She stood firm, refusing to be cowed, her eyes steadfastly on his.

'I'll take the rest of the fares, and I'll come back to you . . . so have your money ready.' She tried to inject as much authority as she was able and moved to the next passenger before he could answer, her heart pounding. Two of the men in the group were now standing in the aisle.

'You all right, duckie?' said her next passenger, an anxious-looking woman with a brightly coloured shawl thrown around her shoulders. Connie didn't want to add to her fears, so she smiled and pressed on.

After she had taken the last fare at the front of the tram, she hesitated, wondering whether to knock on the window separating her from Bert. That would be cowardly. Whenever the talk at the depot had turned to matters of safety, she had spoken out that clippies did not need male colleagues to protect them. She hadn't envisaged encountering a group of drunken lads barely out of school, and yes, they were lads in her opinion. They certainly weren't acting like grown men.

188

She started back down the aisle. Two of the lads had their heads together, whispering and laughing. As she approached, one of them nudged another in the back. As one, they turned towards her.

'Here's the little conductorette again.'

A loud burp and more giggles followed this.

Connie held her head up high. 'I need to take your fares, please, otherwise the company will have you taken to the magistrate.' The ringleader blocked her way, sneering. Only two other passengers remained, a woman who looked to be in her forties sitting part way down the saloon on the left, and a white-haired man right at the front.

Connie glanced past him towards Bert, but he wasn't looking. The woman seemed intent on making herself as small as possible. Neither of the two passengers were likely to come to her aid, she felt. She could not admit that a clippie needed assistance or protection. She edged forward, but the boy in front of her barred her way, effectively cutting her off from Bert. Her hands became sweaty, and her tongue dry. Why, oh why, hadn't she knocked on Bert's window when she'd had the chance?

It was when she saw the boy's eyes go down to her money bag that she fully understood the very real danger she was in. It was strapped underneath the ticket machine and couldn't be stolen.

She pushed forward, hard. The ringleader made a grab for her bag. Realising he couldn't get it, he froze. Another boy pushed her towards the platform.

She swung a fisted hand and caught someone's cheekbone. A man cried out. She struggled against someone who had caught hold of her arm. She felt the nearest body rear up, and she kicked as hard as she could, hoping that the white-haired gentleman would come to her aid.

Someone's foot nudged her ankle. She tripped and lost her footing, landing on her knees, narrowly avoiding hitting her head on the back of the tram. She felt herself pushed forward as her hat came down over her eyes.

'Leave me alone, you brute,' Connie shouted at the top of her voice.

The boy forced her on to her back and pushed his arm into her neck. He grabbed a handful of coins from the bag. The more she struggled, the harder his arm pressed against her neck and shoulder. She stared into his eyes. Matthew's eyes glinted back. The Matthew who had grabbed her arm and forced her into confession.

She tried to get her hand to the bell, but it was too high to reach.

'Get off me,' she yelled, struggling against his weight. Matthew's face disappeared and the boy's face was coming closer. 'Bert! Bert!'

That was where the boy made his big mistake. With his elbow holding her down and one hand in the bag, he had left himself vulnerable. Connie brought her knee up hard into his groin.

'Argggh. Bloody bitch!'

He doubled up in agony and had to let her go. She kicked out to hit anyone nearby.

'If any of you buggers come anywhere near me, you'll regret it.' She screamed in anger rather than fright.

'You tell 'em duck,' shouted the woman passenger, raising her fists, but staying firmly where she was.

The tram screeched to a halt with such a jolt the

boys crashed into each other. The whole gang jumped down from the tram and made off with a few handfuls of cash.

Connie wasn't too sure what happened next. She remembered footsteps running away and thought she heard Bert following them.

She laid her head on the floor of the tram, her chest heaving, eyes closed. It took a few seconds before she regained control. Everywhere was quiet, the tram stationary. She heard footsteps inside the tram getting closer and opened her eyes wide, ready to start again.

The man who had been sitting in the saloon had come forward and was bending over her.

'You all right, duck?'

Thank God, it was over.

She looked up at him, dazed. It was then she realised. He was blind.

'I . . . yes, thank you.'

He helped her to her feet just as Bert appeared on the platform.

'Sod it!' said Bert, bending over, gasping for breath. 'Couldn't catch the buggers.'

Connie took hold of the blind man's hand and shook it. 'Thank you, sir. I appreciate your help.' Tears weren't very far away. The shock was catching up with her. She struggled to get to her feet. Her legs wobbled.

'I only wish I could've done more, lass,' said the blind man.

Bert took both passengers' names and addresses and advised them that they may be needed as witnesses.

The woman handed the man his white stick, and he descended from the tram, muttering to himself.

Bert put his arm under Connie's elbow as her legs gave way.

'At alrate, duck?' he asked. His other hand was shaking and touching his red face until Connie became concerned for his well-being too.

'We'll have to report it. Mr Adams'll want to get 'em up before the magistrates,' he panted. 'You all right to sit on yer own while I drive back? Conner take no passengers with you in this state.'

He helped her to a seat then strode off towards the front of the tram before she could say anything more. He was probably right. The incident had shaken her more than she realised.

Bert escorted Connie into the depot building and left her sitting on a chair in the office while he searched out Mr Adams. Miss Norton had gone home, and the late evening sunshine lit the room. Connie made herself a cup of tea and sipped it slowly, feeling calmer. The waves of panic she had experienced on the way back to the depot became a trickle as the hot tea entered her body and her breathing slowly returned to normal. Heaven only knew what Mr Adams would say. She tried desperately to persuade herself she wasn't partly to blame for her determination to sort it out herself.

Voices in the corridor beyond the door made her sit up. She dabbed her eyes with the finely embroidered handkerchief she kept in her greatcoat pocket. She would not let Mr Adams see how shaken she had been by her experience. She should have banged on the window when she had the chance, and that was definitely her fault, and all because of her pride, because she didn't want to appear as a fragile woman relying on a man to save her. Served her right for thinking she could deal with it herself.

'What have we here? Connie, are you in distress?'

Mr Adams spoke quietly, his face creased with worry.

'Some drunken youths got a bit above themselves on the tram, Mr Adams. They attacked poor Connie and shoved her to the floor, then tried to take her money bag and made off with some cash,' said Bert, sweat on his forehead. 'She fought 'em off as best she could, Mr Adams.'

Mr Adams knelt in front of her and patted her hand as if she was a child.

'I am quite well, Mr Adams. It was a shock, nothing more,' she said, determined to make light of it. She wasn't about to admit how frightening it was. Suffragettes stood up for themselves. She held one trembling hand down on her lap with the other.

'Did you ring the bell for Bert?'

'She couldn't reach it, Mr Adams. To be fair, the boys were in the middle of the saloon,' muttered Bert. 'I run after 'em, but they was too fast.'

'I was too far fr-fr-from the platform and Bert's window.' She did her best to control the stammer but couldn't stop the quiver of her lips.

'They could've done you some serious damage. We'll look into it. It's not the first time, and I daresay it will not be the last. We must protect our lady conductors. Think what would happen if news got out.'

Mr Adams got up and paced back and forth. 'You shouldn't have to put up with such behaviour.'

Bert nodded grimly. 'Got the witnesses' names in me notebook.'

'Good, I'll have it for the time being.'

Bert handed the notebook over.

193

'We'll leave it there for now.'

Connie looked up at him. He was watching her closely and his face had narrowed.

'Gerroff home, the pair of yer and we'll take it further on Monday. Dunner bother about yer weekend shifts and don't talk about it to anyone. I want you both to write down everything you remember tonight while it's still fresh in your minds. You know, how many were in the group, did they say any names, have you seen them before, and did you encourage their lewd behaviour somehow . . .'

'I most certainly did not encourage them.' The look of disdain Connie gave him left him in no doubt that she was above all of that.

'Sorry, Connie, but better I ask you than someone else.'

'I understand, but do you need to make it official, Mr Adams?' said Connie, struggling stiffly to get to her feet. Her shoulder was aching. It seemed she might have a few bruises to take care of with a touch of witch hazel when she got home. 'They were young lads and not used to having money in their pockets. They probably spent all their wages on ale. I don't want to be responsible for them getting in trouble with the police. It could ruin their lives.' She knew that more than anyone.

'The boys should've thought about that themselves when they attacked you. They need discipline. We can't let them get away with it. Think of the other clippies. After all, you're giving your time for the war effort. They'll soon toe the line when they get conscripted. No one should be treated like you were. We'll soon catch 'em. You mark my words!'

It was when she arrived home and readied herself

for bed that she remembered Ginnie would be coming for her first reading lesson the following day. She couldn't put it off. Ginnie would feel rejected and that would be an end to it. She would have to tread very carefully.

She undressed cautiously, touching the deep red bruises on her arms, neck and wrists gingerly with witch hazel. She would not let anyone see them, least of all her mother, who would put a stop to her job in an instant.

★ ★ ★

Connie woke early on Monday morning to the sound of birds in the garden. She lay back thinking about what could have happened, feeling inadequate. She was vulnerable to violence in just the same way as every other human being. What frightened her the most was the violence in the boy's eyes — the same violence she had seen in Matthew's eyes on that Thursday evening before her wedding.

She looked at herself in the mirror. The bruises on her neck were more painful today.

A knock came on the door and Alice walked in.

'Brought you a cup of tea.' Alice laid a tray on the bedside table and then drew back the curtains. The sun shone brightly through the windows at this time of day. 'How do yer feel this morning? Oh, my word . . .'

Connie burst into tears. Alice sat on the side of the bed and hugged her. Connie recovered her composure.

'Whatever's happened?'

Connie ran through the events of Friday briefly. 'The whole thing frightened me more than I had thought.' She wiped her eyes with the sleeve of her nightgown, feeling rather silly to be crying in front of Alice. 'So much violence over so little money. I don't know if I can face work, today or ever.'

'Course you can. You're the strongest woman I know. Yer bound to be all shook up at the moment. Get this cup of tea down yer and then have some breakfast before you go to work.'

Connie dressed in her uniform and walked into the kitchen.

'Thank you, Alice. I just needed to let it all out. I'll be fine now. I'll show them that this particular clippie is not going to be intimidated by violence.' And, as if to prove her new-found determination, she rode her bicycle to work that day.

* * *

A few hours later, Connie and Bert sat in the rest-room, waiting for Mr Adams. Connie took scant comfort that she felt better than Bert looked. He was nervous and fiddling with the brim of his cap.

'I'm that sorry I couldn't do more for yer, duck,' he mumbled, cap in hand.

She put a hand on his shoulder and patted it. 'It's not your fault, Bert. I should've knocked for you when I got a whiff of what they were up to. Thank you for bringing me back. I was a bit shaken by the experience; I can't say otherwise.' She smiled.

Bert's mouth grinned, but his eyes didn't.

News of the assault had swept through the depot. Everyone had words of comfort for her. Betty was horrified and sat with her as long as Mr Adams would allow. Given the circumstances, he seemed in no

196

hurry to send Betty away, especially as she had all but finished her shift.

'Thanks, Betty.' Connie felt weepy at her concern. 'I feel stupid. I should've banged on Bert's window when I had the chance. I wanted to show the bosses —'

'Jean told me yesterday what happen to you. I was bloody angry; I can tell yer. I don't think them boys would've done anything more. It sounds as if they were only after the money so as they could get more boozing done,' retorted Betty. 'Pigs that they are! And don't you go saying as it's your fault when you see Inspector Caldwell, Connie. Cos it weren't. You just say as you was too far away from the window to knock on it. Bloody good job that blind man did, mind you. Talk to Inspector Caldwell. You'll be fine with him. He'll see you right.'

Connie couldn't believe her ears. Another clippie singing his praises. Was Betty talking about the same man, the man who had stood next to Connie during her test, as silent as the grave?

'This'll be a lesson to us all,' Betty carried on in an apocryphal tone. 'No trying to be bloody martyrs in the future!'

22

May 1917

It was two o'clock before Inspector Caldwell arrived. He was coughing as he walked into the depot. Connie was in the yard doing some maintenance checks with Bert to pass the time and heard him before she saw him.

When Bert excused himself to visit the privy for the third time in the space of half an hour, Connie realised that the incident might have affected him more than she had thought. He was in his fifties, after all. And he'd given chase.

Mr Adams appeared at the office door and asked where Bert was. Connie nodded toward the privy. 'Send him to the office when he comes out, will yer?'

Bert was with him for a goodly time because Connie had finished her chores when he reappeared. He said nothing and went outside. Miss Norton called Connie into the office where Inspector Caldwell was waiting. Connie closed the door, and he beckoned her to sit in the chair placed in front of the desk.

In front of him was a cup of tea, and he was no longer coughing, for which she was thankful. She vaguely recognised that the cup he was drinking from was made by Chamberlain's Pottery, where Ginnie worked. Most of the people who worked on the pots would turn the saucer upside down to look at the maker's mark. How strange that it should come to her at such a time.

She gazed into those blue-grey eyes, thinking what an extraordinary colour they were. They still haunted her. How could —

'Connie? Did you hear what I just said?'

His head was on one side, staring at her.

Her face burned. He would think her a complete nincompoop.

'Sorry, Mr Caldwell?'

'I asked how you are feeling?'

His voice, although a little distant, was softer than she was expecting. It almost brought tears to her eyes. It must be the shock of Friday's ordeal.

She sat up straight. 'I am quite well, Inspector Caldwell.'

He smiled. 'I'm glad to hear it. I'm afraid I have to take you back to the unfortunate matters of Friday, Connie. I hope it won't be too painful for you, but it's something we must do quickly before your mind loses sight of it.' He spoke quietly, his voice gentle as if he understood her anxiety.

She nodded.

They sat together, him asking questions and Connie doing her best to answer them as truthfully as she was able. When she came to the part when she thought about attracting Bert's attention, she stumbled and said that she hadn't been entirely sure that anything was going to happen and didn't want to cause the passengers any alarm.

'Yes, Connie . . . but even if there was a slim chance, it might have been better for you to call for assistance. Nobody would have thought any the less of you.'

'Pardon me for saying so, Inspector —'

'Please call me Robert.'

'As I was about to say . . .' she paused, 'Robert, it's all very well for you to say that no one would blame me for asking for help, because you are a man and it suits you to believe that women need protecting.'

He frowned. 'I don't follow?'

'Women have to fight for the right to be treated properly and men, most men, would say you were asking for trouble putting a woman in charge of a tram. Some would say it was my fault for putting myself into that position in the first place.'

He looked surprised at her candour; there was even a trace of admiration in his eyes. 'I don't believe anyone is at fault here, apart from the young men who attacked you. It is the Potteries Tramway Company who needs to pursue this matter on behalf of an employee who was engaged in doing their job. I would say the same to any man who was in your position too.'

His words took the wind out of her sails.

'Well . . . I mean . . . that's fine. As it should be.'

The questioning continued. How many young men were on the tram? Did she do anything to stir up trouble? Why didn't she raise Bert, the driver sooner? Was she flirting?

'But I've already answered these questions in my statement to Mr Adams. What more can I add?'

He looked away, clearly embarrassed. 'Please do as I say, Connie. I am required to collect all the information available. It is not your job to question me.'

It was Connie's turn to flush. With tight lips, she reiterated her conversation with Mr Adams in as formal a tone as she could muster. Inspector Caldwell had her statement. He appeared to be following her closely. When she stopped momentarily, he didn't speak, merely waited for her to continue. She stumbled again when she came to the part when she was held down, and the boy grabbed some money from the bag. She shuddered violently as the scene came into her mind. She could almost feel his arm pressing against her throat as she tried to swallow. The weight of his body. The smell of beer. His hot breath on her face. All came back to her in that moment.

He glanced up at her. 'Do you feel able to continue, Connie?' His voice sounded warm and sympathetic.

'I'm fine Inspector Caldwell, please carry on.' Connie was determined not to falter and look away. She had nothing to hide. She had done nothing to provoke the situation. She was the victim.

After a few more questions, it was over.

'Now that wasn't so bad, was it?'

His smile was warm. He looked rather handsome. He appeared different in every way to Matthew. Maybe that was a good thing, but the thought had startled her.

'As I said, I have to satisfy myself as to the nature of the crime committed. Lady conductors are under intense public scrutiny due to the nature of their work and being alone on buses and trams. All instances of crimes against PTC are required to be investigated and reported, and those against our female staff claim particular attention.'

'And, as I said . . . Robert, I don't think lady conductors should be treated any differently to male conductors. Their jobs are the same, are they not? To look after the tram and its passengers? If you think we need special attention, you are undermining us.'

It was her best suffragette voice, and he squirmed in his seat. Again, there was admiration written on his

201

face. It pleased her to see it. Still, she raised her eyebrows, searching for answers to the questions she had fired at him although she could no longer look him in the eye.

'Quite right. But it's my job to see that all the people under my jurisdiction are safe at all times. Even you must agree with that?'

His question required a response.

'I thought the company would be more concerned about losing the money.'

'I can assure you that's not the case. This company values the safety of staff highly, Connie. It cannot allow this sort of behaviour to go unpunished. You can be carrying, at least to some people, large sums of money and if we allow a robbery such as this to go unpunished, it will be a signal to every petty thief who wants a bit of extra cash that the tram is the place to go. Next time, the conductor may not be so fortunate. Do you not agree?'

He smiled at her, and she smiled back, somewhat surprised. Suddenly, her heart was racing, and she could hardly breathe. He looked . . . he looked rather . . . charming. A sudden rush of blood to her face had her gasping for breath. She wondered how often he smiled.

'Now then, Connie, can you give me your full name? You didn't put it on your statement.'

'Connie Copeland.'

'Connie Copeland? Connie Copeland — now, where have I heard that name before?'

Connie went cold.

'Might we have met somewhere?' He shook his head. 'Perhaps not. I'm sure I would have remembered those green eyes.' His face flushed a deep red as he spoke. He stared down at the papers he was shuffling together. Connie was pleased that she had raised a response in this reserved man.

'Mr Adams has been to see the witnesses. They have corroborated your statement. He has reported the incident to the constables and left the witnesses' names and addresses with them. They will no doubt be in contact again. Neither of the witnesses knew the boys or had any idea where they live. They were both in agreement that they had a Potteries accent but I'm afraid that unless we get some more concrete evidence, we won't be able to take this any further.'

Connie was surprised things had moved so swiftly.

He gave her a quick smile that was almost shy, and that was her undoing. For the life of her, Connie could not speak. She stood up quickly, gave him a gracious nod and hurried from the room before her glowing face gave a hint of her unsettled mind.

How on earth did she come to react like that? Fear and attraction. Fear that he might be set to discover her secrets and end her employment? He thought he recognised her green eyes and her name rang a bell. Could that be to do with her previous suffragette activities? Would he find out about her spell in prison? She wasn't ashamed of her past, but it was still having its impact on her life. Despite the trauma of the last few days, she was enjoying her work more than she could have thought possible. To lose it so soon would be terribly upsetting.

That shy smile of Robert's appeared rarely. It made her skin tingle. Was it attraction? She didn't know. There was so much against him. She couldn't allow herself these thoughts. If she did, how soon would it be before he discovered one or all of those secrets she desperately wanted to keep? And hadn't she promised herself that she would let no man get close enough to hurt her as Matthew had?

Such a pity though; he could be so nice.

* * *

Betty and Jean were all agog when they got together, wanting to know how she had coped with the inspector, what he said and how he acted towards her. They knew she didn't like him.

'He asked me what happened and took a lot of notes. But he was very fair and seemed anxious for my well-being. I'm glad to have got it over with.'

Betty had to start her shift and left. Jean nudged Connie and whispered in her ear.

'Connie, did anything happen?'

'Whatever do you mean?'

'During your meeting with the inspector? You were very flushed when you came out.'

She tried to stay calm, but Jean was like a dog with a bone.

'Something did happen. Come on, Connie Copeland. Spill the beans.'

'It was nothing untoward, Jean. I swear it.'

'So, something did happen?'

Jean was too persistent for her own good. 'He was . . . sympathetic, kind . . . and, I suppose different from how I had originally thought of him.'

'Do you mean you fancy him?'

Connie blushed violently. 'I didn't say that.'

Jean smiled. 'You didn't have to. They do look rather handsome in their uniforms, don't they?'

'Who do?'

'Well . . . Inspector Caldwell and Mr Adams.'

'Mr Adams is pleasant enough,' said Connie. 'But I believe Inspector Caldwell is trying to hide something. He rarely speaks, rarely smiles, rarely does anything. He is trying to keep himself to himself. He doesn't even talk to Fred or Bert.'

'Perhaps he's shy? He knows full well that whatever he says in confidence will be all round the depot in no time.' Jean thought for a moment. 'Was he sympathetic? Do you think he understood how frightening it could be for any clippie to be in that position?'

'Yes. He seemed genuinely concerned about the conductors' welfare. He told me to call him Robert.'

'You called the inspector Rob —'

'Well, he told me to. He didn't see it as a problem. I suppose he was being considerate, given my frightening experience. He did go on about protecting the clippies. I said it was his job to ensure the safety of all the conductors irrespective of whether they were ladies or not.'

'For goodness' sake, Connie, do you want to keep this job, or are you trying to find a way out?'

'Of course not. Even with what's happened. I really do like the job, Jean.'

'What is it that disturbs you so much about him?'

'He made me feel . . . I don't know.' Connie shrugged. 'If you must know . . . he was different than I expected. And . . . I . . . I might have been wrong about him.'

Jean frowned. 'Well that's good, isn't it? I don't see what the problem is?'

'I . . . I thought I wouldn't like him. He seemed too aloof, and I thought he did his job under sufferance.'

'And now?'

'As I said, I might have been wrong, and I don't like it!'

Jean burst out laughing. 'Is that all? Yer a funny one, Connie Copeland, I'll give yer that.'

Connie pursed her lips. She wasn't used to being laughed at.

23

May 1917

Tuesday was her first day back on the tram. She wasn't at all sure how she would react. She went to Miss Norton to pick up her float and ticket machine and walked to her tram where Bert was waiting.

'We're working together again, Bert. That's a coincidence.'

'Just the luck of the draw, duck.'

'How are you feeling today?' Connie asked in a quiet voice as they made ready to depart.

'Nowt wrong wi' me, duck. Gorra keep working. Need the money.'

'But do be careful, won't you, Bert?' Connie insisted. He still looked peaky, although she could appreciate his need to work.

He nodded. 'How did yer get on at your interview with the inspector? It surprised me that they called 'im in. I thought Stephen Adams would do it.'

'I wish it had been Mr Adams, too. Inspector Caldwell went over my statement again and told me that the constables were involved.'

'Are yer worried about being on the tram late at night? Has it put yer off?'

'It unnerved me a little, Bert, I can't deny it. But I'll be ready next time, and you can be sure of that.'

'Good for you, lass. Best get going now.'

She stepped onto her platform, took a deep breath

207

and let it out as slowly as she could. No way was she going to let anyone see how she felt.

As the tram lurched forward, it shook her. She clutched her money bag tightly as a sudden rush of fear surged through her. She stared at the empty seats and steadied herself. She walked the length of the saloon and back, breathing slowly in and out, making sure the back rests of the seats were facing in the right direction.

At the first stop she welcomed four passengers including a young man, not unlike those she had encountered. Her breath came quickly. Keeping a wary eye on him, she moved forward to collect the first fares of the day. When she got to the lad, she forced herself to look him in the eye. They were hazel, not the deep brown she remembered. It wasn't him. She beamed at him, and he grinned, no doubt taken aback by the radiance of her smile.

When she returned to the depot, Jean and Betty were waiting for her, anxiety written on their faces. She hurried over to them, wanting to reassure them that she was fine.

'We were ever so worried, weren't we, Jean?' said Betty.

'You shouldn't have come in today.'

Jean's eyes moved to and fro between them. 'If we keep reminding her, Betty, she's never going to get over it.'

Connie nodded strongly. It had been a big hurdle she had overcome today, and she felt proud of herself. 'I quite agree.'

And she hoped that was the end of the matter.

★ ★ ★

The following day, Mr Adams came into the depot just as Betty was making her final checks before starting her afternoon shift. 'Bert isn't in today.'

'Is he poorly?' shouted Betty over the noise of the compressor. 'Who'll be me driver, then?'

'Got one of the blokes from the Longton depot coming. He should be here shortly.'

'But I'll be late . . .'

'Dunner werrit, lass. Conner be helped.'

Betty shrugged. 'No rush then,' she said to his departing back.

Connie grinned. 'Lazy start for you then, Betty Dean. It was hectic this morning; I'll be glad to get home. Don't you complain.'

'As if!'

A few minutes later they were joined by Doris. She was the first clippie to work at the depot and knew almost everything about almost everybody and what she didn't know wasn't worth knowing. She had been helpful to all the new clippies, including Connie.

'How's tricks, Connie?'

'Oh, not too bad, Doris. Feet are killing me. I have been busy this morning. Got to cash up and then I'm off home.' Connie was relieved that Doris did not ask how she felt after the assault.

'When I get home I'm going to soak me feet,' Doris muttered. They both burst out laughing.

Just then, Jean's tram pulled into the yard with the new driver.

'What's he doing here?' said Doris.

'Do you know him?' said Betty.

'That's Joe Cumberbatch. Well known trouble-maker. He was a driver when I did my training down at Longton. If there was ever any trouble in the depot,

209

he was usually in the middle of it.'

'What sort of trouble?' asked Connie.

'Always trying to take on the bosses. Has plenty to say and not all of it useful. He's a big union man — at least that's what he says. I think he just likes stirring things. Got an eye for the ladies an' all. Our Mr Adams mustn't have had much choice.'

'Is he married?' asked Betty, watching him descend from the cab.

'Best keep well clear of 'im, duckie,' said Doris.

When Jean introduced the three of them to Joe, his face perked up.

'Nice ter meet yer, Joe.' Betty, head on one side, gave him a welcoming smile. 'Are you planning ter be here long?'

He beamed at her. 'Might be? I'm covering for those blokes you lost last week. Always like to help out where I can.'

'That's not like you, doing two men's work. You normally struggle to do one!' said Doris.

Connie smothered a grin. Betty couldn't take her eyes off him.

'Hello, Doris, fancy seeing you here. Tongue as sharp as ever I see. I've come to keep you company, by the looks of it.'

'I don't need your sort of company, Joe. Still stirring it whenever you can, are yer?'

'Have to keep the bosses on their toes. With all you women working 'ere they'll be after reducing our wages.' He turned to Connie. 'Are you the lass what got hurt on the job a few days back?'

Connie nodded. She didn't want to talk about it.

'Shame. Have the constables caught the lads?'

'No,' replied Connie.

'You had a word with the union yet?'

Connie frowned. 'No, why would I? I'm not in the union.'

'Well, we'll have to see about that. It's up to the bosses to keep workers safe. If you were in the union, they'd take your case up and get you compensation.'

'Mr Adams and Inspector Caldwell are doing all they can to find the culprits.'

'And you believe that, do yer?' Joe sneered.

'I do believe it, Mr Cumberbatch, and might I remind you that you've only just arrived here. I believe I know both of them better than you.' It surprised her that she felt the need to defend them both against this interloper. It didn't stop her green eyes flashing with annoyance. 'And you should get your tram out if you want to keep your job.'

It was Connie at her best. So much so that Betty transferred her gaze from Joe to Connie. Connie wasn't sure if her expression registered surprise, admiration or something else. She flushed as she saw the look and decided that to say more would be dangerous.

Joe grinned. 'You're posh for a clippie! That were some speech. I'll consider myself told off, ma'am. Fancy joining the union?'

She walked off towards the office, glad to be away from him. It hadn't taken him long to latch onto her problem. Doris was right. He's a troublemaker, and she would do well to keep away from him.

★ ★ ★

Connie worried about Bert. Because he didn't live far from the depot, he was often called in at short notice if someone was unable to work their shift. He

211

was missed when he wasn't around. He hadn't been in for a few days now and he lived alone. Had he suffered any after-effects after giving chase to the boys? If anything happened and she hadn't checked on him, she wouldn't forgive herself. She enlisted Fred's help.

'It's a shame for poor Bert, isn't it, Fred? Supposing he's seized up and can't get around? Do you think he might be partial to a cake or some fruit? I would like to thank him for his support. It's probably down to me that he's off work. I'd like to see he's all right.'

'He's not so young as he used to be. Could be suffering but wunner admit it to nobody. And he can be a cantankerous old sod when he's feeling under the weather. Pardon my swearing, Connie, but it's the best way to describe the bugger.'

Connie had to laugh. At last, Fred was beginning to treat her like she was one of them and that was indeed progress. 'Where does he live?'

'Bailey Street, number twenty-two. It's one of them streets on yer left through Goldenhill going towards Tunstall; it's about a mile away. Having a visit from you might well cheer him up. It'd certainly make my day if you were to visit me,' he grinned.

Connie laughed loudly. 'I'm sure you don't need looking after at the moment, Mr Parsons.'

'Mmm. Pity, that!' He grinned broadly.

★ ★ ★

Connie decided to visit Bert instead of going straight home. She hummed as she cycled along Bailey Street to Bert's house, one of a terrace of two-up two-down houses built for pottery workers and miners. Ginnie lived in the same type of house. One tap with cold

212

running water, and a range to heat the water and do the cooking. In winter, the range was the only form of heating. Although each room had a fireplace, coal was too expensive to buy. In summer it was only lit twice a week, once on Friday, for bath night and on Monday for the washing. Clothes were washed in a tin bath with a scrubbing board and hung to dry in the back yard. If it was wet, they were dried inside on the clothes-horse.

She knocked on the door. It took some seconds for Bert to answer, and she was almost ready to turn away. Noise from inside the house stayed her feet, and she waited patiently with a smile on her lips.

The door opened a couple of inches. Connie could only see half of Bert's face.

'Hello, Bert. It's me, Connie. I've popped along to see how you are. I wanted to check you're all right?'

He nodded. 'I'm all right.' But the door remained as it was.

Slightly disappointed, Connie tried again. 'You looked after me so well. I thought I would do the same for you.' She waited for him to open the door, which he showed no signs of doing. He wasn't the most communicative of souls, but he wasn't usually this unsocial.

'Bert, are you sure you're all right?'

She frowned and took a step forward and tried to see more of his face. She heard him sigh, a sigh that seemed to travel through his entire body. A few more seconds went by, but Connie stood her ground. He was not going to get rid of her that easily. She would do what she had come to do whether he wanted her company or not. She owed him that.

The door opened. Bert looked unlike she had ever

213

seen him before. His shirt was creased, with food stains on his chest, his trousers held up with a piece of string around his midriff. His hair looked as if it hadn't seen a comb for days. He was so different from the proud Bert she saw in his uniform at the depot.

'Thank you for opening the door, Bert.'

He led her through the sparsely furnished front room and into the kitchen. The sink was full of dishes, some of which looked as if they had been there for days. Three plates were stacked together on the table, possibly the remains of three days of food. It seemed that all the dishes and plates he owned were now dirty and spread across his kitchen.

'Bert, whatever's the matter? Are you unwell?'

He slumped on a chair by the table and held his whiskery head in his hands. Connie looked around, unable to say any more, shocked by his appearance and the state of the house.

Slowly, she sank onto the only other chair that was empty. She sat with her hands on the table, which felt a little sticky, and she couldn't help but move them along a little in the hope that she might find somewhere cleaner.

They sat in silence until Bert raised his head. His eyes looked bloodshot, as if he hadn't slept. Connie got the impression he wanted to talk, but his eyes didn't seem to want to meet hers.

'You don't look at all well, Bert. Did you hurt yourself when you chased the boys?'

He was silent.

'Tell me. Maybe I can help.'

He shook his head. 'You can't.'

She was disappointed that she couldn't get through to him. 'Are you in pain?'

He laughed, but there was no humour in it. 'Am gettin old, Connie. That's what it's all about. Too old ter do me job. When I chased them lads me heart nearly give way.'

'Oh, Bert, why didn't you say? Maybe I could have helped you.'

'And give 'em an excuse to get rid o' me? If I lose me job, I'll lose this place.' He waved his arm around the room. 'I know it's nowt ter look at. But, if I lose me job, I'll lose this an' all. It's brought it all 'ome ter me. I'm in me fifties, duck. You clippies are not the only ones what might be out of a job when the boys come 'ome from the war. Stands ter reason.'

'Oh no. Have you got any family?'

He shook his head. 'Never got wed. Mother died last year. Got a brother but we lost touch after Mam died. He could be anywhere . . . if he hasn't got himself killed over there in France. He's younger than me.' Bert went quiet.

Connie stared around the kitchen. 'We'll have a cup of tea, Bert.'

She scooped up some cups and gave them a thorough wash under the tap, trying not to notice the detritus around her. The teapot was brown inside. She scrubbed it hard. If she gave him a minute or so on his own to recover, there was a chance she might get through to him. When she turned around, he was wiping his face with a towel and breathing in loudly to clear his nose.

'Here we are, Bert. A nice cup of tea for you.'

She placed it in front of him and sat down. The silence grew. It was all she could do not to speak. He was still hunched up.

'Bert, would you mind very much if I spoke to Mr

Adams? Tell him you're not quite right after running after those boys. I'm sure he'll only want to help you.'

'Can't be no worse than I am now,' he said.

The ride home helped to clear her head and think about all she had heard.

Alice met her in the hall. Connie took off her jacket and hat, which Alice hung up in the cupboard.

'My word, you look hot and bothered. You're late. Have you done an extra shift?'

'No, it was such a lovely day I decided to take a leisurely cycle home. But after a full shift, I think the ride was probably too much. Where are Mother and Father?'

'They're visiting the Welches, in Bucknall. They said they'd be back in time for dinner.'

'I shall be in my room, Alice. Can you call me when dinner is ready?'

She sat on her bed, deep in thought. Bert was clearly suffering, anxious about losing his home, a home where he lived all alone. And all because he had tried to help her. She would discuss Bert's situation with Mr Adams tomorrow.

★ ★ ★

'Poor bugger. Pardon me, Connie. But he must 'ave been desperate to open up to you. He's a very proud man.'

'I think everything must have got on top of him and he'd had enough. I can't bear the thought that it's all because of me.'

'It's not your fault. Wait until I get my hands on them lads. I'll show 'em what for.'

'Can you help him, Mr Adams? I think he'll take it

216

more to heart from you than from a woman. Persuade him to come back to work when he's feeling better.'

'I never meant to get rid of 'im. Dunner know where he's got that idea from.'

'I think he's just built it up in his mind. He's seen clippies settle in and get on with the job and he's worrying whether his job is safe.'

'Leave it with me, Connie. I'll make sure as he's all right. And thank you for bringing it to my attention.'

Connie left knowing she had done the right thing and sincerely hoping that Bert would return to work in the very near future.

★ ★ ★

Jean was definitely developing an attraction to Mr Adams. Connie didn't know if the feeling was mutual, and she was worried about her friend. She had heard that soldiers returning from the war often had problems which could not be seen or readily understood. Jean couldn't have had much experience of men. She deserved to know what she was letting herself in for before she got too involved.

Stephen must have been devastated to lose his younger brother, and she would have been surprised if he didn't feel terribly guilty that he had been injured and had not given his life for his country. And what about his poor mother? Three lives ruined in one family. Walking with a stick would be a constant reminder of all he had lost.

It had been difficult to wheedle information out of Jean in the early days, whereas Betty had been very open about herself.

Connie recalled a conversation the three of them

217

had had when waiting for their cash to be counted one Friday night, about a month after they started.

Betty was part of a large family and had been forced into service as soon as she could leave school.

'Stands to reason,' she'd said, nonchalantly. 'One less mouth to feed and a bit of extra cash. Mother jumped at the chance of getting rid of me.'

'That's terrible, Betty. You poor thing,' said Connie, shocked.

'I think she loved me. But she couldn't cope with all of us. So, when I was old enough, I had ter go into service, you know, live in.'

'Did you come from service to here? Must have been strange for you.'

'No. I left after a few months.' She turned away, rubbing her hands. 'But then I got a live-out job, which was much better, but I needed somewhere to stay. As luck would have it, I rented a room two streets away from Jean and we became friends. It was me what suggested we become clippies because the money's much better.'

'I'm glad you did,' Connie said, warmly. 'What about you, Jean?'

'I left school and went straight into the pots.' Jean shrugged as if, with these few simple words, she had told her life story.

'What did you do? I have a friend who works on the pots in Burslem.'

'I was a flower maker. It was a nice job as far as it went, but the money wasn't much good. I probably would've stayed an'all if it hadn't been for Betty here.'

Jean never mentioned her family. If she had opened up to Betty, she never said.

Connie could understand Jean's need for privacy

—wasn't she guilty of exactly the same? She had deliberately kept quiet about her suffragette past for obvious reasons and hadn't spoken of herself, where she lived, or what she'd done in the past. She'd managed to change the subject before things became too personal. The only thing she felt able to share was her friendship with Ginnie — because Ginnie was one of them.

Relationships were so complicated. She still hadn't resolved the problem of whether or not to say anything about Stephen to Jean. She was considering it because Jean was a friend and friends had to be helped.

Connie thought long and hard throughout the evening. In the end, she concluded that she had to tell Jean what she knew of Stephen's background before her friend got in too deep. She would leave it to Jean to decide what to do about it.

Her second meeting with Mrs Adams came to mind. She had seemed a nice, homely sort of woman, forced to take her place at the head of a diminished family. Connie felt sure that they would take Jean in as part of the family with no trouble at all. But suppose Jean wasn't ready for the responsibility of caring for a damaged former soldier?

★ ★ ★

Everyone was glad to see Bert back in the fold again a few days later. Jean and Betty made a point of mentioning it to Connie.

'I wonder how come he's picked up all of a sudden? Hardly used to get a smile, and now look at 'im. He's like a dog with two tails,' said Betty. 'Me dad 'ud say as he was up to summat.'

'Perhaps he's feeling better because he's had a break away from all of us. He's back now and I, for one, say we should put everything behind us. What happened in the past should be left in the past,' Connie said to end the speculation.

At that moment, Bert joined them.

'Welcome back, Bert,' said Jean warmly.

'Who's with me today then?' Bert's glance took all of them in. 'Can't have yer fighting over me.'

Everyone burst into fits of laughter as he climbed into the driver's seat.

Connie hummed to herself as she took the fares, thankful that all was well again. Bert's confidence seemed to have increased and Connie made sure to include him in conversations. She had even made an excuse to call at his house one evening with one of Alice's boiled fruit cakes and was mightily relieved to find the house in a tidier, cleaner state than previously. On the whole, he appeared to be a much happier person, and Connie couldn't stop smiling the whole way home.

★ ★ ★

Connie had agreed to meet Jean in Hanley in a little teashop just down from Parliament Square. The meeting place was Jean's suggestion; she used to frequent it when she worked as a flower maker on the pots. Down a narrow, cobbled street, it had tiny mullioned windows and was quite dark inside. Lamps were lit even in the middle of the day.

A hand waved.

'I wondered if you were still coming,' Jean said quickly.

'I'll get us some tea.'

Connie worried about how to introduce the delicate subject of Stephen Adams and what her intentions might or might not be. After all, if Jean had no desires on him, Connie need not say anything at all. It was going to be challenging to get her to open up.

After ordering refreshments, Connie looked around the small room. People were sitting at four of the six tables, adequately dressed, smart but not grandly so. Connie and Jean would need to keep their voices low.

After general mutterings about the weather and other unimportant matters, Jean was quiet for a moment. This is it, thought Connie. She knows she has been asked here for a reason.

'Is something troubling you, Connie? Do you need someone to talk to? I'm a good listener.'

Connie almost burst out laughing. Jean thought she was the one with the problem. 'There is something I need to talk to you about.'

Jean's eyebrows lifted, and she laid one hand on top of the other on the table and waited.

'I . . . I have a friend who has a dilemma,' Connie began slowly, her thoughts only briefly in front of her words. 'She has discovered that a friend of hers has begun to have feelings for a man she works with.'

Jean nodded, concentrating hard and drinking in every word.

'They are both very nice people and my friend thinks they could be happy together. But . . . my friend has discovered something about the man in question that might cause heartache for her friend, and now she doesn't know whether to warn her friend because the thing she has discovered is a secret.'

'Hmm. And how did your . . . friend discover this secret?'

'She was told in confidence.'

'You mean . . . your friend was asked to keep it quiet and not tell anyone?'

'Well, yes, I suppose.'

'Then you have your answer, Connie. Shouldn't your friend respect those wishes?'

'But supposing her friend gets hurt and my friend knew all along?'

'It's difficult, I agree. And who told your friend?'

'Another person who works with them both.'

'Why doesn't that person tell?'

'Because he . . . because they were told not to.'

'So two friends of a third friend have told you that a secret is a secret?'

During this whole saga, Connie was finding it difficult to remember which friend was which, but Jean seemed to be keeping up with the story. 'I-I believe . . . I mean . . . I think so.' Oh, dear. This was not going as she had planned. She should have kept her mouth shut as she'd been told to do.

'Forget about it, Jean. I shouldn't have said anything. I see that now.'

Jean suddenly laughed out loud, surprising Connie who realised she had never heard Jean laugh like that. She could feel the confusion on her face and thought she must look comical to Jean. Was that why she was laughing?

'Oh, Connie! You do look funny.'

The laughter carried on, and people turned in their seats to look at them. Connie felt a little annoyed. Everyone was now looking at them and she, Connie, was only doing this to stop this very friend

222

from getting hurt.

'I'm sorry, Connie. I know you have my best interests in mind.'

'You? You mean you knew all along what I'm trying to tell you — or not, I suppose? Why didn't you say earlier? I've been going round in circles trying to say something without incriminating anyone. Really, Jean Wright!' Quite put out about the whole thing, Connie decided there and then not to go poking her nose into other people's business in the future.

Jean stopped laughing, although the grin remained. 'I didn't realise what you were going to talk about until you started going on about a friend of a friend. I suppose I wanted to see how you could tell me without letting on who you were talking about.'

'Well, I suppose it's out now.'

'Not quite. Let me get this straight. You don't want to tell me something that you think I should know because it involves someone else who we both know. Am I right so far?'

Connie nodded.

'Is it about Stephen?'

Again, Connie nodded.

'What about him?'

'Well, I still can't tell you, can I?' Connie's frustration was growing. 'I mean . . . you still might not know . . . just because it happens to be about Stephen.' Connie leaned forward and spoke in a low voice. 'Look, do you care for him . . . I mean really care for him, Jean?'

Jean flushed. She looked down and scuffed her foot along the floor, looking serious. 'I do, Connie . . . and before you say anything, I know he's far older than me. But he's kind, and he's a gentleman. I've met his

223

mother . . . I mean apart from when she tested us all on the trams, and she's very nice.'

'You never told me you were courting.'

'No, but you must keep it quiet. It is against company rules for Stephen to walk out with female employees.'

'That seems unfair?'

'It was brought in when they started to employ clippies working in close proximity with drivers.'

'Has Mr Adams spoken to you about his brother?'

'Walter? It was one of the first things he told me.'

Connie heaved a sigh of relief. Thank heavens for that. All her worrying had been for nothing, but she wouldn't have had it any other way. She felt protective of both Jean and Betty. Betty could take care of herself. She was not so sure about Jean.

'I felt it would be a huge responsibility for you to take on if you didn't already know.' Connie could feel her face reddening. 'You and Betty are like the sisters I never had, and I have this urge to protect you both.' She looked directly into Jean's face. 'And I'm not apologising for it even if you think I'm an interfering old —'

'You're not old! It's very thoughtful of you, and I appreciate it. And it brings tears to my eyes that you think of us as sisters.'

Connie meant it too. Her own eyes were bright. She put her hand over Jean's, and they sat still, each in their own world.

'As I said, Stephen is a lovely man. He lost Walter in the war.'

'You don't have to tell me, Jean —'

'But I want to. You deserve to know. You have my best interests at heart, and I can trust you. Walter was

224

the youngest, and they were inseparable. Their father had died in 1913, so Stephen was the man of the house. When they both went off to war, Mrs Adams made Stephen promise to look after Walter.'

'But that's unfair! How could —'

'Unfair, but understandable, Connie. She had lost her husband and couldn't stand to lose her children too. Think about it, Connie — both of your sons marching off to war a couple of years after losing a husband. How painful that must have been. They were only on the Western Front for about two months when Walter was killed in action.'

'You don't have to go on, Jean.'

'I want to. Need to. Then you'll understand, and I won't have to mention it again.'

Connie gave her a sympathetic smile, feeling the anguish Jean was going through but knowing it would be a relief for her to talk about it.

'Two months later, Stephen was hit in the knee while out on patrol. Shrapnel, it was. Someone managed to get him to a Casualty Clearing Station before he lost too much blood.' Jean shuddered and had to gather herself together to continue. 'Then, of course, it was a case of waiting for a transfer home.'

'Poor Mrs Adams. How awful for her.'

'When he could walk again, he returned to his old job back here at the depot. There was no question of him returning to the Front. The company was pleased to get him back, he said. They were running out of men. At the end of the year, they started taking on us clippies.'

All of the pieces were beginning to fit into place now; why Stephen was working in the depot, why his mother helped out with the testing, why she was

225

wearing black and why Stephen kept himself to himself.

'Fred said he used to be the life and soul of the party. He might get back there again someday. It'll just take time, I think.' Jean sighed. 'Like I said, he's a lovely man, and if I can help him become the man, I know he can be, I want to do that.'

Connie had to blink suddenly. Tears threatened. How brave Jean was. She sounded so grown-up. How did girls bear it?

'I'm sure he knows how lucky he is having someone like you to care for him. Thank you for sharing it with me. It will go no further, I promise.'

That night, Connie went through the details of the day. Her thoughts kept returning to Stephen and his lost brother. How did he cope with losing his brother in such a horrendous manner? Which was better, to love someone and lose them, or never to love at all?

24

June 1917

It was Connie's birthday and she had agreed to meet her mother for a meal at the Victoria Hotel in Hanley. It was, perhaps, the most frequented hotel in The Potteries and although it was expensive, the cuisine was excellent, and was considered by many to be money well spent. Her father had been invited, but he wouldn't be home in time and had suggested they go without him. She was surprised he was content to miss the outing. He'd missed a few things recently.

Arm in arm, they walked into the dining room and were seated by smartly dressed waiters. Mother took out her spectacles to read the intricate but rather beautiful script of the extensive menu. After ordering their meals, Connie relaxed and looked around, surprised at the number of seats already taken.

'Now then Constance . . . sorry, Connie. I'm afraid it is going to take a while to get that name fixed into my head. You'll have to forgive me, Connie. Are you sure you are fine working on the tramcars, dear? You look a trifle peaky to me. You seem to be in and out all the time these days and have hardly any time to yourself. Is that wise? And do you think you should protect yourself from the heat, so you do not suffer from freckles?'

'I'm fine, Mother. For the first time, I feel I am doing something worthwhile but different. So do

227

stop worrying. I'm enjoying myself. And Constance is fine — as long as you remember that my name at work is Connie.'

'Hello, Miss Copeland. How are you?'

Connie closed her eyes. She didn't need to look to realise that the deep voice behind her belonged to Inspector Caldwell, the very last person she would have expected to see in this hotel. Worse still, what would he think of finding a mere clippie eating here? How could she possibly afford it on a clippie's pay? And, if he had heard her last words, whatever would he think?

It surprised her that he should make himself known outside of work. She would have expected him to ignore her.

'Hello Inspector, I am quite well, thank you,' she said, starting to rise.

'No, don't get up.' He laid a hand on her shoulder. A hand that burned through her dress to her neck and sent a shiver down her spine. The touch seemed too personal since they barely knew each other. As it was, she had no alternative but to introduce him to her mother, which she did with alacrity.

'I'm very pleased to make your acquaintance, Mrs Copeland.' He took her mother's hand and brought it to his lips, an action much appreciated, judging by the broad smile on her mother's face. His smile took in both of them and Connie was glad she was sitting down.

'Would you care to join us . . . Mr . . . ?'

Connie stared at her mother, horrified.

'Caldwell, but please call me Robert. I'm afraid I can't. I have a guest of my own. I felt I must take the opportunity to introduce myself and to say that your daughter is an asset to the company.'

This was awful. Connie wanted to bury her head in her hands.

'It's good to know that, Robert. She tells me she is enjoying the work.'

'It's a pity she's had such a bad experience —'

'— Of the weather.' Connie interrupted him quickly. 'It could have been better, couldn't it? But everything's fine now. You can't work on a tram and be upset by the weather, can you, Inspector?'

Two lines of a frown appeared each side of his nose and then disappeared as he understood that her mother didn't know about the assault.

'We are here for Constance's birthday celebration. She is twenty-two, Robert.'

'Mother! I'm sure Inspect . . . Robert doesn't need to know that!' Connie didn't know which way to look. It was going from bad to worse.

He looked confused. 'Constance? Oh, you mean Connie?'

'Of course, you know her as Connie. I keep forgetting that she's only Constance at home. I'm afraid I can't keep it in my head. She continues to remind me, of course, don't you, dear?'

Connie groaned. 'We must let . . . Robert go, Mother. He has someone waiting for him.' She glanced at him desperately.

He took the hint. 'I will see you tomorrow, Connie — or should I call you Constance since we're not at work? Enjoy your meals, both of you.'

That was one of the most embarrassing few minutes she had ever experienced. Was he surprised by her mother's revelation? She had managed to make it sound quite underhanded. That was the trouble in having a sociable mother; she could and would talk to anybody about anything.

She watched him return to his seat opposite a well-dressed young lady only to discover she too looked familiar. It was none other than Matthew's cousin, Louisa Pendleton. How on earth did Louisa know Robert Caldwell? Surely he, a tram inspector, wouldn't mix in the same circles. This was just about as bad as it could possibly be. By tomorrow morning Robert would know all about the wedding and, heaven forbid, why it had been cancelled.

Louisa stared back. There was no look of recognition on her face as far as Connie could tell, but Louisa was a good way away. As she watched, Louisa's face appeared to light up inside and looked quite beautiful. She was clearly smitten by him.

When she turned back to her mother, Connie realised that she too had had him under scrutiny the whole time.

'Mother! Don't stare so.'

'He seems to be a nice, well brought up young man. Does he work in the same building?'

'No, he doesn't. He's an inspector, and he comes occasionally to check we are doing our jobs.'

'He's your superior?'

'No!' She said that too sharply. 'He's not my boss. But he does ensure that everything is running satisfactorily.'

'Well, I think he seems nice and smart. You could do worse.'

'Mother! Really! He's with someone else. You saw he was. Besides, we don't even like each other.'

'He didn't have to come to our table to introduce himself, did he? He could have joined us and brought his guest with him.'

'Mother! Do you realise who she is?'

'Should I?'

'Before you get carried away, you should know that her name is Louisa Pendleton. She's a cousin of Matthew's.'

'Really! Oh, my word, Connie, you might have said! What on earth is he doing with her?'

'Firstly, you didn't give me the chance to tell you, Mother.' Connie stopped talking for a moment. 'And secondly, I've only met her once, so I hardly know her.'

She hoped that would be an end to the conversation. She was enormously thankful that her father had not been present, for Robert, spruced up like that, had become quite a gentleman.

As they continued to eat, her thoughts rampaged through her mind. She had spent a long time worrying that Robert would find out about the white feather. Now, it appeared that the rest of her exploits as a suffragette would be her undoing. Louisa was bound to tell Robert why she had been jilted at the altar and all her secrets would come out.

'He does look a charming young man,' said Mother, smiling.

25

June 1917

Connie settled herself in the restroom with a pack of Alice's sandwiches for her dinner, and a book. There seemed to be plenty going on. She could hear a high-pitched singing out in the yard, followed rapidly by a deep male voice and she was tempted to go out and join in. She had a notion the two, most likely Betty and Joe, would not take kindly to her joining them. That was another budding romance in the offing. It seemed the trams attracted young love, although only time would tell if it would last. She leaned her head back against the cream-painted wall and closed her eyes, letting nothing into her mind except the singing.

The door to the restroom opened with a bang. She sat up quickly, noting subconsciously that the singing had stopped, to find Robert standing in front of her. She blushed and hoped that she had not been sleeping with her mouth open.

She hadn't seen him since her birthday lunch at the Victoria Hotel. What was she going to say to him?

'I was told I'd find you in here,' he said, his tone a little on the short side.

It immediately put her back up, and she was sharper than she intended. 'It's dinnertime and I have to eat somewhere, Inspector.'

He stared at her blankly.

She waited for a moment, but he said nothing. 'Do

you want to speak to me — or do you plan to eject me from the restroom?'

It was self-defence, and she knew she was being difficult. Given her position, she also knew it was the very last approach she should take. 'I beg your pardon, I'm afraid I haven't been sleeping too well,' she said quietly, but unable to look at him.

'Do you mind if I join you, momentarily?' he asked.

She gathered together the remains of her dinner and motioned him to sit. There was still a sandwich untouched, and his eyes rested on it. 'Have you eaten, Robert? Here you are . . .' She pushed it over to him, but he declined. 'I'm not likely to eat it, so you're more than welcome.' She couldn't help but smile as his stomach growled.

'If you have taken your fill, I would be happy to take it off your hands.'

His smile was most engaging. She caught her breath and watched him take a mouthful. Once he had devoured it, she spoke again, but it came out as a squeak. 'Do you wish to talk to me?'

'Did you enjoy your birthday meal with Mrs Copeland?'

'My birthday . . .' It surprised her that he should want to talk to her about their meeting. 'Why . . . yes, I suppose I did, thank you.' There were palpitations where her heart should be.

'I was intrigued to discover your change of name — you are Constance at home, if I remember correctly? Are you a spy in disguise?'

He was smiling, but his eyes watched her keenly. She swallowed and decided to tell the truth. 'It must've sounded rather strange to you. Let me explain. I call myself Connie at work because I thought it sounded

233

less aloof. I wanted to fit in as a clippie and not be seen as a toff playing at work. A clippie named Constance doesn't sound quite right, I was told.'

Her cheeks felt hot.

'And that's the only reason? You can imagine my surprise. To be told that someone was working for the company under an assumed name.'

'But I'm only using a short form of my name. It's hardly a matter for your concern.'

'Under normal circumstance, it wouldn't be. But, I don't think this is normal.'

'What do you mean?'

'People can have several reasons for telling only half a story with a half-truth. Do you know what I mean, Miss Copeland? For example, is Connie Copeland, a clippie of the Potteries Tramway Company, the same person as Miss Constance Copeland? Who was due to marry a man named Matthew Roundswell?'

His face was closed to her. What was he thinking?

Connie's face drained. He had lured her into a false sense of security. Just what had he discovered?

'I have matters to discuss with you Connie — or Constance, whichever you prefer. Do I have your permission to call on you this evening?'

'I don't think that would —'

'I believe this is a personal matter, and I wish to discuss it away from the depot.' His blue-grey eyes held hers. 'I suggest that it's in your interests to agree.'

She searched his face for any traces of what was going through his mind. There was none. She had no option but to agree to his request. She nodded. 'Very well. Would half past seven be convenient?'

He nodded and rose to his feet as she wrote down

her address for him. 'I will see you later. Good afternoon to you.'

With that, he let himself out of the room, leaving Connie dumbstruck. How on earth was she going to get out of this mess?

* * *

Connie said nothing to her mother of Robert's reason for calling on them that evening. She wanted to keep everything to herself until she knew the extent of the problem. She told her parents that Inspector Caldwell from the Potteries Tramway Company would be calling on a matter of confidential business. Her father had looked surprised and pleased at her apparently elevated position.

'Oh, you mean that nice gentleman we met at the Victoria Hotel on your birthday?' Her mother managed to get the words out before Connie could stop her.

'We'll need some refreshments. Come with me, Mother.' Connie drew her mother out of the drawing room before she could say more.

On the way to the kitchen, Connie said, 'I don't want you to say anything about meeting Robert in the hotel to anybody, Mother. So, please don't speak of it. We're meeting on confidential business, as I said.'

Her mother looked put out but agreed.

Connie left Mother to talk to Alice and went into the library. It seemed strange to be entertaining a man in Father's domain. It was a large room with five tall, narrow sash windows on two sides, each flanked by floor to ceiling bookcases. As it was summer, the fireplace was empty. It was a man's room with a lingering odour of cigar smoke.

It had been a tiring day. She'd had argumentative passengers on each of the last two runs and, quite frankly, she'd had about as much as she could take. It was wearing to be pleasant to passengers who were determined to be annoying, although she was experienced enough to stand up for herself and now would have no hesitation in calling for the driver if necessary.

Now she must be pleasant to Robert Caldwell.

★ ★ ★

Connie had taken care in dressing, wanting to create an air of confidence. She wore a slim dark-green skirt and a white long-sleeved blouse, close-fitted at the neck. Alice had put her hair up in the way she would normally wear it on a day off. She glanced in the mirror and satisfied herself that she looked like a capable young woman who was very much in control of herself.

If Connie's suspicions were correct and he had discovered her suffragette activities, what was she going to say to him? She had gone over and over the subject in her mind. If Louisa had spoken to him of Connie's supposed wedding to Matthew there was every possibility he would know it had never happened, and why. Should she try to maintain secrecy, or was it time for all to be revealed?

This was not going to be a pleasant meeting. It crossed her mind that she could sit in her father's chair behind the desk but decided instead they should sit in the two leather armchairs either side of the fireplace, to create a more friendly atmosphere.

Connie heard voices in the hall. There was no

mistaking who it was. There was a knock on the library door, and Alice appeared with Robert Caldwell.

'Good evening, Robert.' She didn't add that she was pleased to see him because she didn't know if she was.

'Good evening, Connie.' He stared around the room, taking everything in, no doubt confirming his suspicions about who and what she was.

'Please, do sit down,' she said and motioned him towards the other chair by the fireplace. She couldn't believe how nervous she felt, waiting for him to speak.

Alice reappeared with a tea tray and placed it on the table between them. 'Will that be all, miss?'

'Yes, thank you, Alice.'

Connie turned to Robert. 'Would you like some tea?'

'Thank you,' he said.

Under his steady gaze, her hand felt sweaty, and the handle of the teapot almost slipped as she lifted it to pour the tea. It was all she could do not to blurt out everything, but she held her tongue. Soon, it would be in the open and he could make of it what he wanted. She passed the cup and saucer to him and waited.

In the end, she said, 'You asked to see me, Robert?'

'Yes, I did.'

He leaned forward in the chair, bringing his face closer as if he was trying to see inside her soul.

'You have probably guessed it's about our meeting at the Victoria Hotel.'

'How can I help?' she asked. She took a sip of her tea and tried to stop the cup from rattling in the saucer.

'That funny little conversation we had about you having two names, Connie and Constance. This morning you said it was to help you to better fit in with your fellow workers.' He made a point of looking around the room. 'It might surprise you, but I can see why you decided to keep all of this quiet.'

She nodded, although her breathing was becoming laboured.

'Was there any other reason?'

She shook her head. 'Why would you think that?'

'My lunch guest, Louisa Pendleton, informs me that you were acquainted with her cousin, a gentleman by the name of Matthew Roundswell and that you intended to marry him.'

'Did she tell you that?' She started to flounder a little. 'I can't . . . what do you . . . I mean . . . what exactly did she tell you?'

'That you had a whirlwind romance with him and that he had called the wedding off when he discovered you had been to prison for wrongdoing.' He stopped talking.

'What else?'

'Isn't that enough?'

'Forgive me if I'm wrong, but I don't see that it is anything to do with you.'

'I beg to differ. Being sent to prison and failing to mention it to Mr Adams when he took you on is very much to do with me.'

'But he never asked me.' She bit her lip at the thought that she might be getting Mr Adams into trouble. 'This morning you said that I was wrong for not giving my full name too. My name is my choice, Robert. As I said, I gave my name as Connie because I genuinely believed it might be helpful to my work.'

'Very well. So, let us go back to the prison sentence then, shall we? How did that come about?'

'Did you ask Louisa?'

'I don't think she knows the details. That's why I'm asking you.'

'I don't think I am obliged to tell you, Inspector.'

Robert lifted his head at the return to formality. 'It was sufficiently serious for your husband-to-be to call off his wedding.'

She winced. Perhaps it might be better if she gave her side of the story. She would probably lose her job anyway, so what did it matter?

'It happened a long time ago. As a suffragette, I used to distribute pamphlets, and an associate would deliver speeches. It was something I truly believed in, Inspector; I would never have involved myself otherwise.'

Robert relaxed into the chair. 'Go on.'

'I was handing out pamphlets near the bandstand in Burslem when I first met Matthew. He was with Louisa. We barely spoke but he came back the following week, and we got talking about the suffragettes.'

'So, how did you get yourself into prison?'

'Well before I met Matthew. It was in 1913, not long after the death of Emily Davison. Do you remember her?'

'I do. There was some controversy around her death, I believe.'

Connie nodded. 'Well, a month later a march was arranged in London and I wanted to hear Sylvia Pankhurst speak. I know the family.'

'You know them?'

'Yes, I used to live in Manchester, and I attended some of their meetings with my mother.'

He groaned and rolled his eyes. 'So . . . it runs in the family, does it?'

'I went to London and joined the march. I got to Whitehall and lost sight of Miss Pankhurst. There was a riot. I was pushed several times, and the constables were accosting another lady. She was hurt, bleeding, but they carried on mauling her. I did the first thing I thought of. I picked up a stone and threw it through a window. I wanted them to stop hurting her. Nothing more. I swear to you.'

'And did it feel good to throw stones at the windows of government buildings?'

'It didn't happen like— How did you know it was a government building?'

'It was the window of my office that you smashed. You could've killed me.'

'Your office?'

'The War Office. Papers relating to suffragettes and other troublemakers passed my desk for cataloguing. That's how I found your name. But I hadn't associated Connie Copeland with the Constance Copeland referred to in the report.'

How much worse could it get? 'I didn't do it to hurt anyone. Nobody would be working on a Sunday,' she finished lamely.

'And you went to prison.'

Connie blanched at his statement of fact. 'Yes,' she said in a small voice. Then her head shot up. 'But it was only for a month, and I paid for what I did.'

She held her head high.

'So, is it correct to say then, Miss Copeland, that you were economical with the truth about both your prison sentence and your change of name when Mr Adams interviewed you?'

'It wasn't like that —'

'Stephen Adams didn't take up references, did he?

Did you persuade him not to? I will have to talk to him before taking any decisions on your conduct. I have to say that, in normal circumstances, you would be dismissed.'

Connie stared at him. 'In normal circumstances, Inspector Caldwell, this conversation should be taking place in the depot, not in my house.'

They both got to their feet. Robert glowered. Connie folded her arms beneath her breasts.

'I believe it is time for you to leave, Inspector Caldwell. You must do what you think is best.'

Connie pushed the bell at the side of the fireplace and a few moments later, as rehearsed, a suitably servile Alice appeared with his hat and coat.

'Inspector Caldwell is just leaving, Alice. Would you escort him to the door.'

'Yes, miss.' Alice did a little curtsey.

Robert took his hat and coat and followed her to the door. He turned back to Connie. 'Good evening to you, Miss Copeland.' He looked as if he was about to say more but changed his mind.

Connie nodded. She had hoped he would say something to give her hope but feared that she had gone too far.

Only time would tell.

★ ★ ★

Two weeks had passed since their discussion at Holmorton Lodge. Each day she had gone into work fully expecting to be dismissed. How could Inspector Caldwell do anything else? She had received a prison sentence and had not disclosed it. It was as simple as that and she had probably got Mr Adams into trouble

241

too. It crossed her mind more than once that it might be better if she left of her own accord. Much better than waiting for Inspector Caldwell to sack her. At least that way she was in charge.

When she heard him talking to Miss Norton, Connie's heart sank. She avoided the office and went into the restroom. Moments later, Robert popped his head around the door and beckoned to her to join him in Mr Adams's office. This is it, thought Connie. In a way, she was relieved that she would not be required to wait any longer.

Robert sat in Mr Adams's chair and motioned her towards the visitor's chair. Once she had settled, he started to talk.

'How are you this morning, Miss Copeland?'

'As well as can be expected, Inspector, given the circumstances. How are you?'

He nodded at her but didn't speak.

'Inspector Caldwell, I have decided to —'

He held up his hand. 'Wait, before you speak. You don't know what I am going to say.'

His interruption startled her.

'I have spoken to Mr Adams about your interview and have ascertained what went on. He agreed that he decided you were a lady of integrity and that the need to take up references was less important than getting you in quickly to allow you to train with the other new clippies. Waiting for references would have slowed the process down, and he had no reason to suppose you were unsuitable. He believed that had he asked the question about your background, you would have told him about the prison sentence, which was not for a job-related offence. The fact that you failed to give your full name was your choice. He admitted that it would, likely or not, have been shortened by everyone working in the depot.'

Constance sent a whispered thank you to Mr Adams. He could have been so angry at his misplaced trust. She nodded and was about to say more when Robert began to speak again.

'I haven't finished, Connie.'

Her blood ran cold. This was it. The end of the road for her. She closed her eyes and waited for the inevitable.

'In light of this, Mr Adams felt it would be unfair to dismiss you. He did confirm that he'd had sight of your birth certificate a few days after you started and that your full name is Constance Copeland.' His voice softened. 'So, it is down to the interpretation of the events. You felt you had done nothing wrong: I felt you were sparing with the truth to your own advantage. I think this is an example of where people's personal perceptions can influence their interpretation of the facts to suit their needs.'

Connie's eyes widened. Had she heard him correctly? He wasn't going to sack her. Her hands felt sweaty as a wave of relief came to her.

'I believe Mr Adams has been lenient with you and I think you have been lucky, Miss Copeland.'

'You mean —'

His voice became formal again. 'I can confirm that, as far as the company is concerned, the matter is closed. Regarding what you call yourself and why, as you so rightly say, it should be of concern to nobody except yourself. However, I appreciate that, as a suffragette, you had certain principles to maintain and, while I can't condone their violent activities, I do understand they were fighting for a cause they believed in.' He smiled thinly. 'It may surprise you to know, Connie, that I also have principles — I assume you are still Connie in the depot?'

She nodded, his sarcasm not lost on her. 'And please, Robert, you won't say anything to the others about my . . . circumstances? I swear I was telling the truth when I said that I became Connie because I really wanted this job.'

He looked at her steadily. 'You have my word.'

She sat in silence, as he left the room and closed the door.

She let out a huge shuddering gasp, quite frankly amazed that she still had a job.

It was over.

26

September 1917

It was warm and the sun strong in the evening sky. It had been a little oppressive on the tram, and Connie's feet ached. She would need to bring them back to life by giving them a good soaking.

She had tried to keep out of Robert's way, feeling uncomfortable in his presence and embarrassed at the position she had put him in. Some weeks he was barely around the depot and they had not encountered each other on the trams. Annoyingly, she felt piqued at his disinterest in both her and her job.

When Connie opened the door of Holmorton Lodge that evening, Alice came hurrying towards her, her face heavy with anxiety.

'Alice, what is it?'

'I don't know where to start. Your father's in the library. Shut himself in there. And he's drinking. Your mother's beside herself in her bedroom. I think she's making herself proper poorly. When I went into the library, Mr Copeland was standing by his desk with a bottle of whisky in one hand and a nearly empty glass in the other, and he was filling up again. I went in to ask him if he was all right, but he shouted at me to get out. He's never done that before. He's always a gentleman. Well, I ran out 'cos he didn't 'alf upset me, I don't mind saying.'

'Oh, dear. I'm so sorry, Alice.'

'I went to see yer mother. She was that pale I thought she was going to faint, so I got her some water. I think you'd best go and see her. She's in her bedroom.'

'Thank you, dear Alice. I'm sorry Father shouted at you. Something awful must have happened. I'm sure he didn't mean it.'

Alice nodded and disappeared to the kitchen. Connie picked up her skirts and ran swiftly upstairs to her mother's room. She tapped on the door, and a faint voice answered. She opened the door to find her mother sitting upright on the bed.

'Mother! What's happened. Are you all right?' She hurried over to the bed and grasped her mother's hand firmly.

'I'm fine, Constance . . . I mean Connie. Have you seen your father?'

'No. I came to see that you're all right and to check what happened first. Alice said Father has been drinking.'

Tears welled up in her mother's eyes. Connie couldn't remember ever seeing her cry. She was usually so strong.

'I'm afraid your father's in a spot of bother.'

'What do you mean? What sort of bother?'

'It's this dreadful war. He went to see Mr Railsford, our solicitor. He didn't say why but it must be something terrible.'

With a sharp intake of breath, Connie said. 'Is it to do with money?'

Mother nodded. 'I believe so, but it's not as straightforward as that.'

Connie sat slowly on the bed. 'What's going on, Mother?'

Agatha's hands covered her cheeks. Connie smoothed her mother's hair and waited.

'I don't know how bad it is, Connie. He was rambling about some shares. We shall have to get to the bottom of it tomorrow.'

'I shall go to see him . . . right n —'

Her mother shook her head and caught hold of Connie's arm. 'No, leave him tonight. He'll have passed out by now. We'll both talk to him in the morning.'

Back in her room later, Connie went through all that had happened at work and now it looked as if there were more troubles at home. Thank goodness she still had her job. Nevertheless, there was something, in the pit of her stomach, gradually building, catching at her breath until she realised she was almost panting.

★ ★ ★

She woke suddenly and listened, but heard nothing. She lay silently, waiting for her bedroom to gradually flood with light. It was barely five o'clock.

Her mouth felt dry. She decided to go downstairs to make a cup of tea, and then maybe she would be able to go to sleep again. She was convinced she had been awake more than she had slept.

She slipped into her dressing gown and opened the bedroom door. The lack of windows made the landing silent and dark. Slowly, she crept down the stairs, feeling her way until she reached the hallway where a light shone through the semi-circular arch of tinted glass at the top of the door.

All was still.

The door to the kitchen was ajar. Her mother

wasn't likely to be out of her room, so maybe Alice was up. She walked into the kitchen.

Alice stood in the centre with a saucepan at the ready.

'Connie! Oh, thank God, it's you. I didn't expect you to be up this early.'

'I couldn't sleep.'

'Neither could I. I thought I may as well get up,' said Alice, shakily returning the saucepan to its hook by the oven.

'How about you have a cup of tea with me?'

'I'll not say no to that.'

Alice looked almost back to her old self when the tea was ready, and both of them had sat down with their steaming cups.

''Ave you spoken to Mr Copeland yet?' Alice ventured.

Connie shook her head. 'I talked to Mother, and she thought it best to leave it until tomorrow — well, I should say today, now. But you need not concern yourself. We will get to the bottom of this mess.'

'Poor Mr Copeland. I do hope it's something and nothing.'

* * *

Connie had dark circles under her eyes. Worry and the lack of sleep had drained her. She decided not to go into work that morning. She couldn't have concentrated on the price of the tram tickets and being nice to everyone while her mind was at home with her parents. She hoped Mr Adams would be sympathetic over a family crisis.

On top of everything else, she had received a short

letter from Ginnie. Mabel's husband, Frank, had been killed in action on the Western Front near a village called Passchendaele. Mabel was in pieces, and Ginnie worried about what she might do. And there was poor little Florrie to think about.

Bloody Germans. Bloody war.

Connie dressed soberly and descended the stairs for breakfast. Mother was already sitting at the table. Alice was busy fluttering around her, checking to see she had everything she needed.

'What can I get yer, Miss Connie?'

'I don't feel hungry, Alice. Ginnie has received some bad news. Her brother-in-law has been killed. Her sister must be devastated.'

'Oh, no. Poor girl.'

The door opened to admit her father, looking rather the worse for wear. His face was grey and his eyes bloodshot and partially closed, as if it hurt to keep them open. His clothes were creased and he hadn't shaved. He walked towards the table and put up a hand to shield his eyes.

'Good morning, Agatha. Constance.'

'That will be all, thank you, Alice,' said Mother. 'We shall not need you. You may take the rest of the morning off.'

'Shall I wait for the cups first, Mrs Copeland?'

'No, dear. You may go now.'

'Thank you, Mrs Copeland.' Alice moved swiftly to the door.

Once Mother heard it close, she sat with a straight back and a set face. 'Well, Edwin? Dare I ask how you are this morning?'

He lifted his eyebrows. 'You may, as long as you moderate your voice.' He sighed. 'I'm deeply sorry about my actions yesterday. It was unforgiveable of me to succumb to drink in such a manner.'

'I believe you owe us an explanation regarding recent matters.'

'We need to talk alone first, Agatha.'

'No, Edwin. Constance is a grown-up member of this family and must be party to what is happening,' said Mother firmly. 'Last night I told her, very briefly, that we had a problem with some of our investments — in Government Bonds and shares.'

At first, he looked surprised, then nodded his agreement. 'It's this damn war. Everything was going according to plan until the war started. After buying and renovating this house, I needed to invest the rest of the money I got from selling the business in Manchester. Something safe, not too risky. Bonds were ideal, although the interest rate was low. So, I invested half the money in bonds and half in shares, where the return isn't guaranteed but the dividend rate is higher. It would give us a good life, and you a good education to prepare you for your future. In the beginning we did spend a little more than our income, but not significantly so.'

It was as her mother had said and she took it in steadily.

'Once the war started, it affected interest rates and the value of investments went down and dividends declined, but the cost of living increased. I'm afraid to say that, since then, we have been living beyond our means and I've had to break into our capital.'

Father stopped as if he was thinking carefully about what to say next. Not a word was spoken. Having considered, he continued.

'I was advised by my stockbroker to take this

opportunity to invest while share prices were lower at the start of the war. His advice seemed sound, as share prices would recover to their pre-war value quickly. The war was supposed to end after a few months. I have to admit that Railsford was against this idea from the outset, but sometimes you have to take risks. Prices of shares continued to fall and even now they are lower than the price I paid. My father and I took risks when we set up the business, and those risks have funded this family until now.'

'But, Father . . . why didn't you say? We could have done something — I could have done something.'

'Why do you think I haven't replaced the servants who have left us?'

'But we could have done more to help.'

He stared at her momentarily. Connie couldn't work out his thoughts.

'Where does that leave us now, Edwin?' Mother spoke quietly and calmly.

'Yesterday, I instructed Railsford to sell the last of our bonds to meet our outgoings until the spring. We still have our shares, but their return is lower than ever. Our income is now only half our expenditure.'

Both Connie and her mother gasped.

'The damnedest thing is, once the war is over, their value will increase again, I'm sure of it.'

He looked them both in the eye. 'Railsford thinks that will take many years — and I must agree with his arguments. If that should happen . . . I'm sorry to say that we shall run out of money and will have to sell up.'

'I see.'

Connie couldn't believe what she was hearing and her mother's quiet acceptance worried her more than her father's stark words. 'You mean sell the house?'

'And how soon would that be?' Her mother continued.

'No, no dear. We can continue like this for two or maybe three years. We have plenty of time to find a smaller house and bring our expenditure into line with our income and share prices might increase once this damn war is over. In any case, this is an attractive house which we should be able to sell for a good profit. But we do need to start cutting our expenditure drastically. I'm afraid Alice and Mrs Williams will have to be given notice. In any case, Mrs Williams should have retired years ago. Her arthritis is really bad and she can live with her daughter, she's always telling us about.'

Connie stared at both of them and watched her father's ashen face as he shook his head, his eyes closed to shut out the faces he was not ready to see. Her mother's bottom lip quivered as she tried to hold herself in check.

How could this happen to them? And what about Alice? She had nowhere else to go.

Later, Connie wandered around the house, in and out of the rooms she had, so far, taken for granted, and it came to her that she loved this house. Had loved it ever since the family had moved here from Manchester back in 1910.

Connie did not want to think about the prospect of leaving at this stage.

In the meantime, she would rack her brains to think about how they might get out of this terrible mess.

27

September 1917

Connie had so much to think about. She was quiet at work. Jean gave her funny looks. It was obvious she wanted to ask Connie what was troubling her. Connie appreciated her concern but wasn't quite ready to share her feelings and she managed to stay out of her way.

A couple of days later, her father appeared to be back to his old blustery self, issuing instructions to Mrs Williams, and to Alice who was scampering back and forth trying her best to please him.

'Is everything all right, Father?' Connie asked with a frown.

'Of course it is,' he snapped. 'I'm trying to organise this house, but I seem to be the only one who cares.'

He strode into the library. Connie sent a quick sympathetic smile to Alice who looked at her wits' end and ran after Mrs Williams, who was chuntering her way back to the kitchen.

Connie took a deep breath and walked in to the library, closing the door quietly behind her.

'Father dear, has something happened?'

'What more can happen, Constance? I'm trying to get this family out of an unholy mess and everyone seems to be carrying on as normal.'

Connie rolled her eyes. 'Do we need to reduce our circumstances immediately? Take care of what we spend?'

'We do, but we have to maintain appearances. We can't let word get out. I'm hoping the war will end before much longer and everything can be as it used to be.'

'That's rather fanciful, Father. When you made us aware of our financial troubles, I got the impression something needed to be done immediately. How can we know when the war will end?'

'Constance. If we can just marry you o —'

'Father! You ask too much. I will not be a pawn to be used in such a way. I will decide when and whom I should marry.'

'We have given you everything in life. You should be grateful that we want you to marry well.'

'*You* want her to marry well, Edwin.'

Connie's father spun round to find her mother standing in the doorway. You could hear a pin drop.

'I don't know what you heard, Agatha, but it's not what —'

'I know what I heard, and I don't like it. Constance is our daughter, not a commodity. Neither is her role in life to get us out of trouble. You always think you know what's best, don't you? Because you're a man, you believe you are in charge of our lives.'

'Agatha! How dare you talk to me —'

'We have spoken of this matter before, and you promised it was over, Edwin.'

'As I said before, we will have to get rid of Mrs Williams and Alice. I will go and tell them now.'

'No, wait Edwin. I agree it is right that Mrs Williams should retire. In fact, I have just been speaking to her and I think she is relieved. Her daughter wants Mrs Williams to live with her and we have agreed that she will leave at the end of the month —'

'Oh, and what about Alice?' Connie cut in quickly. 'Mrs Williams says Alice is perfectly capable of cooking our meals and looking after the household. Recently she has been doing more and more. I can't say whether her cooking will be as good as Mrs Williams', but it will be adequate for our needs.'

Father shook his head. 'But what about her wages, Agatha?'

'I'll give you something towards her wages. She doesn't have to know that anything's changed. We can't put her out on the streets,' said Connie.

'Edwin, I have never cooked anything in my life, and I don't intend to start now. We will keep Alice and that is the end of it. Or perhaps you could volunteer to do Alice's job.'

Father dropped his head.

'Can I tell her, Father? Please?'

'Yes . . . yes.' He sounded defeated but when he answered, he was back in charge again. 'I have decided your mother is right. We shall keep Alice on as long as we can.'

* * *

Alice was stoking up the fire in the kitchen as Connie walked in. She looked up and grinned. 'Yer don't half look pleased with yerself, if yer don't mind me saying so?'

'I have some news for you. Sit down for a moment.'

Alice's grin disappeared but she did as she was bid.

'I'm afraid we have to make economies within the household because of the war. Mrs Williams has decided to live with her daughter but Father has decided to keep you on.'

Alice's mouth fell open. 'Does that mean I'm taking Mrs Williams's job? I can't do that, Connie. It wouldn't be right.'

'No, Alice. Mrs Williams should have retired by now. She stayed on to train you. She says you have become a fine cook and a good housekeeper.'

Alice's eyes lit up at the praise.

'The only problem is that you will need to do the housework as well as the cooking initially. Once the war is over, and things are back to normal, we will employ someone to help you. Would you be willing to do that?'

Alice's eyes watered. She sat heavily on a stool by the grate. 'I don't know what ter say, Connie. I've been that worried.'

'Then say yes.'

Alice threw her arms around her, making further words unnecessary.

★ ★ ★

When she arrived at the tram depot Connie discovered, much to her dismay, that Robert Caldwell was in the office talking to Mr Adams. No one knew why. He had just turned up.

She boarded a tram with Harry, one of the older drivers. It wasn't busy, and she had plenty of time to think about matters at home. It was at times like this that she wished she wasn't alone in the saloon; that she had someone to talk to. When their last journey finished, she made her way wearily to the restroom and sank into a chair. The enormity of her situation bubbled up inside. She had told Alice her job was safe, but what would happen to her if they had to sell the house? What if this war went on for years? She caught a sob before it exploded into a shower of tears. It couldn't be happening.

She heard voices outside the door and jumped up quickly, wiping her eyes on her sleeve before searching for her handkerchief.

'Right, Stephen. If that's all, I'll be in touch as soon as I can.'

Robert's voice was getting closer. She turned away from the door, so he couldn't see her face. Apart from normal work duties, inspections and the like, she hadn't seen Robert to speak to since he confirmed she would be staying.

'Connie, are you ill? You look dreadful.'

He put his arm around her shoulder and guided her to the chair she had just a moment before been sitting in.

If it had been any other time, she would've made some sarcastic comment about not greeting a lady in such a manner, but his show of concern was her undoing. The tears she had attempted to control burst forth, and she sobbed into his shoulder.

'Please sit and rest awhile.'

He moved away and appeared to stare through the window for ages, giving her time to gain control once more. She appreciated his thoughtfulness. When he turned, she was surprised at the anxiety lining his face.

Breaking down in front of him and in such a fashion shocked her, but he had met her with such a kindly voice that her emotions had got the better of her.

'I'm sorry, Robert. I don't know what came over me.'

'Think nothing of it. But, what has caused you so much stress today? Have you had another assault?'

'No. No, nothing like that at all. But thank you again for your concern.'

He stared at her. 'Is there anything I can do to help?'

'No. I can assure you it's nothing to do with work.' Tears welled up again, much to her annoyance.

'Are there matters at home that are troubling you?'

She nodded before she could stop herself.

'Do you feel able to share them?'

'I don't want to burden you with my personal troubles.'

He smiled again and pulled up a chair to sit beside her. 'I want to help if I can. Of course, if you think I'm interfering, please say so.'

'You're not interfering. I appreciate that you are trying to help a hysterical woman.' She spluttered as she tried to make a joke of it. It was the only thing she could do. She dabbed at her eyes again.

'That's better.' He reached into his jacket pocket and handed her a clean white handkerchief. 'Here, take this. It'll be drier than the one you're using. I keep a supply close at hand. Not that I tend to have young ladies in tears too often, I might add. I have this cough, but I assure you the handkerchief is unused,' he added quickly.

He was so quiet after that she felt obliged to speak.

'In the last couple of days, I have discovered a problem at home. It's nothing to do with me exactly, but it affects my family. I want to help, but I don't know how,' she ended.

He stared at his scarred hands and nodded but didn't speak.

She had to say something to fill the silence. 'We have some money problems at the moment, and I don't quite know how to resolve the matter.'

'Oh, I see.'

'We have to start making economies. It is going to be quite an effort for the family, something we have never expected and something we are not used to.'

'Well, if there is anything I can do, please get in touch with me at the Stoke office and they'll leave me a message.'

Connie wiped her eyes once more with the borrowed handkerchief. 'Thank you for listening, Robert. I appreciate it very much. I promise to return your handkerchief in a better state than it is now!'

He waved her comment away and stood up. 'I meant every word, Connie. I am at your service.' He opened the door and looked back once, and then he was gone.

It took a minute or so before she felt able to leave the restroom. How nice he had been, not forcing her into a conversation until she was ready. She had been wrong about him. She had allowed his solemnness and lack of social skills to completely mask his finer qualities, such as those he had shown today. Look at how he was with Jean during her test, and now Jean would have no one speak against him. And when he had told Matthew about her prison sentence, he had done so to protect his friend, not to hurt anyone.

She closed her eyes momentarily. His concerned face appeared before her, like a photograph imprinted on her mind.

Jumping to conclusions about people was a failing of hers. She prided herself on being right most of the time. She was beginning to realise that some people could be both right and wrong.

A thought crossed her mind which made her feel helpless. She had told Robert she didn't know what to do, but that was not quite right. She knew that she could solve the family's problems by doing what Father had always wanted her to do: by marrying a rich man. But even that was now more difficult than ever. Betty was right; there was going to be a shortage of men.

Connie had gained a prison sentence, worked in an unsuitable job for a woman of her class, and had no money — not a glowing reference to give to any man, let alone a man of substance.

So it would not be easy, by any means. Nor did she wish to sign her life away to someone she did not love simply for money. On the other hand, there was no doubt it would save her family. Perhaps she shouldn't be so quick to rule it out.

28

November 1917

Connie was not starting work until two o'clock, so she had time for a proper breakfast, and to read the newspaper or whatever she wanted to do. If they weren't burdened with financial problems and the war, she might have said it was an enjoyable period. Her life was full, with her job and new friends. Even Robert had shown his kindly side.

She was chatting to her mother while Alice cleared away the dishes. Alice had taken on the role of housekeeper and was doing very well, although she did need a lot of reassurance. She would soon have the confidence to work more on her own. Connie felt proud of her.

Father walked in holding the newspaper. 'Well, that's torn it, I have just finished reading about this Bolshevik revolution in Russia and turned to the financial pages to be greeted by this.' He flicked the page.

Connie gave her mother a worried glance. Mother's eyebrows creased and she held herself stiff, suspecting the worst.

Father continued before they had a chance to look at the article.

'It says here: *The Amalgamated Iron and Steel Company has posted a loss for the second year running. The Board of Directors have issued a statement saying that*

261

there will be no final dividend for the 1916–17 financial year. Furthermore, there will be no interim dividend for 1917–18 year.'

Father paused and looked down at his tea.

'How bad is that for us?' asked Agatha.

'It's one of our larger investments. I was counting on the dividends for the housekeeping and Alice's wages. With that gone, I hope some of the other shares pay a higher dividend than I expect, otherwise I shall have to sell more shares.'

'Then we will have to make economies,' said Mother.

'I think we have no choice but to put the house on the market.'

'Edwin, not before Christmas.'

'Well, I suppose two months is not going to make any difference. But I'll speak to Railsford. He might have contacts looking for a property like this.'

Alice dropped a cup. Her anxious eyes flitted back and forth between them as she placed dishes, cups and saucers on a tray slowly, as if she wanted to speak but couldn't bring herself to open her mouth.

That her father could speak about such a delicate matter in front of Alice, showed Connie how agitated he was.

'It may not be as bad as we fear.' Her mother spoke firmly. 'If we all rein in our expenditure and the war ends, we will overcome our present difficulties. Only one of those possibilities is within our control, so we need to concentrate our efforts there. We will manage.'

Connie could well believe that no one would disagree with her, not even Father.

'I hope you're right, Agatha.' He strode out, shaking his head.

Mother turned to Alice. 'Now Alice, my dear, when you have finished clearing the table, I would like you to join Constance and myself in the morning room and bring your accounts book and anything you have from the tradesmen. I believe Connie and I should familiarise ourselves with some of the housekeeping matters.'

'Very well, Mrs Copeland.' Alice scuttled away as quickly as she was able with a full tray.

Alice looked a little more in control of herself when she entered the morning room carrying her books.

'Sit down, Alice.'

Connie smiled as Alice gave a wobbly grin.

Mother began. 'You heard the conversation at breakfast. Our financial difficulties, due to this war, have not gone away. My husband indicated we might have to sell the house, as a last resort. We must avoid that at all costs.'

'Yes, Mrs Copeland.'

'So that we might understand, tell us what exactly happens when you spend money for the household.'

'I do the same as what Mrs Williams taught me. I write everything down in this book.' She waved a black book with crinkled pages in front of Mrs Copeland's face. 'Mrs Williams said as I should, what with being new to it all. She didn't need to 'cos she kept everything in her head.'

'I see.'

'I 'ave lists of what I need to buy because I 'ave ter. Then I 'ave a list of what would be nice to have if there's a few coppers to spare. The last list is for luxuries, but I don't often get a chance to buy stuff from that list.'

Connie smiled, but her mother looked serious.

'That sounds excellent, Alice, but I'm afraid we will have to do much more in the future.'

'Yes, Mrs Copeland.'

'Tell me how you go about it.'

'Well, I work out the menus for the week and when you've agreed as it's all right, I work out what I need to buy. I take a list round to the butcher, the grocer and the greengrocer, and they put it up and bring it here. At the end of the week, they send me a bill. I check it and give it to Mr Copeland so as he can pay it.'

'That sounds very efficient, Alice. So, you always have a good idea of what we are spending.'

'Pardon me, Mrs Copeland, but that's not all. We have lots of other bills to take care of from the laundry, tobacconist, wine merchant, bakery, window cleaner, gardener, electrician, gas, dairyman, greengrocer, coalman, odd-job man, plumber —'

'So many!' Connie's eyes opened wide. She hardly noticed these people when they called. It all . . . just happened.

'They don't come every week, but it can be expensive when they do come — and it's not always essential.' Now that Alice had opened up, she was anxious to get her point across. 'Take the window cleaner — he comes every week and there's lots of windows to do. But we could easily manage if he came once a fortnight. I don't suppose anyone would notice, what with the sooty air, an' all. They just as soon get dirty again.'

'But it's not much in the way of savings,' Connie shrugged.

'I know — but if you make lots of savings, they all add up. And, if you don't mind me saying so,' Alice licked her lips, 'I don't think you know how ter save

264

money, if I'm honest.'

'Alice!' Connie felt a rush of annoyance. How could Alice say such things? She had got a job, hadn't she? And it was partly her wages paying for Alice's employment, although she'd never said as much.

'I don't want no trouble but if I don't say it now, I won't ever say it. What you think is essential, I would say was a luxury, like your dresses and hats and shoes. You can manage with less, but you don't, because you've never had to.'

'She's right, Constance. I think Alice might teach us a lot about making economies.'

Connie thought about Ginnie, Betty and Jean. No doubt each of them would have their own ideas on what was essential. The key seemed to be whether it could be justified.

'The same goes for Mr Copeland too, if I might say. Somebody needs to speak to him an' all.'

Two pairs of eyes turned towards Connie's mother.

Alice had a lot more to say before they finally parted, leaving each of them plenty to think about.

29

December 1917

It was three months since they first learned about their financial situation. Father had taken it badly, blaming himself for events outside his control. It was a pity he hadn't spoken earlier, as then they might have started to make economies sooner.

Connie had begun to make her own economies. No more visits to the milliner's or dressmaker's. Dresses would have to be worn more than once or twice and then altered to change the colour or style. She had rummaged through her wardrobes and drawers and discovered items she didn't know she had. Did it really matter if they were not the latest fashions?

It had been snowing all morning. Connie looked out of the drawing room window to where Sneyd Road should be, now marked by slushy black lines where carts and carriages had travelled.

'Yer'll not stop it snowing, Connie, no matter how many times yer look through the window,' grinned Alice.

Connie sighed. 'I'm working on a late shift today and I don't know if I will get to the depot. And even if I do, the trams may not be running or I may not get home again. I might have to bed down in the restroom.'

Alice's mouth fell open. 'Surely not! Whatever will yer father say?'

'I know. It's quite an adventure, isn't it?' Connie looked through the window again. 'Mr Adams says that if we can get into the depot, we should. If the company cancels the trams, we'll get paid for the day. If we don't go in, we'll lose a day's pay. I can use the telephone to contact the depot, but I wonder what the rest of the clippies do in this situation?'

'I never have trouble getting to work!' said Alice.

They both laughed. Connie had organised several dresses of hers to be altered by Ginnie, for Alice to use. As her position was now that of housekeeper, it would not be correct for her to dress in the black uniform normally worn by lower servants.

'What'll yer do about the Christmas Dance on Saturday?'

'I am going to Jean's house and will sleep there if the weather is bad. We plan to meet Betty at the Victoria Hall. It's only a five-minute walk. It'll be good having friends to go with. We can stretch our legs and have a good time. Take our minds off the war and work, and just enjoy ourselves.'

Alice nodded. 'I know how yer feel. I thought I might get out ter meet me mates, but they 'ave ter work. One of them can't have time off because her mistress is having a big do. It can't be helped.'

'Poor you for missing out,' said Connie with a sympathetic smile.

'Never mind. I've got plenty ter keep me busy. I was going ter put the Christmas tree up and decorate it but it'll have to stay outside until it's dry.'

Alice joined Connie at the window.

'We need something, Alice, to keep us from worrying about what's happening to our lads on the Western Front, don't we?'

Connie concentrated on the small, soft flakes floating slowly towards the ground. They were getting smaller. It might not be such a bad day, after all. 'You can put the Christmas tree up at any time, Alice. Why don't you come with us?'

Alice stared at her. 'Me come out with you, Jean and Betty?'

'Yes, that's just what I mean. You'll have a great time. Betty's such a laugh. We can never be too sad when she's around.'

Connie could see Alice's mind whirling, and then she shook her head.

'What about your mother and father? They'll need someone to look after them. I wouldn't be back ter light the fires if the snow's bad. No, it wouldn't be right. I'll stay here and maybe read a book to Mrs Copeland. She enjoys a good ghost story these winter nights.'

'Isn't that a bit boring? I appreciate very much you staying with Mother, but you need to get out and have a good time too, Alice.'

'Yes, I'll maybe organise something for next week. Don't go bothering about me. I hope as you can get out, or else I might be reading to you an' all.'

★ ★ ★

As it turned out, Connie didn't have to spend the night in the restroom and the snow had almost gone by the evening of the dance.

Connie and Jean finished work at the same time and were able to get to Jean's house without any trouble. Jean rented a room in a boarding house on Ware Street. Her room was on the first floor and was well

268

furnished and tidy, as Connie would have expected.

Connie readied herself for the walk to the Victoria Hall with boots, a long coat, scarf and hat.

'By gum, Connie, we're only going round the corner,' said Jean.

Connie was wearing the green dress she had not worn since her showdown with Matthew just before the wedding that didn't take place. She had looked on it as a bad omen and had refused to wear it. Today, she had run out of dresses she hadn't already worn and decided that this was to be the day when it would re-enter the world.

'I am being prepared, Jean, in case the weather turns bad.'

The girls walked briskly towards the Victoria Hall. The sky was starting to clear, and Connie could see the occasional star through the smog. It would be icy later, so they had better watch their step on their return.

Betty stood on the steps of the Hall, hugging herself against the bitter wind. 'Hiya girls, are you ready to enjoy yourselves?'

'Have you two got your tickets ready?' Connie grinned back.

Betty's eyes sparkled. 'I asked Joe if he fancied coming tonight but he said, maybe next time. Wonder if there'll be any soldiers home for Christmas?'

'You're always talking about men,' Jean laughed. 'You're obsessed.'

'Jean, there are loads of women out there, all looking for husbands. We've got to get in quick and find a bloke before they're all taken. Mind you, the way you butter up to Stephen Adams, I bet you're planning on walking him up the aisle, aren't you?'

With a red face, Jean sniffed. 'I'm not buttering up to him, Betty Dean. He's a nice bloke, and if he likes me, I'm not going to ignore him.' Jean flounced off, keeping her distance.

'Stop arguing, you two. We're here to have a good time for Christmas. Don't spoil it.'

'It's all right for her, Connie, she's as good as wed. It's me and you what's still looking.'

'Shut up, Betty, for goodness' sake. We are going to have the best of times tonight,' said Connie, linking arms with them. 'Who knows how long we three will be together? We're friends, aren't we?'

Betty and Jean looked at one another sheepishly and nodded. They showed their tickets to the doorman and he let them in.

Crowds of people were packed into the large hall. The three friends glanced around to see if they could glimpse anyone they knew, but were disappointed.

Many of the chairs laid out against the walls were occupied. Betty refused a seat and wandered off, eyeing up any man she saw to ascertain whether or not he had a partner. Jean shook her head, but this time, she had a smile on her face.

Connie smiled too. Something felt good about the evening. An older woman tapped Jean on the shoulder. Jean turned to speak to her and Connie continued to move around the chatting groups.

She had almost reached the opposite wall when she saw Robert sitting with Louisa Pendleton, engrossed in conversation. She hadn't had the opportunity to speak to him since he had been so kind to her over the money troubles at home. She certainly couldn't speak to him with Louisa holding court and lapping up his company. A little twist in her stomach surprised her.

She wondered how she would feel if he looked at her the way he looked at Louisa.

Robert glanced up momentarily, his face serious.

Connie was sure her face had coloured, and she backed away. To her great relief, she found Jean again but didn't let on that she had seen Robert with Louisa.

The band was playing a foxtrot. A few groups away, Betty was dancing with a soldier, causing Jean and Connie to laugh. It seemed that Betty had had her own way after all.

Connie had a couple of dances and then flopped down next to Jean. 'Are you enjoying yourself, Jean?' she asked, waving her hand briskly in front of her in an attempt to cool down.

'Yes, I am. I had a dance with a bloke whose hands needed a bit of control,' Jean said primly.

'Jean! You took Betty's advice then?'

'I was taller than him, so I stood upright and looked down on him and his hands stopped wandering after that.'

Connie burst into laughter as she pictured the scene. On hearing it, Betty soon joined them.

'Oh, girls, I aren't 'alf enjoying all this. What on earth are we all going to do when we finish on the trams?'

★ ★ ★

It must have been half an hour later when Connie crossed paths with Robert and Louisa again. She had done her best to stay out of their way. Suddenly, there they were, in front of her.

'Oh, my word, it's Miss Copeland, I do believe,'

said Louisa in a haughty manner.

'Good evening, Miss Pendleton.' She couldn't bring herself to ask if Louisa was well — because she didn't care.

'Good evening to you too, Connie.'

She felt ridiculously happy that Robert had chosen to call her by her clippie name. It brought them together and left Louisa on the margin. She thought she saw a hint of admiration in his eyes and was glad she had decided to wear the dress.

'Oh, my word. You've changed your name, Constance. I can't imagine why.'

Connie ignored the gibe and smiled at Robert. 'Thank you, Robert. I hope you are enjoying the evening too?'

He smiled and nodded. Then looked around. 'Are you on your own?' His voice held a note of surprise. 'Would you like to join us?'

To say that Louisa looked annoyed would have been an understatement. Connie smothered a grin. How she wished she could have said she would love to join them, just to see the look on Louisa's face.

'Thank you for your invitation, but I am here with my friends.' At that point, both Jean and Betty came to stand with her, one on each side.

Connie was sure she detected a flash of disappointment on Robert's face at her reply, but she was probably wrong.

'Quite right, Miss Copeland wouldn't want to let her friends down, Robert. We must allow her to rejoin her . . . friends.'

'What's that supposed ter mean?'

Louisa stepped back, putting her hand to her mouth as if shocked at Betty's abrupt tone.

Connie watched the emotions running across Louisa's face, the sneer spreading as she looked at Betty and Jean. Jean had noticed too and her face reddened. Connie grew embarrassed for her class. She was one of them, but the people she called friends were not. So, what did that make her? Working as a clippie hardly made her wife material for someone like Matthew, and the men Louisa associated with. Perhaps there were more benefits to being a clippie than she had realised! Should she place Robert in that category too?

'Oh, Inspector Caldwell, I didn't see yer. Am sorry for butting in.'

Robert nodded to Betty, but his eyes were still on Connie.

'We must leave you to enjoy the rest of your evening, ladies. I bid you good evening.'

With that, Robert gave a quick nod to each of them and, with his hand under Louisa's elbow, he steered her away.

'How did you get talking to 'im?' Betty wanted to know. 'And who's she, anyroad?' she asked, with narrowing eyes.

Connie shrugged. 'He just appeared with her.' She was about to change the subject when Betty did it for her.

'Well, let's get back to enjoying ourselves, girls. He's one person we definitely dunner have to think about tonight.'

★ ★ ★

Holmorton Lodge had survived its first austere Christmas.

Alice decorated the house as normal, despite Father's moaning that he didn't think there was anything to celebrate. She had produced a Christmas dinner that was every bit as good as Mrs Williams's. The bird was adequate but much smaller than they would usually have and Alice had complemented it with a substantial and rather tasty stuffing to fill out the plate. Mother had spoken to Father of the economies as she had promised and the only spirit to be found in the house was the Christmas spirit. The pungent smell of cigar smoke was also missing. Connie imagined that the negotiations that had taken place between them had been as difficult as those between warring countries. But in the end, Mother had had her way and Father agreed these economies were necessary.

It looked now as if they could manage to continue to live at Holmorton Lodge for a little longer, and maybe ride out the war. Peace was what they really needed.

30

March 1918

The peace they needed seemed to be a long way off. The war had been going for over three years. Three years at a time in her life when Connie should have been making plans for the future. She had seen loved ones taken from their families too early, and young women denied their rights to a family because there were too few men to join with them.

There had been some very good times, of course, but more and more bad news was coming from Flanders. Battles were won and lost, ground taken and lost around Ypres, a place that had appeared to have seen continuous fighting since the beginning. How terrible that sounded.

The Russians had finally signed a peace treaty with the Germans although they hadn't had their heart in the war since the abdication of the tsar. Now even more German troops would move from the east to fight in the west. Connie had heard it said that with the American forces in France, the war would be over at Christmas. But she had heard such optimism before.

There was some good news — legislation had finally been passed to allow women to vote in a general election for the first time, if they had property and were over thirty. Not equality with men, but some recognition of their worth.

Connie called at Ginnie's house to give her the

good news. When Ginnie threw open the door, her face was aglow with happiness. At long last she had received a letter from Sam, just a few lines, she said, and burst into tears giving release to all the pent-up emotion she had lived with for so long.

'When it come and I saw Stevo's writing after all this time, I was feared to read it in case it was bad news. But it wasn't.'

How wonderful it was to see Ginnie reading the letter for herself, to have played a part in Ginnie's happiness. It hadn't taken Ginnie too long to learn once she had conquered her shame. It was only the occasional new word that caused her to stumble now.

It was a very happy Connie who pushed open the door of Holmorton Lodge later. She ran upstairs to sit by herself awhile. The tears she had been holding back threatened to burst out, and she wanted to be alone when it happened. She didn't know why she felt like this. She should be overcome with joy, not holding back tears. She shut the door behind her and let the tears flow. Sam was safe, and that was all that mattered.

After the happiness of hearing from Sam, Ginnie became more of her old self again and Connie was thankful. She had gone along to the odd dance and had encouraged Alice to accompany them too. It was such a happy time.

31

June 1918

It was now June and the war did not look like ending soon. For the past two months, the Germans had carried out a series of attacks on Allied forces. Although the newspapers underplayed their significance, the casualty lists said otherwise. The location of many of the battles seemed to be as close to Paris as they were in 1914. There may not be a front for the Americans to fight on if the German successes continued.

Connie rode down to Burslem but she hardly noticed the beauty of the day. Her thoughts were on what was happening at the Front, and with dear Sam. Ginnie had received a telegram — *Missing in Action — 30 May 1918*, it said. It gave hope but Ginnie feared the worst. How could Ginnie bear it?

Connie brought her bicycle to a stop by a gate overlooking the fields between Sandyford and Goldenhill. It was all too much. She needed a moment to gather herself. The wind on her face was refreshing. She wished she could stay here all day and forget what was going on in the world. But she didn't. She had responsibilities.

★ ★ ★

She clocked on and walked into the yard, ready to start her shift. Joe Cumberbatch was standing in the middle of a small group of clippies. Betty was standing so close to him their uniforms melded into one with two heads.

'I'm calling a meeting of all the clippies, we've got a problem about yer pay,' said Joe, frowning.

When he looked like that, trouble usually followed, Doris said.

Ever since he had started to work at the depot, he'd been trying to get as many of the workers and especially the women to join the union, insisting it was for their own good. Connie could see the merit of it, but believed he was going about it in the wrong way. He was getting people's backs up and pushing them in the opposite direction.

'But we already get equal pay. What's the problem, Joe?' asked Doris.

'Come to the meeting an' you'll find out, you'll be glad yer did.'

Connie said, 'We should go along and see what he has to say, Betty. You too, Jean. Then we'll be prepared.'

'Mr Adams will see us —' said Jean.

'Let's just go and no harm done,' insisted Connie.

Jean flushed. 'But we'll be going behind his back.'

'What if we are? We're looking out for ourselves, aren't we?' chimed in Betty.

'But I don't want . . .' Jean's voice trailed off as her face grew redder.

'Dunner worry, he'll not think less of yer.' Betty's voice was getting louder and louder.

'Ssh . . .' Jean covered her face as if mortified.

Connie stood between them. 'Leave her alone, Betty. You do go on sometimes.'

Betty walked off in front, swaggering and turning

back every few seconds to gloat. 'He's so old.'

Connie put her arm around Jean as they followed Betty into the restroom where twelve clippies had squeezed into the small room, the three of them and Joe making sixteen altogether. Even in that crowded space, Betty had managed to stand next to Joe.

'Think of the poor passengers waiting for their tram while we're all sat in here listening to 'im,' murmured Jean.

She did have a point, but Connie's curiosity had been raised.

Joe clapped his hands for silence. 'Now listen, you lot. We're working on the trams and earning a decent wage, aren't we?'

Two or three of the clippies nodded, and one shrugged her shoulders unwilling, apparently, to commit herself one way or another.

'We've got ourselves a situation. I've just heard that the Committee for Production in London has agreed that *men* will be getting a five-shilling war bonus this year.'

A few shouts of hurrah went up.

Joe remained silent. He seemed to be waiting for the news to sink in.

Connie watched his face. 'What about us, Joe?'

'I'm afraid there'll be no bonus for clippies.'

Uproar broke out.

'What d'yer mean?'

'We was promised.'

'How can they go back on their word?'

'It's not right.'

Joe held up his hand for silence. 'They say as you girls get the same pay as us men. And that's right! War bonus is different. It gets paid to the men 'cos they're breadwinners with families to support.'

'But what about us? We have ter look after us families an' all.'

'They say as you women, what's got husbands in the Colours, already get separation allowance.'

Arguments broke out around the room.

'Excuse me, Joe?' Connie moved forward. 'Are you saying that all men will get the bonus and all the women will not?'

Joe nodded. His eyes were alight as the tension rose.

'So, single men like Fred and Bert with no families to support will get it, but widows with children won't.'

'That's about it.'

'But how can that be right?'

'That's what I'm saying. You women have got to join the union. If yer don't, I've a feeling they'll start to split the work so's they can say you women aren't doing the same work as the men and they'll cut yer pay. Thin end of the wedge, if you ask me. It's about time we showed 'em we're not about to roll over and do what they say.'

Connie, Jean and Betty looked at each other. Could they trust him to put up a fight for their cause?

Jean turned to Connie. 'You know what to do, don't yer, Connie.' She stared around the room. 'She was a suffragette, and she knows how to get things done.'

Connie closed her eyes. How did Jean know? Still, it was too late to do anything about it now. It would be all around the depot in five minutes.

Jean coloured.

Connie took a breath. She might as well accept it. 'We may have the vote, but it's still not on the same terms as men.'

'Yes, but we got it, didn't we? Thanks to the likes of

you,' said Jean, boldly now.

'But it's not enough. I'll find out what's going on. We need to be sure of what we're fighting against before we do anything,' said Connie. 'A war bonus for the men should mean war bonuses for clippies too.'

As the group disbanded, Connie called an embarrassed Jean over. 'How did you find out about me being a suffragette?'

'I so sorry, I didn't mean to. When I was talking to Stephen —'

'I might have guessed, but who told Stephen?'

'I don't like to say.'

'Come on Jean, we're friends. I'm not going to hold it against you.'

'Inspector Caldwell. But, I didn't know you wanted to keep it a secret. You could be such a help. I had to say something.'

'Thanks, Jean. Forget about it, I just needed to know. I'd better go and see Mr Adams.'

'Please don't tell him I've spoken out of turn. I wasn't supposed to say anything. I wouldn't have done it if it was important, I swear, Connie.'

★ ★ ★

Connie rapped on the office door and opened it before a response came. Mr Adams was sitting behind the desk, his head resting in his hand as if he had fallen asleep.

'What d'yer want . . . oh, it's you, Connie.'

His voice held a touch of exasperation, but Connie wasn't put off. 'I need to talk to you. We've been talking —'

'Who's been talking?'

'The clippies have had a meeting.'

'And?'

'When we were taken on, we were told it would be on the same pay as the men we were replacing.'

He nodded. 'So?'

'Well, the Committee of Production has granted the men a five-shilling war bonus, but they're not giving it to the women.'

'But you're getting the same wages for the same hours. That's what we agreed. The war bonus is for the cost of living. Nowt to do with wages.'

'How can you say that, Mr Adams? We're all suffering from the rise in the cost of living.'

'Yes, but men have got families to feed and look after.'

'And women don't?'

'Yes . . . no . . . I mean, you women are getting separation allowances so's you can look after kids an' all.'

He rubbed the back of his neck as if to loosen tension, took a deep sigh and then sat back in the chair with his arms crossed.

Connie pressed home her advantage. 'What about women with children and no husband?'

'You 'ave to stop somewhere, Connie. Else everybody would get it. Where'd this country be then? Gone to the dogs, I shouldn't wonder.'

Connie straightened her back, lifted her chin and set her mouth in a grim line. 'You don't believe that, do you, Mr Adams?' She folded her arms.

'I can't say nowt else. My hands are tied.' He stared at the papers on the desk in front of him. 'Sorry, Connie. You know how it is.'

She was afraid she did.

She returned to the yard and advised the clippies to join the union. They were going to have to fight.

32

July/August 1918

'Connie . . . Connie . . .' hissed a voice from the far side of the yard.

Joe was cleaning a tram and beckoned her over. She sighed.

When she reached him, he grabbed her arm and pulled her towards the cab. She must have looked startled because he let go almost as soon as her gasp escaped.

'Sorry, Connie.' He looked as if he meant it too.

'What's so important, Joe?'

'Thanks for getting the clippies to see sense.'

'We'll still be here doing the same jobs. Why are you so concerned?'

'I dunner trust the bosses. I know they had no choice but to pay the same rate at the start or else their trams would have stopped running. But now, you clippies have proved you can do the job as well as men. But you don't do the same job as conductors do.'

'Yes, we do.'

'No. Connie, you don't change the points, turn the tram or move the trolley head. So now there's a difference between what the conductor job was before the war and now. They might say that you are doing less skilled work and pay yer less. Who's to say they don't keep it that way when the blokes come home. Don't forget, not all of the lads who went to war will come back, so there will be new men who know no better. D'yer want that to happen to them what's been fighting for their country?'

'No, I suppose not. But how do you know it will happen?'

'Cos I've seen it in other places. You conner trust bosses.'

He grinned, and Connie could see why Betty was attracted to him. Whenever Betty and Joe were together, it was easy to see the frisson between them. When Joe was in the depot, Betty stationed herself close by, with the likely exception of the privies. Connie smothered her grin.

'Why did you choose to talk to me?'

'Cos you used to be a suffragette. We're on the same side, aren't we?'

★ ★ ★

'We need you to speak up for us, Connie,' Jean said later. 'You can talk to anybody. Joe's been trying to get Betty to fight for the rights of clippies. Of course, she was chuffed he'd asked her, but we both thought that you would do it best. You know the right words to say.'

In other circumstances, Connie would have been flattered by Jean's remarks. But this would give Robert more reason to think her a troublemaker and would put them on opposite sides.

★ ★ ★

'They're out! Can you believe it? The buggers in London are on strike.' Joe waved a newspaper in the

284

air then took off his cap and slapped it against his thigh. 'I'll be damned!'

Connie's eyes grew like saucers. 'You probably will, Joe Cumberbatch.'

She took the newspaper off Joe and scanned it for herself. The strike started on 17 August at a bus garage in London. It was a Saturday, and it took everyone by surprise. The strike spread like wildfire through bus and tram depots and left London almost without public transport.

Betty grabbed hold of Joe's arm, and they did a barn dance around the yard.

Connie smiled. 'At least it's a start.'

Betty and Joe came to a halt. 'What d'yer mean? If people agree as the women should get this war bonus, then they'll have won.'

Connie shook her head. 'What about next year? Will there be another fight to get it? This is just the start, Betty. And they haven't got it yet. What's important is that the bosses, and even the Committee of Production, agree that women should have the same pay for doing the same job, otherwise this argument will go on and on, year after year, just like the vote. Women always have to prove —'

'Connie darling, it's a start. Who knows what this can lead to?' Joe frowned. 'Anyroad, we'll see where it takes us. And support them in London where we can. We might have ter come out on strike with 'em.'

Connie felt dismayed. She didn't know if she had the strength to begin to fight another battle to show that women are men's equals.

In an attempt to cheer up, she raised her arm. 'Come on, girls, we can do this. We'll join the fight.'

A sudden hush surrounded them. Connie closed

285

her eyes. Someone had come in behind her. Someone important.

She counted to ten under her breath and slowly turned. Of all the people to hear her rallying cry, it had to be Robert Caldwell. In his stony face, the blue-grey eyes were dark, like the sea on a grey day.

He didn't move. Didn't speak.

She straightened her shoulders, determined not to lose her self-respect.

One by one, the rest of the workers moved away and returned to work. The last to leave her were Jean and Joe, although a stark glance from Robert sent Jean on her way with a sympathetic tremble of her lips.

Joe stood, legs apart, arms folded.

Connie wished he'd go.

'Inspector Caldwell!' quipped Joe, grinning. 'We was having a union meeting, and you'll be pleased to see that the clippies are all on board. They've all joined the union. We've bin hearing about the goings-on down in London and, what goes for them, goes for us 'ere an' all.'

'Mr Cumberbatch, I'm sure you have given everyone both sides of the story, as always.' Robert's voice was ice-cold.

Joe lifted his chin and stared back as if waiting for more to be said.

'You've got work to do, Mr Cumberbatch. I suggest you go and attend to it now.'

Joe hesitated, then turned to Connie. 'I'll be in touch about everything,' he said, and then he left.

Robert turned to Connie. 'Miss Copeland, you want to be careful who you associate with. People have their own agendas. You should know that. I want to see you at the end of your shift today.' He raised his hand as she was about to speak. 'No arguments.'

He turned on his heel and left.

Blast Joe Cumberbatch.

Reluctantly, Connie dragged herself to the office at six o'clock that evening. She knocked and walked in. Robert didn't ask her to sit but looked at her steadily.

'You wanted to see me, Inspector?'

'Yes, I do.' He leaned forward in his chair. 'When you were talking to Joe Cumberbatch earlier, you sounded as if you were rallying the troops for a mutiny. Would you care to explain yourself?'

'It was nothing. Joe showed us the newspaper about the strike in London over the war bonus. All the workers, men and women alike, have come out on strike to support the women in London who will not receive the war bonus despite promises of equal pay.'

'Go on.' He never took his eyes off her face.

'That's all.'

'Was it?'

'It was just a conversation. I think I said something about —'

His voice got louder. 'Throwing your arm up as if you're some kind of Joan of Arc? Are you trying to incite a riot within this company, Miss Copeland?'

'No. No! I think women should choose what they want to do for themselves. But they need enough information to make that choice. I do believe in the right to choose.'

She glared at him. She couldn't help it. If he'd caught someone else doing as she had done, would he have been so quick to take them to task? She doubted it. She had been asked to help her colleagues, and that was what she was doing.

'I too believe in the right to choose, Miss Copeland. However, there is a big difference between having a choice and starting a riot. One is acceptable — the other is not. I don't believe we need the union here. We have always been able to talk to our employees.' His eyes narrowed. 'What I will not have, Miss Copeland, is a clippie who thinks she knows how to run this company and coerces her fellow workers into doing something they don't feel comfortable with. In future, if you do have . . . information you wish to pass on to your fellow clippies, perhaps you could talk to me or Mr Adams about it before making a full-scale charge?' His face was stone cold. 'Do I make myself clear, Miss Copeland?'

She pulled herself up as tall as she could make herself and looked him in the eye. 'Perfectly, Inspector.'

'If I have cause to speak to you again of this or similar matters, I will have no choice but to terminate your employment with this company.'

He must have seen the shock wave that hit her, but he said nothing else.

Connie didn't think she could hold her anger back much longer. Her green eyes blurred and she blinked to clear the tears away, ready to argue her point, but maybe now was not the time or place to make a stand. 'May I go now?' she said.

'You may.'

Connie turned and opened the door.

'You know something? I'm sure I've seen you before you came here.'

It was too much. On top of everything else, there was still the white feather.

'I think you are mistaken,' she said and closed the door.

The first person to come crashing through the doors to the depot the following day was Joe, his eyes lit up and happier than she had seen him for days. Everyone laid down their tools.

'Hey! Listen, you lot. You'll never believe it! The strike's spreading. During this last week, more and more have come out across the south. And it's coming north, I've been told. My mate in Birmingham's out now, and I'll make sure we're out if nowt changes. Who knows, the whole country'll be on strike if they keep on like this.'

'Who's come out then, Joe?' asked Jean.

'Bath, Brighton, Hastings, Bristol. Oh, and Birmingham, like I said. They conner let it carry on else no one'll be able to get nowhere. Serve 'em right. Eighteen thousand women they reckon are on strike. The bosses are going to have to do summat now.'

At that moment, the door opened and in walked Mr Adams. He looked pale and leaned on his walking stick more heavily than usual. Connie couldn't help but glance at Jean, who stared at him with an anxious gaze. It must be awful for her, Connie thought, caring for someone and not being able to show feelings for them.

He blew loudly on a whistle and beckoned everyone together. 'Now listen, you lot. I've had a message from them in Stoke. They're looking into matters and will come back to us when they've found out what's going on.'

'I'd 'ave thought as they should know already, Mr Adams,' piped up Joe, more politely than Connie had expected.

'What makes you think that?'

'Well, it's hardly new, is it?' said Joe. 'This talk's been going on for a while. It's only new 'cos them women 'ave gone and done summat about it if you ask me.'

'I want you to hold off for the time being. I'll have some more to say about it tomorrow.'

'Well, if yer don't, I'll be calling the clippies out and us drivers'll follow.'

'Are you threatening me, Joe?'

'No, not you. I'm telling yer as you'll leave us no choice if you dunner sort it out. These clippies here,' Joe pointed at Connie, Jean, Betty, Doris and others who had come to join them, 'were took on with the promise of a man's wage. And if a man is entitled to a five bob war bonus, then it stands to reason that the clippies should get it an' all.'

A general murmur of agreement passed through the group. Joe folded his arms and waited. Betty moved to stand next to him and whispered something in his ear. He grinned back.

'I understand your feelings, Joe. I understand all of you.' Stephen Adams's gaze took in each of them. 'Just bear with me for a little while longer, and I'll see what I can do.' He raised an eyebrow as if asking for their approval. A general murmur went around the group, and they gradually dispersed. 'Oh, Jean, can you come to the office. I need a word.'

Jean's face went a bright pink at being singled out and followed him.

Joe perked up. 'Tomorrow, Mr Adams. I'll expect an answer tomorrow. And if it ain't satisfactory, then we're all out!'

★ ★ ★

Connie was taking tea with Ginnie, but she was having difficulty controlling her thoughts which, annoyingly, seemed to be intent on returning to Robert. Of course she knew he hadn't deliberately scuppered her marriage and that, when he chastised her at work, he was only doing his job, but it didn't stop her from feeling put out about it. He treated her as he would treat any other clippie and she would have to respect him for that.

If she ignored her latest telling off she could have said that they passed the time of day together with the odd short conversation at work, but that was all. On the odd occasion they met outside the depot, he was polite and friendly but, she realised, she wanted more from him. He was well-read and in her mind she could imagine the two of them talking over a wide range of topics. What would it be like to grow close to him, to kiss him having convinced herself for so long that she disliked him. That was no longer true. She knew also that she was jealous of Louisa. Robert and Louisa had been seen together a few times now.

'Did you ever hear any more from Matthew, Connie?' Ginnie asked, breaking into her thoughts.

Connie shook her head. 'I never expected to. I'm only sorry I didn't stop the ceremony before he did.'

Ginnie grinned. 'And there's nobody else?'

Connie looked away, but she knew Ginnie had seen the sadness creeping over her face. She hadn't admitted it to herself yet.

'Oh, Ginnie. Things keep going wrong.'

'Is this about that Robert you've spoken of?'

'What makes you say that? I haven't said much about him recently.'

291

Ginnie smiled warmly. 'Yer don't have to say nothing. There's summat in yer face what changes when yer speak of him.'

'Am I so easy to read?'

'Perhaps to me, but not to nobody else what doesn't know yer like I do.'

'Oh, Ginnie. I don't know what to do. It's a mess.'

A look of alarm crossed Ginnie's face.

'I told you that I threw a stone through a window at the War Office. Well, it turns out that Robert worked in that office and he just happens to be a friend of Matthew's. He knows it was me, Ginnie.'

'Oh, heavens above! How's he found out?' Ginnie's eyes opened wide.

'Louisa Pendleton. She's Matthew's cousin. When I had my birthday meal at the Victoria Hotel last year, Robert and Louisa were there together. She recognised me and couldn't wait to tell him that I had been to prison. Until that moment, I had no reason to think that Robert, the friend of Matthew's who told him about my prison sentence, and Inspector Robert Caldwell were the same person.'

Connie recounted the full story.

'What's it like between you and Robert now?'

'Odd conversations about work mainly,' she sighed. 'I think I could have handled things better, Ginnie. He thinks I am a liar, I'm out for what I can get, I incite people to riot and deliberately throw stones through the windows of government buildings.'

Despite everything, Ginnie grinned. 'You think you might want to be friends, or summat more than friends? And you'll not take kindly to waiting for him to come round to that way of thinking. I know you have a problem with patience, Connie, and I think

292

you know too.'

Unwillingly, Connie's lips began to twitch. 'You little —'

'Well, he let you stay at the depot, didn't he? He hasn't told anyone else as far as you know, otherwise, you would have heard summat by now. Has it occurred to you that he might want to keep you there for some other reason?'

Connie shook her head. 'I suppose not.'

'So, what's the problem?'

Connie gave a deep sigh. 'Apart from being aloof and a bit above himself, he seems to be quite a decent man and can be very nice under that moody exterior of his. He's . . . well, different —'

'Are you falling for him, Connie?'

'No, of course not. I'm just saying —'

'It's what you're not saying that I'm interested in,' said Ginnie, her eyes full of mischief.

★ ★ ★

Connie was outraged.

One of the national newspapers reporting on the strike had referred to the clippies as 'girl conductors'. How dare they? They never described men as 'boy strikers', so why denigrate women in this way? Even after all this time, women were not taken seriously when it mattered. What was the point of it all? Women always had something to prove in this world run by men.

The first thing to happen the following morning was Mr Adams telling them that the matter regarding the payment of war bonuses had been resolved and the strike was now over. Clippies would receive the same war bonus as their male counterparts and, as a consequence, the strikers had gone back to work.

A cheer went up. The women were relieved. Many had been wondering how they would manage if the strike went ahead. They didn't want to let their fellow workers down but feeding their families had to come first.

Everyone patted Joe on the back as if he'd been responsible for sorting out the whole thing single-handedly. He was full of himself and Connie suspected he had begun to believe that it was all down to him. Betty hung around him, waiting for him to notice her. Silly girl! Joe wanted all the glory, whether deserved or not.

Connie still wasn't sure that a real victory had been won. Yes, they were going to be five shillings better off this year, but there was no mention of men and women receiving the same wages for doing the same jobs, and that was where the real fight lay. If the war carried on, would they have the same fight every year?

In normal circumstances, Connie would have considered challenging Mr Adams with her views, but she didn't want to speak out for fear of adding mutiny to the accusations of gossip-mongering and inciting riots! There would be time to discuss which jobs were equal when everything had settled down.

Connie had been watching Mr Adams and how he was when Jean was around. His eyes followed her when they were both present. Jean hadn't given anything away since their little chat about Mr Adams's background, except for the little smirk that found its way there when she thought no one was looking. Even Mr Adams smiled more often these days.

33

Autumn 1918

To take Ginnie's mind off Sam, who had now been missing for over three months, Connie had taken her to Burslem Picture House on a couple of occasions, and both had been enthralled with the stories they saw unfolding. The picture house usually smelled of stale smoke and sweat, but now the main smell was of the disinfectant used to combat the 'flu outbreak. Ginnie would go every single week if she could afford to, she said. Now that she could read the words on the screen, she wanted to fill her head with more stories. She could even go by herself if she had a mind to.

Connie thought of Ginnie every day as she got ready for work and prayed for Sam every night, hoping that the next day there would be a letter from him to say that all was well.

★ ★ ★

Everything went pretty smoothly after the strike ended. It had brought Betty and Joe closer together and to say that Betty was delighted with the chain of events was an understatement. They spent time in each other's company and seemed to get on well enough. Joe took her out regularly, and Betty was always beaming.

Today was Betty's birthday, and she was twenty years old. Connie arranged to meet Betty and Jean for tea at the tea rooms in Parliament Row. It would be their first opportunity to go out together for a while.

Once they had settled in their seats, Betty said, 'You two need to get a move on. I told you when we started work that we need to keep an eye on the men if we don't want to end this war as spinsters.'

Connie rolled her eyes. 'You're not still on about that, are you?'

'Look at you, Connie. You're older than us, and there's no sign of any blokes running after you. And yer pretty enough. You should be able to catch yourself a man. And you, Jean, you're just as bad. You want to snap up Mr Adams before yer lose him. Both of you should take lessons from me,' she said triumphantly, leaving Connie and Jean to ponder what she meant.

'We don't need a man. We are quite happy the way we are,' said Connie.

'Of course, you want a man. You don't want to work all your lives, do you? Once you've got a man, then he'll be the breadwinner,' said Betty as if she was speaking from experience.

'That's if he dunner spend all his money in the pub and belt you when he gets home. There are women where I come from not much older than you, Connie, who have seven kids, and a husband they would love to see the back end of. It's not all fun, Betty,' said Jean.

'I'm too young to think about children. I want to enjoy myself first,' said Connie.

'This war cannot go on forever, so dunner werrit yourself, Betty. You've plenty of time to find yer man,' said Jean.

'But if you leave it too long there won't be no men left. Or at least the men left will all be cripples,' blurted out Betty and then, realising what she had said, put her hand up to her mouth.

'Betty, how can you say that? Mr Adams has done his bit, and he will make someone a nice husband. The fact he has to use a stick makes him no less of a man,' countered Jean.

'But it's true, can't you see that? Look at the men at the depot. Joe's the only decent bloke amongst them, who is close to my age,' said Betty.

Jean poured out the tea, and Connie stared at Betty. She was probably right. And yes, it depressed her to think in that way. However, she questioned Betty's taste in men.

'Why isn't your Joe in the army, Betty?' asked Jean.

'I haven't a clue. Never asked him. If he was in the army, he wouldn't be here with me now.'

They chatted away until the waitress told them it was closing time. They hadn't realised how much time they had been in there. They made their way toward the tram stop on Lichfield Street. Betty stopped to do a spot of window shopping at the milliner's.

'Constance! Constance!'

She was so used to being called Connie that she very nearly ignored the shouts behind her.

When the call came again, she turned to see Louisa trying to catch up with her without running, as would befit a lady. Connie grinned to herself even though Louisa Pendleton was the last person she wanted to talk to.

'Were you ignoring me on purpose, Constance?' Louisa was having great difficulty in breathing and speaking at the same time.

'No. I'm more used to Connie now. Constance is rather a mouthful when you're working.'

'Robert told me you had changed your name for some reason. How are you?'

'I'm well, thank you. But I'm sure you haven't stopped me to ask about my health, have you?'

Jean stared at Louisa, no doubt trying to remember who she was, so Connie decided to enlighten her. It was probably about the right time.

'Jean, this is Louisa Pendleton. You might recall seeing her with Robert Caldwell at the Christmas dance last year?'

Jean stared at her. 'Vaguely, I think,' she said.

Louisa looked uncomfortable, expecting a different answer.

Betty chose that moment to re-join them. 'Don't I know yer? Think I saw yer a while back. Louisa something or other?'

'I . . . I . . . Well, never mind,' Louisa turned her back on Betty and spoke again. 'Constance, we must catch up on matters. We must have a chat when you are less busy.'

With that, Louisa marched off, leaving Connie nonplussed. She was pleased that Jean and Betty were with her. She had a feeling that talking with Louisa would not end positively.

★ ★ ★

Connie was working on the long Goldenhill to Meir route. The tram pulled up at the stop in Tunstall where four people were waiting. A woman rushed to join the queue. Connie groaned. It was Louisa Pendleton. A month had passed since they'd met in the street and, as far as Connie was concerned, they had little to say to one another. She was glad she was working and wouldn't have the time to converse with her.

Louisa sat erect in her seat, slightly breathless, and waited until Connie stood beside her before speaking.

'Good morning, Constance.'

'Good morning, Louisa. Fancy seeing you again so soon. Could I have your fare please?'

Louisa turned to look her up and down in a contemptuous manner. 'That was quite convenient, noticing you were on this tram. How interesting to see you in your work clothes, Constance. The uniform suits you.'

Connie refused to rise to the bait. 'Which stop do you require, Louisa?' she said in her best tones.

Louisa delved into her purse to find coppers for her fare. 'Tell me, when do you get a break from your labours? There is a matter I wish to discuss with you. I was going to talk to you when I saw you, but your friends put a stop to that.'

'I don't think we have anything to say to each other.'

'Oh, I think we do. I think you will be very interested in what I have to say.'

Connie's curiosity got the better of her, as Louisa knew very well it would. She was annoyed with herself. 'I have a short break in Hanley, at eleven thirty?'

'Very well, I shall meet you outside Webberley's, the new bookshop on the corner of Percy Street.' Louisa dropped her coins into Connie's outstretched hand. Connie nodded, gave her a ticket, and moved on. She could hardly wait to hear what Louisa had to say, although the matter of which she spoke was unlikely to be good news.

The time soon passed and before she knew it, Connie was heading speedily towards the bookshop. There was no sign of Louisa. Connie glanced at the books in the window, wishing she had time to browse.

'Good day, Constance.'

Almost immediately, Louisa appeared at Connie's side. 'Good day, Louisa. How did you know I was on that tram?'

'I saw you on the platform. It was pure chance and I took it.'

'What news do you have for me? I'm afraid I don't have much time.'

'Then shall we walk?' suggested Louisa.

They both turned and took a few steps. Still Louisa said nothing.

'Do you really have something to tell me, Louisa?'

'Of course. I would hardly try to see you if I didn't. I want to talk to you about Robert.'

'Robert Caldwell? I'm sorry, but why should I want to talk to you about him?'

'Do you like him?'

Connie stopped walking and stared at her. 'What on earth does that have to do with you?'

'We didn't exactly meet at the Victoria Hotel but I saw you there when I was Robert's guest. He stopped at your table to talk to you, passing the time of day, most probably. It was quite a novelty to see a clippie in that establishment. No doubt Robert thought so too.'

Connie started walking again, leaving Louisa to follow. 'But that was ages ago. What are you trying to say, Louisa?'

'I saw you watching him when he came back to me. You couldn't take your eyes off him.'

Connie flushed. 'Louisa, I work with him. Why shouldn't we speak when we meet?'

'What did you talk about?'

The audacity of the woman! Connie shook her head. 'Whatever we did or didn't talk about is no concern of yours. If that's all you want to speak to me about, then I shall take my leave of you and return to work.'

'I think we have quite a lot to discuss if you will only listen. I assure you, it's in your interests to pay attention to my words.'

Louisa paused briefly — for effect most likely, thought Connie.

'Robert and I have become well acquainted. He's quite taken with me. We've been together for a number of months now.'

She was actually preening! Connie couldn't believe it. Of course, she was aware that the two of them appeared to enjoy each other's company. They had been seen together often enough.

'It's quite obvious, looking at your face, that you have feelings for him, Constance.'

Connie willed herself not to cover her red face with her hands. How could she even look at him again after Louisa's insinuations? After his dressing-down at work, he'd be glad to rid himself of her, she was sure.

'Whatever I think of Robert is none of your business, Louisa. Now if you will excuse me —' She turned to walk away.

'If you listen to what I have to say, you might change your mind,' Louisa continued. 'My dear Constance . . . I don't want you to get hurt — again.'

Connie flashed a wary stare.

Louisa smiled. 'Yes, I know all about your most upsetting wedding day. As a cousin of Matthew's, I was in the church. You must have been devastated, you poor girl. That's why I felt I should talk to you on your own.'

Connie shook her head and began to walk away. How much more did she know? 'Is that all you have to say? That you feel sorry for me?'

Louisa narrowed her eyes. 'I know Matthew let you down at the altar. I also know why. Your past misdemeanours, Constance. No doubt you are hoping that I have kept them to myself.'

'Who do you think you are? My misdemeanours, as you call them, have absolutely nothing to do with you.'

'Oh, but Constance, I didn't want dear cousin Matthew to get hurt.' Her voice had taken on a hurt tone.

'Why talk to me about it now?'

'It's about Robert and me. I don't have to spell it out for you, do I?'

It was quite ironic — Louisa warning her off Robert when they were barely speaking to each other. She laughed. 'Honestly, Louisa . . . you have no idea.'

'I think it's you who has no idea, Constance.'

'I have absolutely nothing to do with Robert except working with him, on occasion. He knows about Matthew. For your information, I could hardly be attracted to the man who told Matthew about my past and caused him to call off my wedding. If you're thinking of telling him, forget it. He already knows.'

The look on Louisa's face had changed to a more engaging smile. 'Well, at least you've been truthful with him, which is more than you were with Matthew and more truthful than Robert has been with you.'

Connie frowned. 'What do you mean?'

'You were a suffragette.'

'I don't see —'

'You were probably one of those crazy women who gave out white feathers —'

Connie's jaw dropped. Louisa couldn't possibly know . . . She didn't dare say anything.

Louisa studied Connie's face and gave her a quizzical look. It seemed to take an age before Louisa spoke again. 'Did Robert tell you he didn't believe in war? Do you know he comes from a military family? His father disowned him because he refused to join the army and fight back in 1914. How does that sit with your high and mighty suffragette principles, Constance? How does that make you feel?'

Connie did her best to conceal her relief — and her shock. Relief that Louisa didn't know about the white feather she had given to Robert — and shock to hear from Louisa's lips that Robert did not believe in war and was a coward.

She forced words out. 'Why are you telling me this?'

'Robert tells me everything now that we are . . . together. You're young, Constance, dear. Not experienced in the ways of the world. I thought it my duty to tell you before you get hurt again. You see, him being a conscientious objector does not worry me. But you, being a suffragette . . . well, what can I say?'

Connie stared at her. Robert had talked about principles and doing the right thing. If Louisa was right, then his principles were obviously not the same as hers.

Louisa's eyes bored into hers, appearing to enjoy every second of her discomfiture.

'I have to go now.' Connie had to get away from Louisa's sympathetic but fixed smile.

She could barely concentrate on the job in hand for the rest of her shift. She went over and over it in her mind but failed to come to any conclusion. Why had Louisa sought her out to talk about Robert Caldwell? If she hadn't known better, she would have said that Louisa was jealous. She could think of no other reason for Louisa to tell her about Robert and his family.

Louisa's information was staggering, implying that Robert was a coward while trying to give the impression that she was looking after Connie's interests. Was she warning her away?

34

November/December 1918

The war that was to end by Christmas 1914 was finally over. The German kaiser had abdicated and at eleven a.m. on the eleventh day of the eleventh month an Armistice was declared.

Connie had made her last journey of the day. Her passengers chatted to anyone prepared to listen, even momentarily. There was much gaiety in the tram depot. Someone had made a cake and biscuits, and another had brought in their cheese ration to put on oatcakes cut up into small pieces, so there was enough of the pancake-like Potteries staple to go around. Ale was still in short supply and watered down, and everyone joined in, even those who never drank. Once off the tram, Connie felt as if her feet wanted to dance all the way home. She hardly noticed the chilly November air. Men on their own whistled for want of company. She beamed at everyone she passed, and it felt good to be alive.

On arriving home, Connie hugged Alice, and together they danced a jig around the kitchen.

Mother joined them, but declined the jig.

'Oh, Mother, we can finally begin our lives again. No more wondering, no more telegrams, no more men who are no more than boys going off to war leaving their families and friends.'

Her mother lifted a hand to Connie's face and

gently smoothed her cheek. 'My darling girl, your generation has had so much heartache and has been forced to grow up far too soon — a generation of lost childhoods. Maybe the last few years have taught us something so that we never have to go through this terrible ordeal again. Will you pray with me, Connie? Pray for all the mothers who have lost a child, all the young women who will never have the opportunity to experience the love of a child and the grandmothers who will never be.'

Connie's eyes watered. She too might be one of those. She must, like so many women, now plan a future that may lack the closeness of a man. Her mother's eyes too were wet. She placed a kiss on her mother's forehead and laid her cheek next to the papery softness of her face.

In the evening Connie, Mother and Alice went down into Burslem to join in the celebrations. The covers on the streetlights were off, and shop windows lit, for tonight only, they were told. Bunting and flags appeared as if from nowhere, and the centre of Burslem was a sea of people and Union Jacks. So much excitement and celebration, people losing the heavy burdens they had carried for so long. Smiles on faces, noise — so much noise — but who cared about that?

Many of the factories had knocked off work at the news and there was a holiday feeling in the air. Everywhere, there was a profound thankfulness for the Allied victory and relief that the men who had fought were now safe. Christmas indeed would be celebrated this year and ever after.

It was only an Armistice. Alice asked what the difference was. Connie explained that the Allies and

Germans had only agreed to stop fighting, not to peace. Fighting could restart, but the Germans were beaten. The Kaiser had gone, and everybody wanted peace. The armies wouldn't be returning home immediately as there was much to be sorted, not least how to get the mass of soldiers back home again, but there would be no fighting, no deaths.

She called to see Ginnie on Sunday afternoon with some trepidation. There had been no word from Sam for months. How could Ginnie be excited the war was over when her sweetheart was still listed as missing in action?

Ginnie looked as cheerful as someone might be who was trying to celebrate the end of something when she had no real ending of her own. She had Mabel, who was only going through the motions of celebrating herself, knowing her Frank was one of those who would never return. At least they had four-year-old Florrie to light up the household.

'So, what yer going to do with yourself next, Connie?' said Ginnie.

Connie sighed. 'I've been thinking about it long and hard. The only thing that comes into my head is office work. I have got used to having money of my own and I don't want to be a burden to my family.'

She still hadn't told Ginnie how serious the family's financial worries were. With Sam still missing, she couldn't burden her friend with her own troubles.

★ ★ ★

A month had passed since the Armistice had been declared. Connie's time on the trams would be coming to an end soon and she couldn't put off thoughts of a new job any longer. Plans she had entertained about teaching had gone up in smoke. She couldn't put such a responsibility on her family.

She hadn't broached the matter of a job with Father; he would say one word — marriage.

Was she being selfish? Her parents had taken care of her all her life. They had paid for her schooling. Should she at least think about marrying someone who could help them through their troubles? But how could she agree to an option she had fought against for so long? When the time came, she wanted to marry for love. If her husband had money, then so be it.

She could, of course, choose whatever job she wished because she would, more than likely, have to give it up if she became a married woman. She would be expected to devote all of her time to her husband and family — so what would be the point of looking for a career? It was all so unfair. Why shouldn't a woman have a family and a career?

Connie sighed. Certain women, older women, voted for the first time this month after all those years of campaigning — a step in the right direction. But the road was long and the walking hard. And still, women had to fight for everything they wanted in life. A man or a career? It would be the first time in her life that she had to think about either and it needed careful consideration. Still, there was time yet.

She entered the depot for her evening shift. Bert and Fred were talking beside the only tram still in there. Jean and Joe were out somewhere in the borough. Betty was on a split shift and was one of three clippies still in the depot.

'Hiya, Connie. How's things?'

'Not so bad, thanks, Betty. What about you?'

'A bit fed up. I never thought as I'd feel this way when I finished here.'

'I don't suppose it'll happen quite yet. Have you any idea what you're going to do next?'

'To be honest, I was hoping I wouldn't be working at all.'

A quizzical look must have passed over Connie's face because she carried on talking.

'I was hoping I might meet a decent bloke and be married by the time the war was over. Everybody I know seems to be getting wed in no time at all. And I'm not that bad-looking, am I?'

Connie smiled. 'You're not bad at all, Betty. But don't you want to have a career or find your way in the world before you settle down?'

'Nope. People like me don't get careers, Connie. They get jobs. Whatever pays well that don't require too much brain and then they get wed.'

'Betty! Please don't say that. You're worth so much more. Are you saying that you would find a man, any man, and marry him, so you don't have to find a job?'

'That's it in a nutshell.'

Connie shook her head. 'You're selling yourself short, Betty.'

'It's all right for you to talk. You can do as you like — college, university even or a posh job in an office. That don't happen to us. No point in wanting what you can't 'ave, is there? Anyroad, we'd best get our thinking caps on 'cos we've had our letters, telling us we're finishing.'

'So soon?' Connie's mouth fell open. She turned on her heel and ran across the yard and into the office. Sure enough, there were still a handful of envelopes on the desk, including one with her name written on it in neat copperplate handwriting. Emily Norton smiled at her uncertainly.

'I've had one too, Connie. We're all out, but we don't know when. I'm here to make sure everything's tidy for the man who comes in to take over the office and show him the ropes. You know, all the improvements I've made since I've been here.'

There was bitterness in her voice, and her lips were just a thin red line. She patted Connie's shoulder, leaving her alone with an unopened envelope.

The end had come. She couldn't believe it. Yes, she had begun to think about her future after clippie life, but she'd assumed she would have a month or two to get her mind around it.

She picked up a knife from the desk, slit open the envelope and, through blinking eyes, read the letter.

11th December 1918

To: Miss C. Copeland, Lady Conductor

You were made aware at the beginning of your employment with the Potteries Tramway Company Ltd that your service would terminate at the end of the war.

The Government, on 9th December 1918, announced its plans for demobilising the Forces. They will begin immediately. Given the scale of the operation, Forces personnel will be split into groups according to their importance to the recovery of the nation. Men who have jobs to come back to will be amongst the first to return. We're in the process of identifying former PTC employees who are in this category and will ensure each man will have a job offer. Any vacancies remaining at the end of the process will go to returning servicemen.

The PTC has decided that current employees will be retained until these men return to take up their former jobs. We will, therefore, extend your employment until your position is filled. This means we will not be in a position to confirm the date on which your employment with the PTC will end. We anticipate it will be for an additional month or two. We will, of course, inform you as soon as we are able.

We thank you for stepping forward at our time of need and throwing in your support fully and with great cheer. The men who have given so much to help this country to a glorious victory are anxious to return to the duties you have so willingly undertaken on their behalf.

As you move forwards into the next period of your life, we hope that you will look back on your time with us with satisfaction on a job well done.
Signed: Mr Stephen Adams
Depot Manager
Potteries Tramway Company Ltd

And that was it.

Her eyes moved slowly around the room, taking in her surroundings. Everything she had taken for granted. Everything she had come to love. And there was Robert.

It hurt her to think she would not see him again to talk to. That terrible scene with Louisa had shocked her to the core, but now she'd had time to think about it all, it was probably for the best that she would be leaving soon. Even if she did like him, she could never look on a conscientious objector as a close friend, Louisa was right about that.

There were heavy footsteps outside and in walked Mr Adams. He stopped short when he saw Connie.

'Oh, I didn't know you were in here.'

She stared at him, motionless, her face showing what she could not say.

He glanced down at her hand. 'You knew it was coming, Connie,' he said by way of apology.

'Yes, we knew it was coming, Mr Adams. But now it's here, it has suddenly become real. I do so like this job.'

'My hands are tied. We don't know when the men will return; what we know is that when they do return, they are getting a month's leave. So it won't happen straight away. You should get some notice.'

★ ★ ★

Christmas 1918 should have been so happy, but the demobilisation programme had not started well. The government was already behind its targets. Transport, especially ships, seemed to be the biggest problem. Men desperate to return couldn't get transport home.

Poor Ginnie was still waiting to hear from Sam — she seemed convinced he was coming back even though he was still officially missing. Connie had done her best to keep her friend's spirits up, but it had been so long, she wondered if she should have been preparing her for the worst.

Connie had watched Betty closely whenever they had been on the same shifts. She was quiet, hardly said a word. Joe had been sent back to Longton so she couldn't ask him. Maybe that was part of the problem.

Betty was already sitting in Jean's living room when Connie arrived on the Sunday, for what they had agreed would be their Christmas party. Connie brought some mince pies and a few other treats and a bottle of sherry.

This would probably be the last time they got together and certainly their last Christmas. It was nearly two years since they had met on the tram on their first day at work. Three strangers from different backgrounds — who would have thought they would become firm friends?

Jean asked about Connie's journey and chipped in with the odd comment but Betty remained silent.

'It's lovely to see you both outside of work. I'm sure we have lots to talk about.' Connie smiled at both of them expectantly. 'Any thoughts on what you are going to do next?'

'Not really, how about you, Connie?' said Jean, shrugging her shoulders.

'We know what you'll do.' Betty grinned and winked at Connie.

'I don't know what you mean.'

'Come off it, Jean. We've both seen how you look at Stephen and how he looks at you. You'll be Mrs Adams inside six months, I'll bet.'

Connie smiled. 'He's a good man, you could do a lot worse, Jean.'

'He's so old, he's hardly going to sweep yer off your feet.'

'I'll have you know, he's a very nice man.'

Betty laughed and pointed her finger at Jean. 'So, there is something between you two.'

Jean's face flushed a violent red and she refused to say any more.

'I left school at fourteen,' said Betty wistfully, 'and me mum took me straight into service. One less mouth to feed and a few bob coming in. That was what I was to her.'

'Oh, that's terrible.'

'No, Connie, that's life.'

'I think the sherry's going to our heads, we all need a cup of tea.' Jean stood up and disappeared into the kitchen, leaving Betty to speak to Connie.

'You were a suffragette and stood up to the bosses. Until I met you, I had one plan. To find a man and get married. My only hope was that he didn't knock me about too much. The only men I had ever known were always good with their fists. But now, I'm going to do something with my life. I just don't know what yet. But it will be something for me. If I need a man to get it, then so be it.'

'Betty, I don't know what to say, it's such a sudden change.'

'I've been thinking about it for a while, I just haven't spoken about it. Less questions that way.'

'Do be careful, Betty.'

Jean returned with three cups of tea. 'So what are your plans, Connie?'

'I am planning to apply for an office job. It won't be as exciting as working on the trams, but it'll be a job. I have some experience and can type. Needs must, I suppose.'

'You can do better than that, Connie,' said Jean.

'No seriously, I may have had an education, but it was an education aimed at getting a man and marrying him. Nothing to do with real life, I now understand.'

'Well you don't really need to work, so that must be a relief.'

'That's not really true. Things have not been good for my mother and father during the war. We may have a nice house, but we have financial problems.'

The other two gasped in unison.

'Yer mean proper broke like what we are, or just broke like you can't afford a new hat every month?'

'Yes, probably the last one.' Connie threw a cushion at Betty. 'A few years ago I would have thought that we were proper broke, but now I realise we are still so fortunate. We have a roof over our head and food on the table and that makes us rich. We may have to sell our house next year, though. Please don't tell anyone.'

'So what are your plans, Betty?' said Jean.

'I need a job so as I can pay the rent and eat. I dunner care what it is or where it is, so long as I get paid, but I'll not go back into service.'

'That means you'll leave The Potteries?'

'Yes, if that is what it takes.'

'What does Joe think?'

'I dunner know, I've never asked him.'

'So what about this idea of getting a man and marrying him?'

'Oh, that's still going to happen, we'll have to wait and see. But I'll tell yer this much — he's not going to be poor.'

'Be careful, Betty, whatever you do. I think a loveless marriage for money might be the worst thing.'

'No. Jean, being poor, that's the worst thing.'

315

35

January 1919

Connie looked up from her book to see Jean hovering by the door of the restroom.

'Hello Jean, have you finished your shift?'

'Yes, about ten minutes ago. I want to have a word with you.'

'Of course. Have a seat.' Connie patted the chair next to her.

Jean closed the door and sat down.

'I've had my letter, Connie. I shall be leaving sooner than I thought.'

'Oh, Jean. When is it?'

'The tenth of February. It feels strange to know I am definitely going. I will miss it. Miss you.'

'But that's only two weeks away!' It shocked Connie that Jean was leaving so soon. She couldn't imagine working at the depot without her. 'Mr Adams warned us that we could be leaving quickly, but I thought we'd have longer. It's so final.'

'I know and I'm so sad an' all, being the first of us to leave.'

'We must make plans to keep in touch. I do hope we can still be friends.'

To Connie's surprise, Jean's face had become pink. She put her head on one side.

'Jean? Do you have some more news? You're not leaving The Potteries altogether, are you?'

Jean shook her head. 'I'm not going nowhere, but I do have some more news. And it's much better.' She sounded breathless. 'Stephen has asked me to marry him, and I've said yes.'

Connie jumped to her feet. 'That truly is wonderful news, Jean. I'm so pleased for you.' She threw her arms around Jean and hugged her. 'You're a dark horse. I knew you had an affection for each other, but marriage? How did you manage to keep it so quiet?'

'It was difficult. I wanted to say something at Christmas, but I was sworn to secrecy. It's an unwritten rule that the bosses don't fraternise, I think Stephen called it, with their staff. It's frowned upon because of favouritism and causing problems.'

The words caught Connie by surprise. She never thought that an employer would have such rules, but she supposed it made sense.

'I am so pleased for you. I am sure you are making a good choice.'

'No concerns then? We have your approval?'

Connie laughed. 'No, Jean, absolutely no concerns.'

'I have one.' Jean looked at her steadily. 'We are getting married in Hanley Registry Office, and I need a witness. Do you know of anyone who might fit the bill?'

Connie let out a shriek. 'It's got to be me, Jean. I would be so pleased to do it.'

'I've asked Betty too. We'll be like The Three Musketeers. It would be odd if one of us wasn't there, wouldn't it?'

'Have you had thoughts on a date yet?'

'Yes, 16th April, so I hope your calendar isn't fully booked.'

'If it is, I'll un-book it straight away!'

317

It seemed only a few days since Jean had told Connie she would be leaving and now, that day had arrived. Connie felt as if something had lodged itself in her throat as she tried to swallow.

The rotas had been arranged so that the three friends could spend the last hour together in the depot to say their goodbyes and, hopefully, arrange to meet after all three had left.

Connie had bought Jean a little trinket which she said was from both her and Betty, to remind her of all the good times they'd had at PTC. The Christmas sing-song sprang to mind, as did the time when the water in the privy froze and they had to run over to those at the Three Castles while keeping their legs tightly shut. It wasn't funny at the time, and several clippies learned some new swear words, but afterwards, they saw the funny side, being in the same boat, together.

And now it was over. Although Jean was the quietest of the three, Connie thought she would miss her the most. Betty had just received her letter and would leave in the middle of March, and Connie had tried to ready herself for her own letter, which, no doubt, she would get soon.

Betty had sneaked a small bottle of sherry into the depot, to help them celebrate. No one asked where it had come from because everyone knew she hardly had two pennies to rub together. Betty poured out a large mug of sherry, out of which they all took a sip and passed it on.

At the end, there were hugs all around, faces streaked with tears, and the promise that they would meet again soon.

'Be sure to stay in touch, Jean. We have things to plan,' Connie whispered in Jean's ear.

'This is the very best day I've ever had,' Betty whimpered.

'I'll pop round to see you when I can,' said Jean. 'Stephen doesn't want me to work so I'll likely have some time on me hands. You'll both be at my wedding. We'll have a wonderful time.'

Betty's eyes filled with tears. 'You will take care of yourself, won't you? And look after that man of yours. You don't know how lucky you are.'

Connie put an arm around Betty's shoulder. 'We should all look out for each other. Just like the Musketeers.'

Stephen shouted to Jean that he was ready to leave.

She gave them both one last hug and ran to hold Stephen's hand, and they walked out of the depot.

It felt like the end of something. As Jean looked into Stephen's eyes, Connie smiled. It was also the beginning.

36

March 1919

'Good morning, Miss Norton,' said Connie, a little bit out of breath. 'You wanted to see me?'

'Good morning, Connie. Do you know where Betty is? I need to ask her about next week's rota,' she said with a smile.

'No, I don't. I thought she would be at work now.'

'Never mind, it will have to wait until later or tomorrow. She has not clocked in this morning so might be ill.'

When Betty didn't turn up for work the following day, Connie began to worry. She resolved to visit Betty that evening to see if she was well. She would ask Alice if she wouldn't mind accompanying her. And if she wasn't there, she could call at Jean's house. If anyone knew where she was, it would be Jean.

At home, there was a letter for her on the post table. She was surprised to find it was from Betty. She sliced it open, desperate for news.

Dear Connie,

I am very sorry for leaving without telling you what was happening, but I couldn't take the chance that you might try to stop me. I would have liked to tell you at Christmas but our plans were not fully made. Yes, 'our plans', as in Joe's and mine. We have

*decided to leave The Potteries to make a new life for
each other. What I said about my life at Christmas
still matters, so I agreed with Joe that we would go
somewhere to make a new start. Everyone says two
can live as cheaply as one.*

*We are going to live together as brother and sister.
It is easier to get accommodation and stops people
from asking questions. Joe knows the score, but he
has his own plans. We can help each other and at
least we will know someone in our new life and he's
a good friend.*

*You and Jean have been so good to me, but I
cannot tell you anything more. I will be careful, but
I am determined to get on in this life or die trying.*

*Say goodbye to Jean for me. I wish I could be
with her for her wedding, but I think Mr Adams
will look after her. She is very lucky but she deserves
it. I hope you find what you want to do with your
life. I would not have been able to tell you this to
your face, but do not push Mr Caldwell away from
you. I can see from the way he looks at you that he
has feelings for you. Just think about it.*

*I know you will both be angry with me,
and I wouldn't blame you. But I hope you will
understand.*

*Your friend
Betty*

Living together as brother and sister! Did the silly girl
know what she was doing?

Connie did not bother to change out of her uniform; she caught the next tram to Burslem and then
to Hanley and knocked on Jean's door.

'Hiya, Connie, what brings you here? Come in.'

321

'Have you had a letter from Betty?'

'No. Why, have you?'

'Read this!' Connie thrust the letter into Jean's hand and paced up and down. The smile disappeared off Jean's face as quickly as it had come.

'What the . . . what's she gone and done?'

Jean read through the letter again and rubbed her forehead. 'Let's see if she's still at her lodgings.'

The two set off for the few minutes walk to Betty's. When they got there, the landlady greeted them and confirmed that Betty had done a moonlight flit owing two weeks rent. She had taken all her clothes which did not amount to very much, but had left a parcel for a Mr Adams. Connie promised she would deliver it to him.

'She owes me a pound. Will the tram people be paying me?'

'I think not and neither will we.'

Next, they caught the tram to Longton. The news was similar. Joe's landlady said he had paid all the rent he owed, packed his things and left the very same evening.

'They clearly planned for this to happen,' said Connie.

'Where could they have gone?'

'She didn't give you any ideas at all?'

Jean shook her head. 'She never said a thing.'

★ ★ ★

The world was a complicated place, Connie decided. She had sat and pondered about Betty's disappearance. There was a vast difference between telling the truth and lying, telling part of the truth, telling lies for the right reasons and lying by omission. All could be put to good use or the exact opposite, and she had been on both ends of this during her life. She had no real sense of what she should do; whether she should seek help or leave Betty and Joe to sort it out for themselves. Her brain said it was not her problem; she didn't know the full story. No point in wading in.

Connie began to cry. She couldn't help it. The silly, silly girl. She remembered the happy-go-lucky girl she had first met, and the clippie that had gone dancing. What terrible damage the war had done. Even now, when it was all over, the war had not finished its assault on hearts and minds.

★　★　★

'Connie, Connie, you'll never guess! Sam's back home!'

Alice rushed into the drawing room and pulled up short on seeing Connie talking quietly to her mother. 'So sorry, Mrs Copeland. I've just 'eard and I thought Connie'd want to know.'

'Of course I do!' Connie sprang up and the two hugged each other. Alice had got caught up with Ginnie's story; she was nearly as pleased as Connie was. 'How did you find out?'

'I saw her neighbour, Mrs Scott, in the butchers. She told me. Cock-a-hoop she was.'

'That's wonderful news. I can hardly take it in after all this time. Thank you, Alice dear, you've made my day.'

★　★　★

323

Oh, the thrill of seeing Ginnie's beaming face when she called to see her that very afternoon.

Ginnie had opened the door with a smile stretching from ear to ear.

Connie threw her arms around her friend, tears of relief streaming down their faces.

'I'm so happy for you, dear Ginnie. When did you find out?'

Ginnie turned back to the door. Sam's face appeared, and behind him was Mabel.

''Ow do, ladies?'

And there he was, nervously moving his army cap from hand to hand.

Connie's eyes opened wide. 'Sam! After all this time. I am so glad for you both. Ginnie has been out of her mind with worry.'

'I know. I was an' all, wondering what her'd be thinking all this time. Got back soon as I could and hoped she was still waiting for me.'

'Course I was. I said I would, didn't I?'

They were all laughing and crying, with a rather bemused Sam taking centre stage. He chuckled, and the chuckle became a loud laugh. All four joined in a type of barn dance, but Sam was limping and couldn't keep it up.

'Stop . . . stop. We'll have poor Sam worn out at this rate,' cried Connie.

'I knew he'd come home . . . I knew it,' Ginnie gasped. 'But I didn't dare say nothing for fear it wouldn't come true. I can't believe he's real. I 'ave ter touch him ter make sure.'

'I'm sure that's not the only reason,' Connie said, her eyes bright with tears. 'My dear Ginnie and Sam. I'm so happy for you both. When did you . . . where are you . . . what . . . oh, never mind, questions can wait.'

'I got back yesterday morning an' slept for the best part of the day. After I give me girl a few hugs. Your Mabel made herself scarce an' all, didn't she, Ginnie?'

'She went bright red. Never seen our Mabel looking so . . . shy.'

'Your Mabel shy? I'd never have said that,' said Connie grinning at Mabel, who went a shade of pink.

'Gerroff with yer,' said Mabel, smiling back.

'He's been catching up with some sleep, and when he's awake, Mabel's topped him up with food. Her's building yer strength, isn't she, Sam? She's been so good, Connie, and I believe she's forgiven him for being a workhouse boy.'

Connie let out a happy sigh. 'Good news is quite exhausting,' she said, sitting down in a chair so that Ginnie and Sam could sit together. Ginnie's hand kept straying to him, touching him as if she wasn't sure he was real and when their eyes met, Connie could swear that, for them, there was no one else in the room.

'I think you will be in need of a good rest, Sam. Where are you staying?'

'Dunno. I come straight 'ere yesterday, so I had nowhere to go.'

Ginnie smiled. 'And yer can stay here tonight and the rest, until we get yer sorted out.'

'You can stay with us if you like, Sam?'

Sam chuckled. 'I dunno, all that time on me own with no bed at all and now I've got the both of yer, offering me one. It could go to a bloke's head.'

'Don't you go getting no ideas, Sam White,' Ginnie protested. 'Else I'll clip yer round the earhole.'

Sam laughed outright. A deep, contented laugh of

a man who had found his way home.

They talked for hours, catching up on lost time on that glorious day in March when, for once, they were all together, and everyone was beaming.

37

April 1919

A couple of days later, Ginnie had more news, and Connie was overjoyed for her dearest friend. She knew Ginnie must have something of great importance to disclose because they weren't due to meet again until the weekend.

There were stars in Ginnie's eyes and she didn't seem to care who saw them.

'You'll never guess. Sam's remembered that funny little saying what I told you about not long after we met? About the buttercup what could tell if you was going to get wed? I'd kept it in my carpetbag and showed it to him when he came back, along with my other tranklements. Well he's made it all come true, Connie — he's asked me to marry him as soon as we can arrange it.'

Connie had been expecting the news. Of course, she had. But it didn't stop her own tears welling. And Connie's tears started Ginnie off until the two of them were sobbing in each other's arms.

'Hey, you'll 'ave us drowning,' Ginnie let Connie go with a chuckle.

'Oh dear, why do we cry when we're happy? I'm so happy for you and Sam.'

★ ★ ★

That one happy event was followed soon after by another — Jean and Stephen's wedding, a low-key affair as neither of them had close family ties, and Jean was not the type of woman to be at the centre of everyone's attention for long.

Stephen spent his last bachelor night with his mother. Mrs Adams had welcomed Jean into the family with open arms, and Jean had come to think of her as someone rather special. How incredible that her mother-in-law would be the woman who tested them when they started to work on the trams.

Jean had given up her rented room a week before the wedding and stayed with Connie. The two had great fun and Betty was missed. Knowing Betty's love of company, they both appreciated that her decision to leave had not been taken lightly.

The wedding was to take place at Hanley Registry Office at midday followed by a short celebration at a nearby public house. In the evening they would join the Easter Dance at the Victoria Hall. Connie delighted in her role as witness for the bride and she wasn't surprised to discover that Robert would fulfil the role for Stephen. After the wedding Jean would move into Stephen's family home overlooking Tunstall Park.

The evening before the wedding, Connie sat with Jean in the drawing room enjoying a celebratory glass of sherry to the sound of giggling and laughter.

'I can hardly believe it, Connie. Me, Jean Wright, about to be married. I thought I'd die an old maid.'

'Come on now, Jean. Why should you think that? You are a lovely young woman, kind and considerate, and a true friend.'

'I've never had much confidence. I know I look as if

I should, being tall and a bit ungainly. I'm taller than most of the women I meet. I used to try and make myself smaller so as I wouldn't stand out.'

'Jean, you are not ungainly. Since you started to work as a clippie, you have acquired maturity and confidence. Any man would be proud to have you on his arm.'

With a flushed face, Jean grinned, and it set them off giggling again. She became serious. 'I do wish Betty was here. I thought she'd write and tell us how she's getting on and, maybe come to the wedding. We've been friends for a good while, and it's not like her to miss out on celebrations. She may come over strong and capable, but she isn't.'

'I know what you mean. I think about what she might be up to most days.' Connie stopped talking for a moment wondering where Betty was now. She sighed. 'I've had my letter from the PTC by the way. I leave in two weeks. A serviceman back home from the Navy is starting next week.'

'Will you be sorry to go, Connie?'

'I thought I would be but it's not the same without you and Betty. I love working on the trams, but I miss the banter we used to have. Nearly all the conductors are men now and it's not the same. Betty would have loved it.'

They laughed, but their laughs held affection.

'I've started to apply for office jobs. I'll have to see what turns up.'

Alice appeared at the door with a laden tray of tea and cakes and laid them on the table.

'Do come and join us, Alice. We are having such a jolly time.' Connie jumped up and pulled her towards a chair.

'Won't I be in the way?'

'Of course not.' Jean looked shocked. 'I want you to.'

And so, a smiling Alice became part of the happy group.

When Connie was lying in bed later, she couldn't help but think about Robert. It had been nearly a year since they had spoken to each other in anything other than a formal way, at work. Outwardly, he treated her as he would any other employee. But things were not right between them, and it made Connie feel uncomfortable. Now, her mind strayed back to Betty's letter warning her not to push him away. Could her friend see something that she could not?

Connie had tried to find out more about his background because he intrigued her. Was he a pacifist as Louisa had told her? Was a pacifist automatically a coward? Was Robert involved in the war, where did he get the burns from and what about that cough? If anyone she knew was party to this information, they were keeping their mouths firmly shut.

She only knew what Louisa Pendleton had told her. In the early days, Robert and Louisa had seemed inseparable but, recently they had not been seen together. It made her wonder if they were no longer walking out. The thought pleased her.

To be fair, Robert had been very busy since the end of the war, ending the clippie contracts, welcoming back the men and training them all. She might have felt bitter about that, but she'd known all along that it would be so. And if it put an end to Louisa's friendship with Robert, she couldn't have been happier.

From what little she knew of both of them, Connie couldn't believe they had much in common. Robert was reserved and didn't draw attention to himself. Louisa, on the other hand, was happy to be the centre of everyone's attention. Working as an inspector on the trams, Robert would hardly be in a position to keep Louisa in the luxury she was no doubt looking for.

* * *

Connie and Jean readied themselves for the wedding. Jean had chosen to wear a smart, fitted suit that she had kept for best and her Sunday hat decorated with a rose made from ribbons. Connie chose a conservative approach, not wanting to out-do Jean on her special day. She had bought a lovely outfit with clean lines and a long jacket in a pale green a week before the war started and not had the opportunity to wear it, which embarrassed her now, when she thought about their economies.

They arrived in Hanley early. The shops were already busy. The sun was shining, and the two of them linked arms and wandered casually towards the nearest shop, which happened to be a draper's. They both stared through the window, but Connie didn't take it in. She was still thinking about Robert, couldn't get him out of her head. Since receiving her notice, she had been thinking about him more and more. She had been so angry with him when he had chastised her about leading the clippies in a revolt. She even understood why he'd done it, but it had dented her ego and she couldn't allow that to happen. Not after Matthew. She shook herself. She must put him out of her mind. This was Jean's day and she wasn't about to spoil it.

They strolled back to the Registry Office and up the steps to find Stephen, Robert and Mrs Adams in the hall waiting for them. For the first time, Connie saw Stephen's face redden with . . . what? Pride, love, surprise, when he saw his intended. The blush that lit up Jean's face was a pleasure to behold.

Connie couldn't relax around Robert and she had suddenly become rather nervous after spending part of the day thinking how she would feel when he was no longer around. Despite everything Louisa had said, she couldn't put him out of her mind. Why hadn't he come to the wedding with Louisa? It would have been a perfect time to announce their romance to the world.

Suddenly, Robert was at her side.

'Connie . . . ?' he said in a low voice. 'If I might be allowed a dance later, I would like to talk to you.'

Connie tried, in vain, to think what she might have done to cause him to ask to see her, but she couldn't. He had caught her unawares.

Her heart skipped a beat. She nodded. 'I'll look forward to it,' she said. She hoped he didn't want to speak about work. It would be nice to talk to him about something other than what she might have done wrong.

She turned her attention to her duties as the bride's witness to hide her blushes. The ceremony was short and didn't feel like a true wedding, but the faces of the bride and groom said otherwise.

Her thoughts turned to Louisa and concluded she might be joining Robert later.

At the end of the ceremony, the bride and groom took their first steps as man and wife. Connie couldn't stop the smile spreading from cheek to cheek at their happiness. She followed them out of the Registry Office and was joined by Robert. He took her arm as they followed their friends into the street. His touch sent shivers up and down her spine. The thought that she could be dancing with him later thrilled her. She looked at his handsome face, wishing they were on better terms.

An employee of the Registry Office stood just inside the door and reminded them that rationing had made it a criminal offence to throw rice at the happy couple. They would have to find some other way to celebrate.

They crossed the road to the public house opposite. Jean's face was a picture. Flushed a delicate pink, eyes shining, her hair in a flattering bob, she looked every inch the happy bride.

Connie hugged her tightly. 'I do hope you will be happy, Jean.'

'I know I shall. I only hope that you and Betty can look forward to the same good fortune.' Jean's eyes slid towards Robert, and her eyebrows lifted suggestively.

Connie shook her head. 'I don't think so, Jean. There's a little ill-feeling between us. Can't really talk about it. Maybe I'll meet someone sometime. Until then, I shall have to practise becoming an old maid.'

Jean laughed outright, attracting the attention of everyone, including Robert. 'You, an old maid! Well I never, Connie Copeland.'

Connie's flush started in her neck and ran up her face in waves. Robert frowned. Connie sighed. Oh, no, not again. If he could get annoyed at such a little incident, then she didn't wish to know him!

The rest of the afternoon passed quickly. There was lots of conversation, and jokes flew around the room as they toasted the new Mr and Mrs Adams, but there was no chance of speaking to Robert alone. Whatever he wanted to talk to her about would have to wait.

Connie had to admit that seeing Robert away from work and in the more relaxed atmosphere of the public house was a new experience. His blue-grey eyes twinkled in a most surprising manner as his smiles grew broader. If he could control his manner a little more, he might turn out to be special.

The wedding party moved on to the dance at the Victoria Hall. They sat at a table near to the dancing but not so close as to have people bumping into them as they made their way to the dance floor.

Stephen's eyes followed Jean everywhere, as if he couldn't believe his luck. It was easy to see he adored her. As she watched, Connie felt jealous. It was almost funny that she had warned Jean about taking on the relationship and now, here they were, Jean married and Connie . . . well, alone.

Couples took to the floor almost immediately. Women danced together and glanced enviously at those who had male company. Connie closed her eyes and concentrated on the music playing softly. Stephen led his new wife onto the dance floor, no doubt wanting to show her off. He had left his walking stick at their table and relied on Jean to help him. As more and more people took to the floor, Connie leaned her elbows on the table and rested her head in her hands, listening to the music.

A hand touched her shoulder. She turned. It was Robert. She sat upright quickly.

'Don't worry, I'm not going to send you to the naughty corner!' He smiled at her.

'I'm glad to hear it. Before you sit down, are you

talking to me as Robert Caldwell or Inspector Caldwell?'

He looked rather startled. 'I very much hope it's Robert's turn tonight, Miss Copeland, if you will allow it?'

She smiled. 'Then please take a seat, Robert.'

He sat beside her, but his eyes were on the dance floor. Their little table was a pocket of silence in a sea of noise. She couldn't think what to say. It was up to him. He had asked to speak to her, hadn't he?

'You're due to finish work soon?'

A question. A question to which he already had the answer.

'Yes I am.' What did he want to say to her? He looked . . . uncomfortable, to say the least.

'I wanted to say that you have done an excellent job as a clippie, and I will be more than happy to supply you with a reference.'

Connie held her head high. 'I thought you said Robert was joining me, not the inspector, Inspector?'

He leaned forward. 'I am Robert, at least, I don't think the inspector would talk to you about what I have in mind.'

Connie stared at him. He had his head on one side and a grin on his mouth. She tried to suppress the giggles rising in her throat but couldn't.

'That's better,' he said. 'I know we've had bad times together for the last few months — since we first met, I suppose.' He gave a wry smile. 'I hope we can put them aside and start again.'

Connie smiled at him. 'I would like that too.'

'Most of the time it was because of the job, Connie. Things that, as a manager, I couldn't ignore —'

'I —'

'No, don't interrupt me — there's more. I couldn't ignore some of your actions and I don't think you would have expected me to, if you're honest with yourself.'

Connie opened her mouth and shut it again. What he said was true, but why should she give him the satisfaction of agreeing with him?

'Now that you're leaving, I don't want to lose you, Connie. You drive me mad sometimes, but I wouldn't want to think that I would never see you again. I'd like to think we could get on well together without arguing.'

'Oh!' She hadn't expected that.

'It can't come as a surprise to you, surely? I should have sacked you when you neglected to tell Stephen about the prison sentence. But I couldn't bring myself to do it.'

He was right. She had been amazed to keep her job but had refused to see it because she wanted him to be in the wrong. 'I'm sorry I have caused you so much trouble, Inspector. Do you think Robert could come back again?'

'And you don't mind sitting here talking to me?' She smiled broadly. 'I don't think I do, Robert.'

'Do you know what you intend to do next?'

'No. I only wish I did.'

'Enough talking, we should be dancing, Connie.'

He took her hand and walked her towards the dance floor. Her heart thumped. He turned to face her and she looked into his blue-grey eyes. Her own became misty as he opened his arms to her. His touch was electrifying. She must be positively glowing. Almost immediately, everything cleared as she realised her thoughts were a mere fantasy that might never come to pass.

He bent his head towards her until his lips just touched her ear. She could scarcely breathe. He might have said something, but her heart pounded so hard, she couldn't make out his words.

She had almost forgotten what it felt like to dance with a man and she loved every minute. She had come alive, their bodies touching, hers in tune with his. And she wanted more.

They sat out most of the more energetic dances. Robert said he liked to dance but preferred to watch rather than to compete for space on the dance floor. Connie was content to sit with him — and she needed to talk to him about Louisa.

She tried to hold back, not wanting to spoil the evening, but she had to ask, even if she didn't like the answer. She couldn't risk being hurt again. He had sought her out and she needed to know what his intentions were, before she could commit herself.

'Robert, tell me what's happening with you and Louisa?'

'Me and Louisa — what do you mean?'

'You and Louisa are . . . together?'

'What ever gave you that idea?'

'Louisa.'

'When?'

'Just before the Armistice, she asked to talk to me. She told me that you were romantically linked and that I should know because she didn't want me to get hurt again.'

Robert raised his eyebrows. 'Did she now? There is nothing and never has been anything between Louisa and me. She's Matthew's cousin. She can be a little . . . flighty, so Matthew asked me to look after her when she comes up to Stoke. I'm doing him a favour,

337

nothing more than that.'

'A favour?'

'She's actually his second cousin and, I believe, she dotes on him. We spent time together when we were younger. Matthew and I were both day boys. I was often invited to his house after school and during holidays. Louisa was there sometimes, and we became friends. Once the war started it was natural to accompany each other from time to time.'

'So you had no designs on Louisa?'

Robert laughed. 'She's very pretty, but she's like a sister to me, and a troublesome one at that.' He sighed. 'She's the type of woman who needs to have a man in attendance. She could never be like these.' He pointed around the walls of the room where women without partners sat. Wallflowers.

Connie understood; Louisa was a middle-class version of Betty. 'I think she is well suited to Matthew. They both want the same things in life. She's just what his mother wants for him. They deserve each other.'

Connie's head was spinning. Louisa had lied and if she could tell a lie about them being together, what other lies had she told during that conversation in Hanley? Surely this changed everything about Robert and what he was or wasn't? She had to find out the truth. It would affect the whole of her life. She needed time to think it through.

The traditional last dance was a slow waltz from The Nutcracker. She turned towards Robert to find he was staring at her. She had to put it out of her mind for the time being. He put out his hand, and she took it, gladly. A tingling sensation travelled up her arm. She swallowed, determined this dance would not be the last time she spent in his arms. She wanted to feel

338

the warmth of his body close to hers for a long time to come.

He took her into his arms, and they melded together as one whole being — him leading, her following. She knew in her heart that it didn't matter who was following and who was leading as long as they were together. It was where she wanted to be.

Her head was resting on his shoulder when she opened her eyes, and she found she was looking directly at Jean, who looked so happy on this, her special day. Their eyes met and Connie knew, in an instant, that happiness was written all over her face and there was no way Jean would believe her if she tried to say otherwise.

⋆ ⋆ ⋆

Leaving the PTC was a bit of an anticlimax. Her last run finished at the depot at about three o'clock. She had a lump in the throat when she jumped down from her tram for the last time. She patted the red and cream paintwork and had to blink quickly.

She cast her eyes around for Robert, but he was not to be seen. Her heart sank. By the time she got to the office she had regained her composure.

'Good afternoon Ernest, are we ready to cash up?'

'Yes, Connie. Your last time, isn't it? We'll do the cash and tickets first and then deal with the rest of the paperwork after you have changed into your civvies.'

Connie returned a few minutes later with her two uniforms neatly folded and her boots on the top.

'I've stamped your uniform chitty to say everything's in order, but it hardly matters as there are only two of you left and that's the end of the clippies,' grinned Earnest. 'You'll be glad for a rest, I've no doubt.'

Normally, she would have thrown a sarcastic remark at him, but today was very different.

'I've put your letter of commendation and reference from Mr Adams along with the chitty in this envelope. That's you done.'

The restroom had been invaded by men. New faces chatted to her but without the camaraderie that working with the clippies had brought. In a way, she was glad her time had come to an end.

As she rode her bicycle out of the yard for the final time, there was nobody to see her leave.

38

May 1919

Connie had applied for three jobs so far, two assistant clerk positions, and a role as a junior secretary, but had not heard from any of them. She had thought it would be as easy as it had been when she became a clippie. Now she was beginning to doubt her ability.

She found she could concentrate on very little as Louisa's words and Robert's denial swam around her head. Mother suggested she visit Uncle James at the family home in Lancashire. After working so hard at the depot, her mother felt she needed a holiday before embarking on another job.

Connie thought it an excellent idea. Time away from The Potteries was sorely needed. It would take the pressure off and distance her from Robert when she most needed it.

She sent a short note to Robert thanking him for a lovely time at the wedding, explained where she was going, and said she was looking forward to seeing him again when she returned.

Uncle James made her welcome. His wife had died in childbirth many years ago, and he had two grown-up daughters who now lived in the south of England. He saw them only occasionally. Connie could see he missed them.

The weather was particularly lovely and to be away from the grimy city atmosphere of The Potteries was a pleasure. They went out for walks and visited museums and even had a chance to visit the coast at Southport. The fresh air of the coast suited her, and she felt alive to the new possibilities waiting for her when she returned home.

Connie had been with Uncle James for nearly two weeks. She decided to stay for another two weeks as he suggested a driving tour of the Yorkshire Dales and maybe a visit to Scotland. Plans were made and they departed on the 12th. They expected to be away for a week, and she would spend a further week in Lancashire before returning home.

She enjoyed long conversations with him. He told her lots about when he and her mother were children. She laughed at some of the scrapes they'd got themselves into and couldn't believe such behaviour of her mother.

One evening they were having dinner in the dining room of their hotel. They seemed to have driven a long way that day and the sights they had seen were breathtaking. In the relaxed company of Uncle James, Connie began to talk about Robert, telling him all she knew about his past and what Louisa had said and implied about his principles and beliefs.

'What do you think I should do?'

'I'm an old fuddy-duddy so you're probably asking the wrong person. It's a long time since I was married. But I'll say one thing — whatever your young man's views are, he must hold them strongly. It can't have been easy for him.' Uncle James paused and thought for a moment. 'But I also think you don't know the full story. You are relying on this Louisa's testimony which, at best, could be exaggerated and at worst, downright lies. The woman sounds unhinged to me. He may have been involved in the war, but didn't actually fight. Many soldiers go to war, but with a pen and paper or a ladle and a pot. It doesn't mean they're cowards. Fighting a war's a team effort. Not everybody in a team has a starring role.'

'Do you think I should ask him?'

'In normal times, I would definitely say yes. But these are not normal times and many men have real problems with discussion of what they did during the war. To ask him outright might be just too much, but I believe you do need to know.'

'The suffragettes in the Stoke-on-Trent branch had many different views on the war, covering all the spectrum. I have to admit, I would not normally have had any time for such a person and would have labelled him a coward. Oh, Uncle James — I did label him coward because I gave him a white feather. But this feels different, there is something more about him. I must get to the bottom of Louisa's accusations and I must also tell him about the white feather. Until then we cannot progress.'

'Then you have answered your own question. I think your heart has already been given.'

'Maybe so, maybe so . . .'

* * *

Uncle James decided to return to Lancashire by way of the Lake District. Connie felt encouraged to re-read the poems of Wordsworth while she could still picture the hills and lakes of this most beautiful countryside.

'It's been lovely to see you again after all this time. You have grown into a fine young woman, just like your mother. I wish I could have seen more of her

343

over these last few years, but . . .'

He stopped talking and became thoughtful.

'Are you all right, Uncle James?'

'Yes, my dear. I'm only thinking of what might have been.'

'What do you mean?'

Uncle James shook his head. 'Don't worry, Connie. It's just me being maudlin. Tell Agatha she's in my thoughts every day. I'll never forget her. She'll want for nothing.'

Connie frowned. He seemed depressed, unlike his usual self. 'I will be sure to tell her, Uncle James.' She put a hand on his arm.

'You look so like her, Connie.' He patted her hand and looked her in the eye. 'If you ever need me, I will be here for you and so will your family. Never forget that.'

They pulled through the gates of Urmston Hall at about five o'clock. They were greeted by the house-keeper, Mrs Rawlinson. She asked if they had enjoyed themselves and how the weather had been.

'I'll need to get changed for dinner, so I will go to my room now.'

'Miss Connie, I have put your post on the dressing table.'

Connie went upstairs to her room which overlooked the gardens. There were three letters on a silver tray. She recognised Jean's handwriting on two of them. The third looked official and she opened it immediately. It was an appointment for an interview on 14th May. Her first interview — and she had missed it. Depressed, she tore it up and then had second thoughts and scooped the pieces up again. She would contact them to tell them what had happened and to

344

confirm the job had been filled.

She was actually quite tired after the journey from Lancaster and decided to have a nap. She would save Jean's news until later.

It was nearly ten o'clock when she returned to her bedroom. She got undressed and jumped into bed. She took up the first letter, post marked 12th May 1919, the very day they had departed Urmston Hall. She opened it and started to read.

> *9 Park Road*
> *Tunstall*
> *Stoke-on-Trent*
> *9th May 1919*

Dear Connie,

I hope this letter finds you well and enjoying the countryside of Lancashire with your uncle.
I'm afraid I have some disturbing news for you. At least I think it will be because you and Robert seemed to have put aside your differences at my wedding.

Robert has been quite ill. About a week after you went on holiday, Stephen received a message from him to say he wouldn't be in work as he was unwell. The following evening Stephen went to see Robert at his home. Robert looked quite poorly. Stephen suspected it was the 'flu and called for a doctor who confirmed his suspicion.

Robert has been admitted to Bucknall Isolation Hospital where he will stay for the next two weeks. He is not allowed any visitors so it is pointless you returning home. I will write to you again and let you know how he is progressing.

Love Jean

Connie grabbed the second letter and ripped it open quickly. The words blurred and she had to blink a few times before she could see to read.

9 Park Road
Tunstall
Stoke-on-Trent
19th May 1919

Dear Connie,

I have good news about Robert. He has improved greatly. It was only a mild attack of the 'flu but it was complicated by his bad chest from the war. Stephen said he was not surprised, but hasn't told me why.

The doctor has said he will be released from Bucknall to the London Road Hospital, where he will receive further treatment for his lungs, and should be well enough to return home by 28th May.

As you haven't replied to my first letter, I don't know whether you are interested in Robert in the way I am assuming you are. When you get back, please call on me and we will catch up on all our news together.

Love Jean

Without thinking, Connie ran to see Uncle James, who was reading the newspaper in the library. He looked up, startled to see her in her nightclothes.

'What's to do, Connie?'

'Poor Robert has the 'flu and is in hospital. Jean says he has been very ill.' Connie told Uncle James what she had gleaned from Jean's letters. 'Oh, Uncle James, I have to catch the first train in the morning. I can't leave him on his own. I must go to him.'

'No point in rushing back if he's just come out of isolation and is still in the hospital. Best to return in a couple of days.'

Connie stared at him. How could he suggest that she continue her holiday? Who would look after Robert when he went home? 'I'm sorry but must go Uncle James. I can't bear to leave him on his own.'

'If you're sure you have to go, I'll not stand in your way, love.'

'I must be there to look after him and see he's taken care of when he comes out of hospital.'

★ ★ ★

The next morning Connie dispatched two telegrams, one to Jean telling her she would be returning on 26th May and would come straight to her house from Tunstall railway station. The other she sent to her mother telling her she was returning. What a pity they'd taken out the telephone as one of their economies. It was such an inconvenience.

★ ★ ★

Connie got off the train and checked her luggage into the left-luggage office before rushing the few hundred yards to Jean's house. The houses were built in the mid-nineteenth century for professional people and managers from the potbanks. Stephen's father must have been a man of substance.

She knocked loudly on the door.

It was Jean herself who welcomed her. 'Oh! Connie, I'm so glad to see you. Come in straight away.'

Jean threw her arms around her and guided her to

the parlour at the front of the house, overlooking the park.

Connie did not wait for the normal polite conversation. 'Is there any news of Robert?'

Jean smiled. 'Yes, he came home yesterday. He's still very weak but is much improved. It was a mild case of 'flu but once you are in isolation, you have to stay there. They were more concerned about his chest. Did you know about that?'

'He's always had a cough, but he never told me why.'

'So, I gather from your eager and sudden return that I was right to contact you?'

'Oh, yes. I was so disappointed that he had not written to me after your wedding. I thought he wasn't interested and had been caught in the moment at the dance. Your letters arrived while Uncle James and I were on a touring holiday. When we got back, your letters were waiting for me. I hoped I would be back before he came out of hospital but it's good news too isn't it?'

Jean and Connie went through to the kitchen and made a cup of tea. Connie did not feel like eating and they returned to the parlour.

'Where is Mrs Adams?'

'I'm here,' said Jean, laughing. 'The other Mrs Adams has gone shopping in town. She always gets her food from the same shops, and always will. She likes a good chat with the shopkeepers to keep up with what's happening.'

Jean seemed quite at home as the lady of the house. They talked about how things had gone since the wedding and how she was settling in.

'Is Mrs Adams difficult to live with?'

'I felt like an outsider at first. But she treated me like a daughter rather than her son's wife. She even told me to call her Mother,' Jean began. 'Before the wedding she said she would continue to organise everything in the house until I felt confident. I wasn't concerned, I think I needed all the help I could get. I enjoy being busy and learning all these new things. In my rented room, nothing took very long to do. Washing clothes, making meals, sweeping the floor. Now I live in a palace compared with that, and it is all a little frightening. So, Mother has been passing jobs onto me ever since. But the shopping in Tunstall is part of her social life, so we might start to do that together.'

'Alice organises everything for us, but we have taken on some things now that Alice is on her own.'

'That's the advantage of being rich. Stephen says they used to have a maid, but she left 'cos she could earn more money in the munitions factory. Mrs Adams was probably quoting from experience when she set us that little test. Although Stephen hasn't said anything to me, I think this house is all that they've got, so it's just Stephen's money coming in until I get a job. A servant's out of the question.'

'Are you happy, Jean?'

Jean beamed. 'I couldn't be happier, Connie. He's so good and kind. And Mrs Adams is a dear. I know she's trying to help me, for Stephen's sake and I love her for it.'

'Has Betty been in touch?'

'No. Stephen asked some of the drivers who knew her to keep their eyes open. But no luck so far.'

'Does Stephen talk about the depot very much or are you too busy for talking?'

Jean blushed. 'You're getting as bad as Betty

would have been.'

Soon after, Connie collected her bags from the railway station and made her way home. In the familiar setting of the tram, she thought back to what might have happened to Robert. She now knew the feelings she had for him were nothing like those she had possessed for Matthew. They went much deeper. Ever since she had first met him she had been fighting her feelings for him.

She was glad when the tram stopped at the top of Moorland Road. She needed time to herself — time to think.

★ ★ ★

Connie let herself into the house.

'Alice, are you there?'

Alice popped her head around the door of the kitchen. 'Hiya, Connie. You're back. I've missed you.'

They embraced each other.

'Have yer seen Jean, Connie?'

'I've just got back from seeing her and catching up about Robert. She told you, didn't she?' Alice nodded anxiously and Connie continued. 'I need to see him. I have to check that he is looking after himself.'

'Certainly. You should go after dinner. I bet you haven't had a decent meal all day.'

Connie sank onto the chair in the hall. 'I feel dizzy, Alice. I think I do need something.'

'It's the shock. Your mother and father are in the drawing room. Go to see them and I'll bring you a pot of tea and some sandwiches. We'll go to see him tomorrow morning. You can't go on your own in any case, it wouldn't be proper.'

After breakfast, the two women made their way to Robert's house in Tunstall, a larger than average terrace with a tiny front garden edged by a red-brick wall. It looked well cared for. Now that she had arrived, Connie felt embarrassed for being there. What if he regretted showing her so much attention at the wedding and didn't want to see her? Supposing she was being too pushy in turning up at his door in such a way?

Alice tutted and took the matter in hand. She knocked on the door. Connie tried her best to be patient. The door opened slowly.

Robert looked pale and drawn and his eyes were two slits as if he was trying to keep out the sun.

'Hello, Robert.'

'It's you, Connie. Come in, come in.' His voice sounded cracked, but he managed a smile. He moved to one side and she stepped inside.

'You've met Alice before,' she said, motioning Alice to follow her.

He gave Alice a smile and a nod and closed the door. He led the way into his parlour and motioned them to sit on the settee under the front window.

'I called to see Jean earlier and she told me you had been ill. You still look poorly, Robert. Are you looking after yourself?'

'I'm feeling much better now. Apart from a cough and feeling as helpless as a baby.'

They were quiet, as if wondering what to say next. Connie stared at the bookshelves beside the fireplace. He was well-read. The shelves were overflowing with books and Connie would have liked to thumb through the pages of some of them.

'If you are happy for me to go into yer kitchen, Mr Caldwell, I'll be glad ter make yer both a cup of tea?'

It was Alice's way of giving Connie and Robert some time together privately. When Alice closed the door, Connie's words burst out. 'Oh, Robert, I was so worried when I read Jean's letters. I had to come to see you. I hope you don't mind.'

Robert smiled. 'I'm glad you came. Stephen called to see me once I was out of isolation. He said you had gone to stay with someone.'

'My Uncle James. He lives in Lancashire. He's my favourite uncle. I sent you a letter — well two, actually.'

'They were here when I returned,' he said. 'I was hoping to come to see you but I'm still very weak.'

Connie smiled. 'And I don't suppose you admit that lightly.'

Robert laughed, and began to cough.

Alice took that as a cue and entered with steaming cups of tea.

'You'll need some more milk, Mr Caldwell. I'll just pop out and get some for yer.'

'That's good of you, but you don't —'

'No trouble at all.' She nodded her head towards Connie. 'Best you two have a chat while I'm away.'

She grinned and the door banged shut.

Robert looked tired. He tried his best to sit and talk but anyone could see he was too weak.

'I'm sorry I wasn't here for you, Robert. If only I had known I would have come straight back.'

'You wouldn't have been able to see me. I was in isolation.'

She took his hand and fingered the scars lightly. His

352

skin was so pale they stood out in vivid red contrast.

'I'll visit you every day and do what I can to help.'

'But you can't, not on your own. What about your reputation?'

Connie laughed. 'It's never stopped me before from doing something I have to do.'

He smiled at her. His eyes closed.

When Alice returned, they busied themselves tidying a little and making up a couple of meals, thanks to Alice, for him to eat if he should feel hungry.

When they had finished, Connie decided it was time to leave. The two of them put on their coats. 'Robert, would you mind if I called again tomorrow?' She didn't care if she was being forward.

He looked surprised at first. 'I would look forward to that very much, and Alice is invited as well. I am fortunate indeed to have not one but two pretty ladies waiting on me.'

Connie beamed back and they left.

'He's a nice bloke, but he's going to have a lot of milk in the house when he goes back to work,' Alice quipped. 'Have to try bread tomorrow!'

She had to suffer Alice's jokey remarks all the way back home but she didn't care. It had turned out to be a wonderful day after all.

★ ★ ★

After that first visit to Robert, the two approached Connie's mother.

'Mother dear, Alice and I went to see Robert today. He is still very weak and can barely look after himself. Would you mind very much if Alice accompanies me to help me nurse him back to health?'

Mother raised an eyebrow. 'You may take Alice with you, Connie. I agree, you would be better not to go to a man's house alone. I'm surprised you gave a thought to your reputation.'

Connie grimaced. 'I will help Alice with whatever she needs to do so she doesn't get behind with her work.'

Her mother laughed. 'Alice dear, you might regret letting Constance help. None of her schooling has ever involved housework.'

Alice was a godsend. She always found something to busy herself with, whether it was fetching bread or milk, so Connie could have a few stolen minutes alone with Robert.

39

June 1919

Within a week Robert was much improved, so much so that he was starting back to work on Monday. On the Sunday before, they walked into Tunstall, around the park, and back. Alice had said she wanted to give the house a good cleaning so they could take as long as they wanted.

'I don't know what I would've done without you and Alice,' he said softly. His arm, linked through Connie's, felt quite natural.

'We wanted to come. How could I leave you to fend for yourself? It wasn't as if I was working.'

'And that's my good fortune.' He covered her hand with his own. His blue-grey eyes twinkled. 'Would it be too forward of me to say I want to kiss you?'

His words came out of the blue. Words she had given up on hearing. She had wondered what it would feel like to be kissed by him ever since she had returned from her visit to Uncle James, but his illness had prevented it. Now, there was no such obstacle.

She pretended to think. 'I believe we should try it before coming to a decision.'

His arm came around her and he pressed her to him. His kiss took her breath away and she was clinging to him.

He lifted his lips from hers, slowly. 'Connie . . . you have no idea how long I have been waiting to do that.

I couldn't do it when you worked with the PTC. Relationships with other employees weren't allowed.'

'That's what Stephen said to Jean.'

'And you've no idea of the turmoil I went through. I desperately wanted you to finish, but I had to keep you working in case it all went wrong and I never saw you again.'

'We've been a little obsessed with our problems, Robert, you and I. How much time we've wasted.'

★ ★ ★

Not surprisingly, Connie had seen very little of Ginnie recently; with Jean's wedding, the holiday, and then Robert's illness, it had been an eventful year. Now that he was well, she would have to start looking for a job again. She had thought long and hard about her discussion with Uncle James and had concluded that she would say nothing of Louisa's assertions until she had spoken to Robert. She didn't know yet whether she was ready for his answer.

When she eventually caught up with Ginnie, they were able to have the sort of heart-to-heart talk that can only happen between close friends.

'It's lovely having my Sam back home again. But he's different from the Sam what went away.'

'How do you mean?'

'He's changed. I expected as much after what he's been through, but there's summat else, summat he's keeping back from me. He told me a bit about what happened to him over there when he first came home, but now he's clammed up. Won't talk about it at all.'

'He must have seen a lot of bad things. It's to be expected. And how do you feel about him?'

'I was sixteen when he went away, and he's come back a man, a man I hardly know. I feel that shy when I'm with him, but he's still my Sam, and I love him, Connie.'

'Nobody would doubt that for a moment.'

'I told yer he moved into my bedroom and that I'm sleeping with Mabel and Florrie? It seemed daft to pay for a room for him when he could share at ours. It's a bit of a squeeze, but never mind. He has some terrible nightmares, Connie. He told me that he's usually in the dark, and hears men crying in pain. He says there's continuous noise, night after night, and he feels helpless. Sometimes he sits up all night and waits for the morning. I know what nightmares are like, Connie, but these are so bad, I couldn't help but cry when he told me.'

'Oh, Ginnie, my darling. I had no idea. Poor Sam — and poor you.'

'I run into his bedroom,' Ginnie blushed, '. . . and cuddle him like a kid until it all goes away. In the mornings he can't wait to get outside, as if he feels hemmed in. He goes into himself, and I conner get a word out of him.'

Deep sadness lay heavy in Connie's heart, but she let Ginnie continue. She was sure her friend had been bottling it up and it would do her good if she could let it go.

'His limp's so much better now, and if yer looked at him you'd swear there was nowt wrong. It's his eyes what give it away. He's getting back to being the old Sam gradually, and I want him back so much.' Ginnie's eyes filled. She shook tears away.

'He's feeling stronger every day. He's got a job tending to the gardens in Burslem Park and he loves it. Suits him being outside. He dunner care about the weather; he just needs to take in air what somebody else hasn't taken in before him, even if it's mixed with smoke and soot. That card you told us to put up in the greengrocer's and the newspaper shop was a good idea. He's managed to get some local work looking after some of the big gardens at the back of the houses on Waterloo Road. He's used to tending the soil and growing vegetables and we've spent time just walking through Burslem Park, learning about the flowers what grow there. That's how he got the job in the park. The pay isn't much, but it's regular.'

'Well, I'm glad things are starting to improve for you at long last.'

'I never dared to be as happy as I am right now,' Ginnie hugged her knees. 'It's like I'm reading one of those stories from your library.'

Connie smiled. 'It's your very own story, Ginnie, complete with a happy ending. At least we won't have to endure another war. People will learn from their mistakes. We'll have many happy years ahead of us.'

After hearing of Sam's problems, Connie was glad she hadn't burdened Ginnie with hers.

40

July 1919

Ginnie's wedding was set for Wakes Week, the annual Potters' Holiday in the second week of July. She said they could wait no longer.

Connie helped to arrange it, given the short time-scale, helping her plan what to wear, who to invite to celebrate with them and what to eat — since most things were either rationed or in short supply, even though the war was over.

'I dunner care,' said Ginnie, grinning broadly. 'Don't see as I could miss what I've never had and I'm quite sure as Sam would say the same an' all. And I want you to be my bridesmaid, Connie. No buts —' she said as Connie tried to interrupt.

'What about Mabel?'

'Our Mabel's going to walk me down the aisle and give me away.'

'Then, of course, I'll be honoured to be your brides-maid, dearest Ginnie.'

The girls hugged each other.

'Yer'll bring Robert along, won't yer? I want ter meet him.'

'Yes, of course. It will be our first real engagement, as a couple,' she said coyly.

'I haven't heard you talk about nobody else.'

Connie was enjoying the time spent with Robert. She had chosen to believe him rather than Louisa, but Louisa's claims that he was estranged from his family because he was a conscientious objector were still on her mind. A suffragette and a conscientious objector — could that work? It would certainly be a problem for her father.

'You're miles away, Connie. Who yer thinking about — as if I couldn't guess!'

'It's a bit depressing to think that I was planning my marriage around this time three years ago and still you beat me to it.'

'Sorry, Connie.'

'Don't be. You and Sam are meant for each other. You deserve to be happy.'

'You'll find somebody. Mind you, I'm sure you have already,' said Ginnie with a grin.

Connie's eyes misted. 'I hope so. I would love to go home to a man who is not my father!'

★ ★ ★

The day of Ginnie's wedding dawned, and Connie was up early. She had bought Alice a dress to wear that befitted the occasion, neat and comfortable, but not flashy or inappropriate. A dress she would be able to wear after the wedding too.

Ginnie had insisted on making her wedding dress. She was becoming quite a seamstress and now made most of her clothes. Connie had given her plain white tablecloths and lace to edge seams to make it a little special. After the wedding, Ginnie would dye it and turn it into a dress that she could wear on Sundays and special events.

Connie collected flowers and some greenery from the garden and arranged them into a bouquet. She laughed to herself. That was one skill she learned at her posh school which had come in useful. Carnations were not included. They were the flowers Ginnie had taken, as keepsakes, from her parents' graves and held sad memories. Connie wanted this day to be full of joy for her special friend.

She arrived at Mabel's house at ten o'clock. Mabel opened the door with a very excited Florrie clinging to her skirts.

'Hello, Mabel . . . and hello to you too, Florrie.'

A big grin appeared on the little girl's face, although she pressed herself further behind Mabel as Connie walked in.

'Look here,' said Connie. 'I've got some beautiful flowers for your Aunty Ginnie to take to the church. Aren't they pretty?'

Five-year-old Florrie nodded and looked up at Mabel.

Mabel couldn't help but return the smile, and a happy Florrie ran into the back kitchen shouting for Ginnie.

'Florrie hasn't sat down all morning. Her's that excited I don't know what to do with her. Hope her manages to stay awake at the church else she'll have to be content to go to sleep on the floor.'

Connie laughed. She and Mabel were both the same age, but you wouldn't think so to look at them. Connie felt so much younger, more aligned to Ginnie than her sister. Mabel adhered to the class structure, and she would never have presumed to consider a middle-class young woman among her friends. To Ginnie, it had felt strange, but she hadn't been put off and as a consequence, they had become the best of friends, despite the difference in age and class.

Ginnie let out a squeal of excitement as Connie followed Florrie into the kitchen. The two women hugged each other tightly.

'I can't believe I'm so nervous,' said Ginnie.

Connie placed the flowers on the table. 'You've got no reason to worry. Your Sam is yours forever. I've never seen anyone so besotted as that young man.'

'You think so?'

'I know so.'

'I love him so much, Connie.'

'And it shines out of you. Sam is a very lucky man.'

'Can I get my new frock on now?' interrupted Florrie. 'Please Mummy? Please?'

'You must be very careful not to get it dirty. You must sit like the good girl you can be,' said Mabel.

Ginnie looked surprised. 'Do you know, Florrie, I remember my mother saying the same to me when I was little and wanted to wear my best frock.'

Florrie grinned, no doubt realising that she would have her way.

'Very well then,' said Mabel, 'but if you go and dirty it or rip it, you'll 'ave ter go to our Ginnie's wedding in yer petticoat.'

'Come on, Connie. Let's get changed.'

Connie needed no second invitation.

★ ★ ★

'You look beautiful, Ginnie. I'm so pleased for you. Just think — the rest of your lives will begin from today.'

'You do an' all, Connie.'

Connie was wearing a very pale yellow dress made from organza, that fell to her ankles in soft gathers,

362

another from the back of her wardrobe. She insisted it was plain, not wanting to outshine Ginnie on her special day.

Ginnie stared at herself in the mirror. 'Never liked making plans, you know. Remember how I always felt — that good things were always followed by bad? Do you think it'll happen again?'

Connie stared back. 'No one can say that bad things won't happen, Ginnie. But you're wrong to say they always follow good things. We'd never do anything if that was the case. We have to make the most of the good times, for they make life worth living.'

Ginnie nodded and wiped her eyes.

Florrie's eyes were like saucers when she saw Ginnie in her finery. She hid behind Mabel's legs, peeping out to see what was happening. Connie followed Ginnie down the steep staircase, trying not to tread on Ginnie's dress. 'You look a treat, our Ginnie,' said Mabel.

'You look like a princess, Aunty Ginnie.'

Connie grinned. 'Let me do something with your hair. We'll put it up. It'll make you look taller.'

'I'd like you to do something with this.' Ginnie held out a red ribbon and flushed a similar colour.

'Wait a minute — I recognise that,' said Mabel, taking the ribbon out of Ginnie's hand.

'It's the one you gave me when I went into Haddon Workhouse. I've kept it with all my tranklements — my favourite things — in my carpetbag.'

Mabel put her hands to her face and turned away. Ginnie pulled Mabel and Connie close and the three of them hugged each other.

'Away with yer, our Ginnie. We're never going to get to this 'ere wedding if yer don't get a move on,' sniffed Mabel and scurried to the kitchen to busy her-self.

Ginnie sat in a chair in the parlour — definitely a more peaceful place to be — and Connie slowly brushed her dark hair until it settled in a halo around Ginnie's face, then plaited it and interwove the ribbon through.

'There, Ginnie, how do you like it?' Connie passed her the hand mirror borrowed from Mabel's bedroom.

Ginnie sat in silence.

'Do you like it? I can easily do —'

'Don't say another word. I love it. You've made me look pretty.'

Connie shook her head. 'I've merely made the most of what was already there. You are beautiful and car-ing, and it shines out of you. Don't ever forget that.'

'I'm so glad to have you as a special friend, Connie. Even if you are a toff.'

'I may be a toff, but I'm a rich toff to count you and Sam as friends.'

Mabel breezed back in. 'Come on, you two. Have you got everything?'

The friends nodded tremulously.

'Right then, best get off to the church. Don't want to be running there now, do we?'

Mabel opened the front door and stepped into the street to the happy sounds of their neighbours clapping. She stood to one side as Ginnie and Florrie emerged, followed by Connie. Mabel closed the door, and the party moved along the street through the well-wishers outside the house. The rain that had threatened held off and the sun had decided to show its face.

Connie had never seen Ginnie so happy.

The two church weddings she had attended had

involved the bride arriving in a coach and four with guests dressed in the latest finery. Here, there was no carriage, just well-wishers enjoying the day almost as much as those taking part. The wedding party turned into Queen Street and was greeted by strangers as they passed the shops. Connie watched all that happened, convinced her wealthy friends had no more happiness to show for their fancy weddings than this tiny group of which she was one small part.

The party entered the church to the sound of the organ playing softly. With Mabel on one side of the bride and Florrie the other, the wedding party moved down the aisle. Connie followed behind and was able to see Sam waiting with Peter, his mate from the Parks Department. The minister nodded to Sam, who turned to look at the group. The look on his face made Connie's heart swell with pride. Ginnie had her soulmate back. She would never be alone again.

And there too was Robert, his face a picture when he saw her. He was sitting at the aisle end of the second row, and she almost felt as if she was the one getting married, and she was walking toward her future husband. Suddenly, the face changed, and she was walking towards Matthew Roundswell. She closed her eyes and very nearly fainted.

When she opened them again, it was Robert who was waiting, with bright eyes as she walked towards him.

★ ★ ★

When the service was over Connie caught up with Robert. The light in his eyes told her all she wanted to see, but she needed him to say the words too.

'I think we did Ginnie and Sam proud, didn't we?'

'No doubt about it. Connie, you look . . . amazing. I might have to kiss you again.'

'I'm beginning to enjoy it, although I may need to test you from time to time.'

The party was small in number but included those who had meant something to Ginnie at some point in her life. There were even fewer of Sam's friends. He had been moved around and, with his time overseas, there hadn't been time to make new ones. The only real friend he'd made was Stevo, who had helped him write his letters home. But Stevo had died of the 'flu when he set foot back in England, leaving his wife with a young baby to raise.

Ginnie's friends helped her to uncover the food laid out on the backroom table which had been moved into the parlour in honour of the occasion. There was a lot of giggling going on. It was good to hear their laughter.

Connie's eyes met Robert's, and she trembled all over again, feeling very much like a girl suffering from her first crush. She knew without a shadow of a doubt that she had never loved Matthew. This was what true love felt like.

Ginnie pushed her way through the rest of them and arrived at Connie's side.

'My dear Ginnie, this is Robert Caldwell, a former colleague from work, and . . . a friend.'

Robert took Ginnie's hand in his and gave her a warm smile. 'How do you do, Mrs White, or may I call you Ginnie?'

With the broadest of smiles, Ginnie placed her other hand over the top of his. 'I'm glad to meet yer, Robert. I've heard a bit about you.' She took a sideways mischievous glance at Connie, who had turned bright red at her words. 'Am still getting used to me new name so I mayn't answer if you go calling me Mrs White. It'll take a good while to get used to it. Best call me Ginnie.'

When he laughed out loud, Connie realised he didn't laugh enough. A breath caught in the back of her throat. She struggled to gain control and turned it into a short cough.

'Now then, Connie,' Ginnie quickly turned her back on Robert and gave Connie a huge wink and a nod. 'I'll have to see to my other guests.' She turned back and now her broad smile included Robert too. 'I would very much like to meet you again . . . Robert.'

Connie looked at Robert and raised her eyebrows questioningly.

'Thank you, Ginnie. I should like that very much.'

Ginnie disappeared, leaving the two of them staring at each other.

'I didn't know how you would feel, coming here, Robert,' said Connie after a moment.

'Why not?'

'This is a different world. They haven't got much between them, but they are good working-class people and I've never felt more comfortable anywhere.'

'So you invited me because you didn't think I'd come?'

There was a wry smile on his face, and she couldn't help but smile back. 'Of course not. I invited you because you are good company. Of course, there is always a chance I invited you because I couldn't think of anyone else.' She beamed at him.

How well he got on with the other guests! She had never seen him so relaxed. No one could ever call him snooty or above himself. He could talk to just about anyone and, importantly, they all responded to him, even little Florrie. He got on with Sam very well too. Connie smiled as she watched their faces, each moving from smiling, to serious, to sad and back as they talked, no doubt about the war.

'Connie? Mind if I have a word?' It was Ginnie. Connie grinned; she had a very good idea of what was on her friend's mind.

When they were out of earshot of Robert, Ginnie whispered in her ear. 'I just wanted to tell yer that Robert is a true gentleman.'

Connie flushed. 'I hoped you would like him. I wasn't sure for a long time, but I couldn't get him out of my head.'

'Must get back to me guests, Connie duck. I'll call round soon.'

They hugged each other.

Connie returned to Robert's side and soon after, they said their goodbyes as they left.

'Do you have a carriage coming to take you home?'

'No,' she said a little too quickly. 'I was going to get the tram.'

'It's such a lovely evening. Let us walk to your house. I see enough of trams.'

As they strolled up Moorland Road, she smiled inwardly. He really was a very nice man. Why, oh why hadn't she seen it from the start?

Robert walked her to the front door of Holmorton Lodge. The evening air was still, and there was hardly a sound apart from the songs of the blackbirds and thrushes and the occasional scraping of tram wheels travelling along the main road.

'Thank you for accompanying me, Robert.'

'It was my pleasure, Connie. Think no more of it.' He stared at her. 'You have lovely green eyes, Connie. They remind me of someone. I've thought that ever since we first met —'

'Oh, surely not. I must go inside.' Her heart thumped at the possibility that he might remember where he had seen her green eyes. Their unusual colour would always be a giveaway. 'Mother will be waiting for me. She likes to know I'm home.'

He laughed and shook her hand. Everything about him made him a gentleman.

Then he pulled her into his arms. 'This is becoming a habit, I'm afraid.'

'Some habits are most acceptable. I'm not complaining.'

'If you look at me like that, you'll never get rid of me.'

It was with much reluctance that they drew apart. Her lips tingled from his touch. Connie knew her shining eyes could not keep her feelings a secret.

'Goodnight, Robert.'

She stood on the step and watched him walk away. Then she opened the door and went into the house. Closing the door quietly behind her, she leaned against it.

She still had two important matters to talk to him about. Louisa had said he was a pacifist and estranged from his family and exactly what did he do in the war? The other matter was the white feather she had given to him before they had even met. There was no point in thinking about a relationship as long as it was hanging over her. She couldn't live with the guilt. Would anything be gained by confessing to that? It was a long time ago and it wouldn't necessarily benefit him to know.

She had already suffered from keeping secrets. Could she, should she . . . try to keep another, or risk losing a friendship she was beginning to enjoy very much?

41

July 1919

'A penny for your thoughts?' said Robert.

They had walked to Ford Green and were on their way back to Holmorton Lodge. It was a beautiful day. The sun was hot on Connie's face, and she closed her eyes to concentrate on the warmth permeating her skin.

'Do you mind if I ask if your father still has money problems?'

'We have made some economies. Father is hopeful that our interests will improve now the war is over. I hope he's right. I have also tried to get a job. I have contacted a number of offices without success. There are still too many former soldiers looking, and women who worked in offices during the war. My father insists that if I hadn't been so set on becoming a clippie, I might have gained more useful experience.'

Robert smiled wryly. 'Parents believe they are always right.'

She spied her chance. 'You never talk about your family, Robert. If you don't mind, I would like to know a little about them.'

He became serious and thought for a moment.

'I come from a family with a strong military background. My grandfather was in the Indian Army and was part of the relief force for Lucknow. He eventually became a sergeant major in the Royal Warwickshire

371

Regiment. Naturally, he wanted the same for his sons. My father joined the same regiment and was in the army for twenty-one years before being invalided out after an accident during training. With the money he had saved and his leaving gratuity, he bought a draper's business in Newcastle-under-Lyme.'

Connie was surprised his family were so close. She had assumed they were a distance away, probably because he never spoke of them.

'I have two older brothers, Stanley and Andrew. They're regular soldiers in the Royal Warwickshire's. They both enlisted over ten years ago. I've not seen either of them since 1914, although I do get letters occasionally. They both saw action in and survived the war. My last letter from Andrew was about a year ago, from Egypt.'

'I suppose you get to see your parents regularly, living so close to them, as you do?'

Robert paused for a moment and looked away. Connie put her hand on his shoulder, and as he turned around, she could see the pain on his face.

'My brothers were very much like my father. When I was eleven, I won a scholarship to Newcastle Priory School. That's where I met Matthew. It wasn't the pleasantest place to be, full of boys from privileged families who looked down on me because I was from a non-commissioned officer background and definitely not a member of their club. Matthew and I got on reasonably well and, because we were both day pupils, he'd invite me home to his family for meals, so I got to know Mrs Roundswell.

I passed the entrance exam for Oxford in 1907 and Mother was so pleased. When we told Father, he wanted to know why I was talking of college when

372

I would be joining the army. He had it all planned out. I would join the Royal Warwickshire Regiment. With my academic achievements, I would get a recommendation for officer training. He was so proud of having a potential officer in the family even though he believed it was the sergeants that made the officers what they were.

'Father refused to pay for Oxford so I decided to sit the Civil Service entrance exam and got a position in the War Office. My plan was to save and pay my own way through university. But it was not to be.'

'What did you do there? If you can tell me.'

'It was interesting, if not exciting. I worked with five other clerks, reading and cataloguing reports passing across our desks. It was when I was going through several documents about the suffragettes that I came across your arrest report. At least now I knew the name of the person who threw the stone.'

He grinned at that point.

'Do you see your parents at all?'

'I haven't seen any of my family since July 1914. I refused to join the army when war broke out so Father refused to have anything to do with me. Mother's very loyal and wouldn't go against him.'

Connie's heart skipped a beat. So, Louisa was right about him not going to war.

'We have similar backgrounds, you and I, Robert. Fathers that have plans for us, plans which we are required to fulfil that are not of our choosing.' She couldn't keep the disappointment out of her voice.

He gave her a sharp glance but she didn't trust herself to look at him.

They turned into Sneyd Road and were very nearly home when he spoke again.

'So, you know pretty much everything you need to know about my family . . . a strange lot, aren't we?' Without waiting for an answer, he continued, 'I have told you a lot more than I have shared with anyone else —'

His admission made her feel warm inside, special, to be trusted by this very private man. Was the issue of him not believing in war important now it was all over? She needed to speak to her mother, to help sort out the chaos in her mind.

'More than even Louisa?'

'Yes!' Then he caught the playful glint in her eye and broke into a broad smile.

'Besides, she knows I've met someone else and am waiting until the time is right.'

'You've met someone else?'

He stopped walking and turned her to face him. 'And she's standing in front of me. Oh, Connie, you are annoying and frustrating but you're like no one else I know.'

They arrived at Holmorton Lodge and Connie opened the gate. She turned to look at him and there was no doubt in her mind that he meant every word. As they reached the front door, he pulled her into his arms.

'Connie, I've had feelings for you from the first day I bumped the door against your hand. I might have been in Louisa's company, but it was you I talked about. And now the war is over, my duty towards Louisa has ended.'

'As I told you at the wedding, she led me to believe that you and she were . . . she said some things that were not very nice, about you and your family, Robert. She said she was warning me as a friend.'

'I don't begin to understand how women's minds work, or what her intentions were Connie. Believe me, she knows how I feel about you.'

He bent his head and kissed her lips, slowly, tenderly. And she knew exactly how she felt about him too.

42

August 1919

It was a few days later and Connie was sitting in the morning room looking very serious. Mother walked in followed quickly by Alice with their morning tea. Once Alice had set down the tray and left, Connie turned to her mother.

'Mother, can I tell you something in complete confidence?'

'Mm. It sounds important to you.'

'It is. But I might regret telling you.'

'Why would that be?'

'Because it might affect the way you look at Robert in the future and I don't think I could bear it.'

'You can only discover that if you tell me what's on your mind. And, if it truly matters to you, you won't care what I say.'

Connie swallowed and rubbed her hands against each other.

'Connie, dear, is it so awful? I don't think you could fall for someone you couldn't talk to me about. And if it's your father you're worried about, we can cross that bridge when . . . if it arrives.'

Connie took a deep breath. 'I believe Robert might be a conscientious objector. It's only a possibility.'

The words were little more than a whisper but seemed to reverberate around the room. Her mother's eyes widened as she silently repeated the words back to Connie. 'Now that's nothing like I was expecting.'

'You do see my concern then, Mother?'

To Connie's dismay, her mother nodded seriously. 'I do.'

Connie had thought her mother would tell her that everything would be fine, and she was worrying needlessly.

'Has he told you himself?'

'Well . . . no.'

'So how did you arrive at this conclusion?'

'Matthew's cousin, Louisa, told me. It was just before the Armistice. She told me that she and Robert were together, Robert did not believe in war, his father had disowned him because he wouldn't join the army in 1914 and that he was a conscientious objector.' The words tumbled out.

'He doesn't sound at all like you have described him, or the gentleman we met at the Victoria Hotel. Is he all of those things?'

'That's where the problem lies, Mother. When I asked him about his relationship with Louisa, he categorically stated that there has never been any relationship and he looked upon her as a troublesome sister. When we went for the walk to Ford Green, he told me about his family and that he hasn't seen them since 1914 because he refused to join the army, which agreed with what Louisa said.'

'So, what about the remaining two assertions, dear?'

'I haven't asked him.'

'Don't you think you should?'

'Won't it be hurtful for him to have to explain to me?'

'You are taking the word of an unreliable person who you hardly know and giving it more credence than your own experience and feelings. Robert, in your eyes, is guilty because of what one person claims. I think your best course of action is to ask him directly. It will not be easy, but you can see the mess you have got yourself into by trying to think of all possibilities.'

'But there is one other thing, Mother.' Connie lowered her gaze. 'In 1915, when I helped give out white feathers, I — I gave him one. He wasn't in uniform. It was the only one I'd ever given. His eyes haunted me afterwards — that's why I know it's him.'

'I always expected that irresponsible policy would lead to problems.'

'I think all this evidence points to him really being a conscientious objector and I really don't want him to be!' Connie broke down in tears. 'Oh! What should I do?'

'When are you meeting him again?'

'On Friday.'

'Take these few days to think about what you are going to do. Review what evidence you have. You are an intelligent woman. Whatever Robert's beliefs and principles are he deserves to be heard. I think your best course of action is to ask him outright.'

Connie was not sure. She would have to think about it.

★ ★ ★

Her mother was right. She was either doing Robert a great disservice or had been right about him all along. For the first time in her life, she didn't want to be proved right.

The wind was warm, and the fresh air caught her cheeks. She had arranged to meet Robert near the bandstand in Burslem Park. She wanted to be sure of no interruptions if she was to tackle this most delicate matter.

She spied him at a distance walking purposefully towards her, although she could see by his face that he hadn't yet set eyes on her. She caught the very moment he spotted her, and his face lit up. He looked smart and so handsome. But that wasn't what affected her heart the most; it was the welcome openness of his face.

He reached her and held out his hand. She took it gladly. They strolled, by mutual consent, away from the bandstand towards the edges of the park where they could talk in peace.

'You look charming, today, Connie.' He linked his arm in hers as if it was the right place to be.

'Thank you.'

'I hope your parents are well?'

'They are fine, Robert. I'd like to talk to you about us.'

Now that the time had arrived, she was full of doubt again. When she asked the question she had so far avoided, would his answer change the way she felt about him? Or did it no longer matter now the war was over?

She caught sight of an empty seat tucked in a corner beside some rhododendrons and headed towards it. They sat in silence, each lost in their thoughts. What was he thinking about?

She decided to jump straight in. 'Thank you for telling me about your family, Robert. I do appreciate it, but I have a couple of questions.' She swallowed. She had come this far and she had to go on. 'Would you mind telling me why you didn't join up in 1914?'

Momentarily, he looked startled.

'I never had any intention of joining the army, Connie. I don't believe in killing another human being, no matter what side they are on — it's as simple as that. It's why I didn't join up in 1907 too. There was no point. I couldn't kill anyone.'

Connie closed her eyes. All this time she had been hoping that Louisa had got it wrong and now he had admitted it. 'You were a conscientious objector. So, Louisa was right? She said —'

'Louisa said what? Why, for heaven's sake? When?'

He had lost control of his speech. He jumped up quickly, his back to her. She had never seen him so angry. He was fighting for control, pressing his arms into his sides, his fists clenched.

'Louisa said a lot of things. She told me that you were a conscientious objector, and you didn't believe in war. If fact she implied, you were a coward.' Connie's mouth was dry and she had spoken with difficulty.

He spun around. 'She said what?'

'You heard what I said, Robert. I swear every word is true.'

'I know she can be vindictive and cruel, but to say that when she knew my feelings for you is unbelievable. I will never understand women.' He shook his head despairingly. 'Connie! Listen to me. First of all, Louisa and I are not, and never have been walking out together, as you put it. Secondly, I'm a pacifist. I cannot, and will not, kill a fellow human being. I am not, and never have been, a conscientious objector. Thirdly, I did my duty like everyone else. I served in France and Belgium as a stretcher bearer until I was wounded and invalided home in 1915.'

Connie stared at him conscious that her mouth was

open. 'Oh, Robert, I am so sorry.'

His blue-grey eyes glittered dangerously. 'What hurts the most, Connie, is that I told you Louisa and I were not together in April and still you chose to believe the rest of what she had to say, even though her veracity was at best in doubt and at worst outright lies. Why, for pity's sake didn't you ask me?'

'Well, I am asking you now! You are such a private man, Robert. I knew so little about you. And when I ask, you give me limited information and I jump to the wrong conclusions.'

'You're saying it's my fault?'

Connie shook her head vigorously. 'No . . . no, I'm not accusing you of anything. But if I had known . . .' Her voice trailed off.

He sat down beside her but the distance between them had grown.

He took a deep breath. 'No man has a right to take the life of another, whether or not that be in war or in peacetime.'

'So, you are a conscientious objector.' Even to Connie's ears the words sounded accusatory.

He continued to stare across the park. 'No. A pacifist.'

'What's the difference?'

'It troubles you, does it? You being a suffragette?'

He sounded sarcastic. She supposed she deserved that, but she was not about to exchange one lie for another. She had to be truthful. 'I'm surprised.' She sat quietly, her mind in a sea whirling with questions. She tried a different tack. 'Please, Robert . . . ?'

'Connie . . . are you ashamed of me?' He stood up.

'No. NO. Please, Robert. Oh, dear. I'm not doing this very well, am I?'

381

Someone chose to walk past them at that moment. They remained silent until the person had moved out of earshot.

'Sit down, Robert — please?' She was relieved when he returned to the wooden bench and leaned back, eyes closed.

'Everyone has a right to life, Connie, wherever they are from.'

'I can see that, and I believe you. Truly I do.'

He took a deep breath. 'When I refused to become a soldier, Father and I had a massive row. He never had the opportunity to go to war. I accused him of wanting me to become a soldier so that he could live his life through all of his sons. He accused me of being a coward.'

Connie gasped. 'Oh, Robert. How awful for you both.'

'We were both so angry and said some terrible things. He told me to get out until I joined the army and prove to him that I wasn't a coward.'

Tears were bright in Connie's eyes.

He smiled at her. 'I take after my mother. I like my books and my music, and don't tend to lose my temper. On that occasion, I think there was a bit of Father's bloody-mindedness coming out of me!

'I didn't want to fight. I value life too much for that. But I wasn't a shirker. I wanted to do something to help. When I heard The Quakers were setting up the Friends Ambulance Unit to send overseas to provide medical facilities to the wounded, wherever they came from, I thought, what better way to serve my country, to save lives rather than end them. So that's what I did. I applied to join them more or less straight away, to carry the injured to field hospitals and the like.'

'You're a Quaker?'

'No, you didn't have to be a Quaker to join, many were, but not all. I had to go to Buckinghamshire for training. We did first aid, stretcher drill, basic sanitation and hygiene and marching — lots of marching — so we were fit to do what was needed and then we were shipped to Dunkirk, in mid-October 1914, as part of the British Expeditionary Force.'

Robert's face was still. 'It was soul-destroying, the numbers we had to look after. Hundreds of wounded men in railway sheds, row after row. All we could do was ease their suffering, where we could. One of the worst places was Ypres. You may have heard of it as Wipers?'

She nodded.

'We were there during the evacuation. Helping to get civilians and children out. Huge numbers of Allied soldiers went missing, and there were thousands of German casualties too. We did what we had to do, improving sanitation and water supplies as well as looking after the ill and the wounded.'

'What did your family say when you told them about what you'd done?'

'I never had the chance to tell my parents.'

'Why not?'

'I never went back. I am what I am, Connie. There were lots of ways to play your part without actually fighting.'

'Oh, Robert — I'm so sorry.'

'For what?'

'For even contemplating that you might be . . .' she couldn't say it, not now.

'A coward?'

Connie closed her eyes, wondering how on earth

383

she was going to get out of the pit she had dug herself into. Robert's face looked strained. It had cost him a lot to say the words, she could see that. He was about to rise, taking her silence for . . . she didn't know what. Disappointment? She covered his hands with hers.

'Are you disappointed . . . that I wasn't a soldier? We cared for everyone, Connie, no matter where they came from or who they were.'

She looked deep into his eyes, wanting to assure him of the sincerity of her words. 'I was confused. You are a man of principles, and I respect them. You did your duty. No one can take that away from you.'

'And you won't be upset to be seen with a pacifist?'

'How could I be upset when I'm in the company of a man who saves lives?'

His eyebrows lifted. His eyes grew bright.

'I was only doing a job, just like everybody else. It's all over now. I know about your criminal past and that you were trying to help someone.' He leaned towards her and whispered against her ear. She could tell by his voice that he was smiling. 'You know that I wasn't in the army or any of the forces for that matter and that I too was trying to help people. We were both acting according to our principles even though others might not agree. So, no more secrets?'

How could she argue when he put it like that? But she still had to tell him about the white feather and then all would be straight between them. She wondered if the scarring on his hands had been caused by the war and if that had anything to do with why he was working at the tram depot and not in France.

'But I need to —'

'We will start again. I'm very happy to make your acquaintance, Miss Copeland.' He held out his hand.

She took it. The time for confessing had gone. 'As am I, Mr Caldwell.'

'No more secrets.' He smiled and kissed her.

★ ★ ★

Connie could put off telling her father about Robert no longer. Ginnie and Mother and Alice knew, and it was only a matter of time before he would find out.

It was after lunch and they were relaxing in the drawing room. Her father had his eyes closed, but wasn't asleep.

Connie took a deep breath. 'I have some news for you both. I have met a gentleman, a well-respected gentleman and I would like you both to meet him.'

'Well, this is a pleasant turn-up, I must say. Who is he?' said Father.

'His name is Robert Caldwell and he's twenty-eight years of age. I've never met his family. He thought he should make your acquaintance first, Father.' At least Father's eyebrows suggested he was impressed.

'Where do the family reside?'

'His parents live in Newcastle-under-Lyme, but Robert lives in Tunstall. One of the turnings at the top of the High Street, I believe. He comes from a military family. His father and both of his brothers were in the army. The whole family has given a lot to this country.'

'What did this . . . Robert do during the war?'

'He worked in the War Office in London for a time. A very important job. Of course, he can't talk about it. He came back to Newcastle. I've known him for a while because he was an inspector when I became a clippie.'

'Trams! I raised you for better than that, Constance. He worked in London, you say. Why didn't he join the Colours? Was he handicapped?'

'As I said, he was working in the War Office and was in a medical unit from the start of the war. You will welcome him, won't you, Father? I rather like him. He's kind and helpful, but he's also reflective and doesn't always say a lot. He takes everything in and is the most considerate of men.'

'Not like Matthew Roundswell then? Never did get on with him.'

That was not what Connie remembered. Her father had been taken in by Matthew's background more than anyone.

'No Father, quite the opposite, in fact.'

She turned to her mother and winked. 'I think you'll get on with him fine, too.'

'I do hope so, dear. I want you to have only the best.'

Connie flew across the room and gave her mother a huge hug. 'I don't know if he's the one, Mother. I'm taking my time before I commit to anything. After Matthew I told myself I would never so much as look at another man.'

'A lesson well learned, my dear. Do you not think so too, Edwin?'

'Provided she's not too well learned. Must I remind you she is twenty-four years of age, Agatha and must surely be thinking of her future? She doesn't want to become an old maid, I assume?'

'There are more distressing things in life than becoming an old maid, Father. At least there would be an absence of men believing they can run my life for me.'

'Agatha! Name me any man who would wish to put up with that sort of comment from his future wife?'

'There you go again, Father. All you speak of is how a man feels. But women feel too, and they have a right to talk about it. Goodness, the suffragettes were arguing about this in the first years of this century. Has their fight for the right to vote meant nothing?'

'In my day a woman was brought up to obey and to respect her husband —'

'So, why did you choose me for your wife, Edwin?' her mother interrupted. 'I very much doubt I met your criteria on any count.'

With two sets of eyes boring into his, he made an excuse and left the room. Connie fancied it was because he had lost the battle of words with the two women who shared his life. She giggled and then shared a smile with her mother.

★ ★ ★

Connie had arranged that Robert would come to dinner ten days later to ensure both he and her father would be available. It would be a long wait. She had talked it over with her mother, about whether she was doing the right thing in bringing them together.

Mother had threatened Father with various sanctions if he did not treat their guest in a friendly and sociable manner. As far as Connie was concerned, her whole future depended on a successful outcome, and she would never forgive him if he caused it to have a different result.

When he arrived on that Wednesday evening, Alice answered the door as Connie entered the hall and heard the banter between them.

'Good evening Alice. How's my favourite nurse? You're looking well.'

As Connie approached them, Alice's face turned blood red.

'And you're looking much better too, Mr . . . Robert. Need any more bread?'

Connie was delighted to see Robert's face was tinged pink. As she walked in front of him, Alice gave Connie an exaggerated wink.

Connie coughed and showed him into the drawing room where her mother and father were waiting. Robert looked impeccable in a dark three-piece suit.

'Mother, Father, I would like to introduce Mr Robert Caldwell to you. Mother, you probably remember meeting Robert at the Victoria Hotel when we went out for my birthday?'

'Of course, I do. You came over to us especially, to tell me how well my daughter was doing at the PTC. I am so glad to meet you again. May I call you Robert?'

Connie smiled. Her mother could be relied on to be gracious at all times. If she could keep her father under control the night should be perfect.

Her father held out a hand. 'I'm pleased to make your acquaintance too, young man.'

'Thank you, Mr Copeland. You have a lovely home. And may I say that the garden looks very well.'

How intelligent of Robert to find a subject her father could talk about for hours! She could have hugged him on the spot. Connie even decided that they were getting on sufficiently well together that she could leave them alone for five minutes while she checked with Alice that everything would be on time.

Alice was beaming in the kitchen and pounced on Connie as soon as she walked in.

'He looks very well now he's recovered, Connie,' she said.

'I'm glad you say that, Alice. I think so too.'

Having checked on the timings for the meal, Connie returned to the drawing room. Robert and her father were still talking about gardening as she went in.

'Is everyone comfortable?' she asked.

Robert smiled. He looked utterly relaxed. Her mother looked up as Connie moved towards her. 'Would you like a drink, Mother?' she asked quietly.

'Just a small sherry, dear.'

When Connie returned with a glass in each hand and bent to put them on the small side table, her mother leaned in closely.

'That young man of yours has more intelligence than you give him credit for. He's had your father eating out of his hand since he arrived. I don't think you have anything to worry about.'

It was as they moved forward into the dining room that the conversation moved on to talk about the war.

'What did you do for the war effort, Robert?' asked her father as he opened the door for her mother and accompanied her to the table.

'Sit next to me, Robert. I don't want to spend this evening talking about war. We've spent enough time on it, and now it's over, surely there are more subjects to talk about?' said Mother.

'I spent most of my time in France, and then Belgium.'

Her father nodded knowingly. 'Good man, good man,' he said.

Surprisingly enough, it was her father who changed the subject back to gardening and, for once, Connie didn't complain.

43

October 1919

Father had looked tired and quite flushed.

He sat in his usual chair in the drawing room while Mother sat with her legs resting on a small footstool. Each of them was happy enough to be together without the need for idle chatter. Connie took out the book she was halfway through and settled into the world building in her mind as she read.

Her father suddenly stood up and began pacing about the room.

'Whatever's the matter, Edwin?'

Her mother sounded a bit cantankerous, and Connie gazed at her in surprise. It wasn't like her.

'There is nothing wrong, my dear. I feel the need to stretch my legs.'

'But you look . . . agitated. Are you sure you're quite well?'

'Agatha, I have said there is nothing the matter. Why do you not believe me? Why do I have to repeat myself continually?'

He stormed out of the room, leaving the two women gazing at each other with their mouths open.

'Do you think I should go and speak to him, Mother? I'm sure something is not quite right.'

Her mother shook her head. 'No. Leave him to his own devices. It's probably something and nothing.'

Even so, Mother looked towards the door every few

minutes, appearing unable to rest.

After an hour had passed and her father had not returned, Connie stood up and stretched. 'Would you like a drink of something, Mother?'

'Go on then, I'll take a small sherry.'

'I'll pop into the library to see if Father would like to join us. He should be with us.'

'Very well.'

Mother closed her eyes, quite rested now. Connie went into the library, but he wasn't there. She had not heard him go out, so she ran upstairs to his bedroom. The door was closed. She tapped quietly. 'Father, are you awake?'

There was no reply.

She tapped loudly. 'Father?'

There was still no answer. A moment of panic hit her between the ribs. She gave a final knock on the door and turned the knob. The room was in darkness. 'Father?'

He was lying on the bed, on his back, with his arms grasping his chest.

'Father?'

She put a tentative hand out to touch him, but something held her back. She stared at his chest, waiting for movement. There was none.

Her heart began to thump.

She didn't want to touch him.

She went hot and cold alternately and adrenaline flooded her, as if her body couldn't make up its mind whether to stay or run away. His eyes were closed. Strangely, the lines that had been such a feature in his face for the last year or so were gone.

She reached out again. The coldness of his forehead shocked her fingertips and her hand sprang back without her bidding. The urge to scream was intense. She backed away. When she arrived at the door, she shot through it and sank to the floor, all of her strength gone in that moment.

She screamed.

★ ★ ★

Alice was sent to get the doctor while Connie comforted her mother.

'How long was he lying there, on his own? I never checked — and I told you not to.' Her mother sobbed into Connie's shoulder. 'Perhaps he'd been ill for a while. Why didn't we notice?'

'We can't blame ourselves, Mother. Perhaps all the worries about finance got to him. Perhaps it was all too much for his heart. Maybe the doctor can throw some light on it for us.'

Her mother shook her head. 'We should've watched him more carefully, Connie, and now he's gone.'

'But he's — he was a grown man, Mother. We couldn't have protected him. He had his life to lead.'

Her mother's bottom lip was trembling, her eyes miles away. 'I loved him, Connie. I know I had a go at him from time to time, but I loved him.'

'I know, Mother. And he knew too. I'm sure he tried very hard to look after us. We must take care of each other now.'

She hugged her mother again and walked slowly down the stairs to meet Alice with the doctor.

'Thank you for coming so swiftly, Doctor.'

'I'm sorry it is in difficult circumstances, Miss Copeland. I take it that you and Mrs Copeland are quite well?'

'Yes indeed, although it has been a terrible shock for Mother.'

He nodded. 'Hm. Quite.'

Together they walked up to Father's room, and they entered. She watched him examine her motion-less father.

'I'm afraid it looks like his heart, Miss Copeland. He's in his sixties, isn't he?'

'Yes, sixty-four, Doctor.'

He looked up and beyond her. Connie turned. Her mother stood in the doorway, her face white, with tears streaming down her cheeks.

The doctor made some notes. 'Death was almost certainly due to his heart failing. It was sudden and would have been over very quickly. Did he have any particular health issues? Had he been worried about anything?' asked the doctor.

'We have suffered money problems because of the war, much the same as many others.' Mother thought for a moment. 'I recall he complained of indiges-tion, but it was usually after he had over-indulged himself.'

'There might need to be a post mortem so I can't give you a certificate this evening. Rest assured, Mrs Copeland, Miss Copeland, we will be in touch as soon as we are able.' He raised his hat to both of them and made for the door.

Alice stood there, taking in everything. 'I'll show you out, Doctor,' she murmured. Connie smiled and whispered a thank you, and then turned back to her mother, her mind a complete blank.

★ ★ ★

Unfortunately, Father had to undergo a post mortem, which confirmed what the doctor had suspected — the cause of death was heart disease. The death certificate was issued two days later. Connie got in touch with the funeral parlour, who organised everything.

That was over a week ago, and now the funeral had to be got through. Father was laid out in his coffin in the drawing room, ready for their guests to say their last goodbyes. Her mother had sat by the coffin staring into space for two hours. Connie wondered if she was praying for his soul or in need of his company.

She was surprised at the number in attendance. She hadn't thought he had so many friends. Mother reminded her that, even though he had retired, he was still a highly regarded and respected member of the community. There were also some people from his old business in Manchester who made the journey.

Connie left her mother in the company of some elderly acquaintances and began her duties as the daughter of the house, thanking some thirty guests and receiving their condolences. She couldn't make up her mind whether to see her father one last time before the lid of the coffin was closed forever.

The church service and burial took place in St John's in Burslem. Mother wanted him to be conveyed there with dignity, and so a horse-drawn hearse and open carriage were requested. It was the last thing she could do for him, she said.

When the hearse arrived, Connie returned swiftly to the drawing room. She had a decision to make.

Her father was alone. She had a feeling she might regret not taking one final opportunity to see him, but she wanted to remember him as he was, not as an unseeing person laid out in a box.

She advanced towards the coffin. Closing her eyes, she said a quick prayer. It was now or never. She opened her eyes and looked inside. He looked relaxed, his face unnaturally still and paler then she was expecting. He was dressed very smartly in his best suit as if he was about to attend some important function. Unlike when she had seen him in the bedroom, he now looked at peace. She kissed her fingers and laid them on his chest, not wanting to feel the cold skin of his cheek.

Her mother, with tears in her eyes, walked up to Connie. Connie opened her arms and hugged her, suddenly surprised at how small her mother felt.

'What will we do, Constance? I have never been alone in my life.'

'You're not alone. We will work together and look after each other.'

Alice appeared with their coats, and they made ready as two attendants came in to close the coffin. As her father disappeared from view, Connie and her mother walked slowly out of the drawing room to join their guests at the hearse to await the coffin.

* * *

Connie had gone for a walk when all the guests had departed. She needed fresh air, and Burslem Park was ideal. She had a lot to think about. The day turned to evening and Connie was tired as she opened the door to Holmorton Lodge. The house felt silent, as if it was asleep.

'Mother? Mother . . . I'm home.'

Alice popped her head around the kitchen door. 'Hiya, Connie. How are yer? Would yer like a cup of tea?'

'No, thank you, Alice. Is Mother in her room?'

'No, I do believe she's in the library.' Alice paused. 'We gave him a good send-off, didn't we?'

Connie nodded, surprised how tired she felt.

Alice turned towards the kitchen, then glanced back towards Connie. 'Did you see Robert at the funeral?'

Connie's head perked up. 'Robert?'

'Yes. He come in at the last minute and sat at the back somewhere. When we came out again, he'd gone.'

Connie's heart jumped. He came. He'd only met her father once, but he still came. He'd done it for her. In the throes of all the bleakness, she smiled, and her heart danced a little. She wanted to see him soon. In the meantime, she must comfort her mother.

Connie entered the library. Her mother was sitting in Father's chair, her eyes closed. As Connie approached, she awoke with a start.

'I thought it was time to go through some of your father's papers. I need to know what to expect over the coming months. I think I must have fallen asleep.'

'Why didn't you wait for me? You shouldn't do this on your own. Relax and I'll make a start after dinner.' They sat talking until Alice appeared to say their meal was ready.

★ ★ ★

'Would you like me to make a start getting things together? Might be quicker for you.' Her mother was tired and had nodded off momentarily.

'No, dear. I should be there. We'll do it now.'

They crossed the hallway and entered the library.

It was still Father's library but he would never be physically present in there again. The thought made

Connie catch her breath. She opened the curtains, feeling suddenly claustrophobic. It was a clear night, she could see the moon, which looked unusually bright.

'Sit by the fire, Mother and I'll go through the desk and pass correspondence to you so you can decide what to do with it.'

Alice came in with a tray of tea and placed it down by Mrs Copeland. 'Shall I pour it now?'

'Yes, please do, Alice.'

While Mother made herself comfortable, Connie took to her father's chair at the desk and gazed helplessly at the stacks of paper, pulling out drawer after drawer full of business papers, some of it incomprehensible. She made new piles separating invoices, correspondence and business letters and put anything that looked personal in a separate pile for her mother to read and take a decision on.

After a couple of hours, her head ached, but she continued regardless. She rubbed her eyes and glanced across at her mother, who had fallen asleep despite trying to keep awake. Connie smiled and turned back to the paperwork. It would take days to go through. Some of it seemed foreign to her, and she had to read it two or three times to get the gist of it — or maybe she was tired and needed a break.

The centre drawer of the desk was locked. She looked for the key but couldn't find it. She spied a small brown jug at the bottom of the nearest bookcase and found the key hidden inside. It was small — less than two inches long, gold in colour, although it was scuffed in places as if it had been well used. She inserted the key into the lock in the top drawer of the desk, and it opened smoothly. Surprisingly tidy, it was full of

397

stationery, inks both black and red, pens, two rulers and the like. The other drawers held paper files and ledgers, which Connie put to one side to inspect later.

She then turned to the drawers on the other side of the desk. When she got to the bottom drawer, she discovered a locked cash box. The lock was tiny, and the box sounded empty. She slid the drawer out and turned it upside down, but there was no sign of the key. Damn. She would wait for her mother to wake up and ask her about it.

She carried on working until her neck ached, and her eyes smarted. She was about to end her activities when a note caught her eye. It had been printed, using a typewriter.

Potteries Municipal Bank
Burslem Branch
64 Newcastle Street
Burslem
3rd October 1919

Dear Mr Copeland,
Firstly, can I take the opportunity to thank you for your valuable business over the years and assure you of our continued assistance.
Following the terms of our loan made to you on 1st November 1918, a sum of £283.12s.6d is due for repayment on 31st October 1919. This amount is made up of the principal, accrued interest and stamp duty.
I would be grateful if you could arrange for the necessary funds to be made available for the repayment. At the same time, the bank will formally release to your brokers the share certificates used to secure this loan.

In the unlikely event that you do not have sufficient funds to make this repayment, the bank has the right to sell the aforementioned investments on the open market with deduction of its costs and the outstanding balance of the loan. Any balance remaining from the sale of the investments will, of course, be returned to you as soon as practicable.

If you require any further information or would like to discuss your repayment, then please do make an appointment to see me at your earliest convenience.

Assuring you of our best service at all times.
George Wilson, Esq.
Manager — Burslem Branch

She willed herself to read to the end, unable to believe it. Why had Father borrowed money? It was the first time since Father's death she had thought about their financial position and their futures. She had thought that their situation had improved with their economies. She rose and went to stand by the window looking out on to Sneyd Road. They would be seeing Mr Railsford in a few days, perhaps things would be clear afterwards.

First and foremost, she must sort out her father's finances so that she knew precisely what capital was left and what income they would have. She had parcelled up all the invoices and letters, leaving the personal documents for Mother, and Alice had taken them round to their solicitor's office in Burslem. Tomorrow, they would have the official reading of the will by Mr Railsford and she hoped he would explain their finances.

She would need to take Mother along with her,

as her father's next of kin and principal beneficiary. Thankfully, she had instructed the undertakers to limit the amount spent on the funeral despite Mother's objections. She had a feeling she may need this type of austerity for a long time.

★ ★ ★

The following day they travelled to Burslem on the tram. Connie didn't recognise the driver or conductor. She was glad. Mother was very quiet.

Mr Railsford welcomed them both as they entered his office in the street behind the Queen's Theatre. He had been a solicitor to the family since their move to Stoke-on-Trent; they had complete trust in him. In his late fifties, his blue eyes looked startlingly clear in his wrinkled face, which held a hint of the sadness he was feeling on their behalf. He had been a good friend to Connie's father, and they had met often for a game of cards or some such at the club on High Lane.

'Come in, Mrs Copeland — Miss Copeland and take a seat.'

They did as requested and Mr Railsford eased himself into the large leather chair at the other side of the desk.

'I would like to express my condolences for your loss to both of you.'

Connie swallowed nervously. Seeing Mr Railsford reminded her so much of her father that she could give way to weeping and that would do no good. She dabbed her eyes with a freshly laundered handkerchief. She carried one most days now for she could never tell when she would break down into hysterical tears. They often came when she wasn't prepared.

400

'Firstly, thank you very much for the papers I received the other day. As you know, this is the official reading of the will of the late Mr Edwin James Copeland of Holmorton Lodge, Sneyd Road, Burslem, in the county of Staffordshire.'

He worked through the straightforward will. In essence, Father left all his assets to her mother as expected.

After the reading was complete, there was silence.

'Have you managed to look through the papers I sent to you?' asked Connie.

'Yes, like all estates, there are always several accounts that remain outstanding. I have taken the liberty of asking Mr Copeland's stockbroker for a detailed statement of your late father's investments and the bank for his latest statement.

'As executor, I must ensure that all debts are paid before distributing the estate to the beneficiaries. In this case, I will make arrangements for the local traders to be paid first so your household can continue to function. I will also ensure the loan to the bank is repaid. Once I have all the information, we will need to meet again to finalise the estate.'

'Mr Railsford, can I ask you how much my father confided in you about his finances?' Connie began.

'Mr Copeland and I met regularly to review his portfolio. We discussed investment strategies and other matters.'

Mr Railsford put on his spectacles; he had a schedule of the debts before him and skimmed through the remaining papers, glancing up at Connie occasionally. Connie tried to read his face, but he was used to keeping matters close to his chest, no doubt.

'Might I suggest that we put any further discussions

401

back until we have information from his brokers and bank. But I do have another matter to discuss with you which I feel may be disturbing.'

Connie looked up and waited for him to continue. When he didn't immediately speak, she glanced at her mother, who slid her eyes away. Did she know something they hadn't spoken of?

Her mother started to play with the gloves on her lap. Connie frowned. 'What are you trying to say, Mr Railsford?'

'Just before he died, your father came to see me. He wanted to discuss taking out a mortgage on your house. Unfortunately for him, he passed away before he could do so. I say 'unfortunately for him' advisedly.

'He said he wanted to raise the money to give time for his investments to recover after the war. I advised him to think about it carefully, as it may be better to sell the investments now and cut his losses. It appears he didn't have time to go through with it. The bank has confirmed he made an application which they were considering. I don't know any more at this stage.'

A heartfelt sigh of relief from Connie made him look up from the papers in front of him. 'Share prices have recovered somewhat since the cessation of hostilities, but profits remain low and therefore dividends also remain low. This means your income is considerably below your outgoings and the only way to continue is to sell shares. Once those shares are sold, the income from them ceases and so you have to sell more shares. It is a downward spiral. Do you have any questions at this time, Mrs Copeland . . . Miss Copeland?'

Both women shook their heads despondently.

'Thank you most kindly, Mr Railsford.'

Mother rose to her feet, then put out her hand,

which was taken up immediately and shaken by the solicitor. Connie also gave him her hand. It was a warm, firm handshake which left her in no doubt that he would be as good as his word.

44

November 1919

The second meeting with the solicitor took place on the 26th November which gave Mr Railsford time to amass the information he needed. Advertisements had been placed in the newspaper asking creditors who believed they might have a claim on the estate of Edwin Copeland to come forward. Once again, Constance and her mother presented themselves to Mr Railsford.

'Good afternoon, Mrs Copeland and Miss Copeland.' He nodded to each of them in turn. 'I hope you are keeping well during this most distressing time.'

Once the pleasantries were out of the way, he swiftly got down to business, firstly summarising the financial situation. Holmorton Lodge would be transferred into her mother's name once she had signed the relevant papers.

'The loan I spoke of at our last meeting was repaid on the due date from our client account. At this point, I have to tell you that Mr Copeland's portfolio of investments has been severely diminished over time. A good deal of the investments have been liquidated and the remaining items are mostly valued below what was paid for them.'

He handed them a neatly written piece of paper and continued.

'This is a list of the investments still owned at the time of your husband's passing. The items underlined were sold to clear the loan and other debts to local traders. The figure by the side of each investment is its current value and the column to the right contains its last dividend payment and when that payment was made. I have also analysed your spending from Mr Copeland's account books which I note is considerably reduced compared with the previous years.'

Connie looked at the paper, then Mother and then Mr Railsford. 'Father explained our situation in 1917. When the war ended, he was more optimistic and expected share values to return and our income to be restored.'

'Unfortunately there are too many people in that situation. Your investments still have a reasonable value on paper and would realise that figure if sold and I am pleased to say are increasing in value. However, their current income is well below what you need. Even with your admirable economies you are still spending more than your income. I asked my clerk, Mrs Winter, to investigate whether your investments could return sufficient income if their dividends returned to pre-war levels. It is possible that they could, but the time taken for their recovery could be many years and, in the meantime, you would have to sell investments to cover your expenditure.'

'I think I understand,' said Connie. 'To live, we have to sell investments and then our income drops so we have to sell investments and so on.'

'That is correct, Miss Copeland.'

Mother also nodded. 'So, what are you recommending, Mr Railsford?'

'Your income will not be sufficient to keep Holmorton Lodge going for the foreseeable future. I am advising you to sell Holmorton Lodge at the earliest opportunity.'

'Oh no!' exclaimed Mother. 'I hoped we might be able to keep the house.'

At that moment a clerk entered with a tray of tea. It was a welcome break. The woman laid the tray on the desk. 'Would you like me to pour the tea, Mr Railsford?'

'No, that will be all, Mrs Taylor, thank you.'

As Mrs Taylor turned to leave, Connie spied a bulge straining beneath her waist. It gave Connie an idea.

Mr Railsford continued. 'If you sell Holmorton Lodge and all your current share investments and invest the proceeds in government bonds it would give you sufficient income to rent a reasonable property in Newcastle or Trentham, if you wish to stay in the city, or a larger property out in the country areas around the city. You could live comfortably, but not extravagantly.'

The office fell silent; Connie could just hear the Town Hall clock striking the hour. 'You could even keep your maid, Miss Tucker, on as well. Also, I have not included any income from you, Miss Copeland, as you are currently not in paid employment.'

'Could we keep Holmorton Lodge if I get a job?'

'No. I'm afraid the gap is too great.'

'But a job would help, wouldn't it, Mr Railsford?'

'Of course, Miss Copeland.'

Connie lowered her voice. 'I ask because I noticed Mrs Taylor is expecting. Do you have anyone to replace her, Mr Railsford?'

He looked startled, as if the question had not

occurred to him.

'I don't believe we do.'

'Then I would like to put myself forward for consideration. I have worked in the offices of the WSPU, and I can type and write very well.'

Mr Railsford hesitated so Connie pressed harder. 'You can give me a trial if you wish. You won't be disappointed.'

'Mrs Taylor still has two months' employment with us.'

'I am happy to fit in with Mrs Taylor's circumstances.' She gave him her best smile. 'I could commence at the beginning of January?'

'I would need to discuss the matter with my colleagues, Miss Copeland. Could you send me a letter of application so that we might consider the possibility in some detail? However, before we do that we must get back to the subject of this meeting.'

Connie beamed.

They asked a few more questions, and then Mr Railsford said that they should wait until after Christmas before making up their minds. Their financial position would not alter in such a short period.

'In conclusion, the final value of the estate excluding the house and investments is £474.10s.9d. I will send a cheque to Mr Wilson, at the bank shortly.'

Nothing much was said on the way home. Back in 1917 Father had told them of the situation, but it still was a shock to hear it officially.

They owned Holmorton Lodge and had investments which fell short of what they needed. They would have to sell up.

★ ★ ★

They arrived home, and Connie helped her mother into the house. Her mother was silent. She looked as if she was in a trance. Connie's heart went out to her. She believed that her mother had truly loved her father at one time but, as the years had progressed, that love had been stretched beyond her ability to cope. Connie detected a trace of guilt too. Guilt that she might have supported him more. Her father was a master of keeping most of his troubles to himself. As head of his household, he believed the burden was all his.

They entered the drawing room and Alice appeared almost immediately.

'Did your meeting go well, Mrs Copeland?'

'Not really, Alice. Our worst fears are true. We will have to sell Holmorton Lodge and everything in it. I can't go on . . .' Mother stopped speaking and just stared at the wall. 'Alice, can we all have a cup of tea, please. The three of us need to talk.'

Alice flushed. 'Of course, Mrs Copeland. I shall be back directly.'

When Alice had gone, Connie's mother sat down and said, 'I should tell her as soon as she gets back. She deserves to know straight away.'

Connie felt sick. All this couldn't be happening. Not to her family. Pray to God that Mr Railsford would be able to persuade his colleagues to employ her after Christmas.

A very pale Alice returned with the tea tray. She handed out each cup and saucer with a solemn glance as if she had guessed what was coming.

'As you know, we have had money troubles for several years.' Mother paused and swallowed with difficulty. 'Today we learned just how bad they are. I'm afraid we need to sell Holmorton Lodge after Christmas and to rent somewhere smaller. We should have sufficient funds to live comfortably.'

'What will happen to me?'

'When I say 'we' I mean the three of us. We took you out of the workhouse and out of the workhouse you will stay. If we move to somewhere smaller, we will not need staff to manage it for us. You will have fewer duties to perform and will have the opportunity to build a life for yourself, Alice. We are on our own now and the three of us we will need to look after each other.'

45

December 1919

Plans were being made for Christmas, the first when most of the fighting men who were coming back were safely home. Connie wanted to make it extra special, where friends and family could come together. It would be a time of profound sadness in many homes, with empty chairs that would never be filled.

For Connie, it was bitter-sweet too. It would most likely be their last Christmas at Holmorton Lodge. The sale would be the last economy they could make and the one to make the most impact on all of their lives.

Connie and Alice sat at the kitchen table eating breakfast. Connie had taken a liking to eating breakfast in the kitchen because it was the warmest place in the house and they could eat together as a family.

'Alice, what do we have to do to get ready for Christmas?'

'Oh, Connie, that's an awful big subject. I started back in October with the Christmas cake and puddings. I made 'em when I could get the ingredients. I've ordered a goose from Askeys as usual, and Mr Sutton, the butcher, will save me a nice piece of pork.'

'You seem to have everything under control, what can I do to help?'

Alice shrugged. 'Not very much. If you start everything at the right time, then Christmas does

410

itself. Mrs Williams always told me that and now I see she was right.'

'Do let me know if I can help. Don't think you have to do it all by yourself.'

They took Mother her breakfast in the dining room as usual.

'Good morning Mrs Copeland,' said Alice.

It was too early for everyone to think about name changes, but Connie hoped it would come over time.

'Good morning to you, Alice and to you, Connie. How are you both?'

All three of them sat around the dining table and planned the upcoming festivities. Alice certainly seemed to be warming to her new place in the family. She even asked how much she could spend. Her accounts book covered much more than the daily shopping list. Everything they had spent was noted. She took every invoice that they received and wrote on it what it was for and which of her lists it had come from. It was very rare now that anything was spent that wasn't on one of her lists.

Alice had reluctantly moved down from the attic room to the room next to Connie. She had been cosy in her little room at the top of the house. She had said it seemed wrong to have such a large room all to herself. Connie had laughed, but she had insisted on it, saying that Alice would soon get used to it and wouldn't want to return to her old room. Not surprisingly, no one yet wanted to use or sleep in her father's room. That too would take time.

This would be the first year that Ginnie would have Christmas with Sam and her first as a married woman. Connie had offered to hold the festivities at Holmorton Lodge where there was plenty of room for guests, but Ginnie had other ideas.

'Thank you for offering, Connie, and I appreciate it, but I want to celebrate Christmas at Mabel's house, my house. We've had few things to celebrate since I got to know Mabel again, and now it's time to make the most of us all being together, except for Frank. It'll be difficult enough for Mabel, and I want her to be part of it all.'

'Of course, I didn't think. But can I help in any way?'

'It's very kind of you, but I want you to come and enjoy yourself and let me and our Mabel welcome you as our guest to share our Christmas. Is that selfish of me?'

Connie hugged her. 'No, it isn't. I don't blame you.'

'And you'll bring your mother and Alice, and Robert of course?'

'Yes, it will be Mother's first Christmas on her own.'

'I would like to see yer mother. She's done a lot for me in one way or another.' Ginnie smiled her warmest smile and said softly, 'And I would be very happy to welcome Robert here again. I want ter get to know the man what's found his way into yer heart. I'm so happy, Connie, and I want the same for you. Your face lights up when you talk about him — regardless of what yer mouth says.'

Embarrassed, Connie changed the subject. 'How's Sam coping? Has he had any more nightmares?'

The smile left her face immediately. 'He's so agitated when he wakes up. It's like he's reliving things that happened and he can't get away from it. He screams and then gets upset that he's worrying me. I hug him, but sometimes he thinks he's been captured and fights me off. He worries he might lash out and hurt me. He told me about the lashing out before we got wed, in case I wanted ter change me mind. As if I'd do that!'

She stopped talking and suddenly seemed miles away. Then she started again. 'You know, Connie, I don't think we'll ever find out what truly happened over there. These men what came back — they're all reliving it, every night and day. I sometimes wonder if they'll ever get over it. Sam's told me a bit. As for the rest . . .' She sighed and shook her head.

'He's not the only one, Ginnie and there's many a woman who wouldn't have the stamina to care for someone they haven't had . . . relations with for years, I'm sure.'

'Sam will want for nothing,' said Ginnie and then blushed violently at her words. 'Even our Mabel's taken to him. I knew she would once she got to know him. So, I'd like you to come along so's I can spoil you for once.'

An idea came into Connie's head, and she beamed at Ginnie.

'What are you thinking about now? Summat mad — I can feel it in me water, Connie Copeland.'

'We've all said that it's a very special Christmas — we can have two Christmases! On Christmas Eve, you and Sam will come to my house. Mother and Alice will be pleased to see you. And so will Robert. You can meet all my clippie friends; I'm still in touch with most of them. Then on Christmas Day, you can have your party, and I'll bring Mother, Alice and Robert, and we can meet some of your pottery friends. Go on . . . say yes.'

Connie watched Ginnie's face. It always gave away what she was feeling. Deep thought cleared away to

413

shining eyes. At one time, the thought of meeting Connie's friends in Connie's house would have panicked Ginnie, but not now. How far she had come during these years. Connie smiled. And Ginnie did love Christmas. Yes, it would be good to have two Christmases this year. She would tell Ginnie it would be their last Christmas at Holmorton Lodge when the celebrations were over.

Connie cycled home and recounted the plan to Mother and Alice. They would have a Christmas Eve party at Holmorton Lodge, Christmas lunch at home and then they would all go to Ginnie's house for Christmas evening.

Alice clapped her hands. She'd never had a Christmas when she was a guest, she said.

★ ★ ★

Connie and Robert were attending the Burslem Christmas Ball. She wore the same dress she had worn at Ginnie's wedding. Alice had done her hair in a new style which framed her face and drew attention to her sparkling green eyes. She would tell him tonight that her family's money troubles had not gone away and that they might have to sell their home and move to somewhere smaller.

When she opened the door and stood in front of him, the smile on his face turned from interest to admiration and wonder, and longing. Her heart bumped painfully in her chest, and she had difficulty drawing her breath as might a startled rabbit frozen in the glow of a streetlight.

'You look . . . wonderful, Connie.'

'And you look . . .' Connie put her head on one side

and pondered. '. . . rather handsome, if I might say so?'

'You might say it as often as you like,' he said, grinning like a schoolboy.

They arrived at the ballroom and were soon enfolded into the atmosphere — food followed by dancing — a night of heaven on the arm of a handsome man. A number of ladies without partners sat around the walls of the room. So few young men. Many ladies danced with each other. Sad as it was to say it, there would be many more old maids attending social functions in the future, just as Betty Dean had feared. Connie still hadn't heard from her friend. She hoped the girl wouldn't be lonely this Christmas.

After the meal and a casual discussion on the weather, the depot, books, and other subjects, Connie swallowed. It had to be now or never.

'Robert?'

He had been watching the other guests. He turned and, as his eyes held hers, she was once more caught in their blue-grey light.

'I er . . .' She couldn't speak. No man, not even Matthew, had had this effect on her.

'Miss Copeland, would you like to dance?'

He held out his hand to accompany her to the dance floor, and they danced a slow waltz. It felt good to be in his arms, and she relaxed into the dance, their footsteps matching perfectly. The next dance was a foxtrot. He was about to lead her away, but Connie pleaded with him to stay on the dance floor. It was exhilarating. She had not felt like this in all these years of the war. She couldn't bear to let it go.

Suddenly, Robert began to cough, as if he had difficulty catching his breath. Should she pat his back?

she wondered. Would it be inappropriate?

His face was turning blue. He gasped for air.

'Help us! Please can someone help?' she shouted frantically.

A man shot across the room and knelt beside Robert as he sank to the floor. 'Relax,' he said and glanced up at Connie. 'I'm a doctor. What's his name?'

'Robert. He was fine during the last dance. Then he started coughing and couldn't stop.'

The dancing stopped. People crowded around, watching.

'His lungs,' the man muttered, half to himself.

'What about them?' she whispered. It sounded all too serious.

'I'm fine.' Robert tried to rise, but the coughing started again. Still, he struggled. 'I can sort myself out. You've no reason to worry,' he gasped.

'Robert . . . you're ill. You must . . .'

'No! Leave me alone, and all shall be well.'

He was right. He sat on the floor while someone brought Connie a chair which she collapsed into with relief.

'Here, drink some water,' said the doctor who had rushed to help. He waited a moment for the coughing to ease. 'How are you feeling now, Robert?'

Robert nodded, his face pale with the effort of trying to breathe.

The doctor stood up and looked towards Connie. 'No more dancing tonight, I'm afraid, miss.'

'Thank you.' Connie's eyes smarted. The whole event had shocked her to the core. She had feared he might be in danger.

When his coughing stopped, Connie offered him her arm, and he rose, unsteadily to his feet.

The music had started up again and dancers made their way to the floor.

'Do you feel able to travel, Robert?'

He nodded, but his face told her the opposite.

'You will come to my house for the night. I'll feel happier if I can look after you. I don't want you out on the streets. The weather's too cold and that cough could get a whole lot worse.'

'I couldn't impose on —'

The coughing started up again.

Connie waited for him to recover. 'Are you sure that's just a cough? It sounds rough. I hope it's not something more serious.'

Robert shook his head. 'Don't worry. I'll be fine. It's very kind of you to offer. Are you sure your mother won't mind?'

'She'd be more worried if I sent you away in that state,' Connie retorted.

He smiled, and Connie's heart fluttered uncontrollably.

'Then your kind offer is accepted.'

They caught the tram home and Robert nodded at the conductor, who grinned and couldn't take his eyes off them. Robert would have some explaining to do when he returned to work.

Once home, she settled Robert in the drawing room with a small whisky and rushed to find Alice, who was ironing in the kitchen. They made a bedroom hospitable for her guest.

'Didn't expect you to bring him home with you, Connie. Shall I get him a hot water bottle, an' all?'

Connie bent her head so Alice wouldn't be able to see her blushes. 'Oh, but he's not well. I couldn't possibly send him home in that state, now could I?'

She looked across the bed at Alice's broad grin as she wholeheartedly agreed.

'Then I do believe you should keep to your bed tonight, miss. No walking down to the kitchen. You never know who you might meet.'

'Alice Tucker! Shame on you!'

Connie showed him to the guest bedroom with Alice close behind carrying a tray holding a pot of tea and a plate of biscuits. His coughing had stopped, and the colour had returned to his cheeks.

Connie smiled. 'You're looking better already.'

'How can I not when I am so well looked after?'

Alice flushed red and backed out of the room. It seemed that she too was quite taken with him.

46

December 1919

The last post before Christmas brought wonderful news. It was a letter from Mr Railsford, inviting her to the office to discuss the appointment of an assistant clerk on Monday, 12th January 1920. Connie couldn't believe it. Someone wanted to employ her at last. She would keep it to herself until after the meeting in case it did not go well.

Robert was one of the earliest guests to arrive on Christmas Eve.

'I wanted to be early so that I wouldn't have to face everyone looking at me when I arrived. Now I can settle myself in a corner and no one will know I'm here. I have a feeling I am going to be one of the highlights!'

Connie thought he was joking. Even so, there was probably an element of truth in it too. He wasn't one to push himself forward, preferring to stay in the background.

Robert had made light of the coughing fit and seemed in good spirits, for which Connie was glad. She wanted everyone to have such a wonderful time this year to make up for the heartache suffered by those who had been away and by those who had waited for them to return.

Connie's mother wore a long black dress that glittered in the evening light. She had a plain row of pearls around her neck, and looked quite regal, every inch the lady of the house.

'Robert!' she called. 'How good to see you.'

He strode over to her side immediately. Connie watched him talking to her mother and felt proud. Tall and straight-backed, except when he bent forward to hear her mother speak, he was both attentive and courteous.

She was unable to wipe the smile from her face as she joined them. He turned to look at her and she knew for certain that he would be the only one for her. She loved him. She had been fighting her feelings, scared to commit to him after what Matthew had done to her. Matthew was someone who had paid her some attention and that had somehow blinded her to his faults.

Alice brushed past her and grinned. 'My word, Connie. I've not seen your man looking so handsome. I think you need to make him yours before somebody else does.'

Next to arrive were Jean and Stephen. Marriage had been good for her. She beamed and hurried to give Connie a warm hug. With their arms spread out, they looked each other up and down.

'You're looking gorgeous —'

'— You're looking gorgeous.'

They burst out laughing.

It was true. Jean was positively glowing. Life with Stephen was treating her very well. Gone were all the doubts she'd had about herself as a clippie. She seemed perfectly at home in her new role as Mrs Stephen Adams.

Connie shook hands with Stephen.

'Good evening Stephen. It seems strange to call you that. I hope you are well?'

'As always. And you.'

'Oh, so so, you know how it is. My father passed away in October. Life has been a little . . . difficult.'

'Jean told me, and I'm sorry for your loss.'

His face was full of compassion and brought tears to her eyes. She shook her head and breathed in deeply. 'There are family things to sort out.'

'Have you made any plans for yourself . . . work-wise?'

Their eyes wandered around the room and lighted on Robert talking to her mother, who was sitting on the chair closest to the fire. Judging by the intense look on both their faces, the discussion was serious, and one not meant for an evening of celebrations.

She blushed. 'I have an interview for a position in January. Do excuse me, Stephen — Mother and Robert look far too serious, I must rescue one of them.'

Stephen laughed. 'You do that. My wife doesn't appear to need me either. I'm sure I can find some-one to bore with my stories.'

At that moment, Ginnie and Sam walked in to be greeted by first Alice, and then Connie.

'Happy Christmas to you both. I'm so glad to see you.' She threw her arms around first Ginnie and then Sam.

'Hey duck, you'll 'ave me chokin' ter death.'

Dear old Sam! The same lovely man as always, and still only nineteen or so. Watching him now, it was difficult to imagine him crying out at night with nightmares. She took both of them by the hand and continued towards her mother and Robert.

Robert immediately stood up and offered his hand to Sam and then turned to Ginnie. 'You are looking particularly well, if I may say so, Ginnie. Married life seems to suit many of Connie's friends.'

Ginnie glowed. 'You should try it for yourself then,' she said, bold as brass.

How daring of Ginnie! Connie blushed furiously. She could feel Robert's eyes on her but couldn't bring herself to look at him. He might be able to read the longing in her eyes. She muttered some excuse and made her way around her other guests.

Fred Parsons walked in, gazing around him. He was alone, which surprised her. He had been one of the more sociable of the men working at the PTC. What a pity Betty hadn't fallen for him instead of Joe. Still, he looked happy enough.

'Hiya duck. Yer never told me yer lived in a palace, Connie. I'd 'ave come chasing after yer if I'd have knowed that.'

'Get away with yer, Fred,' she said, hands on hips, in her best Potteries accent. Fred guffawed, delighted.

Bert arrived with a woman on his arm. Proudly, he introduced her as 'one of the neighbours what kept an eye on me', but Connie could see that there was rather more to it than that.

The woman burst out laughing. 'He dunner actually call me that, although you'd think I never 'ad a name if you listen to 'im. I'm Peggy and I am one of his neighbours, for my sins.'

'I'm very happy to meet you, Peggy.'

'Big house what you've got, Connie,' said Peggy with admiration. 'Lots of cleaning and —'

'Dunner go on, woman. Her dunner do it her'sen.'

'You'll be surprised, Bert,' Connie returned, delighted with the woman who would attempt to look after Bert.

Emily Norton remained in the background. Never a talkative woman, she looked sombre but well turned out. Maybe she could ask Fred to look after her for the evening.

From a spot near the door to the garden, Connie watched her guests. They had all had their difficulties and were now witnessing the beginnings of a new life. Her mind travelled to poor Betty. She was disappointed that she still hadn't written. Who would have thought that happy, sociable Betty would have ended up in such a predicament? In years gone by, Connie would have thought that she had brought it on herself, and maybe there was an element of that. But of late, she had not been so quick to jump to conclusions. Betty might have had any number of reasons for doing what she did. Somewhere, she was out there, hopefully, and one day soon, they might meet again in better circumstances.

'Where are you, Connie? You look miles away.'

It was Stephen again.

'Oh, I was wishing Betty was here. I hate to think of her out there without her friends.'

He rubbed his chin. 'Mm, she was always so full of life. She leaves a bit of a hole. I hope young Joe is to be relied on. Poor girl. It's a nice place you've got here. Not quite the place I'd imagined a former clippie would live.'

Everyone seemed to be making her blush tonight. Maybe she was feeling particularly sensitive. 'I didn't want you to think I was only playing at work, Stephen. I really wanted to do something I enjoyed.'

'Even after yer brush with them lads?'

'I learned to stay on my toes after that. But yes, I liked it even after the brawl. I would have stayed if it weren't for the soldiers coming home.'

Stephen nodded. 'I'll 'ave ter give it to yer, Connie, you clippies did a fine job. All of yer were a credit to the PTC.'

Back came the flushes. Her eyes wandered around the room and rested on Jean. 'Your wife looks very happy.'

'Jean's doing fine. Her and mother get on well. If Mother had set her a housewife test, like she did with you clippies, she'd 'ave passed, no messing.'

He lowered his voice. 'You and Robert see a lot of each other. He thinks the world of yer. He's changed since he's got ter know yer. Happier, more relaxed. Do anything for you, he would.'

The room had grown dimmer, and she hoped he didn't notice the blood rush into her face.

'You do know that, don't yer?' he said softly. When she said nothing, he continued. 'You could do a lot worse. He's one of the bravest men I know.'

The more she found out about Robert Caldwell, the more surprised she became.

'He's been very kind to me,' she said lamely. 'When he was ill . . .' A lump came into her throat and she couldn't go on.

'I wouldn't be 'ere if it weren't for 'im.' Stephen's voice had grown husky, and he blinked a couple of times. 'Did he tell yer as we met when I was in the army?'

'No?'

'We were at a place called Hill 60 near to Ypres. It was the only high ground around, and both the Huns and us wanted it. My squad had come out of the trenches on a recce to see what the Germans were up to. I got shot in me leg, well knee, actually. That's how

I came by me walking stick. I went down. Must've blacked out with the pain. When I came to, Robert was there, and he carried me back to the lines. We were under fire all the time, I was told — I was out of it, but he came and got me anyroad.'

To say she was shocked didn't quite do her reaction justice. She put her hand over her mouth to stop herself from crying out loud.

'And 'e had his problems an 'all. After he took me to the Casualty Clearing Station, he went back out to look for more wounded. The following day, he came under a gas attack. Left him with damaged lungs. That's why 'e was sent home. He told me that he wasn't going to go back to work in London and he was going to return to Stoke. I told him that if he needed a job, to come to me and I'd see him right. He's a bright man, he could have done more with himself.'

Stephen's eyes were moist as he recalled that time. 'As I said, Connie, he's one of the best. You won't go far wrong with him. But if you don't think he's the one for you, let him go. He doesn't deserve to be hurt or messed about.'

'Why are you telling me all this?'

'I told him I wouldn't tell anybody who didn't need to know. He still suffers badly with his chest — some days are worse than others. And you've seen the scarring on his hands. It's all from the gas. I told you because I think you need to know. People can't understand the likes of Robert for not wanting to fight. But he understood more than most that the casualties over there needed help an' all, and he wanted to give it. He was a fighter, but his fight was in trying to keep people alive, and he saved a good number out there.'

'Oh, Stephen. Thank you for telling me. He hasn't

said much about the war.'

'I shouldn't have said nowt. I've gone and got you all upset, and you've got yer guests to look after. I thought he might 'ave said summat to yer be now.'

'He told me he wasn't in the army and I'm afraid I jumped to conclusions at first. The wrong conclusions.'

'He doesn't say much about those days, and it's not something you want to come between you. Get him to tell yer. You'll not regret it.' He patted her shoulder. 'Anyroad, this is supposed to be a party, isn't it? I must spend some time with my wife. Look, I've told yer all yer need to know, duckie. The rest's up to you.'

With a smile, he left her alone.

She rushed up to her bedroom before anyone could see her, closed the door and leaned back against it. She knew now why Jean had been so taken with Stephen. She had also witnessed at first hand the closeness between him and Robert. She ached inside. Had anyone come back home from the war without scars, physical or mental, or both?

She stared long and hard in the mirror, feeling years older than the girl on the trams of only a year ago. She had been so wrong about Robert. And she'd dared to give him a white feather! Sadness and sheer helplessness lay heavy on her shoulders. How could she possibly face him now without giving way to tears for what he had been through. But she must. She couldn't hide up here; she had guests to entertain.

She pinched her pale cheeks to bring back some much-needed colour, tidied a loose lock of auburn hair and headed for the door. She could allow no one to see her so troubled. Walking slowly down the stairs, she could hear the babble of voices coming from the drawing room. She stopped on the bottom stair. Tonight, she too would have to show bravery and play her part.

She painted a smile on her face, opened the door and re-joined the party as if nothing had happened. Robert had a quizzical look on his face. He had noted her absence, but she quickly turned his mind to other things, and he never questioned her.

By the end of the evening, her mind was made up. It was about time that everything was in the open — all the secrets and the pain associated with them. If their relationship was strong, any problems could be over-come.

Going to sleep that night was difficult. She'd had plenty of time to think over matters. She would suggest a walk after lunch, ask him what he had done in the war, and she would tell him about the white feather. If all went well, Ginnie would have four guests that evening. And if it didn't, there would be only three, Connie, her mother and Alice, and she would have to put on a brave face for Ginnie's sake.

47

December 1919

Last night, her plan had sounded good, but in the cold, harsh light of day, Connie had come to realise just how much she would miss him if it all went badly. She knew now the kind of man Robert had been — was still. She would be heartbroken if he put an end to their friendship when truly, she wanted so much more.

Robert arrived at eleven o'clock. Her mother greeted him and wished him the compliments of the season. Connie was glad her mother was there, for it appeared that a cat had got hold of her tongue. He must have known something was amiss.

After a very pleasant and delicious Christmas dinner, Connie knew she could put it off no longer. 'Mother dear, would you excuse us if we go for a walk?'

Her mother looked, surprised, but inclined her head. 'Of course, you two go for your stroll and Alice can keep me company.'

Alice smiled. 'Of course, Mrs Copeland.'

'Alice, don't forget that Ginnie invited you too this afternoon.'

Alice beamed. 'No, Connie, I 'aven't forgot.'

Connie and Robert walked along Sneyd Road, heading towards Moorland Road and the park.

Once outside, Connie breathed deeply. There were some people out, taking in the crisp December air.

'You must be missing your father, Connie. Christmas without a loved one is never easy,' said Robert.

'It's been hard. Mother has been depressed. I'm glad she has Alice as a companion and not just a maid. Alice is capable of so much more.'

'I agree. She's a lovely girl.'

They continued walking until she couldn't put off what she needed to say any longer. 'I . . . I wanted to talk to you about something that has been on my mind for a long time.'

He frowned. 'That sounds ominous. Do I need a seat or should we wait until we return?'

She wanted to laugh but couldn't. 'Could you tell me a little about what you did in the war? I want to understand something of what you went through, and I promise I'll never ask you again.'

His face clouded over. 'What would you like to know?'

'I know that you worked for the War Office in London . . . for obvious reasons . . .'

'Yes, I did for nearly seven years and I intended to make a career of it.'

'Where did you meet Stephen?'

'I suppose he told you?'

'Don't be angry; he thought I should know.'

'Really? I asked him to keep it to himself. I'll speak to him later.'

'Robert, maybe he told me because you couldn't. You'd made him promise only to tell someone when it was important. He thought I should know. He said that you brought him back from no man's land under fire and that he knew nothing about it until later.'

Robert frowned. 'Like I said, we did what we had to.'

429

'How did you become friends?'

'Hm?'

It was evident that his mind had wandered. 'You and Stephen? How did you meet him again?'

'The following day I was out on a mission and got caught up in some fighting and I was gassed. Another stretcher-bearer managed to get me back to safety. It left me with weak lungs and . . . I owe him my life. We had improvised masks after hearing that gas had been used in the area. But they only helped a little. I felt as if I was choking to death, and I couldn't see a damn thing. I was led to the Casualty Clearing Station. When I woke up, I heard a familiar voice; it was Stephen. He was still waiting to be transferred to the Field Hospital.'

He lifted his hands and looked at the scars made by the burning gas. 'I'm told the problems might never go away.'

'How brave you must have been.'

'You find out a lot about a person when you're in a hospital with nothing else to do. Stephen came over as a good, reliable man and, at any other time, I would have been pleased to count him as a friend. As it was, I never expected to see him again. But I ended up in the next bed to him before they shipped me back to England. We talked a lot about our jobs. I told him I didn't know if I could go back to working in the office in London and that I might try something different. At that time, we didn't know whether we would go back to war. As it was, we were both invalided back home. I spent nine weeks in the hospital. But while we were in the Clearing Station, he said that if I fancied going back to The Potteries, he would find me a job. And he was as good as his word. It was good to be back, but I think all of us left a part of ourselves over there.'

'I don't know what to say.' Tears made her eyes smart.

'It's not something I talk about.'

He pulled her towards him and held her tight. 'It's all in the past now. I'm feeling a lot better, although there are times when I feel better than others — you know, chest pain, palpitations, shortness of breath, especially if I get an infection. That's why I was so ill when I caught the 'flu. But I'm all right.'

The big moment had arrived. Time to tell him about the white feather. If he decided to walk away, she would be devastated. But one thing she knew; she couldn't keep it from him a moment longer.

She took a deep breath. 'Robert, I have something of the most import to tell you. And once you know, you might never want to set eyes on me again. And if that happens, I want you to know that I will be truly sorry.'

He looked deep into her eyes as if trying to work out what she was about to say. Those blue-grey eyes that had haunted her ever since she had given him the white feather were full of anxiety at her seriousness. How badly she had wronged him. She wanted him to know she meant every word of what she was about to tell him. When she spoke, her voice wobbled slightly, but it was strong.

'Robert, do you remember, way back in 1915, when the suffragettes were giving out white feathers to men who weren't in uniform?'

His head went back, and a deep frown creased his brow. 'Yes, they ran a campaign. Quite effective at getting young men to enlist too, as I recall. They'd turn up anywhere.'

'And, I was a suffragette . . .'

'Yes, you told me . . . are you trying to tell me that you were involved in giving them out?'

She nodded and looked at the floor. 'I feel so terrible about it. I've come to appreciate that you can't take things for granted and what your eyes see isn't always the truth.'

'If we'd only known then what we know now,' he said. He smiled. 'And it's been on your conscience all this time?'

Again, she nodded. 'But it's much worse, Robert.' Her voice became louder, more wobbly, tearful. 'I can hardly bring myself to tell you. It was me . . . me.'

'What do you mean?' The lightness had gone from his eyes. 'Tell me, Connie.'

'It was me. I believe I gave you the white feather.' She stood with her shoulders back, her eyes aching with the pain of four years of carrying this burden.

'You?' His eyes widened. 'I knew I'd seen those green eyes of yours before.'

'You remember then? Did I hurt you terribly, Robert?'

He walked away from her, and she held her breath. He turned slowly. 'You gave me a white feather because I wasn't in the army? I'd been invalided out by that stage.'

'I saw the look on your face. It's never left me. I've wanted to tell you so many times, but I couldn't bring myself to do it.' She hung her head.

It was quiet for a moment. Then she heard his footsteps close in and she lifted her head. He didn't look angry; he looked sad.

Her legs wobbled and almost gave way. He held her

to stop her from falling. The relief of telling him hit her powerfully. The rest was up to him.

His hand linked through hers. Seeing the scars the war had left behind only added to her misery. She lifted his hand to her lips and kissed it gently. 'Robert, will you accept my humble and heartfelt apologies?'

'I could forgive you for anything, my darling. But I'm afraid I too must ask for forgiveness. I wasn't entirely honest with you about my relationship with Matthew. I told you we went to the same school and were friends. I was a scholarship pupil and was looked down on by the privileged boys. Matthew treated me equally as badly in his own way. He constantly brought up my lack of rich parents, treated me as a poor relation who should be pitied, and his personal servant. His mother was even worse.

'Once we left school, we lost touch. I was working in London and he went to university and then into the family business in The Potteries. So I was surprised to receive an invitation from Matthew to attend his wedding to a Miss Constance Copeland. He didn't want me there as his friend; he wanted to show off his beautiful new bride and have a grand wedding to show how rich and important his family were.

'I didn't go. I wasn't in the mood for another spell of Matthew's friendship. But the name on the invitation reminded me of a Miss Constance Copeland who had thrown the stone through my office window.

'I didn't care whether the Constance Copeland on the invitation and the Constance Copeland that I created a surveillance file for were the same person. To me, she wasn't a person at all. She was a way I could get my revenge on Matthew for all the trouble and heartache he'd caused during my school years.

I sent my apologies for not being able to attend to Mrs Roundswell and I included in that letter a note to Matthew informing him that a Miss Constance Copeland had a criminal record and had been jailed in Holloway Prison in 1913. I knew full well that Matthew and his mother would do everything in their power to find out the full story. His mother wouldn't allow the wedding to go ahead whilst there was any hint of her reputation in society being tarnished, or any breath of scandal relating to Matthew.

'It seemed the right thing to do at the time and I didn't regret it. When I heard he had called off the wedding in such a dramatic fashion I did derive a little satisfaction. I swear I only wanted to disrupt the wedding, Connie, but once we set something in motion, we can't always control its eventual outcome.

'When Louisa Pendleton told me that you were the Constance Copeland her cousin was going to marry, I realised how terribly I must have hurt you.'

Connie stared at him, lost for words. He had deliberately set out to ensure the wedding would not take place and, by his own words, had derived some satisfaction out of it. It wasn't the Robert that she had come to know and respect, and love.

'Say something, Connie. I know I must have disappointed you.'

She watched his face. Saw the pleading in his blue-grey eyes. Instead of thinking about what he had done, she considered the small boy who must have felt so much pain at the hands of a society he had been forced into. He had told Matthew the truth. He couldn't be held responsible for what Matthew had done with the information. Was Robert's behaviour any worse than her own?

'Robert, I can see the pain this whole sorry episode has caused you. Who am I to cast judgement on you? I must have hurt you as much as you have wronged me.'

'Strangely enough, we were both doing what we felt was right, but different paths, and different choices. The thing is, if we hadn't both done what we did, we might never have met and if we had met it might have been too late. But of one thing I'm sure, Connie, we were meant to meet.'

'I can't criticise you, Robert, even though it was a bad time of my life. I had already begun to think that Matthew was not the right person for me. I have something else to tell you.'

'What, more secrets?'

'Not really. You already know part of it.'

She managed a smile.

'What do you mean? You intrigue me.'

'We are still plagued with money problems, Robert. Those . . . money problems I mentioned to you never really went away. I . . . we . . . Mother and I have been advised to sell our house next year and to move to somewhere much smaller where our income from investments will allow us to live comfortably. The good news is that I believe I have found a job, in an office in Burslem. I have a meeting with them after Christmas. I know it's not much, but it will help.'

His eyes were bright, his smile compassionate.

'Dearest Connie, I am so very sad for you and your mother. It must have come as a terrible shock. I will help in any way I can.'

'Oh, Robert, that is so kind of you.'

He frowned. 'Did you think, for one moment, that I would let it come between us?'

She stared at him long and hard, recognising the truth of what he said, laid bare on his face.

'No, I didn't, Robert,' and she realised what she said was true.

She gave him her brightest smile. 'Does that mean that you will still be accompanying Mother, Alice and me to Ginnie's later?'

'If you would allow me to, I should be honoured.'

★ ★ ★

Most things were still rationed, but Christmas Day 1919 was rich in so many ways.

Connie felt the love and affection in Mabel's house encircle her as she entered with Robert, Alice and Mother. It was Mabel's little girl, Florrie, who saw them first and came running. Connie went down on her knees and gave her the biggest of hugs. Then Florrie noticed Robert and squirmed to hide behind Connie, peeping out when she dared.

He smiled. 'Hello, Florrie. Connie here tells me you're five now. That's quite an age, isn't it?'

With a finger in her mouth, Florrie nodded but didn't speak.

'Hiya you two.' Ginnie grinned. The friends hugged each other tightly. Ginnie hugged Connie and then Alice. 'Thank you for coming, Mrs Copeland.'

'Good evening, Ginnie. How lovely to see you in your own home. I'm so pleased for you.'

'It's good to see you an' all, Robert.'

Florrie touched Robert's leg with a finger. 'Will you play with me?' She had a red ball in her hands.

Unable to say no, Robert gave a wry smile and followed Florrie to the door into the kitchen and then towards the yard.

Ginnie called after them. 'Don't let her keep you outside, Robert. You won't see much in the dark and she'll 'ave yer playing as long as you'll put up with it.'

She turned shining eyes to Connie. 'I'm so glad Robert came too. Everybody, listen! This 'ere's Connie Copeland, my very best friend. I'll introduce her to yer in a minute.'

They both turned to each other and, at the same time, said, 'I've got something to tell you.'

Again, they laughed and, judging by the happiness on both their faces, it was easy to guess that, this time, the news on both sides would be welcomed.

Ginnie started to reel off some names: Elsie, who Ginnie knew from Chamberlain's Pottery where she had worked as a mouldrunner and whose husband had died in the war; Ada, who had shared a bed with Ginnie in the workhouse and had got herself a job in the decorating end at Royal Edwards Pottery; and Selina, who had become Ginnie's teacher at Royal Edwards Pottery.

Ginnie returned to her guests, and Connie went out to look for Robert. He was still throwing the ball to Florrie in the tiny back yard. He was smiling, and Connie had never seen him look so well.

Florrie grinned when she saw Connie. 'Look at me! I can catch the ball, Aunty Connie.'

'I think we are about to have tea, Florrie. You must let Robert come in for something to eat.'

Florrie looked up at Robert. 'Are you hungry?'

He grinned down at her earnest face. 'I think we should go in and have a look, don't you?'

Florrie grabbed his hand and led him towards the back door leaving Connie to follow. She chuckled as Robert walked past her, with his new best friend, raising an eyebrow as he went. She had the idea that he was rather pleased.

He looked at her a few times over tea as if expecting her to say something. In the end, he said, 'Have you spoken about us to Ginnie?'

'Just in passing. Do you want me to tell her?'

Robert whispered in her ear. 'I don't think I will quite believe it until people know.'

It surprised her that he sounded less confident than usual. She studied his face. 'Why, Inspector Caldwell, do I detect a trace of concern in your manner? I thought that was the prerogative of ladies!'

His face turned bright red, and it delighted her.

'Ginnie has a lot to do in managing her first gathering. We'll tell her before we leave.'

'Hey up, Connie duck. At ol' rate?'

Connie turned and threw her arms around Sam, startling him. 'Sam! How lovely to see you. It seems ages.'

'How do, Robert. At ol' rate?'

'Not so bad.'

The two men shook hands and started chatting straight away, giving Connie a chance to catch up with Ginnie. She was in the small scullery with Mabel. Connie could hear their chatter and headed towards them.

'And how are you, Mabel?'

'Am ol' rate, duckie,' she said with half a smile.

'And what about your gentleman friend. From the Co-op, isn't he?' said Connie, pleased she'd remembered.

Mabel sniffed. 'An 'e can go back ter the Co-op an' all, for all I care.'

438

'Oh, dear!'

'Come on, Connie. I need to talk to you.' Ginnie pulled Connie away and dragged her to the stairs. 'We'll talk in the bedroom.'

At the top of the stairs, Ginnie pulled her into her bedroom. It felt quite personal, with a few clothes hanging over the back of the chair, washing items on the cupboard and Ginnie's carpetbag, where she kept her special things, in the corner.

Ginnie thrust herself onto the bed, and Connie followed.

'I have to say that married life is treating you very well, Ginnie White.'

Ginnie rubbed her hands together. 'It still sounds mighty strange thinking of meself as Ginnie White and not Ginnie Jones.'

'I would imagine so. You're developing into a different person, Ginnie. You have so much more confidence now.'

'It's all down to Sam. I had special people in my life, but they were always coming and going. I know Sam was away a lot, but he was always there for me. Looking out for me.'

'And you for him too, Ginnie. Don't forget that.'

They sat together, holding hands.

'I wanted you ter be the first ter know, Connie. I think I'm expecting.'

'Why Ginnie — that's wonderful news. I'm so pleased for you and Sam.'

Connie blinked, and tears came to her eyes. She couldn't believe she could be so emotional. Maybe it was the relief of getting her own life in order after all this time.

More hugs followed. Well, hugs and kisses.

'I've told our Mabel. But no one else till I'm sure. I've missed two of my monthlies, so I'm pretty sure. But I told Sam as we'd wait a little bit longer before we tell everyone — just in case anything goes wrong. Sam's all for telling everyone he speaks to, so I don't know how long the secret'll last. We must think about where we're going to live. It'll be a bit crowded to stay here. But Mabel says we can stay as long as it takes.'

Connie felt the tears welling up again as she thought of the pleasure that Sam would get out of knowing he was going to be a dad. His own father had gone back to sea when his mother died and had left him at the workhouse where he met Ginnie. She couldn't think of a better person to become a father. 'When are you due?' She did a quick calculation. 'Around June?'

'S'spect so. And now all we have to do is get you married off an' all.'

Connie got the impression that her friend was observing her when she said it, provocatively, to see if she could raise a reaction. Ginnie wasn't disappointed.

Judging by the tightness of her skin, Connie's face must have turned a brilliant red. Much to her annoyance, Ginnie wore her 'I told you so' look.

'Ever since Stephen and Jean's wedding, you know Robert and I have been getting closer. I believe Louisa Pendleton was jealous and led me down the wrong path with her half-truths, and I was happy to follow because of what I thought I knew about him and I blew that damn white feather out of all proportion. Turns out we both had secrets to hide. This afternoon, I told him what I'd done, and he confessed to telling Matthew about my prison sentence knowing full well he would stop the wedding. He had his reasons.'

'How brave you are. I dunner think as I could have done that.'

'You could, Ginnie. You couldn't have lived with yourself if you didn't. Anyway, the past is over and we are going to hide nothing from each other in the future, and that's how it should be. We discovered that we both have principles that make us who we are, and, in the end, it drew us together. He's made an excellent impression on Mother. I believe he's the one, Ginnie. What do you think of him?'

Ginnie held her gaze, clear and without guile. 'He seems to be a wonderful man, Connie. Truly special, just like my Sam. He thinks the world of you.'

'Is that what he said?'

'No, his mouth's said nothing, but his face says everything. When he looks at you . . . I tell you, Connie, if he ain't in love with yer now, he's very close to it.'

'I think we are falling in love. I hope so, because I've fallen in love with him.'

'Well, thank the Lord for that and about time you two got together, if you ask me.'

They laughed — light, girlish laughter.

When they went back downstairs, Robert was the first person Connie saw.

She walked towards him, and the look in his eyes warmed her heart. Throughout the evening she watched him, how he was with Ginnie's family and friends. How he listened, joined in the party games, and how he gave five-year-old Florrie the time of day whenever she wanted it. Nothing was too much trouble.

She thought back to the white feather that had stalked her for so long. It just didn't matter anymore.

441

He was the kindest, most wonderful man she had met.

She couldn't think of a better man to fall in love with.

He drew her close to him. She patted his arm and gave a deep sigh of complete and utter satisfaction.

'I gather Ginnie approves?'

'Most definitely. She has nothing but praise for you.'

'Quite right too,' he murmured into her hair.

What a strange world it had become since the family had left Manchester and built a new life in The Potteries. Her life had evolved out of her principles — her conviction that a woman was any man's equal. After being let down so badly by Matthew she had followed her own advice and taken charge. Who would have thought that her brief chat with a clippie on a tram could have changed her life so completely?

She had learned that the happiest people in this world were not always the richest and that true friendship was priceless. If it hadn't been for Ginnie and Sam she might never have considered working on the trams, would never have met the friends who had become important to her. Would never have met Robert.

Of course, there had been heartbreak too. Regardless of their money problems, she had loved her father. He may not have been fighting, but she was convinced the war had taken him as surely as any other life that had been lost in these most destructive of times. She had felt him close to her, not quite ready to leave her and at night her heart cried out for him.

Betty chose that moment to enter her mind. Young Betty, so full of life and possibly destroyed by her fear that the war had taken away her chances of happiness with a man. How could anyone not in that position know how it felt? But Connie did, and she yearned to put her arms around her friend. The war had damaged so many people — Sam with his terrible nightmares and Ginnie trying her best to help him to feel safe, Robert with his scars sitting deep within as well as those on his hands, a constant reminder.

On the whole, Connie believed she was grateful she hadn't known so many people lost during the war. But all wars have consequences for those who come back, and those who wait to receive them.

So, she was thankful. Regardless of the anguish and upset her association with the suffragettes had caused, it had helped her become the woman she was today. It had brought her to this place, and to this man.

'You're wandering off again, Connie.'

'Mmm,' she said smiling at him. 'But I'll never be far away from you.'

'Happy Christmas, darling,' he whispered.

She rested her hands on his cheeks and brought his face towards her. When she kissed him, it was as a woman who knew what she wanted.

A letter from Lynn

Lots of authors I have spoken to assured me that I am not alone in thinking the second book to be published is a difficult one. Authors spend a great deal of time titivating their first book to within an inch of its life to make it perfect for their readers. Along comes the second book and it is panic stations — writing book two while editing book one for publication, followed by the launch and publicity — and all the while, the clock is ticking for book two.

During the time I was working on the first book, *The Girl from the Workhouse*, one of the characters, Connie, insisted that she had her own story to tell and so I gave her the opportunity to speak in *Wartime with the Tram Girls*. Needless to say, she wasn't satisfied and has lots more to tell you. She has learned a lot during these pages, not least that she has a habit of jumping to conclusions and that there are many aspects to wealth and not all of them involve money. We shall have to wait and see.

I do hope you have enjoyed catching up with Connie, Ginnie and Sam and their new friends in *Wartime with the Tram Girls*. I have very much enjoyed writing this second book in my series set in the Staffordshire Potteries and am indebted to Keshini Naidoo and Lindsey Mooney for giving me the opportunity to meet them again.

You can find me on my social media pages at:
www.facebook.com/lynnjohnsonauthor
Twitter @lynnjohnsonjots
Website www.lynnjohnsonauthor.com

And my thanks to you for reading their stories.
Best wishes,
Lynn

Acknowledgments

Wartime with the Tram Girls has been tremendously satisfying to write. It catches up with old friends and introduces more characters based in and around Burslem in the Staffordshire Potteries.

It involved a fair amount of research around the Suffragette movement and the First World War. I used information from a range of texts to flesh out the background. The British Newspaper Archives was invaluable in providing snippets of information about the Home Front during those dark days. As always, libraries play a big part and my thanks go to Orkney Library and Archive, and Staffordshire Libraries.

Another fantastic resource was Crich Tramway Museum, Derbyshire, and in particular Hannah Bale, Curatorial Assistant, who patiently answered my many questions during my research phase. I felt I got to know a great deal about trams and clippies at the beginning of the twentieth century and I send huge thanks to the museum staff for their patience. If I have pricked your interest, I would certainly recommend a visit.

Once again, I would like to offer huge thanks to my beta readers who gave me such useful feedback when I was too close to see what needed fixing — Jacquie Rogers, Linda Tyler, Katherine Mezzacappa and to my dear friend Lesley Colclough. My thanks to Jennie Ayres and Keshini Naidoo who, through their careful editing, have helped to bring the book to life.

Many of the places mentioned in the novel are

real although I have changed some street names and buildings. All of the characters, with the exception of Emily Wilding Davison, the Pankhursts and the political figures, are fictional.

The Potteries Electric Traction Company, part of the British Electric Traction Company ran the trams during the first two decades of the twentieth century and the Potteries Tramway Company is loosely based on the PETC as far as its destinations are concerned. However, the Potteries Tramway Company is fictional. The Clippies Strike of 1918 did happen in London and caused chaos in the capital and began to spread to the places I have identified until, a few days later, the clippies got their war bonus. It was not unusual for clippies to be harassed while going about their business due to petty crime and by people who believed the women were taking over men's jobs even though clippies were told their jobs would terminate at the end of the war.

The Friends Ambulance Unit was setup by the Quakers to provide voluntary medical aid to thousands of civilians, and soldiers from both sides. In addition, it helped with water purification, inoculations and quell a typhoid epidemic in Ypres, and so much more. Nearly one hundred volunteers were decorated for bravery.

Some of the buildings referred to in the novel, Stoke Town Hall, Queen's Hall in Burslem, and Victoria Hall in Hanley, are real but the tram depots I have described exist only in my imagination. Any mistakes in interpreting the information I have collected are entirely my own.

Once again, my thanks go to my family, Carol Blood and Pat Beresford who give me encouragement and continue to support me in my writing. Last but not least, my thanks to my lovely husband, Michael, who has become my writing assistant over recent months to keep me on track. My love for him knows no bounds.